Praise for #1 *New York Times* bestselling author Linda Lael Miller

"Linda Lael Miller creates vibrant characters I defy you to forget."

—Debbie Macomber,
#1 *New York Times* bestselling author

"Miller is one of the finest American writers in the genre."

—*RT Book Reviews*

"[Linda Lael] Miller tugs at the heartstrings as few authors can."

—*Publishers Weekly*

Praise for *USA TODAY* bestselling author Michelle Major

"A dynamic start to a series with a refreshingly original premise."

—*Kirkus Reviews* on *The Magnolia Sisters*

"A sweet start to a promising series, perfect for fans of Debbie Macomber."

—*Publishers Weekly* on
The Magnolia Sisters (starred review)

"*The Magnolia Sisters* is sheer delight, filled with humor, warmth and heart.... I loved everything about it."

—*New York Times* bestselling author
RaeAnne Thayne

THE McKETTRICK WAY

#1 *NEW YORK TIMES* BESTSELLING AUTHOR

Linda Lael Miller

HARLEQUIN® SELECTS™

Recycling programs
for this product may
not exist in your area.

ISBN-13: 978-1-335-40989-8

The McKettrick Way
First published in 2007. This edition published in 2021.
Copyright © 2007 by Linda Lael Miller

A Baby and a Betrothal
First published in 2016. This edition published in 2021.
Copyright © 2016 by Michelle Major

This edition published by arrangement with Harlequin Books S.A.

For questions and comments about the quality of this book,
please contact us at CustomerService@Harlequin.com.

Harlequin Enterprises ULC
22 Adelaide St. West, 40th Floor
Toronto, Ontario M5H 4E3, Canada
www.Harlequin.com

Printed in Lithuania

MIX
Paper from
responsible sources
FSC® C021394

CONTENTS

The daughter of a town marshal, **Linda Lael Miller** is a *New York Times* bestselling author of more than one hundred historical and contemporary novels. Linda's books have hit #1 on the *New York Times* bestseller list seven times. Raised in Northport, Washington, she now lives in Spokane, Washington.

Books by Linda Lael Miller

HQN Books

Painted Pony Creek

Country Strong

The Carsons of Mustang Creek

A Snow Country Christmas
Forever a Hero
Always a Cowboy
Once a Rancher

The Brides of Bliss County

Christmas in Mustang Creek
The Marriage Season
The Marriage Charm
The Marriage Pact

The Parable Series

Big Sky Secrets
Big Sky Wedding
Big Sky Summer
Big Sky River
Big Sky Mountain
Big Sky Country

Visit the Author Profile page
at Harlequin.com for more titles.

THE McKETTRICK WAY

Linda Lael Miller

In memory of my dad, Grady "Skip" Lael.

Happy trails, cowboy.

Chapter 1

Brad O'Ballivan opened the driver's-side door of the waiting pickup truck, tossed his guitar case inside and turned to wave a farewell to the pilot and crew of the private jet he hoped never to ride in again.

A chilly fall wind slashed across the broad, lonesome clearing, rippling the fading grass, and he raised the collar of his denim jacket against it. Pulled his hat down a little lower over his eyes.

He was home.

Something inside him resonated to the Arizona high country, and more particularly to Stone Creek Ranch, like one prong of a perfectly balanced tuning fork. The sensation was peculiar to the place—he'd never felt it in his sprawling lakeside mansion outside Nashville, on the periphery of a town called Hendersonville, or at the villa in Mexico, or any of the other fancy digs where he'd hung his hat over the years since he'd turned his back on the spread—and so much more—to sing for his supper.

His grin was slightly ironic as he stood by the truck and watched the jet soar back into the sky. His retirement from the country music scene, at the age of thirty-five and the height of his success, had caused quite a media stir. He'd sold the jet and the big houses and most of what was in them, and given away the rest, except for the guitar and the clothes he was wearing. And he knew he'd never regret it.

He was through with that life. And once an O'Ballivan was through with something, that was the end of it.

The jet left a trail across the sky, faded to a silver spark, and disappeared.

Brad was about to climb into the truck and head for the ranch house, start coming to terms with things there, when he spotted a familiar battered gray Suburban jostling and gear-grinding its way over the rough road that had never really evolved beyond its beginnings as an old-time cattle trail.

He took off his hat, even though the wind nipped at the edges of his ears, and waited, partly eager, partly resigned.

The old Chevy came to a chortling stop a few inches from the toes of his boots, throwing up a cloud of red-brown dust, and his sister Olivia shut the big engine down and jumped out to round the hood and stride right up to him.

"You're back," Olivia said, sounding nonplussed. The eldest of Brad's three younger sisters, at twenty-nine, she'd never quite forgiven him for leaving home—much less getting famous. Practical to the bone, she was small, with short, glossy dark hair and eyes the color of a brand-new pair of jeans, and just as starchy. Olivia was low-woman-on-the-totem-pole at a thriving veterinary practice in the nearby town of Stone Creek, specializing in large animals, and Brad knew she spent most of her workdays in a barn someplace, or out on the range, with one arm shoved up where the sun didn't shine, turning a crossways calf or colt.

"I'm delighted to see you, too, Doc," Brad answered dryly.

With an exasperated little cry, Olivia sprang off the soles of her worn-out boots to throw her arms around his neck, knocking his hat clear off his head in the process. She hugged him tight, and when she drew back, there were tears on her dirt-smudged cheeks, and she sniffled self-consciously.

"If this is some kind of publicity stunt," Livie said, once she'd rallied a little, "I'm never going to forgive you." She bent to retrieve his hat, handed it over.

God, she was proud. She'd let him pay for her education, but returned every other check he or his accountant sent with the words *NO THANKS* scrawled across the front in thick black capitals.

Brad chuckled, threw the hat into the pickup, to rest on top of the guitar case. "It's no stunt," he replied. "I'm back for good. Ready to 'take hold and count for something,' as Big John used to say."

The mention of their late grandfather caused a poignant and not entirely comfortable silence to fall between them. Brad had been on a concert tour when the old man died of a massive coronary six months before, and he'd barely made it back to Stone Creek in time for the funeral. Worse, he'd had to leave again right after the services, in order to make a sold-out show in Chicago. The large infusions of cash he'd pumped into the home place over the years did little to assuage his guilt.

How much money is enough? How famous do you have

to be? Big John had asked, in his kindly but irascible way, not once but a hundred times. *Come home, damn it. I need you. Your little sisters need you. And God knows, Stone Creek Ranch needs you.*

Shoving a hand through his light brown hair, in need of trimming as always, Brad thrust out a sigh and scanned the surrounding countryside. "That old stallion still running loose out here, or did the wolves and the barbed wire finally get him?" he asked, raw where the memories of his grandfather chafed against his mind, and in sore need of a distraction.

Livie probably wasn't fooled by the dodge, but she was gracious enough to grant Brad a little space to recover in, and he appreciated that. "We get a glimpse of Ransom every once in a while," she replied, and a little pucker of worry formed between her eyebrows. "Always off on the horizon somewhere, keeping his distance."

Brad laid a hand on his sister's shoulder. She'd been fascinated with the legendary wild stallion since she was little. First sighted in the late nineteenth century and called King's Ransom because that was what he was probably worth, the animal was black and shiny as wet ink, and so elusive that some people maintained he wasn't flesh and blood at all, but spirit, a myth believed for so long that thought itself had made him real. The less fanciful maintained that Ransom was one in a long succession of stallions, all descended from that first mysterious sire. Brad stood squarely in this camp, as Big John had, but he wasn't so sure Livie took the same rational view.

"They're trying to trap him," she said now, tears glistening in her eyes. "They want to pen him up. Get samples of his DNA. Turn him out to stud, so they can sell his babies."

"Who's trying to trap him, Liv?" Brad asked gently. It

was cold, he was hungry, and setting foot in the old ranch house, without Big John there to greet him, was a thing to get past.

"Never mind," Livie said, bucking up a little. Setting her jaw. "You wouldn't be interested."

There was no point in arguing with Olivia O'Ballivan, DVM, when she got that look on her face. "Thanks for bringing my truck out here," Brad said. "And for coming to meet me."

"I didn't bring the truck," Livie replied. Some people would have taken the credit, but Liv was half again too stubborn to admit to a kindness she hadn't committed, let alone one she considered unwarranted. "Ashley and Melissa did that. They're probably at the ranch house right now, hanging streamers or putting up a Welcome Home, Brad banner or something. And I only came out here because I saw that jet and figured it was some damn movie star, buzzing the deer."

Brad had one leg inside the truck, ready to hoist himself into the driver's seat. "That's a problem around here?" he asked, with a wry half grin. "Movie stars buzzing deer in Lear jets?"

"It happens in Montana all the time," Livie insisted, plainly incensed. She felt just as strongly about snowmobiles and other off-road vehicles.

Brad reached down, touched the tip of her nose with one index finger. "This isn't Montana, shortstop," he pointed out. "See you at home?"

"Another time," Livie said, not giving an inch. "After all the hoopla dies down."

Inwardly, Brad groaned. He wasn't up for hoopla, or any kind of celebration Ashley and Melissa, their twin sisters, might have cooked up in honor of his return. Classic between-a-rock-and-a-hard-place stuff—he couldn't hurt their feelings, either.

"Tell me they're not planning a party," he pleaded.

Livie relented, but only slightly. One side of her mouth quirked up in a smile. "You're in luck, Mr. Multiple Grammy Winner. There's a McKettrick baby shower going on over in Indian Rock as we speak, and practically the whole county's there."

The name McKettrick unsettled Brad even more than the prospect of going home to banners, streamers and a collection of grinning neighbors, friends and sisters. "Not Meg," he muttered, and then blushed, since he hadn't intended to say the words out loud.

Livie's smile intensified, the way it did when she had a solid hand at gin rummy and was fixing to go out and stick him with a lot of aces and face cards. She shook her head. "Meg's back in Indian Rock for good, rumor has it, and she's still single," she assured him. "Her sister Sierra's the one having a baby."

In a belated and obviously fruitless attempt to hide his relief at this news, Brad shut the truck door between himself and Livie and, since the keys were waiting in the ignition, started up the rig.

Looking smug, Livie waved cheerily, climbed back into the Suburban and drove off, literally in a cloud of dust.

Brad sat waiting for it to settle.

The feelings took a little longer.

"Go haunt somebody else!" Meg McKettrick whispered to the ghost cowboy riding languidly in the passenger seat of her Blazer, as she drove past Sierra's new house, on the outskirts of Indian Rock, for at least the third time. Both sides of the road were jammed with cars, and if she didn't find a parking place soon, she'd be late for the baby shower. If not the actual *baby*. "Pick on Keegan—or Jesse—or Rance—*anybody* but me!"

"They don't need haunting," he said mildly. He looked nothing like the august, craggy-faced, white-haired figure in his portraits, grudgingly posed for late in his long and vigorous life. No, Angus McKettrick had come back in his prime, square-jaw handsome, broad shouldered, his hair thick and golden brown, his eyes intensely blue, at ease in the charm he'd passed down to generations of male descendants.

Still flustered, Meg found a gap between a Lexus and a minivan, wedged the Blazer into it, and turned off the ignition with a twist of one wrist. Tight-tipped, she jumped out of the rig, jerked open the back door, and reached for the festively wrapped package on the seat. "I've got news for you," she sputtered. "*I* don't need haunting, either!"

Angus, who looked to Meg as substantial and "real" as anybody she'd ever encountered, got out and stood on his side of the Blazer, stretching. "So you say," he answered, in a lazy drawl. "All of *them* are married, starting families of their own. Carrying on the McKettrick name."

"Thanks for the reminder," Meg bit out, in the terse undertone she reserved for arguments with her great-great-however-many-greats grandfather. Clutching the gift she'd bought for Travis and Sierra's baby, she shouldered both the back and driver's doors shut.

"In my day," Angus said easily, "you'd have been an old maid."

"Hello?" Meg replied, without moving her mouth. Over her long association with Angus McKettrick—which went back to her earliest childhood memories—she'd developed her own brand of ventriloquism, so other people, who couldn't see him, wouldn't think she was talking to herself. "This *isn't* 'your day.' It's mine. Twenty-first century, all the way. Women don't define themselves by whether they're married or not." She paused, sucked in a calming breath. "Here's an idea—why don't you wait in the car? Or, better yet, go ride some happy trail."

Angus kept pace with her as she crossed the road, clomping along in his perpetually muddy boots. As always, he wore a long, cape-shouldered canvas coat over a rough-spun shirt of butternut cotton and denim trousers that weren't quite jeans. The handle of his ever-present pistol, a long-barreled Colt .45, made a bulge behind his right coat pocket. He wore a hat only when there was a threat of rain, and since the early-October weather was mild, he was bareheaded that evening.

"It might be your testy nature that's the problem," Angus ruminated. "You're downright pricklish, that's what you are. A woman ought to have a little sass to her, to spice things up a mite. You've got more than your share, though, and it ain't becoming."

Meg ignored him, and the bad grammar he always affected when he wanted to impart folksy wisdom, as she tromped up the front steps, shuffling the bulky package in her arms to jab at the doorbell. *Here comes your nineteenth noncommittal yellow layette,* she thought, wishing she'd opted for the sterling baby rattles instead. If Sierra and Travis knew the sex of their unborn child, they weren't telling, which made shopping even more of a pain than normal.

The door swung open and Eve, Meg and Sierra's mother, stood frowning in the chasm. "It's about time you got here," she said, pulling Meg inside. Then, in a whisper, "Is he with you?"

"Of course he is," Meg answered, as her mother peered

past her shoulder, searching in vain for Angus. "He never misses a family gathering."

Eve sniffed, straightened her elegant shoulders. "You're late," she said. "Sierra will be here any minute!"

"It's not as if she's going to be surprised, Mom," Meg said, setting the present atop a mountain of others of a suspiciously similar size and shape. "There must be a hundred cars parked out there."

Eve shut the door smartly and then, before Meg could shrug out of her navy blue peacoat, gripped her firmly by the shoulders. "You've lost weight," she accused. "And there are dark circles under your eyes. Aren't you sleeping well?"

"I'm fine," Meg insisted. And she *was* fine—for an old maid.

Angus, never one to be daunted by a little thing like a closed door, materialized just behind Eve, looked around at his assembled brood with pleased amazement. The place was jammed with McKettrick cousins, their wives and husbands, their growing families.

Something tightened in the pit of Meg's stomach.

"Nonsense," Eve said. "If you could have gotten away with it, you would have stayed home today, wandering around that old house in your pajamas, with no makeup on and your hair sticking out in every direction."

It was true, but beside the point. With Eve McKettrick for a mother, Meg couldn't get away with much of anything. "I'm here," she said. "Give me a break, will you?"

She pulled off her coat, handed it to Eve, and sidled into the nearest group, a small band of women. Meg, who had spent all her childhood summers in Indian Rock, didn't recognize any of them.

"It's all over the tabloids," remarked a tall, thin woman

wearing a lot of jewelry. "Brad O'Ballivan is in rehab again."

Meg caught her breath at the name, and nearly dropped the cup of punch someone shoved into her hands.

"Nonsense," a second woman replied. "Last week those rags were reporting that he'd been abducted by aliens."

"He's handsome enough to have fans on other planets," observed a third, sighing wistfully.

Meg tried to ease out of the circle, but it had closed around her. She felt dizzy.

"My cousin Evelyn works at the post office over in Stone Creek," said yet another woman, with authority. "According to her, Brad's fan mail is being forwarded to the family ranch, just outside of town. He's not in rehab, and he's not on another planet. He's *home*. Evelyn says they'll have to build a second barn just to hold all those letters."

Meg smiled rigidly, but on the inside, she was scrambling for balance.

Suddenly, woman #1 focused on her. "You used to date Brad O'Ballivan, didn't you, Meg?"

"That—that was a long time ago," Meg said as graciously as she could, given that she was right in the middle of a panic attack. "We were just kids, and it was a summer thing—" Frantically, she calculated the distance between Indian Rock and Stone Creek—a mere forty miles. Not nearly far enough.

"I'm sure Meg has dated a lot of famous people," one of the other women said. "Working for McKettrickCo the way she did, flying all over the place in the company jet—"

"Brad wasn't famous when I knew him," Meg said lamely.

"You must miss your old life," someone else commented.

While it was true that Meg was having some trouble shifting from full throttle to a comparative standstill, since the family conglomerate had gone public a few months before, and her job as an executive vice president had gone with it, she *didn't* miss the meetings and the sixty-hour workweeks all that much. Money certainly wasn't a problem; she had a trust fund, as well as a personal investment portfolio thicker than the Los Angeles phone book.

A stir at the front door saved her from commenting.

Sierra came in, looking baffled.

"Surprise!" the crowd shouted as one.

The surprise is on me, Meg thought bleakly. *Brad O'Ballivan is back.*

Brad shoved the truck into gear and drove to the bottom of the hill, where the road forked. Turn left, and he'd be home in five minutes. Turn right, and he was headed for Indian Rock.

He had no damn business going to Indian Rock.

He had nothing to say to Meg McKettrick, and if he never set eyes on the woman again, it would be two weeks too soon.

He turned right.

He couldn't have said why.

He just drove.

At one point, needing noise, he switched on the truck radio, fiddled with the dial until he found a country-western station. A recording of his own voice filled the cab of the pickup, thundering from all the speakers.

He'd written that ballad for Meg.

He turned the dial to Off.

Almost simultaneously, his cell phone jangled in the pocket of his jacket; he considered ignoring it—there were a number of people he didn't want to talk to—but suppose it was one of his sisters calling? Suppose they needed help?

He flipped the phone open, not taking his eyes off the curvy mountain road to check the caller ID panel first. "O'Ballivan," he said.

"Have you come to your senses yet?" demanded his manager, Phil Meadowbrook. "Shall I tell you again just *how much* money those people in Vegas are offering? They're willing to build you your own *theater,* for God's sake. This is a three-year gig—"

"Phil?" Brad broke in.

"Say yes," Phil pleaded.

"I'm retired."

"You're thirty-five," Phil argued. "*Nobody* retires at thirty-five!"

"We've already had this conversation, Phil."

"Don't hang up!"

Brad, who'd been about to thumb the off button, sighed.

"What the hell are you going to do in Stone Creek, Arizona?" Phil demanded. "Herd cattle? Sing to your horse? Think of the money, Brad. Think of the women, throwing their underwear at your feet—"

"I've been working real hard to repress that image," Brad said. "Thanks a lot for the reminder."

"Okay, forget the underwear," Phil shot back, without missing a beat. "But think of the money!"

"I've already got more of that than I need, Phil, and so do you, so spare me the riff where your grandchildren are homeless waifs picking through garbage behind the supermarket."

"I've used that one, huh?" Phil asked.

"Oh, yeah," Brad answered.

"What are you doing, right this moment?"

"I'm headed for the Dixie Dog Drive-In."

"The *what?*"

"Goodbye, Phil."

"What are you going to do at the Dixie-Whatever Drive-In that you couldn't do in Music City? Or Vegas?"

"You wouldn't understand," Brad said. "And I can't say I blame you, because I don't really understand it myself."

Back in the day, he and Meg used to meet at the Dixie Dog, by tacit agreement, when either of them had been away. It had been some kind of universe-thing, purely intuitive. He guessed he wanted to see if it still worked—and he'd be damned if he'd try to explain that to Phil.

"Look," Phil said, revving up for another sales pitch, "I can't put these casino people off forever. You're riding high right now, but things are bound to cool off. I've got to tell them *something*—"

"Tell them 'thanks, but no thanks,'" Brad suggested. This time, he broke the connection.

Phil, being Phil, tried to call twice before he finally gave up.

Passing familiar landmarks, Brad told himself he ought to turn around. The old days were gone, things had ended badly between him and Meg anyhow, and she wasn't going to be at the Dixie Dog.

He kept driving.

He went by the Welcome To Indian Rock sign, and the Roadhouse, a popular beer-and-burger stop for truckers, tourists and locals, and was glad to see the place was still open. He slowed for Main Street, smiled as he passed Cora's Curl and Twirl, squinted at the bookshop next door. That was new.

He frowned. Things changed, places changed.

What if the Dixie Dog had closed down?

What if it was boarded up, with litter and sagebrush tumbling through a deserted parking lot?

And what the hell did it matter, anyhow?

Brad shoved a hand through his hair. Maybe Phil and everybody else was right—maybe he was crazy to turn down the Vegas deal. Maybe he *would* end up sitting in the barn, serenading a bunch of horses.

He rounded a bend, and there was the Dixie Dog, still open. Its big neon sign, a giant hot dog, was all lit up and going through its corny sequence—first it was covered in red squiggles of light, meant to suggest catsup, and then yellow, for mustard. There were a few cars lined up in the drive-through lane, a few more in the parking lot.

Brad pulled into one of the slots next to a speaker and rolled down the truck window.

"Welcome to the Dixie Dog Drive-In," a youthful female voice chirped over the bad wiring. "What can I get you today?"

Brad hadn't thought that far, but he was starved. He peered at the light-up menu box under the chunky metal speaker. Then the obvious choice struck him and he said, "I'll take a Dixie Dog," he said. "Hold the chili and onions."

"Coming right up" was the cheerful response. "Anything to drink?"

"Chocolate shake," he decided. "Extra thick."

His cell phone rang again.

He ignored it again.

The girl thanked him and roller-skated out with the order about five minutes later.

When she wheeled up to the driver's-side window, smiling, her eyes went wide with recognition, and she dropped the tray with a clatter.

Silently, Brad swore. Damn if he hadn't forgotten he was famous.

The girl, a skinny thing wearing too much eye makeup, immediately started to cry. "I'm sorry!" she sobbed, squatting to gather up the mess.

"It's okay," Brad answered quietly, leaning to look down at her, catching a glimpse of her plastic name tag. "It's okay, Mandy. No harm done."

"I'll get you another dog and a shake right away, Mr. O'Ballivan!"

"Mandy?"

She stared up at him pitifully, sniffling. Thanks to the copious tears, most of the goop on her eyes had slid south. "Yes?"

"When you go back inside, could you not mention seeing me?"

"But you're Brad O'Ballivan!"

"Yeah," he answered, suppressing a sigh. "I know."

She was standing up again by then, the tray of gathered debris clasped in both hands. She seemed to sway a little on her rollers. "Meeting you is just about the most important thing that's ever happened to me in my whole entire *life*. I don't know if I could keep it a secret even if I tried!"

Brad leaned his head against the back of the truck seat and closed his eyes. "Not forever, Mandy," he said. "Just long enough for me to eat a Dixie Dog in peace."

She rolled a little closer. "You wouldn't happen to have a picture you could autograph for me, would you?"

"Not with me," Brad answered. There were boxes of publicity pictures in storage, along with the requisite T-shirts, slick concert programs and other souvenirs commonly sold on the road. He never carried them, much to Phil's annoyance.

"You could sign this napkin, though," Mandy said. "It's only got a little chocolate on the corner."

Brad took the paper napkin, and her order pen, and scrawled his name. Handed both items back through the window.

"Now I can tell my grandchildren I spilled your lunch all over the pavement at the Dixie Dog Drive-In, and here's my proof." Mandy beamed, waggling the chocolate-stained napkin.

"Just imagine," Brad said. The slight irony in his tone was wasted on Mandy, which was probably a good thing.

"I won't tell anybody I saw you until you drive away," Mandy said with eager resolve. "I *think* I can last that long."

"That would be good," Brad told her.

She turned and whizzed back toward the side entrance to the Dixie Dog.

Brad waited, marveling that he hadn't considered incidents like this one before he'd decided to come back home. In retrospect, it seemed shortsighted, to say the least, but the truth was, he'd expected to be—Brad O'Ballivan.

Presently, Mandy skated back out again, and this time, she managed to hold on to the tray.

"I didn't tell a soul!" she whispered. "But Heather and Darlene *both* asked me why my mascara was all smeared." Efficiently, she hooked the tray onto the bottom edge of the window.

Brad extended payment, but Mandy shook her head.

"The boss said it's on the house, since I dumped your first order on the ground."

He smiled. "Okay, then. Thanks."

Mandy retreated, and Brad was just reaching for the food when a bright red Blazer whipped into the space beside his. The driver's-side door sprang open, crashing into the metal speaker, and somebody got out, in a hurry.

Something quickened inside Brad.

And in the next moment, Meg McKettrick was standing practically on his running board, her blue eyes blazing.

Brad grinned. "I guess you're not over me after all," he said.

Chapter 2

After Sierra had opened all her shower presents, and cake and punch had been served, Meg had felt the old, familiar tug in the middle of her solar plexus and headed straight for the Dixie Dog Drive-In. Now that she was there, standing next to a truck and all but nose to nose with Brad O'Ballivan through the open window, she didn't know what to do—or say.

Angus poked her from behind, and she flinched.

"Speak up," her dead ancestor prodded.

"Stay out of this," she answered, without thinking.

Puzzlement showed in Brad's affably handsome face. "Huh?"

"Never mind," Meg said. She took a step back, straightened. "And I am *so* over you."

Brad grinned. "Damned if it didn't work," he marveled. He climbed out of the truck to stand facing Meg, ducking around the tray hooked to the door. His dark-blond hair was artfully rumpled, and his clothes were downright ordinary.

"*What* worked?" Meg demanded, even though she knew.

Laughter sparked in his blue-green eyes, along with considerable pain, and he didn't bother to comment.

"What are you doing here?" she asked.

Brad spread his hands. Hands that had once played Meg's body as skillfully as any guitar. Oh, yes. Brad O'Ballivan knew how to set all the chords vibrating.

"Free country," he said. "Or has Indian Rock finally seceded from the Union with the ranch house on the Triple M for a capitol?"

Since she felt a strong urge to bolt for the Blazer and lay rubber getting out of the Dixie Dog's parking lot, Meg planted her feet and hoisted her chin. *McKettricks,* she reminded herself silently, *don't run.*

"I heard you were in rehab," she said, hoping to get under his hide.

"That's a nasty rumor," Brad replied cheerfully.

"How about the two ex-wives and that scandal with the actress?"

His grin, insouciant in the first place, merely widened. "Unfortunately, I can't deny the two ex-wives," he said. "As for the actress—well, it all depends on whether you believe her version or mine. Have you been following my career, Meg McKettrick?"

Meg reddened.

"Tell him the truth," Angus counseled. "You never forgot him."

"No," Meg said, addressing both Brad *and* Angus.

Brad looked unconvinced. He was probably just egotistical enough to think she logged onto his Web site regularly, bought all his albums and read every tabloid article about him that she could get her hands on. Which she did, but that was *not* the point.

"You're still the best-looking woman I've ever laid eyes on," he said. "That hasn't changed, anyhow."

"I'm not a member of your fan club, O'Ballivan," Meg informed him. "So hold the insincere flattery, okay?"

One corner of his mouth tilted upward in a half grin, but his eyes were sad. He glanced back toward the truck, then met Meg's gaze again. "I don't flatter anybody," Brad said. Then he sighed. "I guess I'd better get back to Stone Creek."

Something in his tone piqued Meg's interest.

Who was she kidding?

Everything about him piqued her interest. As much as she didn't want that to be true, it was.

"I was sorry to hear about Big John's passing," she said. She almost touched his arm, but managed to catch herself just short of it. If she laid a hand on Brad O'Ballivan, who knew what would happen?

"Thanks," he replied.

A girl on roller skates wheeled out of the drive-in to collect the tray from the window edge of Brad's truck, her cheeks pink with carefully restrained excitement. "I might have said something to Heather and Darleen," the teenager confessed, after a curious glance at Meg. "About you being who you are and the autograph and everything."

Brad muttered something.

The girl skated away.

"I've gotta go," Brad told Meg, looking toward the drive-in. Numerous faces were pressed against the glass door; in another minute, there would probably be a stampede. "I don't suppose we could have dinner together or something? Maybe tomorrow night? There are—well, there are some things I'd like to say to you."

"Say yes," Angus told her.

"I don't think that would be a good idea," Meg said.

"A drink, then? There's a redneck bar in Stone Creek—"

"Don't be such a damned prig," Angus protested, nudging her again.

"I'm not a prig."

Brad frowned, threw another nervous look toward the drive-in and all those grinning faces. "I never said you were," he replied.

"I wasn't—" Meg paused, bit her lower lip. *I wasn't talking to you. No, siree, I was talking to Angus McKettrick's ghost.* "Okay," she agreed, to cover her lapse. "I guess one drink couldn't do any harm."

Brad climbed into his truck. The door of the drive-in crashed open, and the adoring hordes poured out, screaming with delight.

"Go!" Meg told him.

"Six o'clock tomorrow night," Brad reminded her. He backed the truck out, made a narrow turn to avoid running over the approaching herd of admirers and peeled out of the lot.

Meg turned to the disappointed fans. "Brad O'Ballivan," she said diplomatically, "has left the building."

Nobody got the joke.

The sun was setting, red-gold shot through with purple, when Brad crested the last hill before home and looked down on Stone Creek Ranch for the first time since his grandfather's funeral. The creek coursed, silvery-blue, through the middle of the land. The barn and the main house, built by Sam O'Ballivan's own hands and shored up by every generation to follow, stood as sturdy and imposing as ever. Once, there had been two houses on the place, but the one belonging to Major John Blackstone, the original landowner, had been torn down long ago. Now a copse of oak trees stood where the major had lived, surrounding a few old graves.

Big John was buried there, by special dispensation from the Arizona state government.

A lump formed in Brad's throat. *You see that I'm laid to rest with the old-timers when the bell tolls,* Big John had told him once. *Not in that cemetery in town.*

It had taken some doing, but Brad had made it happen.

He wanted to head straight for Big John's final resting place, pay his respects first thing, but there was a cluster of cars parked in front of the ranch house. His sisters were waiting to welcome him home.

Brad blinked a couple of times, rubbed his eyes with a thumb and forefinger, and headed for the house.

Time to face the proverbial music.

Meg drove slowly back to the Triple M, going the long way to pass the main ranch house, Angus's old stomping grounds, in the vain hope that he would decide to haunt it for a while, instead of her. A descendant of Angus's eldest son, Holt, and daughter-in-law Lorelei, Meg called their place home.

As they bumped across the creek bridge, Angus assessed the large log structure, added onto over the years, and well-maintained.

Though close, all the McKettricks were proud of their particular branch of the family tree. Keegan, who occupied the main house now, along with his wife, Molly, daughter,

Devon, and young son, Lucas, could trace his lineage back to Kade, another of Angus's four sons.

Rance, along with his daughters, was Rafe's progeny. He and the girls and his bride, Emma, lived in the grandly rustic structure on the other side of the creek from Keegan's place.

Finally, there was Jesse. He was Jeb's descendant, and resided, when he wasn't off somewhere participating in a rodeo or a poker tournament, in the house Jeb had built for his wife, Chloe, high on a hill on the southwestern section of the ranch. Jesse was happily married to a hometown girl, the former Cheyenne Bridges, and like Keegan's Molly and Rance's Emma, Cheyenne was expecting a baby.

Everybody, it seemed to Meg, was expecting a baby.

Except her, of course.

She bit her lower lip.

"I bet if you got yourself pregnant by that singing cowboy," Angus observed, "he'd have the decency to make an honest woman out of you."

Angus had an uncanny ability to tap into Meg's wavelength; though he swore he couldn't read her mind, she wondered sometimes.

"Great idea," she scoffed. "And for your information, I *am* an honest woman."

Keegan was just coming out of the barn as Meg passed; he smiled and waved. She tooted the Blazer's horn in greeting.

"He sure looks like Kade," Angus said. "Jesse looks like Jeb, and Rance looks like Rafe." He sighed. "It sure makes me lonesome for my boys."

Meg felt a grudging sympathy for Angus. He'd ruined a lot of dates, being an almost constant companion, but she loved him. "Why can't you be where they are?" she asked softly. "Wherever that is."

"I've got to see to you," he answered. "You're the last holdout."

"I'd be all right, Angus," she said. She'd asked him about the afterlife, but all he'd ever been willing to say was that there was no such thing as dying, just a change of perspective. Time wasn't linear, he claimed, but simultaneous. The "whole ball of string," as he put it, was happening at once—past, present and future. Some of the experiences the women in her family, including herself and Sierra, had had up at Holt's house lent credence to the theory.

Sierra claimed that, before her marriage to Travis and the subsequent move to the new semi-mansion in town, she and her young son, Liam, had shared the old house with a previous generation of McKettricks—Doss and Hannah and a little boy called Tobias. Sierra had offered journals and photograph albums as proof, and Meg had to admit, her half sister made a compelling case.

Still, and for all that she'd been keeping company with a benevolent ghost since she was little, Meg was a left-brain type.

When Angus didn't comment on her insistence that she'd get along fine if he went on to the great roundup in the sky, or whatever, Meg tried again. "Look," she said gently, "when I was little, and Sierra disappeared, and Mom was so frantic to find her that she couldn't take care of me, I really needed you. But I'm a grown woman now, Angus. I'm independent. I have a life."

Out of the corner of her eye, she saw Angus's jaw tighten. "That Hank Breslin," he said, "was no good for Eve. No better than *your* father was. Every time the right man came along, she was so busy cozying up to the *wrong* one that she didn't even notice what was right in front of her."

Hank Breslin was Sierra's father. He'd kidnapped Sierra, only two years old at the time, when Eve served him with divorce papers, and raised her in Mexico. For a variety of reasons, Eve hadn't reconnected with her lost daughter until recently. Meg's own father, about whom she knew little, had died in an accident a month before she was born. Nobody liked to talk about him—even his name was a mystery.

"And you think I'll make the same mistakes my mother did?" Meg said.

"Hell," Angus said, sparing her a reluctant grin, "right now, even a *mistake* would be progress."

"With all due respect," Meg replied, "having you around all the time is not exactly conducive to romance."

They started the long climb uphill, headed for the house that now belonged to her and Sierra. Meg had always loved that house—it had been a refuge for her, full of cousins. Looking back, she wondered why, given that Eve had rarely accompanied her on those summer visits, had instead left her daughter in the care of a succession of nannies and, later, aunts and uncles.

Sierra's kidnapping had been a traumatic event, for certain, but the problems Eve had subsequently developed because of it had left Meg relatively unmarked. She hadn't been lonely as a child, mainly because of Angus.

"I'll stay clear tomorrow night, when you go to Stone Creek for that drink," Angus said.

"You like Brad."

"Always did. Liked Travis, too. 'Course, I knew he was meant for your sister, that they'd meet up in time."

Meg and Sierra's husband, Travis, were old friends.

They'd tried to get something going, convinced they were perfect for each other, but it hadn't worked. Now that Travis and Sierra were together, and ecstatically happy, Meg was glad.

"Don't get your hopes up," she said. "About Brad and me, I mean."

Angus didn't reply. He appeared to be deep in thought. Or maybe as he looked out at the surrounding countryside, he was remembering his youth, when he'd staked a claim to this land and held it with blood and sweat and sheer McKettrick stubbornness.

"You must have known the O'Ballivans," Meg reflected, musing. Like her own family, Brad's had been pioneers in this part of Arizona.

"I was older than dirt by the time Sam O'Ballivan brought his bride, Maddie, up from Haven. Might have seen them once or twice. But I knew Major Blackstone, all right." Angus smiled at some memory. "He and I used to arm wrestle sometimes, in the card room back of Jolene Bell's Saloon, when we couldn't best each other at poker."

"Who won?" Meg asked, smiling slightly at the image.

"Same as the poker," Angus answered with a sigh. "We'd always come out about even. He'd win half the time, me the other half."

The house came in sight, the barn towering nearby. Angus's expression took on a wistful aspect.

"When you're here," Meg ventured, "can you see Doss and Hannah and Tobias? Talk to them?"

"No," Angus said flatly.

"Why not?" Meg persisted, even though she knew Angus didn't want to pursue the subject.

"Because they're not dead," he said. "They're just on the other side, like my boys."

"Well, I'm not dead, either," Meg said reasonably. She refrained from adding that she could have shown him their graves, up in the McKettrick cemetery. Shown him his own, for that matter. It would have been unkind, of course, but there was another reason for her reluctance, too. In some version of that cemetery, given what he'd told her about time, there was surely a headstone with *her* name on it.

"You wouldn't understand," Angus told her. He always said that, when she tried to find out how it was for him, where he went when he wasn't following her around.

"Try me," she said.

He vanished.

Resigned, Meg pulled up in front of the garage, added onto the original house sometime in the 1950s, and equipped with an automatic door opener, and pushed the button so she could drive in.

She half expected to find Angus sitting at the kitchen table when she went into the house, but he wasn't there.

What she needed, she decided, was a cup of tea.

She got Lorelei's teapot out of the built-in china cabinet and set it firmly on the counter. The piece was legendary in the family; it had a way of moving back to the cupboard of its own volition, from the table or the counter, and vice versa.

Meg filled the electric kettle at the sink and plugged it in to heat.

Tea was not going to cure what ailed her.

Brad O'Ballivan was back.

Compared to that, ghosts, the mysteries of time and space, and teleporting teapots seemed downright mundane.

And she'd agreed, like a fool, to meet him in Stone Creek for a drink. What had she been thinking?

Standing there in her kitchen, Meg leaned against the counter and folded her arms, waiting for the tea water to boil. Brad had hurt her so badly, she'd thought she'd never recover. For years after he'd dumped her to go to Nashville, she'd barely been able to come back to Indian Rock, and when she had, she'd driven straight to the Dixie Dog, against her will, sat in some rental car, and cried like an idiot.

There are some things I'd like to say to you, Brad had told her, that very day.

"What things?" she asked now, aloud.

The teakettle whistled.

She unplugged it, measured loose orange pekoe into Lorelei's pot and poured steaming water over it.

It was just a drink, Meg reminded herself. An innocent drink.

She should call Brad, cancel gracefully.

Or, better yet, she could just stand him up. Not show up at all. Just as he'd done to her, way back when, when she'd loved him with all her heart and soul, when she'd believed he meant to make a place for her in his busy, exciting life.

Musing, Meg laid a hand to her lower abdomen.

She'd stopped believing in a lot of things when Brad O'Ballivan ditched her.

Maybe he wanted to apologize.

She gave a teary snort of laughter.

And maybe he really had fans on other planets.

A rap at the back door made her start. Angus? He never knocked—he just appeared. Usually at the most inconvenient possible time.

Meg went to the door, peered through the old, thick panes of greenish glass, saw Travis Reid looming on the other side. She wrestled with the lock and let him in.

"I'm here on reconnaissance," he announced, taking off his cowboy hat and hanging it on the peg next to the door. "Sierra's worried about you, and so is Eve."

Meg put a hand to her forehead. She'd left the baby shower abruptly to go meet Brad at the Dixie Dog Drive-In. "I'm sorry," she said, stepping back so Travis could come inside. "I'm all right, really. You shouldn't have come all the way out here—"

"Eve tried your cell—which is evidently off—and Sierra left three or four messages on voice mail," he said with a nod toward the kitchen telephone. "Consider yourself fortunate that I got here before they called out the National Guard."

Meg laughed, closed the door against the chilly October twilight, and watched as Travis took off his sheepskin-lined coat and hung it next to the hat. "I was just feeling a little—overwhelmed."

"Overwhelmed?" She'd been *possessed*.

Travis went to the telephone, punched in a sequence of numbers and waited. "Hi, honey," he said presently, when Sierra answered. "Meg's alive and well. No armed intruders. No bloody accident. She was just—overwhelmed."

"Tell her I'll call her later," Meg said. "Mom, too."

"She'll call you later," Travis repeated dutifully. "Eve, too." He listened again, promised to pick up a gallon of milk and a loaf of bread on the way home and hung up.

Knowing Travis wasn't fond of tea, Meg offered him a cup of instant coffee, instead.

He accepted, taking a seat at the table where generations of McKettricks, from Holt and Lorelei on down, had taken their meals. "What's really going on, Meg?" he asked quietly, watching her as she poured herself some tea and joined him.

"What makes you think anything is going on?"

"I know you. We tried to fall in love, remember?"

"Brad O'Ballivan's back," she said.

Travis nodded. "And this means—?"

"Nothing," Meg answered, much too quickly. "It means nothing. I just—"

Travis settled back in his chair, folded his arms, and waited.

"Okay, it was a shock," Meg admitted. She sat up a little straighter. "But you already knew."

"Jesse told me."

"And nobody thought to mention it to me?"

"I guess we assumed you'd talked to Brad."

"Why would I do that?"

"Because—" Travis paused, looked uncomfortable. "It's no secret that the two of you had a thing going, Meg. Indian Rock and Stone Creek are small places, forty miles apart. Things get around."

Meg's face burned. She'd thought, she'd truly believed, that no one on earth knew Brad had broken her heart. She'd pretended it didn't matter that he'd left town so abruptly. Even laughed about it. Gone on to finish college, thrown herself into that first entry-level job at McKettrickCo. Dated other men, including the then-single Travis.

And she hadn't fooled anyone.

"Are you going to see him again?"

Meg pressed the tips of her fingers hard into her closed eyes. Nodded. Then shook her head from side to side.

Travis chuckled. "Make a decision, Meg," he said.

"We're supposed to have a drink together tomorrow night, at a cowboy bar in Stone Creek. I don't know why I said I'd meet him—after all this time, what do we have to say to each other?"

"'How've ya been?'" Travis suggested.

"I *know* how he's been—rich and famous, married twice, busy building a reputation that makes Jesse's look tame," she said. "I, on the other hand, have been a workaholic. Period."

"Aren't you being a little hard on yourself? Not to mention Brad?" A grin quirked the corner of Travis's mouth. "Comparing him to *Jesse?*"

Jesse had been a wild man, if a good-hearted, well-intentioned one, until he'd met up with Cheyenne Bridges. When he'd fallen, he'd fallen hard, and for the duration, the way bad boys so often do.

"Maybe Brad's changed," Travis said.

"Maybe not," Meg countered.

"Well, I guess you *could* leave town for a while. Stay out of his way." Travis was trying hard not to smile. "Volunteer for a space mission or something."

"I am *not* going to run," Meg said. "I've always wanted to live right here, on this ranch, in this house. Besides, I intend to be here when the baby comes."

Travis's face softened at the mention of the impending birth. Until Sierra came along, Meg hadn't thought he'd ever settle down. He'd had his share of demons to overcome, not the least of which was the tragic death of his younger brother. Travis had blamed himself for what happened to Brody. "Good," he said. "But what do you actually *do* here? You're used to the fast lane, Meg."

"I take care of the horses," she said.

"That takes, what—two hours a day? According to Eve, you spend most of your time in your pajamas. She thinks you're depressed."

"Well, I'm not," Meg said. "I'm just—catching up on my rest."

"Okay," Travis said, drawing out the word.

"I'm not drinking alone and I'm not watching soap operas," Meg said. "I'm vegging. It's a concept my mother doesn't understand."

"She loves you, Meg. She's worried. She's not the enemy."

"I wish she'd go back to Texas."

"Wish away. She's not going anywhere, with a grandchild coming."

At least Eve hadn't taken up residence on the ranch; that was some comfort. She lived in a small suite at the only hotel in Indian Rock, and kept herself busy shopping, day trading on her laptop and spoiling Liam.

Oh, yes. And nagging Meg.

Travis finished his coffee, carried his cup to the sink, rinsed it out. After hesitating for a few moments, he said, "It's this thing about seeing Angus's ghost. She thinks you're obsessed."

Meg made a soft, strangled sound of frustration.

"It's not that she doesn't believe you," Travis added.

"She just thinks I'm a little crazy."

"No," Travis said. "Nobody thinks that."

"But I should get a life, as the saying goes?"

"It would be a good idea, don't you think?"

"Go home. Your pregnant wife needs a gallon of milk and a loaf of bread."

Travis went to the door, put on his coat, took his hat from the hook. "What do *you* need, Meg? That's the question."

"Not Brad O'Ballivan, that's for sure."

Travis grinned again. Set his hat on his head and turned the doorknob. "Did I mention him?" he asked lightly.

Meg glared at him.

"See you," Travis said. And then he was gone.

"He puts me in mind of that O'Ballivan fella," Angus announced, nearly startling Meg out of her skin.

She turned to see him standing over by the china cabinet. Was it her imagination, or did he look a little older than he had that afternoon?

"Jesse looks like Jeb. Rance looks like Rafe. Keegan looks like Kade. You're seeing things, Angus."

"Have it your way," Angus said.

Like any McKettrick had ever said *that* and meant it.

"What's for supper?"

"What do you care? You never eat."

"Neither do you. You're starting to look like a bag of bones."

"If I were you, I wouldn't make comments about bones. Being dead and all, I mean."

"The problem with you young people is, you have no respect for your elders."

Meg sighed, got up from her chair at the table, stomped over to the refrigerator and selected a boxed dinner from the stack in the freezer. The box was coated with frost.

"I'm sorry," Meg said. "Is that a hint of silver I see at your temples?"

Self-consciously, Angus shifted his weight from one booted foot to the other. "If I'm going gray," he scowled, "it's on account of you. None of my boys ever gave me half as much trouble as you, or my Katie, either. And they were plum full of the dickens, all of them."

Meg's heart pinched. Katie was Angus's youngest child, and his only daughter. He rarely mentioned her, since she'd caused some kind of scandal by eloping on her wedding day—with someone other than the groom. Although she and Angus had eventually reconciled, he'd been on his deathbed at the time.

"I'm *all right,* Angus," she told him. "You can go. Really."

"You eat food that could be used to drive railroad spikes into hard ground. You don't have a husband. You rattle around in this old house like some—ghost. I'm not leaving until I know you'll be happy."

"I'm happy *now.*"

Angus walked over to her, the heels of his boots thumping on the plank floor, took the frozen dinner out of her hands, and carried it to the trash compactor. Dropped it inside.

"Damn fool contraption," he muttered.

"That was my supper," Meg objected.

"Cook something," Angus said. "Get out a skillet. Dump some lard into it. Fry up a chicken." He paused, regarded her darkly. "You *do* know how to cook, don't you?"

Chapter 3

Jolene's, built on the site of the old saloon and brothel where Angus McKettrick and Major John Blackstone used to arm wrestle, among other things, was dimly lit and practically empty. Meg paused on the threshold, letting her eyes adjust and wishing she'd listened to her instincts and cancelled; now there would be no turning back.

Brad was standing by the jukebox, the colored lights flashing across the planes of his face. Having heard the door open, he turned his head slightly to acknowledge her arrival with a nod and a wisp of a grin.

"Where is everybody?" she asked. Except for the bartender, she and Brad were alone.

"Staying clear," Brad said. "I promised a free concert in the high school gym if we could have Jolene's to ourselves for a couple of hours."

Meg nearly fled. If it hadn't been against the McKettrick

code, as inherent to her being as her DNA, she would have given in to the urge and called it good judgment.

"Have a seat," Brad said, drawing back a chair at one of the tables. Nothing in the whole tavern matched, not even the bar stools, and every stick of furniture was scarred and scratched. Jolene's was a hangout for honky-tonk angels; the winged variety would surely have given the place a wide berth.

"What'll it be?" the bartender asked. He was a squat man, wearing a muscle shirt and a lot of tattoos. With his handlebar mustache, he might have been from Angus's era, instead of the present day.

Brad ordered a cola as Meg forced herself across the room to take the chair he offered.

Maybe, she thought, as she asked for an iced tea, the rumors were true, and Brad was fresh out of rehab.

The bartender served the drinks and quietly left the saloon, via a back door.

Brad, meanwhile, turned his own chair around and sat astraddle it, with his arms resting across the back. He wore jeans, a white shirt open at the throat and boots, and if he hadn't been so breathtakingly handsome, he'd have looked like any cowboy, in any number of scruffy little redneck bars scattered all over Arizona.

Meg eyed his drink, since doing that seemed slightly less dangerous than looking straight into his face, and when he chuckled, she felt her cheeks turn warm.

Pride made her meet his gaze. "What?" she asked, running damp palms along the thighs of her oldest pair of jeans. She'd made a point of *not* dressing up for the encounter—no perfume, and only a little mascara and lip gloss. War paint, Angus called it. Her favorite ghost had an opinion on everything, it seemed, but at least he'd honored his promise not to horn in on this interlude, or whatever it was, with Brad.

"Don't believe everything you read," Brad said easily, settling back in his chair. "Not about me, anyway."

"Who says I've been reading about you?"

"Come on, Meg. You expected me to drink Jack Daniel's straight from the bottle. That's hype—part of the bad-boy image. My manager cooked it up."

Meg huffed out a sigh. "You haven't been to rehab?"

He grinned. "Nope. Never trashed a hotel room, spent a weekend in jail, or any of the rest of the stuff Phil wanted everybody to believe about me."

"Really?"

"Really." Brad pushed back his chair, returned to the jukebox, and dropped a few coins in the slot. An old Johnny Cash ballad poured softly into the otherwise silent bar.

Meg took a swig of her iced tea, in a vain effort to steady her nerves. She was no teetotaler, but when she drove, she didn't drink. Ever. Right about then, though, she wished she'd hired a car and driver so she could get sloshed enough to forget that being alone with Brad O'Ballivan was like having her most sensitive nerves bared to a cold wind.

He started in her direction, then stopped in the middle of the floor, which was strewn with sawdust and peanut shells. Held out a hand to her.

Meg went to him, just the way she'd gone to the Dixie Dog Drive-In the day before. Automatically.

He drew her into his arms, holding her close but easy, and they danced without moving their feet.

As the song ended, Brad propped his chin on top of Meg's head and sighed. "I've missed you," he said.

Meg came to her senses.

Finally.

She pulled back far enough to look up into his face.

"Don't go there," she warned.

"We can't just pretend the past didn't happen, Meg," he reasoned quietly.

"Yes, we can," she argued. "Millions of people do it, every day. It's called denial, and it has its place in the scheme of things."

"Still a McKettrick," Brad said, sorrow lurking behind the humor in his blue eyes. "If I said the moon was round, you'd call it square."

She poked at his chest with an index finger. "Still an O'Ballivan," she accused. "Thinking you've got to explain the shape of the moon, as if I couldn't see it for myself."

The jukebox in Jolene's was an antique; it still played 45s. Now a record flopped audibly onto the turntable, and the needle scratched its way into Willie Nelson's version of "Georgia."

Meg stiffened, wanting to pull away.

Brad's arms, resting loosely around her waist, tightened slightly.

Over the years, the McKettricks and the O'Ballivans, owning the two biggest ranches in the area, had been friendly rivals. The families were equally proud and equally stubborn—they'd had to be, to survive the ups and downs of raising cattle for more than a century. Even when they were close, Meg and Brad had always identified strongly with their heritages.

Meg swallowed. "Why did you come back?" she asked, without intending to speak at all.

"To settle some things," Brad answered. They were swaying to the music again, though the soles of their boots were still rooted to the floor. "And you're at the top of my list, Meg McKettrick."

"You're at the top of mine, too," Meg retorted. "But I don't think we're talking about the same kind of list."

He laughed. God, how she'd missed that sound. How she'd missed the heat and substance of him, and the sun-dried laundry smell of his skin and hair...

Stop, she told herself. She was acting like some smitten fan or something.

"You bought me an engagement ring," she blurted, without intending to do anything of the kind. "We were supposed to elope. And then you got on a bus and went to Nashville and married what's-her-name!"

"I was stupid," Brad said. "And scared."

"No," Meg replied, fighting back furious tears. "You were *ambitious*. And of course the bride's father owned a recording company—"

Brad closed his eyes for a moment. A muscle bunched in his cheek. "Valerie," he said miserably. "Her name was Valerie."

"Do you really think I give a damn what her name was?"

"Yeah," he answered. "I do."

"Well, you're wrong!"

"That must be why you look like you want to club me to the ground with the nearest blunt object."

"I got over you like that!" Meg told him, snapping her fingers. But a tear slipped down her cheek, spoiling the whole effect.

Brad brushed it away gently with the side of one thumb. "Meg," he said. "I'm so sorry."

"Oh, that changes everything!" Meg scoffed. She tried

to move away from him again, but he still wouldn't let her go.

One corner of his mouth tilted up in a forlorn effort at a grin. "You'll feel a lot better if you forgive me." He curved the fingers of his right hand under her chin, lifted. "For old times' sake?" he cajoled. "For the nights when we went skinny-dipping in the pond behind your house on the Triple M? For the nights we—"

"No," Meg interrupted, fairly smothering as the memories wrapped themselves around her. "You don't deserve to be forgiven."

"You're right," Brad agreed. "I don't. But that's the thing about forgiveness. It's all about grace, isn't it? It's supposed to be undeserved."

"Great logic if you're on the *receiving* end!"

"I had my reasons, Meg."

"Yeah. You wanted bright lights and big money. Oh, and fast women."

Brad's jaw tightened, but his eyes were bleak. "I couldn't have married you, Meg."

"Pardon my confusion. You gave me an engagement ring and proposed!"

"I wasn't thinking." He looked away, faced her again with visible effort. "You had a trust fund. I had a mortgage and a pile of bills. I laid awake nights, sweating blood, thinking the bank would foreclose at any minute. I couldn't dump that in your lap."

Meg's mouth dropped open. She'd known the O'Ballivans weren't rich, at least, not like the McKettricks were, but she'd never imagined, even once, that Stone Creek Ranch was in danger of being lost.

"They wanted that land," Brad went on. "The bankers,

I mean. They already had the plans drawn up for a housing development."

"I didn't know—I would have helped—"

"Sure," Brad said. "You'd have helped. And I'd never have been able to look you in the face again. I had one chance, Meg. Valerie's dad had heard my demo and he was willing to give me an audition. A fifteen-minute slot in his busy day. I tried to tell you—"

Meg closed her eyes for a moment, remembering. Brad had told her he wanted to postpone the wedding until after his trip to Nashville. He'd promised to come back for her. She'd been furious and hurt—and keeping a secret of her own—and they'd argued....

She swallowed painfully. "You didn't call. You didn't write—"

"When I got to Nashville, I had a used bus ticket and a guitar. If I'd called, it would have been collect, and I wasn't *about* to do that. I started half a dozen letters, but they all sounded like the lyrics to bad songs. I went to the library a couple of times, to send you an e-mail, but beyond 'how are you?' I just flat-out didn't know what to say."

"So you just hooked up with Valerie?"

"It wasn't like that."

"I'm assuming she was a rich kid, just like me? I guess you didn't mind if *she* saved the old homestead with a chunk of her trust fund."

Brad's jawline tightened. "*I* saved the ranch," he said. "Most of the money from my first record contract went to paying down the mortgage, and it was still a struggle until I scored a major hit." He paused, obviously remembering the much leaner days before he could fill the biggest stadiums in the country with devoted fans, swaying to his music in the darkness, holding flickering lighters aloft in tribute. "I didn't love Valerie, and she didn't love me. She was a rich kid, all right. Spoiled and lonesome, neglected in the ways rich kids so often are, and she was in big trouble. She'd gotten herself pregnant by some married guy who wanted nothing to do with her. She figured her dad would kill her if he found out, and given his temper, I tended to agree. So I married her."

Meg made her way back to the table and sank into her chair. "There was...a baby?"

"She miscarried. We divorced amicably, after trying to make it work for a couple of years. She's married to a dentist now, and really happy. Four kids, at last count." Brad joined Meg at the table. "Do you want to hear about the second marriage?"

"I don't think I'm up to that," Meg said weakly.

Brad's hand closed over hers. "Me, either," he replied. He ducked his head, in a familiar way that tugged at Meg's heart, to catch her eye. "You all right?"

"Just a little shaken up, that's all."

"How about some supper?"

"They serve supper here? At Jolene's?"

Brad chuckled. "Down the road, at the Steakhouse. You can't miss it—it's right next to the sign that says, Welcome To Stone Creek, Arizona, Home Of Brad O'Ballivan."

"Braggart," Meg said, grateful that the conversation had taken a lighter turn.

He grinned engagingly. "Stone Creek has always been the home of Brad O'Ballivan," he said. "It just seems to mean more now than it did when I left that first time."

"You'll be mobbed," Meg warned.

"The whole town could show up at the Steakhouse, and it wouldn't be enough to make a mob."

"Okay," Meg agreed. "But you're buying."

Brad laughed. "Fair enough," he said.

Then he got up from his chair and summoned the bartender, who'd evidently been cooling his heels in a storeroom or office.

The floor felt oddly spongy beneath Meg's feet, and she was light-headed enough to wonder if there'd been some alcohol in that iced tea after all.

The Steakhouse, unlike Jolene's, was jumping. People called out to Brad when he came in, and young girls pointed and giggled, but most of them had been at the welcome party Ashley and Melissa had thrown for him on the ranch the night before, so some of the novelty of his being back in town had worn off.

Meg drew some glances, though—all of them admiring, with varying degrees of curiosity mixed in. Even in jeans, boots and a plain woolen coat over a white blouse, she looked like what she was—a McKettrick with a trust fund and an impressive track record as a top-level executive. When McKettrickCo had gone public, Brad had been surprised when she didn't turn up immediately as the CEO of some corporation. Instead, she'd come home to hibernate on the Triple M, and he wondered why.

He wondered lots of things about Meg McKettrick.

With luck, he'd have a chance to find out everything he wanted to know.

Like whether she still laughed in her sleep and ate cereal with yogurt instead of milk and arched her back like a gymnast when she climaxed.

Since the Steakhouse was no place to think about Meg having one of her noisy orgasms, Brad tried to put the image out of his mind. It merely shifted to another part of his anatomy.

They were shown to a booth right away, and given menus and glasses of water with the obligatory slices of fresh lemon rafting on top of the ice.

Brad ordered a steak, Meg a Caesar salad.

The waitress went away, albeit reluctantly.

"Okay," Brad said, "it's my turn to ask questions. Why did you quit working after you left McKettrickCo?"

Meg smiled, but she looked a little flushed, and he could tell by her eyes that she was busy in there, sorting things and putting them in their proper places. "I didn't need the money. And I've always wanted to live full-time on the Triple M, like Jesse and Rance and Keegan. When I spent summers there, as a child, the only way I could deal with leaving in the fall to go back to school was to promise myself that one day I'd come home to stay."

"You love it that much?" Given his own attachment to Stone Creek Ranch, Brad could understand, but at the same time, the knowledge troubled him a little, too. "What do you do all day?"

Her mouth quirked in a way that made Brad want to kiss her. And do a few other things, too. "You sound like my mother," she said. "I take care of the horses, ride sometimes—"

He nodded. Waited.

She didn't finish the sentence.

"You never married." He hadn't meant to say that. Hadn't meant to let on that he'd kept track of her all these years, mostly on the Internet, but through his sisters, too.

She shook her head. "Almost," she said. "Once. It didn't work out."

Brad leaned forward, intrigued and feeling pretty damn territorial, too. "Who was the unlucky guy? He must have been a real jackass."

"You," she replied sweetly, and then laughed at the expression on his face.

He started to speak, then gulped the words down, sure they'd come out sounding as stupid as the question he'd just asked.

"I've dated a lot of men," Meg said.

The orgasm image returned, but this time, he wasn't Meg's partner. It was some other guy bringing her to one of her long, exquisite, clawing, shouting, bucking climaxes, not him. He frowned.

"Maybe we shouldn't talk about my love life," she suggested.

"Maybe not," Brad agreed.

"Not that I exactly have one."

Brad felt immeasurably better. "That makes two of us."

Meg looked unconvinced. Even squirmed a little on the vinyl seat.

"What?" Brad prompted, enjoying the play of emotions on her face. He and Meg weren't on good terms—too soon for that—but it was a hopeful sign that she'd met him at Jolene's and then agreed to supper on top of it.

"I saw that article in *People* magazine. 'The Cowboy with the Most Notches on His Bedpost,' I think it was called?"

"I thought we weren't going to talk about our love lives. And would you mind keeping your voice down?"

"We agreed not to talk about *mine,* if I remember correctly, which, as I told you, is nonexistent. And to avoid the subject of your second wife—at least, for now."

"There have been women," Brad said. "But that bedpost thing was all Phil's idea. Publicity stuff."

The food arrived.

"Not that I care if you carve notches on your bedpost," Meg said decisively, once the waitress had left again.

"Right," Brad replied, serious on the outside, grinning on the inside.

"Where is this Phil person from, anyway?" Meg asked, mildly disgruntled, her fork poised in midair over her salad. "Seems to me he has a pretty skewed idea on the whole cowboy mystique. Rehab. Trashing hotel rooms. The notch thing."

"There's a 'cowboy mystique'?"

"You know there is. Honor, integrity, courage—those are the things being a cowboy is all about."

Brad sighed. Meg was a stickler for detail; good thing she hadn't gone to law school, like she'd once planned. She probably would have represented his second ex-wife in the divorce and stripped his stock portfolio clean. "I tried. Phil works freestyle, and he sure knew how to pack the concert halls."

Meg pointed the fork at him. "*You* packed the concert halls, Brad. You and your music."

"You like my music?" It was a shy question; he hadn't quite dared to ask if she liked *him* as well. He knew too well what the answer might be.

"It's...nice," she said.

Nice? Half a dozen Grammies and CMT awards, weeks at number one on every chart that mattered, and she thought his music was "nice"?

Whatever she thought, Brad finally concluded, that was all she was going to give up, and he had to be satisfied with it.

For now.

He started on the steak, but he hadn't eaten more than two bites when there was a fuss at the entrance to the restaurant and Livie came storming in, striding right to his table.

Sparing a nod for Meg, Brad's sister turned immediately to him. "He's hurt," she said. Her clothes were covered with straw and a few things that would have upset the health department, being that she was in a place where food was being served to the general public.

"Who's hurt?" Brad asked calmly, sliding out of the booth to stand.

"Ransom," she answered, near tears. "He got himself cut up in a tangle of rusty barbed wire. I'd spotted him with binoculars, but before I could get there to help, he'd torn free and headed for the hills. He's hurt bad, and I'm not going to be able to get to him in the Suburban—we need to saddle up and go after him."

"Liv," Brad said carefully, "it's dark out."

"He's *bleeding,* and probably weak. The wolves could take him down!" At the thought of that, Livie's eyes glistened with moisture. "If you won't help, I'll go by myself."

Distractedly, Brad pulled out his wallet and threw down the money for the dinner he and Meg hadn't gotten a chance to finish.

Meg was on her feet, the salad forgotten. "Count me in, Olivia," she said. "That is, if you've got an extra horse and some gear. I could go back out to the Triple M for Banshee, but by the time I hitched up the trailer, loaded him and gathered the tack—"

"You can ride Cinnamon," Olivia told Meg, after sizing her up as to whether she'd be a help or a hindrance on the trail. "It'll be cold and dark up there in the high country," she added. "Could be a long, uncomfortable night."

"No room service?" Meg quipped.

Livie spared her a smile, but when she turned to Brad

again, her blue eyes were full of obstinate challenge. "Are you going or not—cowboy?"

"Hell, yes, I'm going," Brad said. Riding a horse was a thing you never forgot how to do, but it had been a while since he'd been in the saddle, and that meant he'd be groaning-sore before this adventure was over. "What about the stock on the Triple M, Meg? Who's going to feed your horses, if this takes all night?"

"They're good till morning," Meg answered. "If I'm not back by then, I'll ask Jesse or Rance or Keegan to check on them."

Livie led the caravan in her Suburban, with Brad following in his truck, and Meg right behind, in the Blazer. He was worried about Ransom, and about Livie's obsession with the animal, but there was one bright spot in the whole thing.

He was going to get to spend the night with Meg McKettrick, albeit on the hard, half-frozen ground, and the least he could do, as a gentleman, was share his sleeping bag—and his body warmth.

"Right smart of you to go along," Angus commented, appearing in the passenger seat of Meg's rig. "There might be some hope for you yet."

Meg answered without moving her mouth, just in case Brad happened to glance into his rearview mirror and catch her talking to nobody. "I thought you were giving me some elbow room on this one," she said.

"Don't worry," Angus replied. "If you go to bed down with him or something like that, I'll skedaddle."

"I'm not going to 'bed down' with Brad O'Ballivan."

Angus sighed. Adjusted his sweat-stained cowboy hat.

Since he usually didn't wear one, Meg read it as a sign bad weather was on its way. "Might be a good thing if you did. Only way to snag some men."

"I will not dignify that remark with a reply," Meg said, flooring the gas pedal to keep up with Brad, now that they were out on the open road, where the speed limit was higher. She'd never actually been to Stone Creek Ranch, but she knew where it was. Knew all about King's Ransom, too. Her cousin Jesse, practically a horse-whisperer, claimed the animal was nothing more than a legend, pieced together around a hundred campfires, over as many years, after all the lesser tales had been told.

Meg wanted to see for herself.

Wanted to help Olivia, whom she'd always liked but barely knew.

Spending the night on a mountain with Brad O'Ballivan didn't enter into the decision at all. Much.

"Is he real?" she asked. "The horse, I mean?"

Angus adjusted his hat again. "Sure he is," he said, his voice quiet, but gruff. Sometimes a look came into his eyes, a sort of hunger for the old days and the old ways.

"Is there anything you can do to help us find him?"

Angus shook his head. "You've got to do that yourselves, you and the singing cowboy and the girl."

"Olivia is not a girl. She's a grown woman and a veterinarian."

"She's a snippet," Angus said. "But there's fire in her. That O'Ballivan blood runs hot as coffee brewed on a cookstove in hell. She needs a man, though. The knot in *her* lasso is way too tight."

"I hope that reference wasn't sexual," Meg said stiffly,

"because I do *not* need to be carrying on that type of conversation with my dead multi-great grandfather."

"It makes me feel old when you talk about me like I helped Moses carry the commandments down off the mountain," Angus complained. "I was young once, you know. Sired four strapping sons and a daughter by three different women—Ellie, Georgia and Concepcion. And I'm not dead, neither. Just...different."

Olivia had stopped suddenly for a gate up ahead, and Meg nearly rear-ended Brad before she got the Blazer reined in.

"Different as in dead," Meg said, watching through the windshield, in the glow of her headlights, as Brad got out of his truck and strode back to speak to her, leaving the driver's-side door gaping behind him.

He didn't look angry—just earnest.

"If you want to ride with me," he said when Meg had buzzed down her window, "fine. But if you're planning to drive this rig up into the bed of my truck, you might want to wait until I park it in a hole and lower the tailgate."

"Sorry," Meg said after making a face.

Brad shook his head and went back to his truck. By then, Olivia had the gate open, and he drove ahead onto an unpaved road winding upward between the juniper and Joshua trees clinging to the red dirt of the hillside.

"What was that about?" Meg mused, following Brad and Olivia's vehicles through the gap and not really addressing Angus, who answered, nonetheless.

"Guess he's prideful about the paint on that fancy jitney of his," he said. "Didn't want you denting up his buggy."

Meg didn't comment. Angus was full of the nineteenth-century equivalent of "woman driver" stories, and she didn't care to hear any of them.

They topped a rise, Olivia still in the lead, and dipped down into what was probably a broad valley, given what little Meg knew about the landscape on Stone Creek Ranch. Lights glimmered off to the right, revealing a good-size house and a barn.

Meg was about to ask if Angus had ever visited the ranch when he suddenly vanished.

She shut off the Blazer, got out and followed Brad and Olivia toward the barn. She wished it hadn't been so dark—it would have been interesting to see the place in the daylight.

Inside the barn, which was as big as any of the ones on the Triple M and boasted all the modern conveniences, Olivia and Brad were already saddling horses.

"That's Cinnamon over there," Olivia said with a nod to a tall chestnut in the stall across the wide breezeway from the one she was standing in, busily preparing a palomino to ride. "His gear's in the tack room, third saddle rack on the right."

Meg didn't hesitate, as she suspected Olivia had expected her to do, but found the tack room and Cinnamon's gear, and lugged it back to his stall. Brad and his sister were already mounted and waiting at the end of the breezeway when Meg led the gelding out, however.

"Need a boost?" Brad asked, in a teasing drawl, saddle leather creaking as he shifted to step down from the big paint he was riding and help Meg mount up.

Cinnamon was a big fella, taller by several hands than any of the horses in Meg's barn, but she'd been riding since she was in diapers, and she didn't need a boost from a "singing cowboy," as Angus described Brad.

"I can do it," she replied, straining to grip the saddle

horn and get a foot into the high stirrup. It was going to be a stretch.

In the next instant, she felt two strong hands pushing on her backside, hoisting her easily onto Cinnamon's broad back.

Thanks, Angus, she said silently.

Chapter 4

It was a purely crazy thing to do, setting out on horseback, in the dark, for the high plains and meadows and secret canyons of Stone Creek Ranch, in search of a legendary stallion determined not to be found. It had been way too long since she'd done anything like it, Meg reflected, as she rode behind Olivia and Brad, on the borrowed horse called Cinnamon.

Olivia had brought a few veterinary supplies along, packed in saddle bags, and while Meg was sure Ransom, wounded or not, would elude them, she couldn't help admiring the kind of commitment it took to set out on the journey anyway. Olivia O'Ballivan was a woman with a cause and for that, Meg envied her a little.

The moon was three-quarters full, and lit their way, but the trail grew steadily narrower as they climbed, and the mountainside was steep and rocky. One misstep on the part of a distracted horse and both animal and rider would plunge hundreds of feet into an abyss of shadow, to their very certain and very painful deaths.

When the trail widened into what appeared, in the thin wash of moonlight, to be a clearing, Meg let out her breath, sat a little less tensely in the saddle, loosened her grip on Cinnamon's reins. Brad drew up his own mount to wait for her, while Olivia and her horse shot forward, intent on their mission.

"Do you think we'll find him?" Meg asked. "Ransom, I mean?"

"No," Brad answered, unequivocally. "But Livie was bound to try. I came to look out for her."

Meg hadn't noticed the rifle in the scabbard fixed to Brad's saddle before, back at the O'Ballivan barn, but it stood out in sharp relief now, the polished wooden stock glowing in a silvery flash of moonlight. He must have seen her eyes widen; he patted the scabbard as he met her gaze.

"You're expecting to shoot something?" Meg ventured. She'd been around guns all her life—they were plentiful on the Triple M—but that didn't mean she liked them.

"Only if I have to," Brad said, casting a glance in the direction Olivia had gone. He nudged his horse into motion, and Cinnamon automatically kept pace, the two geldings moving at an easy trot.

"What would constitute having to?" Meg asked.

"Wolves," Brad answered.

Meg was familiar with the wolf controversy—environmentalists and animal activists on the one side, ranchers on the other. She wanted to know where Brad stood on the subject. He was well-known for his love of all things finned, feathered and furry—but that might have been part of his carefully constructed persona, like the notched bedpost and the trashed hotel rooms.

"You wouldn't just pick them off, would you? Wolves, I mean?"

"Of course not," Brad replied. "But wolves are predators, and Livie's not wrong to be concerned that they'll track Ransom and take him down if they catch the blood-scent from his wounds."

A chill trickled down Meg's spine, like a splash of cold water, setting her shivering. Like Brad, she came from a long line of cattle ranchers, and while she allowed that wolves had a place in the ecological scheme of things, like every other creature on earth, she didn't romanticize them. They were not misunderstood *dogs,* as so many people seemed to think, but hunters, savagely brutal and utterly ruthless, and no one who'd ever seen what they did to their prey would credit them with nobility.

"Sharks with legs," she mused aloud. "That's what Rance calls them."

Brad nodded, but didn't reply. They were gaining on Olivia now; she was still a ways ahead, and had dismounted to look at something on the ground.

Both Brad and Meg sped up to reach her.

By the time they arrived, Olivia's saddlebags were open beside her, and she was holding a syringe up to the light. Because of the darkness, and the movements of the horses, a few moments passed before Meg focused on the animal Olivia was treating.

A dog lay bloody and quivering on its side.

Brad was off his horse before Meg broke the spell of shock that had descended over her and dismounted, too. Her stomach rolled when she got a better look at the dog; the poor creature, surely a stray, had run afoul of either a wolf or coyote pack, and it was purely a miracle that he'd survived.

Meg's eyes burned.

Brad crouched next to the dog, opposite Olivia, and stroked the animal with a gentleness that altered something deep down inside Meg, causing a grinding sensation, like the shift of tectonic plates far beneath the earth.

"Can he make it?" he asked Olivia.

"I'm not sure," Olivia replied. "At the very least, he needs stitches." She injected the contents of the syringe into the animal's ruff. "I sedated him. Give the medicine a few minutes to work, and then we'll take him back to the clinic in Stone Creek."

"What about the horse?" Meg asked, feeling helpless, a bystander with no way to help. She wasn't used to it. "What about Ransom?"

Olivia's eyes were bleak with sorrow when she looked up at Meg. She was a veterinarian; she couldn't abandon the wounded dog, or put him to sleep because it would be more convenient than transporting him back to town, where he could be properly cared for. But worry for the stallion would prey on her mind, just the same.

"I'll look for him tomorrow," Olivia said. "In the daylight."

Brad reached across the dog, laid a hand on his sister's shoulder. "He's been surviving on his own for a long time, Liv," he assured her. "Ransom will be all right."

Olivia bit her lower lip, nodded. "Get one of the sleeping bags, will you?" she said.

Brad nodded and went to unfasten the bedroll from behind his saddle. They were miles from town, or any ranch house.

"How did a dog get all the way out here?" Meg asked, mostly because the silence was too painful.

"He's probably a stray," Olivia answered, between

soothing murmurs to the dog. "Somebody might have dumped him, too, down on the highway. A lot of people think dogs and cats can survive on their own—hunt and all that nonsense."

Meg drew closer to the dog, crouched to touch his head. He appeared to be some kind of Lab-retriever mix, though it was hard to tell, given that his coat was saturated with blood. He wore no collar, but that didn't mean he didn't have a microchip—and if he did, Olivia would be able to identify him immediately, once she got him to the clinic. Though from the looks of him, he'd be lucky to make it that far.

Brad returned with the sleeping bag, unfurling it. "Okay to move him now?" he asked Olivia.

Olivia nodded, and she and Meg sort of helped each other to their feet. "You mount up," Olivia told Brad. "And we'll lift him."

Brad whistled softly for his horse, which trotted obediently to his side, gathered the dangling reins, and swung up into the saddle.

Meg and Olivia bundled the dog, now mercifully unconscious, in the sleeping bag and, together, hoisted him high enough so Brad could take him into his arms. They all rode slowly back down the trail, Brad holding that dog as tenderly as he would an injured child, and not a word was spoken the whole way.

When they got back to the ranch house, where Olivia's Suburban was parked, Brad loaded the dog into the rear of the vehicle.

"I'll stay and put the horses away," Meg told him. "You'd better go into town with Olivia and help her get him inside the clinic."

Brad nodded. "Thanks," he said gruffly.

Olivia gave Meg an appreciative glance before scrambling into the back of the Suburban to ride with the patient, ambulance-style. Brad got behind the wheel.

Once they'd driven off, Meg gathered the trio of horses and led them into the barn. There, in the breezeway, she removed their saddles and other tack and let the animals show her which stalls were their own. She checked their hooves for stones, made sure their automatic waterers were working, and gave them each a flake of hay. All the while, her thoughts were with Brad, and the stray dog lying in the back of Olivia's rig.

A part of her wanted to get into the Blazer and head straight for Stone Creek, and the veterinary clinic where Olivia worked, but she knew she'd just be in the way. Brad could provide muscle and moral support, if not medical skills, but Meg had nothing to offer.

With the O'Ballivans' horses attended to, she fired up the Blazer and headed back toward Indian Rock. She covered the miles between Stone Creek Ranch and the Triple M in a daze, and was a little startled to find herself at home when she pulled up in front of the garage door.

Leaving the Blazer in the driveway, Meg went into the barn to look in on Banshee and the four other horses who resided there. On the Triple M, horses were continually rotated between her place, Jesse's, Rance's and Keegan's, depending on what was best for the animals. Now they blinked at her, sleepily surprised by a late-night visit, and she paused to stroke each one of their long faces before starting for the house.

Angus fell into step with her as she crossed the side yard, headed for the back door.

"The stallion's all right," he informed her. "Holed up in one of the little canyons, nursing his wounds."

"I thought you said you couldn't help find him," Meg said, stopping to stare up at her ancestor in the moonlight.

"Turned out I was wrong," Angus drawled. His hat was gone; the bad weather he'd probably been expecting hadn't materialized.

"Mark the calendar," Meg teased. "I just heard a McKettrick admit to being wrong about something."

Angus grinned, waited on the small, open back porch while she unlocked the kitchen door. In his day, locks hadn't been necessary. Now the houses on the Triple M were no more immune to the rising crime rate than anyplace else.

"I've been wrong about plenty in my life," Angus said. "For one thing, I was wrong to leave Holt behind in Texas, after his mother died. He was just a baby, and God knows what I'd have done with him on the trail between there and the Arizona Territory, but I should have brought him, nonetheless. Raised him with Rafe and Kade and Jeb."

Intrigued, Meg opened the door, flipped on the kitchen lights and stepped inside. All of this was ancient family history to her, but to Angus, it was immediate stuff. "What else were you wrong about?" she asked, removing her coat and hanging it on the peg next to the door, then going to the sink to wash her hands.

Angus took a seat at the head of the table. In this house, it would have been Holt's place, but Angus was in the habit of taking the lead, even in small things.

"I ever tell you I had a brother?" he asked.

Meg, about to brew a pot of tea, stopped and stared at him, stunned out of her fatigue. "No," she said. "You didn't." The McKettricks were raised on legend and lore, cut their teeth on it; the brother came as news. "Are you telling me there could be a whole other branch of the family out there?"

"Josiah got on fine with the ladies," Angus reminisced. "It would be my guess his tribe is as big as mine."

Meg forgot all about the tea-brewing. She made her way to the table and sat down heavily on the bench, gaping at Angus.

"Don't fret about it," he said. "They'd have no claim on this ranch, or any of the take from that McKettrickCo outfit."

Meg blinked, still trying to assimilate the revelation. "No one has *ever* mentioned that you had a brother," she said. "In all the diaries, all the letters, all the photographs—"

"They wouldn't have said anything about Josiah," Angus told her, evidently referring to his sons and their many descendants. "They never knew he existed."

"Why not?"

"Because he and I had a falling-out, and I didn't want anything to do with him after that. He felt the same way."

"Why bring it up now—after a century and a half?"

Angus shifted uncomfortably in his chair and, for a moment, his jawline hardened. "One of them's about to land on your doorstep," he said after a long, molar-grinding silence. "I figured you ought to be warned."

"*Warned?* Is this person a serial killer or a crook or something?"

"No," Angus said. "He's a lawyer. And that's damn near as bad."

"As a family, we haven't exactly kept a low profile for the last hundred or so years," Meg said slowly. "If Josiah has as many descendants as you do, why haven't any of them contacted us? It's not as if McKettrick is a common name, after all."

"Josiah took another name," Angus allowed, after more jaw-clamping. "That's what we got into it about, him and me."

"Why would he do that?" Meg asked.

Angus fixed her with a glare. Clearly, even after all the time that passed, he hadn't forgiven Josiah for changing his name and for whatever had prompted him to do that.

"He went to sea, when he was hardly more than a boy," Angus said. "When he came back home to Texas, years later, he was calling himself by another handle and running from the law. Hinted that he'd been a pirate."

"A *pirate?*"

"Left Ma and me to get by on our own, after Pa died," Angus recalled bitterly, looking through Meg to some long-ago reality. "Rode out before they'd finished shoveling dirt into Pa's grave. I ran down the road after him—he was riding a big buckskin horse—but he didn't even look back."

Tentatively, Meg reached out to touch Angus's arm. Clearly, Josiah had been the elder brother, and Angus a lot younger. He'd adored Josiah McKettrick—that much was plain—and his leaving had been a defining event in Angus's life. So defining, in fact, that he'd never acknowledged the other man's existence.

Angus bristled. "It was a long time ago," he said.

"What name did he go by?" Meg asked. She knew she wasn't going to sleep, for worrying about the injured dog and the stallion, and planned to spend the rest of the night at the computer, searching on Google for members of the heretofore unknown Josiah-side of the family.

"I don't rightly recall," Angus said glumly.

Meg knew he was lying. She also knew he wasn't going to tell her his brother's assumed name.

She got up again, went back to brewing tea.

Angus sat brooding in silence, and the phone rang just as Meg was pouring boiling water over the loose tea leaves in the bottom of Lorelei's pot.

Glancing at the caller ID panel, she saw no name, just an unfamiliar number with a 615 area code.

"Hello?"

"He's going to recover," Brad said.

Tears rushed to Meg's eyes, and her throat constricted. He was referring to the dog, of course. And using the cell phone he'd carried when he still lived in Tennessee. "Thank God," she managed to say. "Did Olivia operate?"

"No need," Brad answered. "Once she'd taken X-rays and run a scan, she knew there were no internal injuries. He's pretty torn up—looks like a baseball with all those stitches—but he'll be okay."

"Was there a microchip?"

"Yeah," Brad said after a charged silence. "But the phone number's no longer in service. Livie ran an internet search and found out the original owner died six months ago. Who knows where Willie's been in the meantime."

"Willie?"

"The dog," Brad explained. "That's his name. Willie."

"What's going to happen to Willie now?"

"He'll be at the clinic for a while," Brad said. "He's in pretty bad shape. Livie will try to find out if anybody adopted him after his owner died, but we're not holding out a lot of hope on that score."

"He'll go to the pound? When he's well enough to leave the clinic?"

"No," Brad answered. He sounded as tired as Meg felt.

"If nobody has a prior claim on him, he'll come to live with me. I could use a friend—and so could he." He paused. "I hope I didn't wake you or anything."

"I was still up," Meg said, glancing in Angus's direction only to find that he'd disappeared again.

"Good," Brad replied.

A silence fell between them. Meg knew there was something else Brad wanted to say, and that she'd want to hear it. So she waited.

"I'm riding up into the high country again first thing in the morning," he finally said. "Looking for Ransom. I was wondering if—well—it's probably a stupid idea, but—"

Meg waited, resisting an urge to rush in and finish the sentence for him.

"Would you like to go along? Livie has a full schedule tomorrow—one of the other vets is out sick—and she wants to keep an eye on Willie, too. She's going to obsess about this horse until I can tell her he's fine, so I'm going to find him if I can."

"I'd like to go," Meg said. "What time are you leaving the ranch?"

"Soon as the sun's up," Brad answered. "You're sure? The country's pretty rough up there."

"If you can handle rough country, O'Ballivan, so can I."

He chuckled. "Okay, McKettrick," he said.

Meg found herself smiling. "I'll be there by 6:00 a.m., unless that's too early. Shall I bring my own horse?"

"Six is about right," Brad said. "Don't go to the trouble of trailering another horse—you can ride Cinnamon. Dress warm, though. And bring whatever gear you'd need if we had to spend the night for some reason."

Alone in her kitchen, Meg blushed. "See you in the morning," she said.

"'Night," Brad replied.

"Good night," Meg responded—long after Brad had hung up.

Giving up on the tea and, at least for that night, researching Josiah McKettrick, and having decided she needed to at least *try* to sleep, since tomorrow would be an eventful day, Meg locked up, shut off the lights and went upstairs to her room.

After getting out a pair of thermal pajamas, she took a long shower in the main bathroom across the hall, brushed her teeth, tamed her wet hair as best she could and went to bed.

Far from tossing and turning, as she'd half expected, she dropped into an immediate, consuming slumber, so deep she remembered none of her dreams.

Waking, she dressed quickly, in jeans and a sweatshirt, over a set of long underwear, made of some miraculous microfiber and bought for skiing, and finished off her ensemble with two pairs of socks and her sturdiest pair of boots. She shoved toothpaste, a brush and a small tube of moisturizer into a plastic storage bag, rolled up a blanket, tied it tightly with twine from the kitchen junk drawer and breakfasted on toast and coffee.

She called Jesse on her cell phone as she climbed into the Blazer, after feeding Banshee and the others. Cheyenne, Jesse's wife, answered on the second ring.

"Hi, it's Meg. Is Jesse around?"

"Sleeping," Cheyenne said, yawning audibly.

"I woke you up," Meg said, embarrassed.

"Jesse's the lay-abed in this family," Cheyenne responded warmly. "I've been up since four. Is anything wrong, Meg? Sierra and the baby—?"

"They're fine, as far as I know," Meg said, anxious to

reassure Cheyenne and, at the same time, very glad she'd gotten Jesse's wife instead of Jesse himself. He'd look after her horses if she asked, but he'd want to know where she was going, and if she replied that she and Brad O'Ballivan were riding off into the sunrise together, he'd tease her unmercifully. "Look, Cheyenne, I need a favor. I'm going on a—on a trail ride with a friend, and I'll probably be back tonight, but—"

"Would this 'friend' be the famous Brad O'Ballivan?"

"Yes," Meg said, but reluctantly, backing out of the driveway and turning the Blazer around to head for Stone Creek. It was still dark, but the first pinkish gold rays of sunlight were rimming the eastern hills. "Cheyenne, will you ask Jesse to check on my horses if he doesn't hear from me by six or so tonight?"

"Of course," Cheyenne said. "So you're going riding with Brad, and it might turn into an overnight thing. Hmmmmm—"

"It isn't anything romantic," Meg said. "I'm just helping him look for a stallion that might be hurt, that's all."

"I see," Cheyenne said sweetly.

"Just out of curiosity, what made you jump to the conclusion that the friend I mentioned was Brad?"

"It's all over town that you and country music's baddest bad boy met up at the Dixie Dog Drive-In the other day."

"Oh, great," Meg breathed. "I guess that means Jesse knows, then. And Rance and Keegan."

Cheyenne laughed softly, but when she spoke, her voice was full of concern. "Rance and Jesse are all for finding Brad and punching his lights out for hurting you so badly all those years ago, but Keegan is the voice of reason. He says give Brad a week to prove himself, *then* punch his lights out."

"The McKettrick way," Meg said. Her cousins were as protective as brothers would have been, and she loved them. But in terms of her social life, they weren't any more help than Angus had been.

"We'll talk later," Cheyenne said practically. "You're probably driving."

"Thanks, Chey," Meg answered.

When she got to Stone Creek Ranch, Brad came out of the house to greet her. He was dressed for the trail in jeans, boots, a work shirt and a medium-weight leather coat.

Meg's breath caught at the sight of him, and she was glad of the mechanics of parking and shutting off the Blazer, because it gave her a few moments to gather her composure.

Normally, she was unflappable.

She'd handled some of the toughest negotiations during her career with McKettrickCo, without so much as a flutter of nerves, but there was something about Brad that erased all the years she'd spent developing a thick skin and a poker face.

He opened the Blazer door before she was quite ready to face him.

"Hungry?" he asked.

"I had toast and coffee at home," Meg answered.

"That'll never hold you till lunch," he said. "Come on inside. I've got some *real* food on the stove."

"Okay," Meg said, because short of sitting stubbornly in the car, she couldn't think of a way to avoid accepting his invitation.

The O'Ballivan house, like the ones on the Triple M, was large and rustic, and it exuded a sense of rich history. The porch wrapped around the whole front of the structure, and the back door was on the side nearest the barn.

Meg followed Brad up the porch steps in front and around to another entrance.

The kitchen was big, and except for the wooden floors, which looked venerable, the room showed no trace of the old days. The countertops were granite, the cupboards gleamed, and the appliances were ultramodern, as were the furnishings.

Meg felt strangely let down by the sheer glamour of the place. All the kitchens on the Triple M had been modernized, of course, but in all cases, the original wood-burning stoves had been incorporated, and the tables all dated back to Holt, Rafe, Kade and Jeb's time, if not Angus's.

If Brad noticed her reaction, he didn't mention it. He dished up an omelet for her, and poured her a cup of coffee.

"You cook?" Meg teased, washing her hands at the gleaming stainless steel sink.

"I'm a fair hand in a kitchen," Brad replied modestly. "Dig in. I'll go saddle the horses while you eat."

Meg nodded, sat down and tackled the omelet.

It was delicious, and so was the coffee, but she felt uncomfortable sitting alone in that kitchen, as fancy as it was. She kept wondering what Maddie O'Ballivan would think, if she could see it, or even Brad's mother. Surely if things had been as difficult financially as Brad had let on the night before, at Jolene's, the renovations were fairly recent.

Having eaten as much as she could, Meg rinsed her plate, stuck it into the dishwasher, along with her fork and coffee cup, and hurried to the back door. Brad was out in front of the barn, the big paint ready to ride, tightening the cinch on Cinnamon's saddle. He picked her rolled blanket up off the ground and tied it on behind.

"Not much gear," he said. "Do you know how cold it gets up there?"

"I'll be fine," Meg said.

Brad merely shook his head. His own horse was restless, and the rifle was in evidence, too, looking ominous in the worn scabbard.

"That's quite a kitchen," Meg said as Brad gave her a leg up onto Cinnamon's back.

"Big John said it was a waste of money," Brad recalled, smiling to himself as he mounted up. "That was my granddad."

Meg knew who Big John O'Ballivan was—everybody in the county did—but she didn't point that out. If Brad wanted to talk about his family, to pass the time, that was fine with Meg. She nudged Cinnamon to keep pace with Brad's horse as they crossed a pasture, headed for the hills beyond.

"He raised you and your sisters, didn't he?" she asked, though she knew that, too.

"Yes," Brad said, and the set of his jaw reminded her of the way Angus's had looked, when he told her about his estranged brother.

Meg's curiosity spiked, but she didn't indulge it. "I take it Willie's still on the mend?"

Brad's grin was as dazzling as the coming sunrise would be. "Olivia called just before you showed up," he said with a nod. "Willie's going to be fine. In a week or two, I'll bring him home."

Remembering the way Brad had handled the dog, with such gentleness and such strength, Meg felt a pinch in the center of her heart. "You plan on staying, then?"

He tossed her a thoughtful look. "I plan on staying," he confirmed. "I told you that, didn't I?"

You also told me we'd get married and you'd love me forever.

"You told me," she said.

"Would this be a good time to tell you about my second wife?"

Meg considered, then shook her head, smiling a little. "Probably not."

"Okay," Brad said, "then how about my sisters?"

"Good idea." Meg had known Olivia slightly, but there was a set of twins in the family, too. She'd never met them.

"Olivia has a thing for animals, as you can see. She needs to get married and channel some of that energy into having a family of her own, but she's got a cussed streak and runs off every man who manages to get close to her. Ashley and Melissa—the twins—are fraternal. Ashley's pretty down-home—she runs a bed-and-breakfast in Stone Creek. Melissa's clerking in a law office in Flagstaff."

"You're close to them?"

"Yes," Brad said, expelling a long breath. "And, no. Olivia resents my leaving home—I can't seem to get it through her head that we wouldn't have *had* a home if I hadn't gone to Nashville. The twins are ten years younger than I am, and seem to see me more as a visiting celebrity than their big brother."

"When Olivia needed help," Meg reminded him, "she came to you. So maybe she doesn't resent you as much as you think she does." There was something really different about Olivia O'Ballivan, Meg thought, looking back over the night before, but she couldn't quite figure out what it was.

"I hope you're right," Brad said. "It's fine to love animals—I'm real fond of them myself. But Olivia carries it to a whole new place. So much so that there's no room in her life for much of anything—or anybody—else."

"She's a veterinarian, Brad," Meg said reasonably. "It's natural that animals are her passion."

"To the exclusion of everything else?" Brad asked.

"She'll be fine," Meg said. "When Olivia meets the right man, she'll make room for him. Just wait and see."

Brad looked unconvinced. He raised his chin and said, "If we're going to find that horse, we'd better move a little faster."

Meg nodded in agreement and Cinnamon fell in behind Brad's gelding as they started the twisting, perilous climb up the mountainside.

Chapter 5

Looking for that wild stallion was a fool's errand, and Brad knew it. As he'd told Meg, his primary reason for undertaking the quest was to keep Olivia from doing it. Now he wondered how many times, during his long absence, his little sister had climbed this mountain alone, at all hours of the day and night, and in all seasons of the year.

The thought made him shudder.

The country above Stone Creek was as rugged as it had ever been. Wolves, coyotes and even javelinas were plentiful, as were rattlesnakes. There were deep crevices in the red earth, some of them hidden by brush, and they'd swallowed many a hapless hiker. But the worst threat was probably the weather—at that elevation, blizzards could strike literally without warning, even in July and August. It was October now, and that only increased the danger.

Meg, shivering in her too-light coat, rode along beside him without complaint. Being a McKettrick, he thought, with a sad smile turned entirely inward, she'd freeze to death before she'd admit she was cold.

Inviting her along had been a purely selfish act, and Brad regretted it. Too many things could happen, most of them bad.

They'd been traveling for an hour or so when he stopped alongside a creek to rest the horses. High banks on either side sheltered them from the wind, and Meg got a chance to warm up.

Brad opened his saddlebags and brought out a long-sleeved thermal shirt, extended it to Meg. She hesitated a moment—that damnable McKettrick pride again—then took the shirt and pulled it on, right over the top of her coat.

The effect was comically unglamorous.

"Where's a Starbucks when you need one?" she joked.

Brad grinned. "There's an old line shack up the trail a ways," he told her. "Big John always kept it stocked with supplies, in case a hiker got stranded and needed shelter. It's not Starbucks, but I'll probably be able to rustle up a pot of coffee and some lunch. If you don't mind the survivalist packaging."

Meg's relief was visible, though she wouldn't have expressed it verbally, Brad knew. "We didn't need to bring the blankets and other gear then," she reasoned. "If there's a line shack, I mean."

"You've been living in the five-star lane for too long," Brad replied, but the jibe was a gentle one. "A while back, some hunters were trespassing on this land—Big John posted No Hunting signs years ago—and a snowstorm came up. They were found, dead of exposure, about fifty feet from the shack."

She shivered. "I remember," she said, and for a moment, her blue eyes looked almost haunted. The story had been a gruesome one, and she obviously *did* remember—all too clearly.

"We're not all that far from the ranch," Brad said. "It would probably be best if I took you back."

Meg's gaze widened, and grew more serious. "And you'd turn right around and come back up here to look for Ransom?"

"Yes," Brad answered, resigned.

"Alone."

He nodded. Once, Big John would have made the journey with him. Now there was no one.

"I'm staying," Meg said and shifted slightly, as if planting her feet. "You *invited* me to come along, in case you've forgotten."

"I shouldn't have. If anything happened to you—"

"I'm a big girl, Brad," she interrupted.

He looked her over, and—as always—liked what he saw. Liked it so much that his throat tightened and he had a hard time swallowing so he could hold up his end of the conversation. "You probably weigh a hundred and thirty pounds wrapped in a blanket and dunked into a lake. And despite your illustrious heritage, you're no match for a pack of wolves, a sudden blizzard, or a chasm that reaches halfway to China."

"If you can do it," Meg said, "*I* can do it."

Brad shoved a hand through his hair, exasperated even though he knew it was his own fault that Meg was in danger. After all, he *had* asked her to come along, half hoping the two of them would end up sharing a sleeping bag.

What the hell had he been thinking?

The pertinent question, he decided, was what had he been thinking *with*—not his brain, certainly.

"We'd better get moving again," she told him, when he

didn't speak. Before they'd left the ranch, he'd given her a pair of binoculars on a neck strap; now she pulled them out from under the donated undershirt, her coat, and whatever was beneath that. "We have a horse to find."

Brad nodded, cupped his hands to give her a leg up onto Cinnamon's back. She paused for a moment, deciding, before setting her left foot in the stirrup of his palms.

"This is a tall horse," she said, a little flushed.

"We should have named him Stilts instead of Cinnamon," Brad allowed, amused. Meg, like the rest of her cousins, had virtually grown up on horseback, as had he and Olivia and the twins. She'd interpret even the smallest courtesy—the offer of a boost, for instance—as an affront to her riding skills.

Forty-five minutes later, Meg, using the binoculars, spotted Ransom on the crest of a rocky rise.

"There he is!" she whispered, awed. "Wait till I tell Jesse he's real!"

After a few seconds, she lifted the binoculars off her neck by the strap and handed them across to Brad.

Brad drew in a breath, struck by the magnificence of the stallion, the defiance and barely restrained power. A moment or so passed before he thought to scan the horse for wounds. It was hard to tell, given the distance, even with binoculars, but Ransom wasn't limping, and Brad didn't see any blood. He could report to Olivia, in all honesty, that the object of her equine obsession was holding his own.

Before lowering the binoculars, Brad swept them across the top of that rise, and that was when he saw the two mares. He chuckled. Ransom had himself a harem, then.

He watched them a while, then gave the binoculars back to Meg, with a cheerful, "He has company."

Meg's face glowed. "They're beautiful," she whispered,

as if afraid to startle the horses and send them fleeing, though they were well over a mile away, by Brad's estimation. "And Ransom. He knows we're here, Brad. It's almost as if he wanted to let us see that he's all right."

Brad raised his coat collar against a chilly breeze and wished he'd worn his hat. He'd considered it that morning, but it had seemed like an affectation, a way of asserting that he was still a cowboy, by his own standards if not those of the McKettricks. "He knows," he agreed finally, "but it's more likely that he's taunting us. Catch-me-if-you-can. That's what he'd say if he could talk."

Meg's entire face was glowing. In fact, Brad figured if he could strip all those clothes off her, that glow would come right through her skin and be enough to warm him until he died of old age.

"How about that coffee?" she said, grinning.

After seeing Brad's kitchen on Stone Creek Ranch, Meg had expected the "line shack" to be a fancy log A-frame with a Jacuzzi and Internet service. It was an actual *shack,* though, made of weathered board. There was a lean-to on one side, to shelter the horses, but no barn, with hay stored inside. Brad gave the animals grain from a sealed metal bin, and filled two water buckets for them from a rusty old pump outside.

Meg might have gone inside and started the fire, so they could brew the promised coffee, but she was mesmerized, watching Brad. It was as though the two of them had somehow gone back in time, back to when all the earlier McKettricks and O'Ballivans were still in the prime of their lives.

Once, there had been several shacks like that one on the Triple M, far from the barns and bunkhouses. Ranch hands, riding the far-flung fence lines, or just traveling overland for some reason, used to spend the night in them, take refuge there when the weather was bad. Eventually, those tiny buildings had become hazards, rather than havens, and they'd been knocked down and burned.

"Pretty decrepit," Brad said, leading the way into the shack.

Things skittered inside, and the smell of the place was faintly musty, but Brad soon had a good fire going in the ancient potbellied stove. There was no furniture at all, but shelves, made of old wooden crates stacked on top of each other, held cups, food in airtight silver packets, cans of coffee.

The whole place was about the size of Meg's downstairs powder room on the Triple M.

"I'd offer you a chair," Brad said, grinning, "but obviously there aren't any. Make yourself at home while I rinse out these cups at the pump and fill the coffeepot."

Meg examined the plank floor, sat down cross-legged, and reveled in the warmth beginning to emanate from the wood-burning stove. The shack, inadequate as it was, offered a welcome respite from the cold wind outside. The hunters Brad had mentioned probably wouldn't have died if they'd been able to reach it. She remembered the news story; the facts had been bitter and brutal.

Like Stone Creek Ranch, the Triple M was posted, and hunting wasn't allowed. Still, people trespassed constantly, and Rance, Keegan and Jesse enforced the boundaries— mostly in a peaceful way. Just the winter before, though, Jesse had caught two men running deer with snowmobiles on the high meadow above his house, and he'd scared them off with a rifle shot aimed at the sky. Later, he'd tracked the pair to a tavern in Indian Rock—strangers to the area, they'd laughed at his warning—and put both of them in the hospital. He might have killed them, in fact, if Keegan hadn't gotten wind of the fight and come to break it up, and even with his help, it took the local marshal, Wyatt Terp, his deputy, and half the clientele in the bar to get Jesse off the second snowmobiler. He'd already pulverized the first one.

There was talk about filing assault charges against Jesse, and later it was rumored that there might be lawsuits, but nothing ever came of either. Meg, along with everybody else in Indian Rock, doubted the snowmobilers would ever set foot in town again, let alone on the Triple M.

But there was always, as Keegan liked to say, a fresh supply of idiots.

Brad came in with the cups and the full coffeepot, shoving the door closed behind him with one shoulder. Again, Meg had a sense of having stepped right out of the twenty-first century and into the nineteenth.

Despite cracks between the board walls, the shack was warm.

Brad set the coffeepot on the stove, measured ground beans into it from a can, and left it to boil, cowboy-style. No basket, no filter.

Then he emptied two of the crates being used as cupboards and dragged them over in front of the stove, so he and Meg could sit on them.

Overhead, thunder rolled across the sky, loud as a freight train.

Meg stiffened. "Rain?"

"Snow," Brad said. "I saw a few flakes drift past while I was outside. Soon as we've warmed up a little and fortified ourselves with caffeine and some grub, we'd better make for the low country."

Had there been any windows, Meg would have gotten up to look out of one of them. She could open the door a crack, but the thought of being buffeted by the rising wind stopped her.

By reflex, she scrambled to extract her cell phone from her coat pocket, flipped it open.

"No service," she murmured.

"I know," Brad said, smiling a little as he rose off the crate he'd been sitting on to add wood to the stove. Fortunately, there seemed to be an adequate supply of that. "I tried to call Olivia and let her know Ransom was still king of the hill a few minutes ago. Nothing."

Another round of thunder rattled the roof, and out in the lean-to, the horses fussed in alarm.

"Be right back," Brad said, heading for the door.

When he returned, he had a bedroll and Meg's pitifully insufficient blanket with him. And the horses were quiet.

"Just in case," he said when Meg's gaze landed, alarmed, on the overnight gear. "It's snowing pretty hard."

Meg, feeling foolish for sitting on her backside while Brad had been tending to the horses and fetching their gear inside, stood to lift the lid off the coffeepot and peek inside. The water was about to boil, but it would be a few minutes before the grounds settled to the bottom and they could drink the stuff.

"Relax, Meg," Brad said quietly. "There's still a chance the snow will ease up before dark."

At once tantalized and full of dread at the prospect of spending the night alone in a line shack with Brad O'Ballivan, Meg paced back and forth in front of the stove.

She knew what would happen if they stayed.

She'd known when she accepted Brad's invitation.

Known when she set out for Stone Creek Ranch before dawn.

And he probably had, too.

She shoved both hands into her hair and paced faster.

"Meg," Brad said, sitting leisurely on his upended crate, *"relax."*

"You knew," she accused, stopping to shake a finger at him. "You knew we'd be stuck here!"

"So did you," Brad replied, unruffled.

Meg went to the door, wrenched it open and looked out, oblivious to the cold. The snow was coming down so hard and so fast that she couldn't see the pine trees towering less than a hundred yards from where she stood.

Attempting to travel under those conditions would be suicide.

Brad came and helped her shut the door again.

On the other side of the wall, in the lean-to, the horses made no sound.

Meg was standing too close to Brad, no question about it. But when she tried to move, she couldn't.

They looked into each other's eyes.

The very atmosphere zinged around them.

If Brad had kissed her then, she wouldn't have had the will to do anything but kiss him right back, but he didn't. "I'd better get some drinking water," he said, turning away and reaching for a bucket. "While I can still find my way back from the pump."

He went out.

Meg, needing something to do, pushed the coffeepot to the back of the stove so it wouldn't boil over and then examined a few of the food packets, evidently designed for post-apocalyptic dinner parties. The expiration dates were fifty years in the future.

"Spaghetti à la the Starship Enterprise," she muttered. There was Beef Wellington, too, and even meat loaf. At least they wouldn't starve.

Not right away, anyhow.

They'd starve *slowly*.

If they didn't freeze to death first.

Meg tried her cell phone again.

Still no service.

It was just as well, she supposed. Cheyenne knew her approximate location. Jesse would feed her horses, and if her absence was protracted, he and Keegan and Rance were sure to come looking for her. In the meantime, though, there would be a lot of room for speculation about what might be going on up there in the high country. And Jesse wouldn't miss a chance to tease her about it.

She was still holding the phone when Brad came in again, carrying a bucket full of water. He looked so cold that Meg almost went to put her arms around him.

Instead, she poured him a cup of hot coffee, still chewy with grounds, and handed it to him as soon as he'd set the bucket down.

"I don't suppose there's a generator," she said because the shack was darkening, even though it wasn't noon yet, and by nightfall, she wouldn't be able to see the proverbial hand in front of her face.

He favored her with a tilted grin. "Just a couple of battery-operated lamps and a few candles. We'll want to conserve the batteries, of course."

"Of course," Meg said, and smiled determinedly, hoping that would distract Brad from the little quaver in her voice.

"We don't have to make love," Brad said, lingering by the stove and taking slow, appreciative sips from his coffee. "Just because we're alone in a remote line shack during what may be the snowstorm of the century."

"You are not making me feel better."

That grin again. It was saucy, but it had a wistful element. "Am I making you feel *something?*"

"Nothing discernible," Meg lied. In truth, all her nerves felt supercharged, and her body was remembering, against strict orders from her mind, the weight and warmth of Brad's hands, caressing her bare skin.

"I used to be pretty good at it. Making you feel things, that is."

"Brad," Meg said, "don't."

"Okay," he said.

Meg was relieved, but at the same time, she wished he hadn't given up quite so easily.

"You wanted coffee," Brad remarked. "Have some."

Meg filled a cup for herself. Scooted her crate an inch or two farther from Brad's and sat down.

The shadows deepened and the shack seemed to grow even smaller than it was, pressing her and Brad closer together. And then closer still.

"This," Meg said, inspired by desperation, "would be a good time to talk about your second wife. Since we've been putting it off for a while."

Brad chuckled, fished in his saddlebags, now lying on the floor at his feet, and brought out a deck of cards. "I was thinking more along the lines of gin rummy," he said.

"What was her name again?"

"What was whose name?"

"Your second wife."

"Oh, her."

"Yeah, her."

"Cynthia. Her name is Cynthia. And I don't want to

talk about her right now. Either we reminisce, or we play gin rummy, or—"

Meg squirmed. "Gin rummy," she said decisively. "There is no reason at all to bring up the subject of sex."

"Did I?"

"Did you what?"

"Did I bring up the subject of sex?"

"Not exactly," Meg said, embarrassed.

Brad grinned. "We'll get to that," he said. "Sooner or later."

Meg swallowed so much coffee in the next gulp that she nearly choked.

"There are some things I've been wondering about," Brad said easily, watching her over the rim of his metal coffee mug. His eyes smoldered with lazy blue heat.

Outside, the snow-thunder crashed again, but the horses didn't react. They'd probably already settled down for the night, snug in their furry hides and their lean-to.

"I'm hungry," Meg said, reaching for one of the food packets.

Brad went on as though she hadn't spoken at all. "Do you still like to eat cereal with yogurt instead of milk?"

Meg swallowed. "Yes."

"Do you still laugh in your sleep?"

"I—I suppose."

"Do you still arch your back like a bucking horse when you climax?"

Meg's face felt hotter than the old stove, which rocked a little with the heat inside it, crimson blazes glowing through the cracks. "What kind of question is that?"

"A personal one, I admit," Brad said. He might have passed for a choirboy, so innocent was his expression, but his eyes gave him away. They had the old glint of easy confidence in them. He knew he could have her anyplace and anytime he wanted—he was just biding his time. "I'll know soon enough, I guess."

"No," she said.

"No?" He raised an eyebrow.

"No, I don't arch my back when I—I don't arch my back."

"Hmmmm," Brad said. "Why not?"

Because I don't have sex, Meg almost answered, but in the last, teetering fraction of a second, she realized she didn't want to admit that. Not to Brad, the man with all the notches on his bedpost.

"You haven't been sleeping with anybody?" he asked.

"I didn't say that," Meg replied, keeping her distance, mainly because she wanted so much to take Brad's coffee from his hand, set it aside, straddle his thighs and let him work his slow, thorough magic. Peeling away her outer garments, kissing and caressing everything he uncovered.

"Nobody who could make you arch your back?"

Meg was suffused with aching, needy misery. She'd been in fairly close proximity to Brad all morning, and managed to keep her perspective, but now they were alone in a remote shack, and he'd already begun to seduce her. Without so much as a kiss, or a touch of his hand. With Brad O'Ballivan, even gin rummy would qualify as foreplay.

"Something like that," she said. It was a lame answer, and way too honest, but she'd figured if she tossed his ego a bone, the way she might have done to get past a junkyard dog, she'd get a chance to diffuse the invisible but almost palpable charge sparking between them.

"I came across one of Maddie's diaries a few years ago," Brad said, still stripping her with his eyes. Maddie, of course, was his ancestress—Sam O'Ballivan's wife. "She mentioned this line shack several times. She and Sam spent a night here, once, and conceived a child."

That statement should have quelled Meg's passion—unlike Sam and Maddie, she and Brad weren't married, weren't in love. She wasn't using any form of birth control, since there hadn't been a man in her life for nearly a year, and intuition told her that for all Brad's preparations, Brad hadn't brought any condoms along.

Yet, the mention of a baby opened a gash of yearning within Meg, a great, jagged tearing so deep and so dark and so raw that she nearly doubled over with the pain of it.

"Are you all right?" Brad asked, on his feet quickly, taking her elbows in his hands, looking down into her face.

She said nothing. She couldn't have spoken for anything, not in that precise moment.

"What?" Brad prompted, looking worried.

She couldn't tell him that she'd wanted a baby so badly she'd made arrangements with a fertility specialist on several occasions, always losing her courage at the last moment. That she'd almost reached the point of sleeping with strangers, hoping to get pregnant.

In the end, she hadn't been able to go through with that, either.

She'd never known her own father. Oh, she'd lacked for nothing, being a McKettrick. Nothing except the merest acquaintance with the man who'd sired her. He was so anonymous, in fact, that Eve had occasionally referred to him, not knowing Meg was listening, as "the sperm donor."

She wanted more for her own son or daughter. Granted, the baby's father didn't have to be involved in their day-to-day life, or pay child support, or much of anything else. But he had to have a face and a name, so Meg could show her child a photograph, at some point in time, and say, "This is your daddy."

"Meg?" Brad's hands tightened a little on her elbows.

"Panic attack," she managed to gasp.

He pressed her down onto one of the crates, ladled some water from the bucket he'd braved the elements to fill at the pump outside, and held it to her lips.

She sipped.

"Do you need to take a pill or something?"

Meg shook her head.

He dragged the second crate closer, and sat facing her, so their knees touched. "Since when do you get panic attacks?" he asked.

Tears stung Meg's eyes. She rocked a little, hugging herself, and Brad steadied the ladle in her hands, raised it to her mouth again.

She sipped, more slowly this time, and Brad set it aside when she was finished.

"Meg," he repeated. "The panic attacks?"

It only happens when I suddenly realize I want to have a certain man's baby more than I want anything in the world. And when that certain man turns out to be you.

"It's a freak thing," she said. "I've never had one before."

Brad raised an eyebrow—he'd always been perceptive. It was one of the qualities that made him a good songwriter, for example. "I mentioned that Sam and Maddie conceived a child in this line shack, and you started hyperventilating." He leaned forward a little, took both Meg's hands gently in his. "I remember how much you wanted kids when we were together," he mused. "And now your sister is having a baby."

Meg's heart wedged itself into her windpipe. She'd

wanted a baby, all right. And she'd conceived one, with Brad, and miscarried soon after he left for Nashville. Not even her mother had known.

She nodded.

Brad stroked the side of her cheek with the backs of his fingers, offering her comfort. She'd never told him about the pregnancy—she'd been saving the news for their wedding night—but now she knew she would have no choice, if they got involved again.

"I'm not jealous of Sierra," she said, anxious to make that clear. "I'm happy for her and Travis."

"I know," Brad said. He drew her from her crate onto his lap; she straddled his thighs. But beyond that, the gesture wasn't sexual. He simply held her, one hand gently pressing her head to his shoulder.

After a little deep breathing, in order to calm herself, Meg straightened and gazed into Brad's face.

"Suppose we had sex," she said softly. Tentatively. "And I conceived a child. How would you react?"

"Well," Brad said after pondering the idea with an expression of wistful amusement on his face, "I guess that would depend on a couple of things." He kissed her neck, lightly. Nibbled briefly at her earlobe.

A hot shudder went through Meg. "Like what?"

"Like whether we were going to raise the baby together or not," Brad replied, still nibbling. When Meg stiffened slightly, he drew back to look into her face again. "What?"

"I was sort of thinking I could just be a single mother," Meg said.

She was off Brad's thighs and plunked down on her crate again so quickly that it almost took her breath away.

"And my part would be what?" he demanded. "Keep my distance? Go on about my business? What, Meg?"

"You have your career—"

"I don't have my career. That part of my life is over. I've told you that."

"You're young, Brad. You're very talented. It's inevitable that you'll want to sing again."

"I don't have to be in a concert hall or a recording studio to sing," he said tersely. "I mean to live on Stone Creek Ranch for good, and any child of *mine* is going to grow up there."

Meg stood her ground. After all, she was a McKettrick. "Any child of *mine* is going to grow up on the Triple M."

"Then I guess we'd better not make a baby," Brad replied. He got up off the crate, went to the stove and refilled his coffee cup.

"Look," Meg said more gently, "we can just let the subject drop. I'm sorry I brought it up at all—I just got a little emotional there for a moment and—"

Brad didn't answer.

They were stuck in a cabin together, at least overnight, and maybe longer. They had to get along, or they'd both go crazy.

She retrieved the pack of cards from the floor, where Brad had set them earlier. "Bet I can take you, O'Ballivan," she said, waggling the box from side to side. "Gin rummy, five-card stud, go fish—name your poison."

He laughed, and the tension was broken—the overt kind, anyway. There was an underground river of the stuff, coursing silently beneath their feet. "Go fish?"

"Lately, I've played a lot of cards—with my nephew, Liam. That's his favorite."

Brad chose rummy. Set a third crate between them for a table top. "You think you can take me, huh?" he challenged. And the look in his eyes, as he dealt the first hand, said *he* planned on doing the taking—and the cards didn't have a thing to do with it.

Chapter 6

It was a wonder to Brad that he could sit there in the middle of that line shack, playing gin rummy with Meg McKettrick, when practically all he'd thought about since coming home to Stone Creek was bedding down with her. She'd practically invited him to father her baby, too.

Whatever his reservations might be where her insistence on raising the child alone was concerned, and on the Triple M to boot, he sure wouldn't have minded the *process* of conceiving it.

So why wasn't he on top of her at that very moment?

He studied his cards solemnly—Meg was going to win this hand, as she had the last half dozen—and pondered the situation. The wind howled around the shack like a million shrieking banshees determined to drive them both out into the freezing cold, making the walls shake. And the light was going, too, even though it wasn't noon yet.

"Play," Meg said impatiently, a spark of mischievous triumph—and something else—dancing in her eyes.

"If I didn't know better," Brad said ruefully, "I'd think you'd stacked the deck. You're going to lay down all your cards and set me again, aren't you?"

She grinned, looking at him coyly over the fan of cards. Even batting her eyelashes. "There's only one way to find out," she teased.

A cowboy's geisha, Brad thought. Later, when he was alone at the ranch, he'd tinker around with the idea, maybe make a song out of it. He might have retired from recording and life on the road, but he knew he'd always make music.

Resigned, he drew a card from the stack, couldn't use it, and tossed it away.

Meg's whole being seemed to twinkle as she took his discard, incorporated it into a grand slam of a run and went out with a flourish, spreading the cards across the top of the crate.

"McKettrick luck," she said, beaming.

On impulse, Brad put down his cards, leaned across the crate between them and kissed Meg lightly on the mouth. She tensed at first, then responded, giving a little groan when he used his tongue.

Her arms slipped around his shoulders.

He wanted with everything in him to shove cards and crate aside, lay her down, then and there, and have her.

Whoa, he told himself. *Easy. Don't scare her off.*

There were tears in her eyes when she drew back from his kiss, sniffled once, and blinked, as though surprised to find herself alone with him, in the eye of the storm.

Like most men, Brad was always unsettled when a woman cried. He felt an urgent need to rectify whatever was wrong, and at the same time, knew he couldn't.

Meg swabbed at her cheeks with the back of one hand, straightened her proud McKettrick spine.

"What's the matter?" Brad asked.

"Nothing," Meg answered, averting her gaze.

"You're lying."

"Just hedging a little," she said, trying hard to smile and falling short. "It was like the old days, that's all. The kiss I mean. It brought up a lot of feelings."

"Would it help if I told you I felt the same way?"

"Not really," she said. A thoughtful look came into those fabulous, fathomless eyes of hers.

Brad slid the crate to one side and leaned in close, filled with peculiar suspense. He had to know what was going on in her head. "What?"

"Lots of people have sex," she told him, "without anybody getting pregnant."

"The reverse is also true," he felt honor-bound to say. "Far as I know, making love still causes babies."

"Making love," Meg said, "is not necessarily the same thing as having sex."

Brad cleared his throat, still walking on figurative eggshells. "True," he said very cautiously. Was she messing with him? Setting him up for a rebuff? Meg wasn't a particularly vengeful person, at least as far as he knew, but he'd hurt her badly all those busy years ago. Maybe she wanted to get back at him a little.

"What I have in mind," she told him decisively, "is *sex,* as opposed to making love." A pause. "Of course."

"Of course," he agreed. Hope fluttered in his chest, like a bird flexing its wings and rising, windborne, off a high tree branch. At the same time, he felt stung—Meg was making it clear that any intimacy they might enjoy during this brief time-out-of-time would be strictly for physical gratification. Frenetic coupling of bodies, an emotion-free zone.

Since beggars couldn't be choosers, he was willing to bargain, but the disturbing truth was, he wanted more from Meg than a noncommittal quickie. She wasn't, after all, a groupie to be groped and taken in the back of some tour bus, then forgotten.

She squinted at him, catching something in his expression. "This bothers you?" she asked.

He tried to smile. "If you want to have sex, McKettrick, I'm definitely game. It's just that—"

"What?"

"It might not be a good idea." Was he crazy? Here was the most beautiful woman he'd ever seen, essentially offering herself to him—and he was leaning on the brake lever?

"Okay," she said, and she looked hurt, uncomfortable, suddenly shy.

And that was his undoing. All his noble reluctance went right out the door.

He pulled her onto his lap again.

She hesitated, then wrapped both arms around his neck.

"Are you sure?" he asked her quietly, gruffly. "We're taking a chance here, Meg. We *could* conceive a child—"

The idea filled him with desperate jubilation, strangely mingled with sorrow.

"We could," she agreed, her eyes shining, dark with sultry heat, despite the chill seeping in between the cracks in the plain board walls.

He cupped her chin in his hand, made her look into his face. "Fair warning, McKettrick. If there's a baby, I'm not going to be an anonymous father, content to cut a check once a month and go on about my business as if it had never happened."

She studied him. "You're serious."

He nodded.

"I'll take that chance," she decided, after a few moments of deliberation.

He kissed her again, deeply this time, and when their mouths parted, she looked as dazed as he felt. Once, during a rehearsal before a concert, he'd gotten a shock from an electric guitar with a frayed chord. The jolt he'd taken, kissing Meg just now, made the first experience seem tame.

She was straddling him, and even through their jeans, the insides of her thighs, squeezing against his hips, seemed to sear his skin. She squirmed against his erection, making him groan.

Never in his life had Brad wanted a bed as badly as he did at that moment. It wasn't right to lay Meg down on a couple of sleeping bags, on that cold floor.

But even as he was thinking these disjointed thoughts, he was pulling her shirt up, slipping his hands beneath all that fabric, stroking her bare ribs.

She shivered deliciously, closed her eyes, threw her head back.

"Cold?" Brad asked, worried.

"Anything but," she murmured.

"You're sure?"

"Absolutely sure," Meg said.

He found the catch on her bra, opened it. Cupped both hands beneath her full, warm breasts.

She moaned as he chafed her nipples gently, using the sides of his thumbs.

And that was when they heard the deafening and unmistakable *thwup-thwup-thwup* of helicopter blades, directly above the roof of the line shack.

Meg looked up, disbelieving. Jesse, Rance, or Keegan—or all three. Who else would take a chopper up in weather like that?

Out in the lean-to, the horses whinnied in panic. The walls of the cabin shook as Meg jumped to her feet and righted her bra in almost the same motion. *"Damn!"* she sputtered furiously.

"That had better not be Phil," Brad said ominously. He was standing, too, his gaze fixed on the trembling ceiling.

Meg smoothed her hair, straightened her clothes. "Phil?"

"My manager," Brad reminded her.

"We should be so lucky," Meg yelled, straining to be heard over the sound of the blades. "It's my cousins!"

They both went to the door and peered out, heedless of the blasting cold, made worse by the downdraft from the chopper, Meg ducking under Brad's left arm to see.

Sure enough, the McKettrickCo helicopter, a relic of the corporation days, was settling to the ground, bouncing on its runners in the deepening snow.

"I'll be damned," Brad said with a grin of what looked like rueful admiration, forcing the door shut against the icy wind. At the last second, Meg saw two figures moving toward them at a half crouch.

"I'll kill them," Meg said.

The door rattled on its hinges at the first knock.

Meg stood back while Brad opened it again.

Jesse came through first, followed by Keegan. They wore Western hats pulled low over their faces, leather coats thickly lined with sheep's wool, and attitudes.

"I tried to stop them," Angus said, appearing at Meg's elbow.

"Good job," Meg scoffed, under her breath, without moving her lips.

Angus spread his hands. "They're McKettricks," he reminded her, as though that explained every mystery in the universe, from spontaneous human combustion to the Bermuda Triangle.

"Are you crazy?" Meg demanded of her cousins, storming forward to stand toe-to-toe with Jesse, who was tight-jawed, casting suspicious glances at Brad. "You could have been killed, taking the copter up in a blizzard!"

Brad, by contrast, hoisted the coffeepot off the stove, grinning wryly, and not entirely in a friendly way. "Coffee?" he asked.

Jesse scowled at him.

"Don't mind if I do," Keegan said, pulling off his heavy leather gloves. He tossed Meg a sympathetic glance in the meantime, one that said, *Don't blame me. I'm just here to keep an eye on Jesse.*

Brad found another cup and, without bothering to wipe it out, filled it and handed it to Keegan. "It's good to see you again," he said with a sort of charged affability, but underlying his tone was an unspoken, *Not.*

"I'll just bet," Jesse said, whipping off his hat. His dark blond hair looked rumpled, as though he'd been shoving a hand through it at regular intervals.

"Jesse," Keegan warned quietly.

Meg stood nearly on tiptoe, her nose almost touching Jesse's, her eyes narrowed to slits. "What the *hell* are you doing here?"

Jesse wasn't about to back down, his stance made that clear, and neither was Meg. Classic McKettrick standoff.

Keegan, used to the family dynamics, and the most diplomatic member of the current generation, eased an arm between them, holding his mug of hot coffee carefully in the other. "To your corners," he said easily, forcing them both to take a step back.

Jesse gave Brad a scathing look—once, they'd been friends—and turned to face Meg again. "I might ask you the same question," he countered. "What the hell are *you* doing here? With *him?*"

Brad cleared his throat, folded his arms. Waited. He looked amused—the expression in his eyes notwithstanding.

"That, Jesse McKettrick," Meg seethed, "is my own business!"

"We came," Keegan interceded, still unruffled but, in his own way, as watchful as Jesse was, "because Cheyenne told us you were up here on horseback. When we got word of the blizzard, we were worried."

Meg threw her arms out, slapped them back against her sides. "Obviously, I'm all right," she said. "Safe and sound."

"I don't know about that," Jesse said, taking Brad's measure again.

A muscle bunched in Brad's jaw, but he didn't speak.

"Get your stuff, if you have any," Jesse told Meg. "We're leaving." He turned to Brad again, added reluctantly, "You'd better come with us. This storm is going to get a lot worse before it gets better."

"Can't leave the horses," Brad said.

Meg was annoyed. Her cousins had landed a helicopter in front of the line shack, in the middle of a blinding whiteout, determined to carry her out bodily if they had to, and all he could think about was the horses?

"I'll stay and ride out with you," Jesse told Brad. Whatever his issues with Brad might be, he was a rancher, born and bred. And a rancher never left a horse stranded, whether it was his own or someone else's, if he had any choice in the matter. His blue eyes sliced to Meg's face. "Keegan will get you back to the Triple M."

"Suppose I don't want to go?"

"Better decide," Keegan put in. "This storm is picking up steam as we speak. Another fifteen or twenty minutes, and the four of us will be bunking in here until spring."

Meg searched Jesse's face, glanced at Brad.

He wasn't going to express an opinion one way or the other, apparently, and that galled her. She knew it wasn't cowardice—Brad had never been afraid of a brawl, with her rowdy cousins or anybody else. Which probably meant he was relieved to get out of a sticky situation.

Color flared in her cheeks.

"I'll get my coat," she said, glaring at Brad. Still hoping he'd stop her, send Jesse and Keegan packing.

But he didn't.

She scrambled into her coat with jamming motions of her fists, and got stuck in the lining of one sleeve.

"Call Olivia," Brad said, watching her struggle, one corner of his mouth tilted slightly upward in a bemused smile. "Let her know I'm okay."

Meg nodded once, angrily, and let Keegan shuffle her out into the impossible cold to the waiting helicopter.

"Smooth," Brad remarked, studying Jesse, shutting the door behind Meg and Keegan and offering a brief, silent prayer for their safety. Flying in this weather was a major risk, but if anybody was up to the job, it was Keegan. His father had been a pilot, and all three of the McKettrick boys were as skilled at the controls of a plane or a copter as they were on the back of a horse.

A little of the air went out of Jesse, but not much. "We'd

better ride," he said, "if we're going to make it out of here
before dark."

"What'd you think I was going to do, Jesse?" Brad asked
evenly, reaching for the poker, opening the stove door to
bank the fire. "Rape her?"

Jesse thrust a hand through his hair. "It wasn't that," he
said, but grudgingly. "Until we spotted the smoke from the
line shack chimney, we thought the two of you might still
be out there someplace, in a whole lot of trouble."

"You couldn't have just turned the copter toward the
Triple M and left well enough alone?" He hadn't shown
it in front of Meg, but Brad was about an inch off Jesse.
Meg wasn't a kid, and if she'd needed protection, he would
have provided it.

Jesse's eyes shot blue fire. "Maybe Meg's ready to forget what you did to her, but I'm not," he said. "She put on
a good show back then, but inside, she was a shipwreck.
Especially after the miscarriage."

For Brad, the whole world came to a screeching, spark-
throwing stop in the space of an instant.

"What miscarriage?"

"Uh-oh," Jesse said.

It was literally all Brad could do not to get Jesse by the
lapels and drag an answer out of him. He even took a step
toward the door, meaning to stop Meg from leaving, but
the copter was already lifting off, shaking the shack, setting the horses to fretting again.

"There—was—a baby?"

"Let's go get those horses ready for a hard ride," Jesse
said, averting his gaze. Clearly, he'd assumed Meg had told
Brad about the child. Now Jesse was the picture of regret.

"Tell me," Brad pressed.

"You'll have to talk to Meg," Jesse answered, putting

his hat on again and squaring his shoulders to go back out into the cold and around to the lean-to. "I've already said more than I should have."

"It was mine?"

Jesse reddened. Yanked up the collar of his heavy coat. "*Of course* it was yours," he said indignantly. "Meg's not the type to play that kind of game."

Brad put on his own coat and yanked on some gloves. He felt strangely apart from himself, as though his spirit had somehow gotten out of step with his body.

Meg had been pregnant when he caught that bus to Nashville.

He knew in his bones it was true.

If he'd been anything but a stupid, ambitious kid, he'd have known it then. By the fragile light in her eyes. By the way she'd touched his arm, as if to get his attention so she could say something important, then drawn back, trembling a little.

He'd still have gone to Nashville—he'd had to, to save Stone Creek from the bankers and developers. But he'd have sent for Meg first thing, swallowed his pride whole if he had to, or thumbed it back to Arizona to be with her.

Tentatively, Jesse laid a hand on Brad's shoulder. Withdrew it again.

After securing the line shack as best they could, they left, made their way to the fitful horses, saddled them in silence.

The roar of the copter's engine and the whipping of the blades made conversation impossible without a headset, and Meg refused to put hers on.

Keegan concentrated on working the controls, keeping

a close watch on the instrument panel. The blizzard had intensified; they were literally flying blind.

Presently, though, visibility increased, and Meg relaxed a little.

Keegan must have been watching her out of the corner of his eye, because he reached over and patted her lightly on the arm. Picked up the second headset and nudged her until she took it, put on the earphones, adjusted the mic.

"I can't believe you did this," she said.

Keegan grinned. His voice echoed through the headset. "Rule number one," he said. "Never leave another McKettrick stuck in a blizzard."

Meg huffed out a sigh. "I was perfectly all right!"

"Maybe," Keegan replied, banking to the northwest, in the direction of the Triple M. "But we didn't have any way of knowing that. Switch on your cell phone. You'll find we left at least half a dozen messages on your voice mail, trying to find out if you were okay."

"What if they don't make it out of that storm?" Meg fretted. Before, she'd just been furious. Now, with a little perspective, she was suddenly assailed by worries, on all sides. The fear was worse than the anger. "What if the horses get lost?"

"Brad knows the trail," Keegan assured her, "and Jesse could ride out of hell if he had to. If they don't show up in a few hours, I'll come back looking for them."

"You're not invincible, you know," Meg said tersely. "Even if you *are* a McKettrick."

"I'll do what I have to do," he told her. "Are you and Brad—well—back on?"

"That is patently none of your affair."

Keegan's grin was damnably endearing. "When has that ever stopped me?"

"No," Meg said, beaten. "We are *not* 'back on.' I was just helping him look for Ransom, that's all."

"Ransom? The stallion?"

"Yes."

"He's real?"

"I've seen him with my own eyes."

"You decided to go chasing a wild horse in the middle of a blizzard?"

"It wasn't snowing when we left Stone Creek Ranch," Meg said, feeling defensive.

"Know what I think?"

"No, but I'm afraid you're going to tell me."

Keegan's grin widened, took on a wicked aspect. "You wanted to sleep with Brad. He wanted to sleep with you. And I use the word *sleep* advisedly. Both of you knew snow's a real possibility in the high country, year-round. And there's the old line shack, handy as hell."

"*So* none of your business. And who do you think you are, Dr. Phil?"

Keegan chuckled, shook his head once. "It probably won't help," he told her, "but if we'd known we were interrupting a tryst, we'd have stayed clear."

"We were *playing gin rummy.*"

"Whatever."

Meg folded her arms and wriggled deeper into the cold leather seat. "Keegan, I don't have to convince you. And I definitely don't have to explain."

"You're absolutely right. You don't."

By then, they were out of the snow, gliding through a golden autumn afternoon. They passed over the town of Stone Creek, continued in the direction of Indian Rock.

Meg didn't say another word until Keegan set the copter down in the pasture behind her barn, the downdraft making the long grass ripple like an ocean.

"Thanks for the ride," she said tersely, waiting for the blades to slow so she could get out without having her head cut off. "I'd invite you in, but right now, I am seriously pissed off, and the less I see of any of my male relatives, you included, the better."

Keegan cocked a thumb at her. "Got it," he said. "And for the record, I don't give a rat's ass if you're pissed off."

Meg reached across and slugged him in the upper arm, hard, but she laughed a little as she did it. Shook her head. "Goodbye!" she yelled, tossing the headset into his lap.

Keegan signaled her to keep her head down, and watched as she pushed open the door of the copter and leaped to the ground.

Ducking, she headed for the house.

Angus was standing in the kitchen when she let herself in, looking apologetic.

"Thanks a heap for the help," Meg said.

"There's not much I can do with folks who can't see or hear me," Angus replied.

"I get all the luck," Meg answered, pulling off her coat and flinging it in the direction of the hook beside the door.

Angus looked solemn. "You've got trouble," he said.

Meg tensed, instantly alarmed. She'd ridden home from the mountaintop in relative comfort, but the trip would be dangerous on horseback, even for men who'd literally grown up in the saddle. "Jesse and Brad are okay, aren't they?"

"They'll be fine," Angus assured her. "A couple of shots of good whiskey'll fix 'em right up."

"Then what are you talking about?"

"You'll find out soon enough."

"Do you have to be so damned cryptic?"

Angus's grin was reminiscent of Keegan's. "I'm not cryptic," he said. "I can get around just fine."

"Very funny."

He chuckled.

Frazzled, Meg blurted, "First you tell me about your long-lost brother, and how some unknown McKettrick is about to show up. Then you say I've got trouble. Spill it, Angus!"

He sobered. "Jesse let the cat out of the bag. And that's all I'm going to say."

Meg froze. She had only one deep, dark secret, and Jesse couldn't have let it slip because he didn't know what it was.

Did he?

She put one hand to her mouth.

Angus patted her shoulder. "You'd better go out to the barn and feed the horses early. You might be too busy later on."

Meg stared at her ancestor. "Angus McKettrick—"

He vanished.

Typical man.

Meg placed the promised call to Olivia O'Ballivan, got her voice mail and left a message. Next, she started a pot of coffee, then picked her coat up off the floor, put it back on and went out to tend to the livestock.

The work helped to ease her anxiety, but not all that much.

All the while, she was wondering if Jesse had found out about the baby somehow, if he'd told Brad.

You've got trouble, Angus had said, and the words echoed in her mind.

She finished her chores and returned to the house, shedding her coat again and washing her hands at the sink before pouring herself a mug of fresh coffee. She considered lacing it with a generous dollop of Jack Daniel's, to get the chill out of her bones, then shoved the bottle back in the cupboard, unopened.

If Jesse and Brad didn't get home, Keegan wouldn't be the only one to go out looking for them.

She reached for the telephone, dialed Cheyenne's cell number.

"I'm sorry," Cheyenne said immediately, not bothering with a hello. "When I passed your message on to Jesse, about checking on your horses if you didn't call before nightfall, he wanted to know where you'd gone." She paused. "And I told him."

Meg pressed the back of one hand to her forehead and closed her eyes for a moment. If a certain pair of stubborn cowboys got lost in that blizzard, or if Jesse had, as Angus put it, "let the cat out of the bag," the embarrassing scene at the line shack would be the least of her problems.

"There's a big storm in the high country," she said quietly, "and Jesse and Brad are on horseback. Let me know when Jesse gets back, will you?"

Cheyenne drew in an audible breath. "Oh, my God," she whispered. "They're riding in a *blizzard?*"

"Jesse can handle it," Meg said. "And so can Brad. Just the same, I'll rest easier when I know they're home."

Cheyenne didn't answer for a long time. "I'll call," she promised, but she sounded distracted. No doubt she was thinking the same thing Meg was, that it had been reckless enough, flying into a snowstorm in a helicopter. Taking a treacherous trail down off the mountain was even worse.

Meg spoke a few reassuring words, though they sounded hollow even to her, and she and Cheyenne said goodbye.

At loose ends, Meg took her coffee to the study at the front of the house and logged onto the computer. Ran a search on the name Josiah McKettrick, though her mind wasn't on genealogical detective work, and she started over a dozen times.

In the kitchen, she heated a can of soup and ate it mechanically, never tasting a bite. After that, she read for a couple of hours, then she took a long, hot bath, put on clean sweats and padded downstairs again, thinking she'd watch some television. She was trying to focus on a rerun of *Dog the Bounty Hunter* when she heard a car door slam outside.

Boot heels thundered up the front steps.

And then a fist hammered at the heavy wooden door.

"Meg!" Brad yelled. "Open up! *Now!*"

Chapter 7

Brad looked crazed, standing there on Meg's doorstep. She moved to step out of his way, but before she could, he advanced on her, backing her into the entryway. Kicking the door shut behind him with a hard motion of one foot.

He hadn't stopped to change clothes after the long, cold ride down out of the hills, and he was soaked to the skin. He'd lost his gloves somewhere, and there was a faintly bluish cast to his taut lips.

"Why didn't you tell me about the baby?" he demanded, shaking an index finger under Meg's nose when she collided with the wall behind her, next to Holt and Lorelei's grandfather clock. The ponderous tick-tock seemed to reverberate throughout the known universe.

Meg's worst fears were confirmed in that moment. Jesse *had* known about her pregnancy and subsequent miscarriage—and he'd let it slip to Brad.

"Calm down," she said, recovering a little.

Brad gripped her shoulders. If he'd been anyone other than exactly who he was, Meg might have feared for her safety. But this was Brad O'Ballivan. Sure, he'd crushed her heart, but he wasn't going to hurt her physically, she knew that. It was one of the few absolutes.

"Was there a child?"

Meg bit her lower lip. She'd always known she'd have to tell him if they crossed paths again, but she hadn't wanted it to be like this. "Yes," she whispered, that one word scraping her throat raw.

"My baby?"

She felt a sting of indignation, hot as venom, but it passed quickly. "Yes."

"Why didn't you tell me?"

Meg straightened her spine, lifted her chin a notch. "You were in Nashville," she said. "You didn't write. You didn't call. I guess I didn't think you'd be interested."

The blue fury in Brad's eyes dulled visibly; he let go of her shoulders, but didn't step back. She felt cornered, overshadowed—but still not threatened. Oddly, it was more like being shielded, even protected.

He shoved a hand through his hair. "How could I not be interested, Meg?" he rasped bleakly. "You were carrying our baby."

Slowly, Meg put her palms to his cheeks. "I miscarried a few weeks after you left," she said gently. "It wasn't meant to be."

Moisture glinted in his eyes, and that familiar muscle bunched just above his jawline. "Still—"

"Go upstairs and take a hot shower," Meg told him. "I'll fix you something to eat, and we'll talk."

Brad tensed again, then relaxed, though only slightly. Nodded.

"Travis left some clothes behind when he and Sierra moved to town," she went on, when he didn't speak. "I'll get them for you."

With that, she led the way up the stairs, along the hallway to the main bathroom. After pushing the door open and waiting for Brad to enter, she went on to the master bedroom, pulled an old pair of jeans and a long-sleeved T-shirt from a bureau drawer.

Brad was already in the shower when she returned, naked behind the steamy glass door, but clearly visible.

Swallowing a rush of lust, Meg set the folded garments on the lid of the toilet seat, placed a folded towel on top of them and slipped out.

She was cooking scrambled eggs when Brad came down the back stairs fifteen minutes later, barefoot, his hair towel-rumpled, wearing Travis's clothes. Without comment, Meg poured a cup of fresh coffee and held it out to him.

He took it, after a moment's hesitation, and sipped cautiously.

Meg was relieved to see that the hot shower had restored his normal color. Before, he'd been ominously pale.

"Sit down," she said quietly.

He pulled out Holt's chair and sat, watching her as she turned to the stove again. Even with her back turned to him, she could feel his gaze boring into the space between her shoulder blades.

"What happened?" he asked, after a few moments.

She looked back at him briefly before scraping the eggs onto a waiting plate. Didn't speak.

"The miscarriage," he prompted grimly. "What made it happen?"

With a pang, Meg realized he thought it might have

been his fault somehow, her losing their baby. Because he'd gone to Nashville, or because of the fight they'd had before he left.

She'd suffered her own share of guilt over the years, wondering if she could have done something differently, prevented the tragedy. She didn't want Brad to go through the same agony.

"There was no specific incident," she said softly. "I was pregnant, and then I wasn't. It happens, Brad. And it's not always possible to know why."

Brad absorbed that, took another sip of his coffee. "You should have told me."

"I didn't tell anyone," Meg said. "Not even my mother."

"Then how did Jesse know?"

Now that she'd had time to think, the answer was obvious. Jesse had been the one to take her to the hospital that long-ago night. She'd told him it was just a bad case of cramps, but he'd either put two and two together on his own or overheard the nurses and doctors talking.

"He was with me," she said.

"He was, and I *wasn't*," Brad answered.

She set the plate of scrambled eggs in front of him, along with two slices of buttered toast and some silverware. "It wouldn't have changed anything," she said. "Your being there, I mean. I'd still have lost the baby, Brad."

He closed his eyes briefly, like someone taking a hard punch to the solar plexus, determined not to fight back.

"You should have told me," he insisted.

She gave the plate a little push toward him and, reluctantly, he picked up his fork, began to eat. "We've been over that," she said, sitting down on the bench next to the table, angled to face Brad. "What good would it have done?"

"I could have—helped."

"How?"

He sighed. "You went through it alone. That isn't right."

"Lots of things aren't 'right' in this world," Meg reasoned quietly. "A person just has to—cope."

"The McKettrick way," Brad said without admiration. "Some people would call that being bullheaded, not coping."

She propped an elbow on the tabletop, cupped her chin in her hand, and watched as he continued to down the scrambled eggs. "I'd do the same thing all over again," she confessed. "It was hard, but I toughed it out."

"Alone."

"Alone," Meg agreed.

"It must have been a lot worse than 'hard.' You were only nineteen."

"So were you," she said.

"Why didn't you tell your mother?"

Meg didn't have to reflect on that one. From the day Hank Breslin had snatched Sierra and vanished, Eve had been hit by problem after problem—a serious accident, in which she'd been severely injured, subsequent addictions to painkillers and alcohol, all the challenges of steering McKettrickCo through a lot of corporate white water.

"She'd been through enough," she replied simply. Brad's question had been rhetorical—he'd known the McKettrick history all along.

"She'd have strung me up by my thumbs," Brad said. And though he tried to smile, he didn't quite make it. He was still in shock.

"Probably," Meg said.

He'd finished the food, shoved his plate away. "Where do we go from here?" he asked.

"I don't know," she said. "Maybe nowhere."

He moved to take her hand, but withdrew just short of touching her. Scraped back his chair to stand and carry the remains of his meal to the sink. Set the plate and silverware down with a thunk.

"Was our baby a boy or a girl?" he asked gruffly, standing with his back to her.

She saw the tension in his broad shoulders as he awaited her answer. "I didn't ask," she said. "I guess I didn't want to know. And it was probably too early to tell, anyway. I was only a few weeks into the pregnancy."

He turned, at last, to face her, but kept his distance, leaning back against the counter, folding his arms. "Do you ever think about what it would be like if he or she had survived?"

All the time, she thought.

"No," she lied.

"Right," he said, clearly not believing her.

"I'm—I'm sorry, Brad. That you had to find out from someone else, I mean."

"But not for deceiving me in the first place?"

Meg bristled. "I didn't deceive you."

"What do you call it?"

"You were *gone*. You had things to do. If I'd dragged you back here, you wouldn't have gotten your big chance. You would have hated me for that."

At last, he crossed to her, took her chin in his hand. "I couldn't hate you, Meg," he said gravely, choking a little on the words. "Not ever."

For a few moments, they just stared at each other in silence.

Brad was the first to speak again. "I'd better get back

to the ranch." Another rueful attempt at a grin. "It's been a bitch of a day."

"Stay," Meg heard herself say. She wasn't thinking of leading Brad to her bed—not *exclusively* of that, anyhow. He'd just ridden miles through a blizzard on horseback, he'd taken a chill in the process, and the knowledge that he'd fathered a child was painfully new.

He was silent, perhaps at a loss.

"You shouldn't be alone," Meg said. *And neither should I.*

She knew what would happen if he stayed, of course. And she knew it was likely to be a mistake. They'd become strangers to each other over the years apart, living such different lives. It was too soon to run where angels feared to tread.

But she needed him that night, needed him to hold her, if nothing else.

And his need was just as great.

He grinned, though wanly. "How do we know your cousins won't land on the roof in a helicopter?" he asked.

"We don't," Meg said, and sighed. "They meant well, you know."

"Sure they did," he agreed wryly. "They were out to save your virtue."

Meg stood, went to Brad, slipped her arms around his middle. It seemed such a natural thing to do, and yet, at the same time, it was a breathtaking risk. "Stay," she said again.

He held her a little closer, propped his chin on top of her head. Stroked the length of her back with his hands. "Those who don't learn from history," he said, "are condemned to repeat it."

Meg rested her head against his shoulder, breathed in

the scent of him. Felt herself softening against the hard heat of his body.

And the telephone rang.

"It might be important," Brad said, setting Meg away from him a little, when she didn't jump to answer.

She picked up without checking the ID panel. "Hello."

"Jesse's home," Cheyenne said, honoring her earlier promise to let Meg know when he returned. "He's half-frozen. I poured a hot toddy down him and put him to bed."

"Thanks for calling, Chey," Meg replied.

"You're all right?" Cheyenne asked shyly.

Wondering how much Jesse had told his wife when he got home, Meg replied that she was fine.

"He told me he and Keegan barged in on you and Brad, up in the mountains somewhere," Cheyenne went on. "I'm sorry, Meg. Maybe I should have kept my mouth shut, but I heard a report of the blizzard on the radio and I—well—I guess I panicked a little."

"Everything's all right, Cheyenne. Really."

"He's there, isn't he? Brad, I mean. He's with you, right now."

"Since I'd rather not have a midnight visit from my cousins," Meg said, "I'm admitting nothing."

Cheyenne giggled. "My lips are zipped. Want to have lunch tomorrow?"

"That sounds good," Meg answered, smiling. Brad was standing behind her by then, sliding his hands under the front of her sweatshirt, stopping just short of her bare breasts. She fought to keep her voice even, her breathing normal. "Good night, Cheyenne."

"I'll meet you in town, at Lucky's Bar and Grill at noon," Cheyenne said. "Call me if you're still in bed or anything like that, and we'll reschedule."

Brad tweaked lightly at Meg's nipples; she swallowed a gasp of pleasure. "See you there," she replied, and hung up quickly.

Brad turned Meg around, gave her a knee-melting kiss and then swept her up into his arms. Carried her to the back stairs.

She directed him to the very bed Holt and Lorelei had shared as man and wife.

He laid her down on the deep, cushy mattress, a shadow figure rimmed in light from the hallway behind him. She couldn't see his face, but she felt his gaze on her, gentle and hungry and so hot it seared her.

Afraid honor might get the better of him, Meg wriggled out of her sweatpants, pulled the top off over her head. Planning to sleep in the well-worn favorites, she hadn't bothered to put on a bra and panties after her bath earlier. Now she was completely naked. Utterly vulnerable.

Brad made a low, barely audible sound, rested one knee on the mattress beside her.

"Hold me," she whispered, and traces of an old song ran through her mind.

Help me make it through the night...

He stripped, maneuvered Meg so she was under the covers and joined her. The feel of him against her, solid and warm and all man, sent an electric rush of dizziness through her, pervading every cell.

She wrapped her arms around his neck and clung—she who never allowed herself to cling to anyone or anything except her own fierce pride.

A long, delicious time passed, without words, without caresses—only the holding.

The decision that there would be no foreplay was a tacit one.

The wanting was too great.

Brad nudged Meg's legs apart gently, settled between them, his erection pressing against her lower belly like a length of steel, heated in a forge.

She moaned and arched her back slightly, seeking him.

He took her with a single long, slow, smooth stroke, nestling into her depths. Held himself still as she gasped in wordless welcome.

He kissed her eyelids.

She squirmed beneath him.

He kissed her cheekbones.

Craving friction, desperate for it, Meg tried to move her hips, but he had her pinned, heavily, delectably, to the bed.

She whimpered.

He nibbled at her earlobes, one and then the other.

She ran her hands urgently up and down his back.

He tasted her neck.

She pleaded.

He withdrew, thrust again, but slowly.

She said his name.

He plunged deep.

And Meg came apart in his arms, raising herself high. Clawing, now at his back, now at the bedclothes, surrendering with a long, continuous, keening moan.

The climax was ferocious, but it was only a prelude to what would follow, and knowing that only increased Meg's need. Her body merged with Brad's, fused to it at the most elemental level, and the instant he began to move upon her she was lost again.

Even as she exploded, like a shattering star, she was aware of his phenomenal self-control, but when she reached her peak, he gave in. She reveled in the flex of his powerful body, the ragged, half groan, half shout of his

release. Felt the warmth of his seed spilling inside her—
and prayed it would take root.

Finally, he collapsed beside her, his face buried between
her neck and the curve of her shoulder, his arms and legs
still clenched around her, loosening by small, nearly im-
perceptible shivers.

Instinctively, Meg tilted her pelvis slightly backward,
cradling the warmth.

A long while later, when both their breathing had returned to normal, or some semblance of that, Brad lifted
his head. Touched his nose to hers. Started to speak, then
thrust out a sigh, instead.

Meg threaded her fingers through his hair. Turned her
head so she could kiss his chin.

"Guess you just earned another notch for the bedpost,"
she said.

He chuckled. "Yeah," he said. "Except this is *your* bed,
McKettrick. *You* seduced *me*. I want that on record. Either
way, since it's obviously an antique, carving the thing up
probably wouldn't be the best idea."

"We're going to regret this in the morning, you know,"
she told him.

"That's then," he murmured, nibbling at her neck again.
"This is now."

"Um-hmm," Meg said. She wanted *now* to last forever.

"I kept expecting a helicopter."

Meg laughed. "Me, too."

Brad lifted his head again, and in the moonlight she
could see the smile in his eyes. "Know what?"

"What?"

"I'm glad it happened this way. In a real bed, and not the
floor of some old line shack." He kissed her, very lightly.
"Although I would have settled for anything I could get."

She pretended to slug him.

He laughed.

She felt him hardening against her, pressed against the outside of her right thigh. Stretching, he found the switch on the bedside lamp and turned it, spilling light over her. The glow of it seemed to seep into her skin, golden. Or was it the other way around? Was *she* the one shining, instead of the lamp?

"God," Brad whispered, "you *are* beautiful."

A tigress before, now Meg felt shy. Turned her head to one side, closed her eyes.

Brad caressed her breasts, her stomach and abdomen and the tops of her thighs; his touch so light, so gentle, that it made her breath catch in her throat.

"Look at me," he said.

She met his eyes. "The light," she protested weakly.

He slid his fingers between the moist curls at the juncture of her thighs. "So beautiful," he said.

She gasped as he made slow, sweet circles, deliberately exciting her. "Brad—"

"What?"

She was conscious of the softness of her belly; knew her breasts weren't as firm and high as he remembered. She wanted more of his lovemaking, and still more, but under the cover of darkness and finely woven sheets and the heirloom quilt Lorelei McKettrick had stitched with her own hands, so many years before. "The *light*."

He made no move to flip the switch off again, but continued to stroke her, watching her responses. When he slipped his fingers inside her, found her G-spot and plied it expertly, she stopped worrying about the light and became a part of it.

* * *

While Meg slept, Brad slipped out of bed, pulled his borrowed clothes back on and retrieved his own from the bathroom where he'd showered earlier. Sat on the edge of the big claw-foot bathtub to pull on his socks and boots, still damp from his ride down the mountainside with Jesse.

Downstairs, he found the old-fashioned thermostat and turned it up. Dusty heat whooshed from the vents. In the kitchen he switched on the lights, filled and set the coffeemaker. Maybe these small courtesies would make up for his leaving before Meg woke up.

He found a pencil and a memo pad over by the phone, planning to scribble a note, but nothing suitable came to mind, at least not right away.

"Thanks" would be inappropriate.

"Goodbye" sounded too blunt.

Only a jerk would write "See you around."

"I'll call you later"? Too cavalier.

Finally, he settled on, "Horses to feed."

Four of his songs had won Grammies, and all he could come up with was "horses to feed"? He was slipping.

He paused, stood looking up at the ceiling for a few moments, wanting nothing so much as to go back upstairs, crawl in bed with Meg again and make love to her.

Again.

But she'd said they were going to have regrets in the morning, and he didn't want to see those regrets on her face. The two of them would make bumbling excuses, never quite meeting each other's eyes.

And Brad knew he couldn't handle that.

So he left.

* * *

Meg stood in her warm kitchen, bundled in a terry-cloth bathrobe and surrounded by the aroma of freshly brewed coffee, peering at the note Brad had left.

Horses to feed.

"The man's a poet," she said out loud.

"Do you think it took?" Angus asked.

Meg whirled to find him standing just behind her, almost at her elbow. "You scared me!" she accused, one hand pressed to her heart, which felt as though it might scramble up her esophagus to the back of her throat.

"Sorry," Angus said, though there was nothing the least bit contrite about his tone or his expression.

"Do I think *what* took?" Meg had barely sputtered the words when the awful realization struck her: Angus was asking if she thought she'd gotten pregnant, which meant—

Oh, God.

"Tell me you weren't here!"

"What do you take me for?" Angus snapped. "Of *course* I wasn't!"

Meg swallowed. Flushed to the roots of her hair. "But you knew—"

"I saw that singing cowboy leave just before sunup," came the taciturn reply. Now Angus was blushing, too. "Wasn't too hard to guess the rest."

"Will you stop calling him 'that singing cowboy'? He has a name. It's Brad O'Ballivan."

"I know that," Angus said. "But he's a fair hand with a horse, and he croons a decent tune. To my way of thinking, that makes him a singing cowboy."

Meg gave him a look, padded to the refrigerator, jerked open the door and rummaged around for something that might constitute breakfast. She'd cooked the last of the eggs for Brad, and the remaining choices were severely limited. Three green olives floating in a jar, some withered cheese, the arthritic remains of last week's takeout pizza and a carton of baking soda.

"Food doesn't just appear in an icebox, you know," Angus announced. "In my day, you had to hunt it down, or grow it in a garden, or harvest it from a field."

"Yes, and you probably walked ten miles to and from school," Meg said irritably, "uphill both ways."

She was starving. She'd have to hit the drive-through in town, then pick up some groceries. All that before her lunch with Cheyenne.

"I never went to school," Angus replied seriously, not getting the joke. "My ma taught me to read from the Good Book. I learned the rest on my own."

Meg sighed as an answer, shoved the splayed fingers of one hand through her tangled hair. Although she'd been disappointed at first to wake up and find Brad gone, now she was glad he couldn't see her. She looked like—well— a woman who had been having howling, sweaty-sheet sex half the night.

She started for the stairs.

"Make yourself at home," she told Angus, wondering if he'd catch the irony in her tone. For him, "home" was the Great Beyond, or the main ranch house down by the creek.

When she came down again half an hour later, showered and dressed in jeans and a lightweight blue sweater, he was sitting in Holt's chair, waiting for her.

"You ever think about wearing a dress or a skirt?" he asked, frowning.

Meg let that pass. "I've got some errands to run. See you later."

The telephone rang.

Brad?

She checked the caller ID panel.

Her mother.

"Voice mail will pick up," she told Angus.

"Answer it," Angus said sternly.

Meg reached for the receiver. "Hello, Mom. I was just on my way out the door—"

"You'd better sit down," Eve told her.

The pit of Meg's stomach pitched. "Why? Mom, is Sierra all right? Nothing's happened to Liam—"

"Both of them are fine. It's nothing like that."

Meg let out her breath. Leaned against the kitchen counter for support. "What, then?"

"Your father contacted me this morning. He wants to see you."

Meg's knees almost gave out. She'd never met her father, never spoken to him on the telephone or received so much as a birthday or Christmas card from him. She wasn't even sure what his name was—he used so many aliases.

"Meg?"

"I'm here," Meg said. "I don't want to see him."

"I knew I should have talked to you in person," Eve sighed. "But I was so alarmed—"

"Mother, did you hear what I just said? I don't want to see my father."

"He claims he's dying."

"Well, I'm sincerely sorry to hear that, but I still don't want anything to do with him."

"Meg—"

"I mean it, Mother. He's been a nonentity in my life. What could he possibly have to say to me now, after all this time?"

"I don't know," Eve replied.

"And if he wanted to talk to me, why did he call you?" The moment the question left her mouth, Meg wished she hadn't asked it.

"I think he's afraid."

"But he wasn't afraid of you?"

"He's past that, I think," Eve said. She'd been downright secretive on the subject of Meg's father from the first. Now, suddenly, she seemed to be urging Meg to make contact with him. What was going on? "Listen, why don't you stop by the hotel, and I'll make you some breakfast. We'll talk."

"Mom—"

"Blueberry pancakes. Maple-cured bacon. Your favorites."

"All right," Meg said, because as shaken as she was, she could have eaten the proverbial horse. "I'll be there in twenty minutes."

"Good," Eve replied, a little smugly, Meg thought. She was used to getting her way. After all, for almost thirty years, when Eve McKettrick said "jump," everybody reached for a vaulting pole.

"Are you going to ride shotgun?" Meg asked Angus after she'd hung up.

"I wouldn't miss this for anything," Angus said with relish.

Less than half an hour later, Meg was knocking on the front door of her mother's hotel suite.

When it opened, a man stood looking down at her, his expression uncertain and at the same time hopeful. She saw her own features reflected in the shape of his face, the set of his shoulders, the curve of his mouth.

"Hello, Meg," said her long-lost father.

Chapter 8

After the horses had been fed, Brad turned them out to pasture for the day and made his way not into the big, lonely house, but to the copse of trees where Big John was buried. The old man's simple marker looked painfully new, amid the chipped and moss-covered stone crosses marking the graves of other, earlier O'Ballivans and Blackstones.

Brad had meant to visit the small private cemetery first thing, but between one thing and another, he hadn't managed it until now.

Standing there, in the shade of trees already shedding gold and crimson and rust-colored leaves, he moved to take off his hat, remembered that he wasn't wearing one and crouched to brush a scattering of fallen foliage from the now-sunken mound.

About time you showed up, he heard Big John O'Ballivan's booming voice observe, echoing through the channels of his mind.

Brad gave a lopsided, rueful grin. His eyes smarted, so he blinked a couple of times. "I'm here, old man," he answered hoarsely. "And I mean to stay. Look after the girls and the place. That ought to make you happy."

There was no reply from his grandfather, not even in his head.

But Brad felt like talking, so he did.

"I'm seeing Meg McKettrick again," he said. "Turns out I got her pregnant, back when we were kids, and she lost the baby. I never knew about it until yesterday."

Had Big John been there in the flesh, there'd have been a lecture coming. Brad would have welcomed that, even though the old man could peel off a strip of hide when he was riled.

One more reason why you should have stayed here and attended to business, Big John would have said. And that would have been just the warm-up.

"You never understood," Brad went on, just as if the old man *had* spoken. "We were going to lose Stone Creek Ranch. Maybe you weren't able to face that, but I had to. Everything Sam and Maddie and the ones who came after did to hold on to this place would have been for nothing."

The McKettricks would have stepped in if he'd asked for help, Brad knew that. Meg herself, probably her mother, too. Contrary as that Triple M bunch was, they'd bailed more than one neighbor out of financial trouble, saved dozens of smaller farms and ranches when beef prices bottomed out and things got tough. Even after all this time, though, the thought of going to them with his hat in his hands made the back of Brad's throat scald.

Although the ground was hard, wet and cold, he sat, cross-legged, gazing upon his grandfather's grave through a misty haze. He'd paid a high price for his pride, big, fancy career notwithstanding.

He'd lost the years he might have spent with Meg, the other children that might have come along. He hadn't been around when Big John needed him, and his sisters, though they were all educated, independent women, had been mere girls when he left. Sure, Big John had loved and protected them, in his gruff way, but that didn't excuse *his* absence. He should have been their big brother.

Caught up in these thoughts, and all the emotions they engendered, Brad heard the approaching rig, but didn't look around. Heard the engine shut off, the door slam.

"Hey," Olivia said softly from just behind him.

"Hey," he replied, not ready to look back and meet his sister's gaze.

"Willie's better. I've got him in the truck."

Brad blinked again. "That's good," he said. "Guess I'd better go to town and get him some dog food and stuff."

"I brought everything he needs," Livie said, her voice quiet. She came and sat down beside Brad. "Missing Big John?"

"Every day," Brad admitted. Their mother had hit the road when the twins were barely walking, and their dad had died a year later, herding spooked cattle in a lightning storm. Big John had stepped up to raise four young grand-children without a word of complaint.

"Me, too," Livie replied softly. "You ever wonder where our mom ended up?"

Brad knew where Della O'Ballivan was—living in a trailer park outside of Independence, Missouri, with the latest in a long line of drunken boyfriends—but he'd never shared that information with his sisters. The story, brought to him by the private detective he'd hired on the proceeds from his first hit record, wasn't a pretty one.

"No," he said in all honesty. "I never wonder." He'd gone to see Della, once he'd learned her whereabouts. She'd been sloshed and more interested in his stardom, and how it might benefit her, than getting to know him. Ironically, she'd refused the help he *had* offered—immediate admission to one of the best treatment centers in the world— standing there in a tattered housecoat and scruffy slippers, with lipstick stains in the deep smoker's lines surrounding her mouth. She hadn't even asked about her daughters or the husband she'd left behind.

"She's probably dead," Livie said with a sigh.

Since Della's existence couldn't be called living, Brad agreed. "Probably," he replied. Except for periodic requests for a check, which were handled by his accountant, Brad never heard from their mother.

"It's why I don't want to get married, you know," Livie confided. "Because I might be like her. Just get on a bus one day and leave."

Just get on a bus one day and leave.

Like he'd done to Meg, Brad reflected, hurting. Maybe he was more like Della than he'd ever want to admit aloud.

"You'd never do that," he told his sister.

"I used to think she'd come home," Livie went on sadly. "To see me play Mary in the Christmas program at church, or when I got that award for my 4-H project, back in sixth grade."

Brad slipped an arm around Livie's shoulders, felt them trembling a little, squeezed. His reaction had been different from Livie's—if Della had come back, especially after their dad was killed, he'd have spit in her face.

"And you figure if you got married and had kids, you'd

just up and leave them? Miss all the Christmas plays and the 4-H projects?"

"I remember her, Brad," Livie said. "Just the lilac smell of her, and that she was pretty, but I remember. She used to sing a lot, hanging clothes out on the line and things like that. She read me stories. And then she was—well—just *gone*. I could never make sense of it. I always figured I must have done something really bad—"

"The flaw was in her, Livie, not you."

"That's the thing about flaws like that. You never know where they're going to show up. Mom probably didn't expect to abandon us."

Brad didn't agree, but he couldn't say so without revealing way too much. The Della he knew was an unmedicated bipolar with a penchant for gin, light on the tonic water. She'd probably married Jim O'Ballivan on a manic high, and decided to hit the road on a low—or vice versa. It was a miracle, by Brad's calculations, that she'd stayed on Stone Creek Ranch as long as she had, far from the bright lights and big-town bars, where a practicing drunk might enjoy a degree of anonymity.

Coupled with things Big John had said about his daughter-in-law, "man to man" and in strictest confidence, that she'd hidden bottles around the place and slept with ranch hands when there were any around, Brad had few illusions about her morals.

Livie got to her feet, dusting off her jeans as she rose, and Brad immediately did the same.

"I'd better get Willie settled in," she said. "I've got a barn full of sick cows to see to, down the road at the Iversons' place."

"Anything serious?" Brad asked, as Livie headed for

the Suburban parked next to his truck, and he kept pace. "The cows, I mean?"

"Some kind of a fever," Livie answered, looking worried. "I drew some random blood samples the last time I was there, and sent them to the university lab in Tempe for analysis. Nothing anybody's ever seen before."

"Contagious?"

Livie sighed. Her small shoulders slumped a little, under the weight of her life's calling, and not for the first time, Brad wished she'd gone into a less stressful occupation than veterinary medicine.

"Possibly," she said.

Brad waited politely until she'd climbed into the Suburban—Willie was curled comfortably in the backseat, in a nest of old blankets—then got behind the wheel of his truck to follow her to the house.

There, he was annoyed to see a black stretch limo waiting, motor purring.

Phil.

Muttering a curse, Brad did his best to ignore the obvious, got out of the truck and strode to Livie's Suburban to hoist Willie out of the backseat and carry him into the house. Livie was on his heels, arms full of rudimentary dog equipment, but she cast a few curious glances toward the stretch.

They entered through the kitchen door. Olivia set the dog bed down in a sunny corner, and Brad carefully lowered Willie onto it.

"Who's in the big car?" Livie asked.

"Probably Phil Meadowbrook," Brad said a little tersely.

"Your manager?" Livie's eyes were wary. She was probably thinking Phil would make an offer Brad couldn't refuse, and he'd leave again.

"*Former* manager."

Willie, his hide crisscrossed with pink shaved strips and stitches, looked up at Brad with luminous, trusting eyes.

Livie was watching him, too. There was something bruised about her expression. She knew him better than Willie did.

"We need you around, Brad," she said at great cost to her pride. "Not just the twins and me, but the whole community. If the Iversons have to put down all those cows, they'll go under. They're already in debt up to their eyeballs—last year, Mrs. Iverson had a bout with breast cancer, and they didn't have insurance."

Brad's jaw tightened, and so did the pit of his stomach. "I'll write a check," he said.

Livie caught hold of his forearm. *"No,"* she said with a vehemence that set him back on his heels a little. "That would make them feel like charity cases. They're good, decent people, Brad."

"Then what do you want me to do?" Half Brad's attention was on the conversation, the other half on the distant closing of the limo door, so he'd probably sounded abrupt.

"Put on a concert," Livie said. "There are half a dozen other families around Stone Creek in similar situations. Divvy up the proceeds, and that will spare everybody's dignity."

Brad frowned down at his sister. "How long has *that* plan been brewing in your busy little head, Dr. Livie?"

She smiled. "Ever since you raised all that money for the animals displaced during Hurricane Katrina," she said.

A knock sounded at the outside door.

Phil's big schnoz was pressed to the screen.

"Gotta go," Livie said. She squatted to give Willie a

goodbye pat and ducked out of the kitchen, headed for the front.

"Can I come in?" Phil asked plaintively.

"Would it make a difference if I said no?" Brad shot back.

The screen door creaked open. "Of course not," Phil said, smiling broadly. "I came all the way from New Jersey to talk some sense into your head."

"I could have saved you the trip," Brad answered. "I'm not going to Vegas. I'm not going *anywhere*." He liked Phil, but after the events of the past twenty-four hours, he was something the worse for wear. With his chores done and the overdue visit to Big John's grave behind him, he'd planned to eat something, take a hot shower and fall face-first into his unmade bed.

"Who said anything about Vegas?" Phil asked, the picture of innocent affront. "Maybe I want to deliver a big fat royalty check or something like that."

"And maybe you're full of crap," Brad countered. "I just *got* a 'big, fat royalty check,' according to my accountant. He's fit to be tied because the recording company promised to parcel the money out over at least fifteen years, and it came in a lump sum instead. Says the taxes are going to eat me alive."

Phil sniffled, pretended to wipe tears from his eyes. "Cry me a river, Mr. Country Music," he said. "I belong to the you-can-never-be-too-rich school of thought. Until my niece suffered that bout with anorexia—thank God she recovered—I thought you could never be too thin, either, but that theory's down the swirler."

Brad said nothing.

"What happened to that dog?" Phil asked, after giving Willie the eyeball.

"He was attacked by coyotes—or maybe wolves."

Livie had lugged in a bag of kibble and a couple of bowls, along with the bed Willie was lounging on now, and she'd set two prescription bottles on the counter, too, though Brad hadn't noticed them until now. He busied himself with reading the labels.

"Why anybody'd want to live in a place where a thing like that is even remotely possible, even if he *is* a dog," Phil marveled, "is beyond me."

Willie was to have one of each pill—an antibiotic and a painkiller—morning and night. With food.

"A lot of things are beyond you, Phil," Brad said, figuring Olivia must have dosed the dog that morning before leaving the clinic, which meant the medication could wait until suppertime.

"He's pretty torn up. Wouldn't have happened in Music City, to a dog *or* a man."

"Evidently," Brad said, still distracted, "you've repressed the gory memories of my second divorce."

Phil chuckled. "You could give all that extra royalty money you're so worried about to good ole Cynthia," he suggested. "Write it off as an extra settlement and let *her* worry about the taxes."

"You're just full of wisdom today. Something else, too."

Uninvited, Phil drew back a chair at the table and sank into it, one hand pressed dramatically to his heart. "Phew," he sighed. "The old ticker ain't what it used to be."

"Right," Brad said. "I was there for the celebration after your last cardiology workup, remember? You probably have a better heart than I do, so spare me the sympathy plays."

"You have a heart?" Phil countered, raising his bushy gray eyebrows almost to his thinning hairline. Even with plugs, the carpet looked pretty sparse. Phil's pate always reminded Brad of the dolls his sisters had had when they were little, sprouting shocks of hair out of holes in neat little rows. "Couldn't prove it by me."

"Whatever," Brad said, dipping one of Willie's bowls into the kibble bag, then setting it down, full, where the dog could reach it without getting off his bed. He followed up by filling the other bowl with tap water. Then, on second thought, he dumped that and poured the bottled kind, instead.

"This is something big," Phil said. "That's why I came in person."

"If I let you tell me, will you leave?" By then, Brad was plundering the fridge for the makings of breakfast.

"Got any kosher sausage in there?" the older man asked.

"Sorry," Brad answered. He'd come up with something if Phil stayed, since he couldn't eat in front of the man, but he was still hoping for a speedy departure.

Next, he'd be hanging up a stocking on Christmas Eve, setting out an empty basket the night before Easter.

"Big opportunity," Phil continued. "Very, very big."

"I don't care."

"You don't care? This is a *movie*, Brad. The lead. A *feature*, too. A big Western with cattle and wagons and a cast of dozens. And you won't even have to sing."

"No."

"Two years ago, even a year ago, you would have *killed* for a chance like this!"

"That was then," Brad said, flashing back to the night before, when he'd said practically the same thing to Meg, "and this is now."

"I've got the script in the car. In my briefcase. Solid gold, Brad. It might even be Oscar material."

"Phil," Brad said, turning from the fridge with the makings of a serious omelet in his hands, "what part of 'no' is eluding you? Would it be the *N,* or the *O?*"

"But you'd get to play an *outlaw,* trying to go straight."

"Phil."

"You're really serious about this retirement thing, aren't you?" Phil sounded stunned. Aggrieved. And petulant. "In a year—hell, in *six months*—when you've got all this down-home stuff out of your system, you'll wish you'd listened to me!"

"I listened, Phil. Do you want an omelet?"

"Do I *want an omelet?* Hell, no! I want you to make a damned *movie!*"

"Not gonna happen, Phil."

Phil was suddenly super-alert, like a predator who's just spotted dinner on the hoof. "It's some woman, isn't it?"

Again, he flashed on Meg. The way she'd felt, silky and slick, against him. The way she'd scratched at his back and called his name...

"Maybe," he admitted.

"Do I need to remind you that your romantic history isn't exactly going to inspire a new line of Hallmark valentines?"

Brad sighed. Got out the skillet and set it on the stove. Willie gave him a sidelong look of commiseration from the dog bed.

"If you won't eat an omelet," Brad told Phil, "leave."

"That pretty little thing who sneaked out of here when I came to the door—was that her?"

"That was my sister," Brad said.

Phil raised himself laboriously to his feet, like he was ninety-seven instead of seventy-seven, and all that would save him from a painful and rapid descent into the grave all but yawning at the tips of his gleaming shoes was Brad's signature on a movie contract. "Well, whoever this woman is, I'd like her name. Maybe *she* can get you to see reason."

That made Brad smile. Meg made him see galaxies colliding. Once or twice, during the night, he'd almost seen God. But reason?

Nope.

He plopped a dollop of butter into the skillet.

Phil made a huffy exit, slamming the screen door behind him.

Willie gave a low whine.

"You're right," Brad told the dog. "He'll probably be back."

Meg stood as if frozen in the hallway of Indian Rock's only hotel, wanting to turn and run, but too stunned to move.

She'd just gathered the impetus to flee when her father stuck a hand out. "Ted Ledger," he said, by way of introduction. "Come in and meet your sister, Meg."

Her sister?

It was that, added to a desire to commit matricide, that brought Meg over the threshold and into her mother's simply furnished, elegantly rustic suite.

Eve was nowhere in sight, the coward. But a little girl, ten or twelve years old, sat stiffly on the couch, hands folded in her lap. She was blond and blue-eyed, clad in cheap discount-store jeans and a floral shirt with ruffles, and the look on her face was one of terrified defiance.

"Hello," Meg said, forcing the words past her heart, which was beating in her throat.

The marvelous blue eyes narrowed.

"Carly," said Ted Ledger, "say hello."

"Hello," Carly complied grudgingly.

Looking at the child, Meg couldn't help thinking that the baby she'd lost would have been about this same age, if it hadn't been for the miscarriage.

She straightened her spine. Turned to the father who hadn't cared enough to send her so much as an e-mail, let alone be part of her life. "Where is my mother?" she asked evenly.

"Hiding out," Ledger said with a wisp of a grin. In his youth, he'd probably been handsome. Now he was thin and gray-haired, with dark shadows under his pale blue eyes.

Carly looked Meg over again and jutted out her chin. "I don't want to live with her," she said. "She probably doesn't need a kid hanging around anyhow."

"Go in the kitchen," Ledger told the child.

To Meg's surprise, Carly obeyed.

"Live with me?" Meg echoed in a whisper.

"It's that or foster care," Ledger said. "Sit down."

Meg sat, not because her father had asked her to, but because all the starch had gone out of her knees. Questions battered at the back of her throat, like balls springing from a pitching machine.

Where have you been?

Why didn't you ever call?

If I kill my mother, could a dream-team get me off without prison time?

"I know this is sudden," Ted Ledger said, perching on the edge of the white velvet wingback chair Eve had had sent from her mansion in San Antonio, to make the place more "homey."

"But the situation is desperate. *I'm* desperate."

Meg tried to swallow, but couldn't. Her mouth was too

dry, and her esophagus had closed up. "I don't believe this," she croaked.

"Your mother and I agreed, long ago," Ledger went on, "that it would be best if I stayed out of your life. That's why she never brought you to visit me."

"Visit you?"

"I was in prison, Meg. For embezzlement."

"From McKettrickCo," Meg mused aloud, startled, but at the same time realizing that she'd known all along, on some half-conscious level.

"I told you he was a waste of hair and hide," Angus said. He stood over by the fake fireplace, one arm resting on the mantelpiece.

Meg took care to ignore him, not to so much as glance in his direction, though she could see him out of the corner of one eye. He was in old-man mode today, white-headed and wrinkled and John Wayne—tough, but dressed for the trail.

"Yes," Ledger replied. "Your mother saw that there was no scandal—easier to do in those days, before the media came into its own. I went to jail. She went on with her life."

"Where does Carly fit in?"

Ledger's smile was soft and sad. "While I was inside, I got religion, as they say. When I was released, I found a job, met a woman, got married. We had Carly. Then, three years ago, Sarah—my wife—was killed in a car accident. Things went downhill from there—I was diagnosed last month."

Tears burned in Meg's eyes, but they weren't for Ledger, or even for Sarah. They were for Carly. Although she'd grown up in a different financial situation, with all the stability that came with simply being a McKettrick, she knew what the child must be going through.

"You don't have any other family? Perhaps Sarah's people—"

Ledger shook his head. "There's no one. Your mother has generously agreed to pay my medical bills and arrange for a decent burial, but I'll be lucky if I live six weeks. And once I'm gone, Carly will be alone."

Meg pressed her fingertips to her temples and breathed slowly and deeply. "Maybe Mom could—"

"She's past the age to raise a twelve-year-old," Ledger interrupted.

He leaned forward slightly in his chair, rested his elbows on his knees, intertwined his fingers and let his hands dangle. "Meg, you don't owe me a damn thing. I was no kind of father, and I'm not pretending I was. But Carly is your half sister. She's got your blood in her veins. And she doesn't have anybody else."

Meg closed her eyes, trying to imagine herself raising a resentful, grieving preadolescent girl. As much as she'd longed for her own child, nothing had prepared her for this.

"She won't go to foster care," she said. "Mother would never allow it."

"Boarding school, then," Ledger replied. "Carly would hate that. Probably run away. She needs a real home. Love. Somebody young enough to steer her safely through her teens, at least."

"You heard her," Meg said. "She doesn't want to live with me."

"She doesn't know what she wants, except for me to have a miraculous recovery, and that isn't going to happen. I can't ask you to do this for me, Meg—I've got no right to ask anything of you—but I can ask you to do it for Carly."

The room seemed to tilt. From the kitchen, Meg heard

her mother's voice, and Carly's. What were they talking about in there?

"Okay," Meg heard herself say.

Ledger's once-handsome face lit with a smile of relief and what looked like sincere gratitude. "You'll do it? You'll look after your sister?"

My sister.

"Yes," Meg said. On the outside, she probably looked calm. On the inside, she was shaking. "What happens now?"

"I go into the hospital for pain control. Carly goes home with you for a few days. When—and if—I get out, she'll come back to stay with me."

Meg nodded, her mind racing, groping, grasping for some handhold on an entirely new, entirely unexpected situation.

"We've got a room downstairs," Ledger said, rising painfully from the chair. "Carly and I will leave you alone with Eve for a little while."

Over by the fireplace, Angus scowled, powerful arms folded across his chest. Fortunately, he didn't say anything, because Meg would have told him to shut up if he had.

Her father left, Carly trailing after him.

Eve stepped into the kitchen doorway the moment they'd gone.

Angus vanished.

"Nice work, Mom," Meg said, still too shaken to stand up. Since a murder would be hard to pull off sitting down, her mother was off the hook. Temporarily.

"She's about the same age as your baby would have been," Eve said. "It's fate."

Meg's mouth fell open.

"Of course I knew," Eve told her, venturing as far as the

white velvet chair and perching gracefully on the edge of its cushion. "I'm your mother."

Meg closed her mouth. Tightly.

Eve's eyes were on the door through which Ted Ledger and Carly had just passed. "I loved him," she said. "But when he admitted stealing all that money, there was nothing I could do to keep him out of prison. We divorced after his conviction, and he asked me not to tell you where he was."

Meg sagged back in her own chair, still dizzy. Still speechless.

"She's a beautiful child," Eve said, referring, of course, to Carly. "You looked just like her, at that age. It's uncanny, really."

"She's bound to have a lot of problems," Meg managed.

"Of course she will. She lost her mother, and now her father is at death's door. But she has you, Meg. That makes her lucky, in spite of everything else."

"I haven't the faintest idea how to raise a child," Meg pointed out.

"Nobody does, when they start out," Eve reasoned. "Children don't come with a handbook, you know."

Suddenly, Meg remembered the lunch she had scheduled with Cheyenne, the groceries she'd intended to buy. Instantaneous motherhood hadn't been on her to-do list for the day.

She imagined making a call to Cheyenne. *Gotta postpone lunch. You see, I just gave birth to a twelve-year-old in my mother's living room.*

"I had plans," she said lamely.

"Didn't we all?" Eve countered.

"There's no food in my refrigerator."

"Supermarket's right down the road."

"Where have they been living? What kind of life has she had, up to now?"

"A hard one, I would imagine. Ted's something of a drifter—I suspect they've been living out of that old car he drives. He claims he homeschooled her, but knowing Ted, that probably means she knows how to read a racing form and calculate the odds of winning at Powerball."

"Great," Meg said, but something motherly was stirring inside her, something hopeful and brave and very, very fragile. "Can I count on you for help, or just the usual interference?"

Eve laughed. "Both," she said.

Meg found her purse, fumbled for her cell phone, dialed Cheyenne's number.

It was something of a relief that she got her friend's voice mail.

"This is Meg," she said. "I can't make it for lunch. How about a rain check?"

Chapter 9

Meg moved through the supermarket like a robot, programmed to take things off the shelves and drop them into the cart. When she got home and started putting away her groceries, she was surprised by some of the things she'd bought. There were ingredients for actual meals, not just things she could nuke in the microwave or eat right out of the box or bag.

She was brewing coffee when a knock sounded at the back door.

Glancing over, she saw her cousin Rance through the little panes of glass and gestured for him to come in. Tall and dark-haired, he looked as though he'd just come off a nineteenth-century cattle drive, in his battered boots, old jeans and Western-cut shirt. Favoring her with a lopsided grin, he removed his hat and hung it on one of the pegs next to the door.

"Heard you had a little shock this morning," he said.

Meg shook her head. She'd never gotten over how fast word got around in a place like Indian Rock. Then again, maybe Eve had called Rance, thinking Meg might need emotional support. "You could say that," she replied. "Who told you?"

Rance proceeded to the coffeemaker, which was still doing its steaming and gurgling number, took a mug down from the cupboard above and filled it, heedless of the brew dripping, fragrant and sizzling, onto the base. Of course, being a man, he didn't bother to wipe up the overflow.

"Eve," he said, confirming her suspicions.

Meg, not usually a neatnik, made a big deal of papertoweling up the spill around the bottom of the coffeemaker. "It's no emergency, Rance," she told him.

He looked ruefully amused. "Your dad walks into your life after something like thirty years and it's not an emergency?"

"I suppose Mom told you about Carly."

Rance nodded. Ushered Meg to a seat at the table, set down his coffee mug and went back to pour a cup for her, messing up the counter all over again. "Twelve years old, something of an attitude," he confirmed, giving her the cup and then sitting astride the bench. "And coming to live with you. Is that going to screw up your love life?"

"I don't *have* a love life," Meg said. Sure, she'd spent the night tangling sheets with Brad O'Ballivan but, one, primal sex didn't constitute a relationship and, two, it was none of Rance's business anyway.

"Whatever," Rance said. "The point is, you've got a kid to raise, and she's a handful, by all accounts. I'm no authority on bringing up kids, but I do have two daughters. I'll do what I can to help, Meg, and so will Emma."

Rance's girls, Maeve and Rianna, were like nieces to

Meg, and so was Keegan's Devon. While they were all younger than Carly, they would be eager to include her in the family, and it was comforting to know that.

"Thanks," Meg said as her eyes misted over.

"You can do this," Rance told her.

"I don't seem to have a choice. Carly is my half sister, there's no one else, and blood is blood."

"If there's one concept a hardheaded McKettrick can comprehend right away, it's that."

"I don't know as we're all that hardheaded," Angus put in, after materializing behind Rance in the middle of the kitchen.

Meg didn't glance up, nor did she answer. She was close to Rance, Jesse and Keegan—always had been—but she'd never told them she saw Angus, dead since the early twentieth century, on a regular basis. Her mother knew, having overheard Meg talking to him, long after the age of entertaining imaginary playmates had passed, and for all the problems Eve had suffered after Sierra's kidnapping, she'd given her remaining daughter one inestimable gift. She'd believed her.

You're not the type to see things, Eve had said after Meg reluctantly explained. *If you say Angus McKettrick is here, then he is.*

Remembering, Meg felt a swell of love for her mother, despite an equal measure of annoyance.

"I'd better get back to punching cattle," Rance said, finishing his coffee and swinging a leg over the bench to stand. With winter coming on, he and his hired men were rounding up strays in the hills and driving the whole bunch down to the lower pastures. "If you need a hand over here, with the girl or anything else, you let me know."

Meg grinned up at him. He'd taken time out of a busy

day to come over and check on her in person, and she appreciated that. "Once Carly's had a little time to settle in, we'll introduce her to Maeve and Rianna and Devon. I don't think she's got a clue what it's like to be part of a family like ours."

Rance laid a work-calloused hand on Meg's shoulder as he passed, carrying his empty coffee mug to the sink, then crossing to take his hat down from the peg. "Probably not," he agreed. "But she'll find out soon enough."

With that, Rance left again.

Meg turned to acknowledge Angus. "We *are* hard-headed," she told him. "Every last one of us."

"I'd rather call it 'persistent,'" Angus imparted.

"Your decision," Meg responded, getting up to dispose of her own coffee cup then heading for the backstairs. She didn't know when Carly would be arriving, but it was time to get a room ready for her. That meant changing sheets, opening windows to air the place out and equipping the guest bathroom with necessities like clean towels, a toothbrush and paste, shampoo and the like.

She'd barely finished, and returned to the kitchen to slap together a hasty lunch, when an old car rattled up alongside the house, backfired and shut down. As Meg watched from the window, Ted Ledger got out, keeping one hand to the car for balance as he rounded it, and leaned in on the opposite side, no doubt trying to persuade a reluctant Carly to alight.

Meg hurried outside.

By the time she reached the car, Carly was standing with a beat-up backpack dangling from one hand, staring at the barn.

"Do you have horses?" she asked.

Hallelujah, Meg thought. *Common ground.*

"Yes," she said, smiling.

"I hate horses," Carly said. "They smell and step on people."

Ted passed Meg a beleaguered look over the top of the old station wagon, his eyes pleading for patience.

"You do not," he said to Carly. Then, to Meg, "She's just being difficult."

Duh, Meg thought, but in spite of all her absent-father issues, she felt a pang of sympathy for the man. He was terminally ill, probably broke, and trying to find a place for his younger daughter to make the softest possible landing.

Meg figured it would be a fiery crash instead, complete with explosions, but she also knew she was up to the challenge. Mostly, that is. And with a lot of help from Rance, Keegan, Jesse and Sierra.

Oh, yeah. She'd be calling in her markers, all right.

Code-blue, calling all McKettricks.

"I'm not staying unless my dad can stay, too," Carly announced, standing her ground, there in the gravel of the upper driveway, knuckles white where she gripped the backpack.

Meg hadn't considered this development, though she supposed she should have. She forced herself to meet Ted's gaze, saw both resignation and hope in his eyes when she did.

"It's a big house," she heard herself say. "Plenty of room."

Rance's earlier question echoed in her mind. *Is that going to screw up your love life?*

There'd be no more overnight visits from Brad, at least not in the immediate future. To Meg, that was both a relief—things were moving too fast on that front—and a problem. Her body was still reverberating with the pleasure Brad had awakened in her, and already craving more.

"Okay," Carly said, moving a little closer to Ted. The two of them bumped shoulders in unspoken communication, and Meg felt a brief and unexpected stab of envy.

Meg tried to carry Ted's suitcase inside, but he wouldn't allow that. Manly pride, she supposed.

Angus watched from the back steps as the three of them trailed toward the house, Meg in the lead, Ted following and Carly straggling at the rear.

"She's a good kid," Angus said.

Meg gave him a look but said nothing.

Just walking into the house seemed to wear Ted out, and as soon as Carly had been installed in her room, he expressed a need to lie down. Meg showed him to the space generations of McKettrick women—she being an exception—had done their sewing.

There was only a daybed, and Meg hadn't changed the sheets, but Ted waved away her offer to spruce up the room a little. She went out, closing the door behind her, and heard the bedsprings groan as if he'd collapsed onto them.

Carly's door was shut. Meg paused outside it, on her way to the rear stairway, considered knocking and decided to leave the poor kid alone, let her adjust to new and strange surroundings.

Downstairs, Meg went back to what she'd been doing when Ted and Carly arrived. She made a couple of extra sandwiches, just in case, wolfed one down with a glass of milk and eyeballed the phone.

Was Brad going to call, or was last night just another slam-bam to him? And if he *did* call, what exactly was she going to say?

* * *

Willie was surprisingly ambulatory, considering what he'd been through. When Brad came out of the upstairs bathroom, having showered and pulled on a pair of boxer-briefs and nothing else, the dog was waiting in the hall. Climbing the stairs must have been an ordeal, but he'd done it.

"You need to go outside, boy?" Brad asked. When Big John's health had started to decline, Brad had wanted to install an elevator, so the old man wouldn't have to manage a lot of steps, but he'd met with the usual response.

An elevator? Big John had scoffed. *Boy, all that fine Nashville livin' is goin' to your head.*

Now, with an injured dog on his hands, Brad wished he'd overridden his grandfather's protests.

He moved to lift Willie, intending to carry him downstairs and out the kitchen door to the grassy side yard, but a whimper from the dog foiled that idea. Carefully, the two of them made the descent, Willie stopping every few steps to rest, panting.

The whole process was painful to watch.

Reaching the kitchen at last, Brad opened the back door and waited as Willie labored outside, found a place in the grass after copious sniffing and did his business.

Once he was back inside, Brad decided another trip up the stairway was out of the question. He moved Willie's new dog bed into a small downstairs guest room, threw back the comforter on one of the twin-sized beds and fell onto it, face-first.

"Who's the old man?" Carly asked, startling Meg, who had been running more searches on Josiah McKettrick on the computer in the study, for more reasons than one.

"What old man?" Meg retorted pleasantly, turning in the chair to see her half sister standing in the big double doorway, looking much younger than twelve in a faded and somewhat frayed sleep shirt with a cartoon bear on the front.

"This house," Carly said implacably, "is haunted."

"It's been around a long time," Meg hedged, still smiling. "Lots of history here. Are you hungry?"

"Only if you've got the stuff to make grilled-cheese sandwiches," Carly said. She was in the gawky stage, but one day, she'd be gorgeous. Meg didn't see the resemblance Eve had commented on earlier, but if there was one, it was cause to feel flattered.

"I've got the stuff," Meg assured her, rising from her chair.

"I can do it myself," Carly said.

"Maybe we could talk a little," Meg replied.

"Or not," Carly answered, with a note of dismissal that sounded false.

Meg followed the woman-child to the kitchen, earning herself a few scathing backward glances in the process.

Efficiently, Carly opened the fridge, helped herself to a package of cheese and proceeded to the counter. Meg supplied bread and a butter dish and a skillet, but that was all the assistance Carly was willing to accept.

"Can you cook?" Meg asked, hoping to get some kind of dialogue going.

Carly shrugged one thin shoulder. Her feet were bare and a tiny tattoo of some kind of flower blossomed just above one ankle bone. "Dad's hopeless at it, so I learned."

"I see," Meg said, wondering what could have possessed her father to let a child get a tattoo, and if it had hurt much, getting poked with all those needles.

"You don't see," Carly said, skillfully preparing her sandwich, everything in her bearing warning Meg to keep her distance.

"What makes you say that?"

Another shrug.

"Carly?"

The girl's back, turned to Meg as she laid the sandwich in the skillet and adjusted the gas stove burner beneath, stiffened. "Don't ask me a bunch of questions, okay? Don't ask how it was, living on the road, or if I miss my mother, or what it's like knowing my dad is going to die. Just leave me be, and we'll get along all right."

"There's one question I have to ask," Meg said.

Carly tossed her another short, over-the-shoulder glower. "What?"

"Did it hurt a lot, getting that tattoo?"

Suddenly, a smile broke over Carly's face, and it changed everything about her. "Yes."

"Why did you do it?"

"That's *two* questions," Carly pointed out. "You said one."

"Was it because your friends got tattoos?"

Carly's smile faded, and she averted her attention again, spatula in hand, ready to turn her grilled-cheese sandwich when it was just right. "I don't have any friends," she said. "We moved around too much. And I didn't need them anyhow. Me and Dad—that was enough."

Meg's eyes burned.

"I got the tattoo," Carly said, catching Meg off-guard, "because my mom had one just like it, in the same place. It's a yellow rose—because Dad always called her his yellow rose of Texas."

Meg's throat went tight. How was she going to help this

child face the loss of not one parent, but two? Sister or not, she was a stranger to Carly.

The phone rang.

Carly, being closest, picked up the receiver, peered at the caller ID panel, and went wide-eyed. *"Brad O'Ballivan?"* she whispered reverently, padding across the kitchen to give Meg the phone. "*The* Brad O'Ballivan?"

Meg choked out a laugh. Well, well, well. Carly was a fan. Just the opening Meg needed to establish some kind of bond, however tenuous, with her newly discovered kid sister. "*The* Brad O'Ballivan," she said before thumbing the talk button. "Hello?"

Brad's answer was an expansive yawn. Evidently, he'd either just awakened or he'd gone to bed early. Either way, the images playing in Meg's mind were scintillating ones, and they soon rippled into other parts of her anatomy, like tiny tsunamis boiling under her skin.

"Willie's home," he said finally.

Carly was staring at Meg. "I have all his CDs," she said.

"That's good," Meg answered.

"We ought to celebrate," Brad went on. "I grill a mean steak. Six-thirty, my place?"

"Only if you have a couple of spares," Meg said. "I have company."

The smell of scorching sandwich billowed from the stove.

Carly didn't move.

"Company?" Brad asked sleepily, with another yawn.

Meg pictured him scantily clothed, if he was wearing anything at all, with an attractive case of bed head. And she blushed to catch herself thinking lascivious thoughts with a twelve-year-old in the same room. "It's a lot to explain over the phone," she said diplomatically, gesturing to Carly to rescue the sandwich, which she finally did.

"The more the merrier," Brad said. "Whoever they are, bring them."

"We'll be there," Meg said.

Carly pushed the skillet off the burner and waved ineffectually at the smoke.

Meg said goodbye to Brad and hung up the phone.

"We're going to *Brad O'Ballivan's house?*" Carly blurted. *"For real?"*

"For real," Meg said. "If your dad feels up to it."

"He's your dad, too," Carly allowed. "And he likes Brad's music. We listen to it in the car all the time."

Meg let the part about Ted Ledger being her dad pass. He'd been her sire, not her father. "Let's let him rest," she said, taking over the grilled cheese operation and feeling glad when Carly didn't protest, or try to elbow her aside.

"How long have you known him?" Carly demanded, almost breathless.

It was a moment before Meg realized the girl was talking about Brad, not Ted, so muddled were her thoughts. "Since junior high," she said.

"What's he like?"

"He's nice," Meg said carefully, slicing cheese, reaching for the butter dish and then the bread bag.

"'Nice'?" Carly looked not only skeptical, but a little disappointed. "He trashes hotel rooms. He pushed a famous actress into a swimming pool at a big Hollywood party—"

"I think that's mostly hype," Meg said, hoping the kid hadn't heard the notches-in-the-bedpost stuff. She started the new sandwich in a fresh skillet and carried the first one to the sink. When she glanced Carly's way, she was surprised and touched to see she'd taken a seat on the bench next to the table.

"Do you think he'd autograph my CDs?"

"I'd say there was a fairly good chance he will, yes." She turned the sandwich, got out a china plate, poured a glass of milk.

Carly glowed with anticipation. "If I had any friends," she said, "I'd call them all and tell them I get to meet Brad O'Ballivan *in the flesh.*"

And what flesh it was, Meg thought, and blushed again. "Once you start school," she said, "you'll have all kinds of friends. Plus, there are some kids in the family around your age."

"It's not my family," Carly said, stiffening again.

"Of course it is," Meg argued, but cautiously, scooping a letter-perfect grilled-cheese sandwich onto a plate and presenting it to Carly with a flourish, along with the milk. She wished Angus had been there, to see her cooking. "You and I are sisters. I'm a McKettrick. So that means you're related to them, too, if only by association."

"I hate milk," Carly said.

"Brad drinks it," Meg replied lightly.

Carly reached for the glass, took a sip. Pondered the taste, and then took another. "You see him, too," the child observed. "The old man, I mean."

Before Meg could come up with an answer, Angus reappeared.

"I'm not that old," he protested.

"Yes, you are," Carly argued, looking right at him. "You must be a hundred, and that's *old.*"

Meg's mouth fell open.

"I *told* you I could see him," Carly said with a touch of smugness.

Angus laughed. "I'll be damned," he marveled.

Carly's brow furrowed. "Are you a ghost?"

"Not really," Angus said.

"What are you, then?"

"Just a person, like you. I'm from another time, that's all."

No big deal. I just step from one century to another at will. Anybody could do it.

Meg watched the exchange in amazement, speechless. Ever since she'd started seeing Angus, way back in her nursery days, she'd wished for one other person—just one—who could see him, too. Being different from other people was a lonely thing.

"When my dad dies, will he still be around?"

Angus approached the table, drew back Holt's chair, and sat down. His manner was gruff and gentle, at the same time, and Meg's throat tightened again, recalling all the times he'd comforted her, in his grave, deep-voiced way. "That's a question I can't rightly answer," he said solemnly. "But I can tell you that folks don't really die, in the way you probably think of it. They're just in another place, that's all."

Carly blinked, obviously trying hard not to cry. "I'm going to miss him something awful," she said very softly.

Angus covered the child's small hand with one of his big, work-worn paws. There was such a rough tenderness in the gesture that Meg's throat closed up even more, and her eyes scalded.

"It's a fact of life, missing folks when they go away," Angus said. "You've got Meg, here, though." He nodded his head slightly, in her direction, but didn't look away from Carly's face. "She'll do right by you. It's the McKettrick way, taking care of your own."

"But I'm not a McKettrick," Carly said.

"You could be if you wanted to," Angus reasoned. "You're not a Ledger, either, are you?"

"We've changed our name so many times," the child admitted, her eyes round and sad and a little hungry as she studied Angus, "I don't remember who I am."

"Then you might as well be a McKettrick as not," Angus said.

Carly's gaze slid to Meg, swung away again. "I'm not going to forget my dad," she said.

"Nobody expects you to do that," Angus replied. "Thing is, you've got a long life ahead of you, and it'll be a lot easier with a family to take your part when the trail gets rugged."

Upstairs, a door opened, then closed again.

"Your pa," Angus told Carly, lowering his voice a little, "is real worried about you being all right, once he's gone. You could put his mind at ease a bit, if you'd give Meg a chance to act like a big sister."

Carly bit her lower lip, then nodded. "I wish you wouldn't go away," she said. "But I know you're going to." She paused, and Meg grappled with the sudden knowledge that it was true—one day soon, Angus would vanish, for good. "If you see my mom—her name is Rose—will you tell her I've got a tattoo just like hers?"

"I surely will," Angus promised.

"And you'll look out for my dad, too?"

Angus nodded, his eyes misty. It was a phenomenon Meg had never seen before, even at family funerals. Then he ruffled Carly's hair and vanished just as Ted came down the stairs, moving slowly, holding tightly to the rail.

It was all Meg could do not to rush to his aid.

"Hungry?" she asked moderately.

"I could eat," Ted volunteered, looking at Carly. His whole face softened as he gazed at his younger child.

It made Meg wonder if he'd ever missed *her,* during all those years away.

As if he'd heard her thoughts, her father turned to her. "You turned out real well," he said after clearing his throat. "Your mom did a good job, raising you. But, then, Eve was always competent."

"We're going to meet Brad O'Ballivan," Carly said.

"Get out," Ted teased, a faint twinkle shining in his eyes. "We're not, either."

"Yes, we are," Carly insisted. "Meg knows him. He just called here. Meg says he might autograph my CDs."

Ted grinned, made his way to the table and sank into the chair Angus had occupied until moments before. Spent a few moments recovering from the exertion of descending the stairs and crossing the room.

Meg served up the extra sandwiches she'd made earlier, struggling all the while with a lot of tangled emotions. Carly could see Angus. Ted Ledger might be a total stranger, but he was Meg's father, and he was dying.

Last but certainly not least, Brad was back in her life, and there were bound to be complications.

A strange combination of grief, joy and anticipation pushed at the inside walls of Meg's heart.

They arrived right on time, Meg and a young girl and a man who put Brad in mind of Paul Newman. Willie, who'd been resting on the soft grass bordering the flagstone patio off the kitchen, keeping an eye on his new master while he prepared the barbeque grill for action, gave a soft little woof.

Brad watched as Meg approached, thinking how delicious she looked in her jeans and lightweight, close-fitting sweater. She hadn't explained who her company was, but looking at them, Brad saw the girl's resemblance to Meg, and guessed the man to be the father she hadn't seen since she was a toddler.

He smiled.

The girl blushed and stared at him.

"Hey," he said, putting out a hand. "My name's Brad O'Ballivan."

"I know," the girl said.

"My sister, Carly," Meg told him. "And this is my—this is Ted Ledger."

Shyly, Carly slipped off her backpack, reached inside, took out a couple of beat-up CDs. "Meg said I could maybe get your autograph."

"No maybe about it," Brad answered. "I don't happen to have a pen on me at the moment, though."

Carly swallowed visibly. "That's okay," she said, her gaze straying to Willie, who was thumping his tail against the ground and grinning a goofy dog grin at her, hoping for friendship. "What happened to him?"

"He had a run-in with a pack of coyotes," Brad said. "He'll be all right, though. Just needs a little time to mend."

The girl crouched next to the dog, stroked him gently. "Hi," she said.

Meanwhile, Meg's father took a seat at the patio table. He looked bushed.

"I had to have stitches once," Carly told Willie. "Not as many as you've got, though."

"Brad's sister is a veterinarian," Meg said, finally finding her voice. "She fixed him right up."

"I'd like to be a veterinarian," Carly said.

"No reason you can't," Brad replied, turning his attention to Ted Ledger. "Can I get you a drink, Mr. Ledger?"

Ledger shook his head. "No, thanks," he said quietly.

His gaze moved fondly between Meg and Carly, resting on one, then the other. "Good of you to have us over. I appreciate it. And I'd rather you called me Ted."

"Is there anything I can do to help?" Meg asked.

"I've got it under control," Brad told her. "Just relax."

Great advice, O'Ballivan, he thought. *Maybe you ought to take it.*

Meg went to greet Willie, who gave a whine of greeting and tried to lick her face. She laughed, and Brad felt something open up inside him, at the sound. When he'd conceived the supper idea, he'd intended to ply her with good wine and a thick steak, then take her to bed. The extra guests precluded that plan, of course, but he didn't regret it. When it finally registered that his and Meg's child might have looked a lot like Carly, though, he felt bruised all over again.

"Any news about Ransom?" Meg asked, stepping up beside him when he turned his back to lay steaks on the grill, along with foil-wrapped baked potatoes that had been cooking for a while.

Brad shook his head, suddenly unable to look at her. If he did, she'd see all the things he felt, and he wasn't ready for that.

"According to the radio," Meg persisted, "the blizzard's passed, and the snow's melted."

Brad sighed. "I guess that means I'd better ride up and look for that stallion before Livie decides to do it by herself."

"I'd like to go with you," Meg said, sounding almost shy.

Brad thought about the baby who'd never had a chance to grow up. The baby Meg hadn't seen fit to tell him about. "We'll see," he answered noncommittally. "How do you like your steak?"

Chapter 10

After the meal had been served and enjoyed, with Willie getting the occasional scrap, Brad signed the astounding succession of CDs Carly fished out of her backpack. Ted, who had eaten little, seemed content to watch the scene from a patio chair, and Meg insisted on cleaning up; since she'd had no part in the preparations, it only seemed fair.

As she carried in plates and glasses and silverware, rinsed them and put them into the oversize dishwasher, she reflected on Brad's mood change. He'd been warm to Ted, and chatted and joked with Carly, but when she'd mentioned that she'd like to accompany him when he went looking for Ransom again, it was as if a wall had slammed down between them.

She was just shutting the dishwasher and looking for the appropriate button to push when the screen door creaked open behind her. She turned, saw Brad hesitating on the threshold. It was past dusk—outside, the patio lights were burning brightly—but Meg hadn't bothered to flip a switch when she came in, so the kitchen was almost dark.

"Kid wants a T-shirt," he said, his face in shadow so she couldn't read his expression. "I think I have a few around here someplace."

Meg nodded, oddly stricken.

Brad didn't move right away, but simply stood there for a few long moments; she knew by the tilt of his head that he was watching her.

"You've gone out of your way to be kind to Carly," Meg managed, because the silence was unbearable. "Thank you."

He still didn't speak, or move.

Meg swallowed hard. "Well, it's getting late," she said awkwardly. "I guess we'd better be heading for home soon."

Brad reached out for a switch, and the overhead lights came on, seeming harsh after the previous cozy twilight in the room. His face looked bleak to Meg, his broad shoulders seemed to stoop a little.

"Seeing her—Carly, I mean—"

"I know," Meg said very softly. Of course Brad saw what she had, when he looked at Carly—the child who might have been.

"She's her own person," Brad said with an almost inaudible sigh. "It wouldn't be right to think of her in any other way. But it gave me a start, seeing her. She looks so much like you. So much like—"

"Yes."

"What's going on, Meg? You said you couldn't explain over the phone, and I figured out that Ledger had to be your dad. But there's more to this, isn't there?"

Meg bit her lower lip. "Ted is dying," she said. "And it turns out that Carly has no one else in the world except me."

Brad processed that, nodded. "Be careful," he told her quietly. "Carly is Carly. It would be all too easy—and completely unfair—to superimpose—"

"I wouldn't do that, Brad," Meg broke in, bristling. "I'm not pretending she's—she's our daughter."

"Guess I'll go rustle up that T-shirt," Brad said.

Meg didn't respond. For the time being, the conversation—at least as far as their lost child was concerned—was over.

Carly wore the T-shirt home—Brad's guitar-wielding profile was silhouetted on the front, along with the year of a recent tour and an impressive list of cities—practically bouncing in the car seat as she examined the showy signature on the face of each of her CDs.

"I bet he never trashed a single hotel room," she enthused, from the backseat of Meg's Blazer. "He's way too nice to do that."

Meg and Ted exchanged a look of weary amusement up front.

"It was quite an evening," Ted said. "Thanks, Meg."

"Brad did all the work," she replied.

"I like his dog, too," Carly bubbled. She seemed to have forgotten her situation, for the time being, and Meg could see that was a relief to Ted. "Brad said he'd change his name to Stitches, if he didn't already answer to Willie."

Meg smiled.

All the way home, it was Brad said this, Brad said that.

Once they'd reached the ranch house, Ted went inside, exhausted, while Carly and Meg headed for the barn to feed the horses. Despite her earlier condemnation of the entire equine species, Carly proved a fair hand with hay and grain.

"Is he your boyfriend?" Carly asked, keeping pace with Meg as they returned to the house.

"Is who my boyfriend?" Meg parried.

"You *know* I mean Brad," Carly said. "Is he?"

"He's a *friend*," Meg said. But a voice in her mind chided, *Right. And last night, you were rolling around on a mattress with him.*

"I may be twelve, but I'm not stupid," Carly remarked, as they reached the back door. "I saw the way he looked at you. Like he wanted to put his hands on you all the time."

Yeah, Meg thought wearily. *Specifically, around my throat.*

"You're imagining things."

"I'm very sophisticated for twelve," Carly argued.

"Maybe *too* sophisticated."

"If you think I'm going to act like some *kid,* just because I'm twelve, think again."

"That's exactly what I think. A twelve-year-old *is* a kid." Meg pushed open the kitchen door; Ted had turned on the lights as he entered, and the place glowed with homey warmth. "Go to bed."

"There's no TV in my room," Carly protested. "And I'm not sleepy."

"Tough it out," Meg replied. Crossing to the china cabinet on the far side of the room, she opened a drawer, found a notebook and a pen, and handed them to her little sister. "Here," she said. "Keep a journal. It's a tradition in the McKettrick family."

Carly hesitated, then accepted the offering. "I guess I could write about Brad O'Ballivan," she said. She held the notebook to her chest for a moment. "Are you going to read it?"

"No," Meg said, softening a little. "You can write anything you want to. Sometimes it helps to get feelings out of your head and onto paper. Then you can get some perspective."

Carly considered. "Okay," she said and started for the stairs, taking the notebook with her.

Meg, knowing she wouldn't sleep, tired as she was, headed for the study as soon as Carly disappeared, logged onto the Internet and resumed her research.

"You won't find him on that contraption," Angus told her.

She looked up to see him sitting in the big leather wing-back chair by the fireplace. Like many other things in the house, the chair was a holdover from the Holt and Lorelei days.

"Josiah, I mean," Angus added, jawline hard again as he remembered the brother who had so disappointed him. "I told you he didn't use the McKettrick name." He gave a snort. "Sounded too Irish for him."

"Help me out, here," Meg said.

Angus remained silent.

Meg sighed and turned back to the screen. She'd been scrolling through names, intermittently, for days. And now, suddenly, she had a hit, more an instinct than anything specific.

"Creed, Josiah *McKettrick,*" she said excitedly, clicking on the link. "I must have passed right over him dozens of times."

Angus materialized at her elbow, stooping and staring at the screen, his heavy eyebrows pulled together in consternation and curiosity.

"Captain in the United States Army," Meg read aloud, and with a note of triumph in her voice. "Founder of 'the legendary Stillwater Springs Ranch,' in western Montana. Owner of the Stillwater Springs *Courier,* the first newspaper in that part of the territory. On the town council, two terms as mayor. Wife, four sons, active member of the Methodist Church." She stopped, looked up at Angus. "Doesn't sound like an anti-Irish pirate to me." She tapped at Josiah's solemn photograph on the home page. Bewhiskered, with a thick head of white hair, he looked dour and prosperous in his dark suit, the coat fastened with one button at his breastbone, in that curious nineteenth-century way. "There he is, Angus," she said. "Your brother, Josiah McKettrick Creed."

"I'll be hornswoggled," Angus said.

"Whatever that is," Meg replied, busily copying information onto a notepad. The Web site was obviously the work of a skillful amateur, probably a family member with a genealogical bent, and there was no "contact us" link, but the name of the town, and the ranch if it still existed, was information enough.

"Looks like you missed something," Angus said.

Meg peered at the screen, trying to see past Angus's big index finger, scattering a ring of pixels around its end.

She pushed his hand gently aside.

And saw a tiny link at the bottom of the page, printed in blue letters.

A press of a mouse button and she and Angus were looking at the masthead of Josiah's newspaper, the *Courier.*

The headline was printed in heavy type. *MURDER AND SCANDAL BESET STILLWATER SPRINGS RANCH.*

Something quivered in the pit of Meg's stomach, a peculiar combination of dread and fascination. The byline was Josiah's own, and the brief obituary beneath it still pulsed with the staunch grief of an old man, bitterly determined to tell the unflinching truth.

Dawson James Creed, 21, youngest son of Josiah McKettrick Creed and Cora Dawson Creed, perished yesterday at the hand of his first cousin, Benjamin A. Dawson, who shot him dead over a game of cards and a woman. Both the shootist and the woman have since fled these parts. Services tomorrow at 2:00 p.m., at the First Street Methodist Church. Viewing this evening at the Creed home. Our boy will be sorely missed.

"Creed," Angus repeated, musing. "That was my mother's name, before she and my pa hitched up."

"So maybe Josiah *wasn't* a McKettrick," Meg ventured. "Maybe your mother was married before, or—"

Angus stiffened. "Or nothing," he said pointedly. "Back in those days, women didn't go around having babies out of wedlock. Pa must have been her second husband."

Meg, feeling a little stung, didn't comment. Nor did she argue the point, which would have been easy to back up, that premarital pregnancies weren't as uncommon in "his day" as Angus liked to think.

"Where's that old Bible Georgia set such store by?" he asked now.

Georgia, his second wife, mother of Rafe, Kade and Jeb, had evidently been her generation's record-keeper and family historian. "I suppose Keegan has it," she answered, "since he lives in the main ranch house."

"Ma wrote all the begats in that book," Angus recalled. "I never thought to look at it."

"She never mentioned being married before?"

"No," Angus admitted. "But folks didn't talk about things like that much. It was a private matter and besides, they had their hands full just surviving from day to day. No time to sit around jawing about the past."

"I'll drop in on Keegan and Molly in the morning," Meg said. "Ask if I can borrow the Bible."

"I want to look at it *now.*"

"Angus, it's late—"

He vanished.

Meg sighed. There were no more articles on the website—just that short, sad obituary notice—so she logged off the computer. She was brewing a cup of herbal tea in the microwave, hoping it would help her sleep, when Ted came down the backstairs, wearing an old plaid flannel bathrobe and scruffy slippers.

Lord, he wanted to talk.

Now, from the look on his face.

She wasn't ready, and that didn't matter.

The time had come.

Dragging back a chair at the table, Ted crumpled into it.

"Tea?" Meg asked, and immediately felt stupid.

"Sit down, Meg," Ted said gently.

She took the mug from the microwave, grateful for its citrusy steamy scent, and joined him, perching on the end of one of the benches.

"There's no money," Ted said.

"I gathered that," Meg replied, though not flippantly. And the dizzying thought came to her that maybe this was all some kind of con—a *Paper Moon* kind of thing, Ted playing the Ryan O'Neal part, while Carly handled Tatum's role. But the idea fizzled almost as quickly as it had flared up in her mind—a scam would have been so much easier to take than the grim reality.

Ted ran a tremulous hand through his thinning hair. "I wish things had happened differently, Meg," he said. "I wanted to come back a hundred times, say I was sorry for everything that happened. I convinced myself I was being noble—you were a McKettrick, and you didn't need an ex-yardbird complicating your life. The truth gets harder to deny when you're toeing up to the pearly gates, though. I was a coward, that's all. I tried to make up for it by being the best father I could to Carly." He paused, chuckled ruefully. "I won't take any prizes for that, either. After Rose died, it was as if somebody had greased the bottom of my feet. I just couldn't stay put, and it was mostly downhill, a slippery slope, all the way. The worst part is, I dragged Carly right along with me. Last job I had, I stocked shelves in a discount store."

"You don't have to do this," Meg said, blinking back tears she didn't want him to see.

"Yes," Ted said, "I do. I loved your mother and she loved me. You need to know how happy we were when you were born—that you were welcome in this big old crazy world."

"Okay," Meg allowed. "You were happy." She swallowed. "Then you embezzled a lot of money and went to prison."

"Like most embezzlers," Ted answered, "I thought I could put it back before it was missed. It didn't happen that way. Your mother tried to cover for me at first, but there were other McKettricks on the board, and they weren't going to tolerate a thief."

"Why did you do it?" The question, more breathed than spoken, hovered in the otherwise silent room.

"Before I met Eve, I gambled. A lot. I still owed some

people. I was ashamed to tell Eve—and I knew she'd divorce me—so I 'borrowed' what I needed and left as few tracks as possible. That got my creditors off my back—they were knee-breakers, Meg, and they wouldn't have stopped at hurting me. They'd have gone after you and Eve, too."

"So you stole the money to protect Mom and me?" Meg asked, not bothering to hide her skepticism.

"Partly. I was young and I was scared."

"You should have told Mom. She would have helped you."

"I know. But by the time I realized that, it was too late." He sighed. "Now it's too late for a lot of things."

"It's not too late for Carly," Meg said.

"Exactly my point. She's going to give you some trouble, Meg. She won't want to go to school, and she's used to being a loner. I'm all the family she's had since her mother was killed. Like I said before, I've got no right to ask you for anything. I don't expect sympathy. I know you won't grieve when I'm gone. But Carly *will,* and I'm hoping you're McKettrick enough to stand by her till she finds her balance. My worst fear is that she'll go down the same road I did, drifting from place to place, living by her wits, always on the outside looking in."

"I won't let that happen," Meg promised. "Not because of you, but because Carly is my sister. And because she's a child."

They'd been over this before, but Ted seemed to need a lot of reassurance. "I guess there is one other favor I could ask," he said.

Meg raised an eyebrow. Waited.

"Will you forgive me, Meg?"

"I stopped hating you a long time ago."

"That isn't the same as forgiving me," Ted replied.

She opened her mouth, closed it again. A glib, "Okay, I forgive you" died on her tongue.

Ted smiled sadly. "While you're at it, forgive your mother, too. We were both wrong, Eve and I, not to tell you the whole truth from the beginning. But she was trying to protect you, Meg. And it says a lot about the other McKettricks, that none of them ever let it slip that I was a thief doing time in a Texas prison while you were growing up. A lot of people would have found that secret too juicy to keep to themselves."

Meg wondered if Jesse, Rance and Keegan had known, and decided they hadn't. Their parents had, though, surely. All three of their fathers had been on the company board with Eve, back in those days. Meg thought of them as uncles—and they'd looked after her like a daughter, taken her under their powerful wings when she summered on the Triple M, and so had her "aunts." Stirred her right into the boisterous mix of loud cousins, remembered her birthdays and bought gifts at Christmas. All the while, they'd been conspiring to keep her in the dark about Ted Ledger, of course, but she couldn't resent them for it. Their intentions, like Eve's, had been good.

"Who are you, really?" Meg asked, remembering Carly's remark about changing last names so many times she was no longer sure what the real one was. And underlying the surface question was another.

Who am I?

Ted smiled, patted her hand. "When I married your mother, I was Ted Sullivan. I was born in Chicago, to Alice and Carl Sullivan. Alice was a homemaker, Carl was a finance manager at a used car dealership."

"No brothers or sisters?"

"I had a sister, Sarah. She died of meningitis when she

was fifteen. I was nineteen at the time. Mom never recovered from Sarah's death—she was the promising child. I was the problem."

"How did you meet Mom?" She hadn't thought she needed, or even wanted, to know such things. But, suddenly, she did.

Ted grinned at the memory, and for just a moment, he looked young again, and well. "After I left home, I took college courses and worked nights as a hotel desk clerk. I moved around the country, and by the time I wound up in San Antonio, I was a manager. McKettrickCo owned the chain I worked for, and one of your uncles decided I was a bright young man with a future. Hired me to work in the home office. Where, of course, I saw Eve every day."

Meg imagined how it must have been, both Ted and Eve still young, and relatively mistake-free. "And you fell in love."

"Yes," Ted said. "The family accepted me, which was decent of them, considering they were rich and I had an old car and a couple of thousand dollars squirreled away in a low-interest savings account. The McKettricks are a lot of things, but they're not snobs."

Having money doesn't make us better than other people, Eve had often said as Meg was growing up. *It just makes us luckier.*

"No," she agreed. "They're not snobs." She tried to smile and failed. "So I would have been Meg Sullivan, not Meg McKettrick—if things hadn't gone the way they did?"

Ted chuckled. "Not in a million years. You know the McKettrick women don't change their names when they marry. According to Eve, the custom goes all the way back to old Angus's only daughter."

"Katie," Meg said. Her mind did a time-warp thing—

for about fifteen seconds, she was nineteen and pregnant, having her last argument with Brad before he got into his old truck and drove away. Late that night, he would board a bus for Nashville.

We'll get married when I get back, Brad had said. *I promise.*

You're not coming back, Meg had replied, in tears.

Yes, I am. You'll see—you'll be Meg O'Ballivan before you know it.

I'll never be Meg O'Ballivan. I'm not taking your name.

Have it your way, Ms. McKettrick. You always do.

"Meg?" Ted's voice brought her back to the kitchen on the Triple M. Her tea had grown cold, sitting on the table-top in its heavy mug.

"You're not the first person who ever made a mistake," she told her father. "I hereby confer upon you my complete forgiveness."

He laughed, but his eyes were glossy with tears.

"You're tired," Meg said. "Get some rest."

"I want to hear your story, Meg. Eve sent me a few pictures, the occasional copy of a report card, when I was on the inside. But there are a lot of gaps."

"Another time," Meg answered. But even as Ted stood to make his way back upstairs, and she disposed of her cold tea and put the mug into the dishwasher, she wondered if there would *be* another time.

Phil was back.

Brad, accompanied to the barn by an adoring Willie, tossed the last flake of hay into the last feeder when he heard the distinctive purr of a limo engine and swore under his breath.

"This is getting old," he told Willie.

Willie whined in agreement and wagged his tail.

Phil was walking toward Brad, the stretch gleaming in the early morning light, when he and Willie stepped outside.

"Good news!" Phil cried, beaming. "I spoke to the Hollywood people, and they're willing to make the movie right here at Stone Creek!"

Brad stopped, facing off with Phil like a gunfighter on a windswept Western street. "No," he said.

Phil, being Phil, was undaunted. "Now, don't be too hasty," he counseled. "It would really give this town a boost. Why, the jobs alone—"

"Phil—"

Just then, Livie's ancient Suburban topped the hill, started down, dust billowing behind. Brad took a certain satisfaction in the sight when the rig screeched to a halt alongside Phil's limo, covering it in fine red dirt.

Livie sprang from the Suburban, smiling. "Good news," she called, unknowingly echoing Phil's opening line. "The Iversons' cattle aren't infected."

Phil nudged Brad in the ribs and said in a stage whisper, "She could be an extra. Bet your sister would like to be in a movie."

"In a what?" Livie asked, frowning. She crouched to examine Willie briefly, and accept a few face licks, before straightening and putting out a hand to Phil Meadowbrook. "Olivia O'Ballivan," she said. "You must be my brother's manager."

"*Former* manager," Brad said.

"But still with his best interests at heart," Phil added, placing splayed fingers over his avaricious little ticker and looking woebegone, long-suffering and misunderstood. "I'm offering him a chance to make a *feature film,* right

here on the ranch. Just *look* at this place! It's perfect! John
Ford would salivate—"

"Who's John Ford?" Livie asked.

"He made some John Wayne movies," Brad explained,
beginning to feel cornered.

Livie's dusty face lit up. She had hay dust in her hair—
probably acquired during an early morning visit to the
Iversons' dairy barn. "Wait till I tell the twins," she burst
out.

"Hold it," Brad said, raising both hands, palms out.
"There isn't going to *be* any movie."

"Why not?" Livie asked, suddenly crestfallen.

"Because I'm retired," Brad reminded her patiently.

Phil huffed out a disgusted sigh.

"I don't see the problem if they made the movie right
here," Livie said.

"At last," Phil interjected. "Another voice of reason,
besides my own."

"Shut up, Phil," Brad said.

"You always talked about making a movie," Livie went
on, watching Brad with a mischievous light dancing in
her eyes. "You even started a production company once."

"Cynthia got it in the divorce," Phil confided, as though
Brad wasn't standing there. "The production company, I
mean. I think that soured him."

"Will you stop acting as if I'm not here?" Brad snapped.

Willie whimpered, worried.

"See?" Phil was quick to say. "You're upsetting the
dog." Another patented Phil Meadowbrook grin flashed.
"Hey! He could be in the movie, too. People eat that animal stuff up. We might even be able to get Disney in on
the project—"

"No," Brad said, exasperated. "No Disney. No dog. No

petite veterinarian with hay in her hair. *I don't want to make a movie.*"

"You could build a library or a youth center or something with the money," Phil said, trailing after Brad as he broke from the group and strode toward the house, fully intending to slam the door on his way in.

"We could use an animal shelter," Livie said, scrambling along at his other side.

"Fine," Brad snapped, slowing down a little because he realized Willie was having trouble keeping up. "I'll have my accountant cut a check."

The limo driver gave the horn a discreet honk, then got out and tapped at his watch.

"Plane to catch," Phil said. "Big Hollywood meeting. I'll fax you the contract."

"Don't bother," Brad warned.

Livie caught at his arm, sounding a little breathless. "What is the *matter* with you?" she whispered. "That movie would be the biggest thing to happen in Stone Creek since that pack of outlaws robbed the bank in 1907!"

Brad stopped. Thrust his nose right up to Livie's. "I. Am. *Retired.*"

Livie set her hands on her skinny hips. She really needed to put some meat on those fragile little bones of hers. "I think you're chicken," she said.

Willie gave a cheery little yip.

"You stay out of this, Stitches," Brad told him.

"Chicken," Livie repeated, as the now-dusty limo made a wide turn and started swallowing up dirt road.

"Not," Brad argued.

"Then what?"

Brad shoved a hand through his hair as the answer to Livie's question settled over him, like the red dust that had showered the limo. He was making some headway with Meg, slowly but surely, but Meg and show business mixed about as well as oil and water. Deep down, she probably believed, as Livie had until this morning, that he'd go back to being that other Brad O'Ballivan, the one whose name was always written in capital letters, if the offer was good enough.

Too, if he agreed to do the movie, Phil would never get off his back. He'd be back, before the cameras stopped rolling, with another offer, another contract, another big idea.

"I used to be a performer," Brad said finally. "Now I'm a rancher. I can't keep going back and forth between the two."

"It's one movie, Brad, not a world concert tour. And you wanted to do a movie for so long. What happened? *Was* it losing the production company to Cynthia, like your manager said?"

"No," Brad said. "This is a Pandora's box, Livie. It's the proverbial can of worms. One thing will lead to another—"

"And you'll leave again? For good, this time?"

He shook his head. "No."

"Then just think about it," Livie reasoned. "Making the movie, I mean. Think about the money it would bring into Stone Creek, and how excited the local people would be."

"And the animal shelter," Brad said, sighing.

"Small as Stone Creek is, there are a lot of strays," Livie said.

"Did you come out here for a reason?"

"Yes, to see my big brother and check up on Willie."

"Well, here I am, and Willie's fine. Go or stay, but I don't want to talk about that damn movie anymore, understood?"

Livie smirked. "Understood," she said sweetly.

At four-thirty that afternoon, the movie contract appeared in Brad's email.

He read it, signed it and emailed it back.

Chapter 11

Carly sat hunched in the front passenger seat of the Blazer, arms folded, glowering as kids converged on Indian Rock Middle School, colorful clothes and backpacks still new, since class had only been in session for a little over a month. It was Monday morning and Ted was scheduled to enter the hospital in Flagstaff for "treatment" the following day. Meg's solemn promise to take Carly to visit him every afternoon, admittedly small comfort, was nonetheless all she had to offer.

"I don't want to go in there," Carly said. "They're going to give me some stupid test and put me with the little kids. I just know it."

Ted had homeschooled Carly, for the most part, and though she was obviously a very bright child, there was no telling what kind of curriculum he'd used, or if the process had involved books at all. Her scores would determine her placement, and she was understandably worried.

"Everything will be all right," Meg said.

"You keep saying that," Carly protested. "Everybody says that. *My dad is going to die.* How is that 'all right'?"

"It isn't. It totally bites."

"You could homeschool me."

Meg shook her head. "I'm not a teacher, Carly."

"Neither is my dad, and he did fine!"

That, Meg thought, *remains to be seen.* "More than anything in the world, your dad wants you to have a good life. And that means getting an education."

Tears brimmed in Carly's eyes. "*My* dad? He's *your* dad, too."

"Okay," Meg said.

"You hate him. You don't care if he dies!"

"I *don't* hate him, and if there was any way to keep him alive, I'd do it."

Carly's right hand went to the door handle; with her left, she gathered up the neon pink backpack Meg had bought for her over the weekend, along with some new clothes. "Well, not hating somebody isn't the same as *loving* them."

With that, she shoved open the car door, unfastened her seat belt and got out to stand on the sidewalk, facing the long brick schoolhouse, her small shoulders squared under more burdens than any child ought to have to carry.

Meg waited, her eyes scalding, until Carly disappeared into the building. Then she drove to Sierra's house, where she found her other sister on the front porch, deadheading the flowers in a large clay pot.

The bright October sunshine gilded Sierra's chestnut hair; she looked like Mother Nature herself in her floral print maternity dress.

Meg parked the Blazer in the driveway and approached, slinging her bag over her shoulder as she walked.

Sierra beamed, delighted, and straightened, one hand resting protectively on her enormous belly, the other shading her eyes. "I just made a fresh pot of coffee," she called. "Come in, and we'll catch up."

Meg smiled. She'd lived her life as an only child; now she had two sisters. She and Sierra had had time to bond, but establishing a relationship with Carly was going to be a major challenge.

"I suppose Mom told you the latest," Meg said, referring to Ted and Carly's arrival.

"Some of it. The gossip lasted about twenty minutes, though—you got beat out by the news that Brad O'Ballivan is making a movie over at Stone Creek. Everybody in the county wants to be an extra."

Meg stopped in the middle of the sidewalk. Brad hadn't called since the barbeque, and she hadn't heard about the movie. That hurt, and though she regained her composure quickly, Sierra was quicker.

"You didn't know?" she asked, holding the front door open and urging Meg through it.

Meg sighed, shook her head.

Sierra patted her shoulder. "Let's have that coffee," she said softly.

For the next hour, she and Meg sat in the sunny kitchen, catching up. Meg told her sister what she knew about Ted's condition, Carly, and *most* of what had happened between her and Brad.

Sierra chuckled at the account of Jesse and Keegan's helicopter rescue the day of the blizzard. Got tears in her eyes when Meg related Willie's story.

Although Sierra was one of the most grounded people Meg knew, her emotions had been mercurial since the beginning of her last trimester.

"So when is this baby going to show up, anyhow?" Meg inquired cheerfully when she was through with the briefing. It was definitely time to change the subject.

"I was due a week ago," Sierra answered. "The nursery is all ready, and so am I. Apparently, the baby isn't."

Meg touched her sister's hand. "Are you scared?"

Sierra shook her head. "I'm past that. Mostly, I feel like a bowling-ball smuggler."

"You know," Meg teased, "if you'd spilled the beans about whether this kid is a boy or a girl, you wouldn't have gotten so many yellow layettes at your baby shower."

Sierra laughed, crying a little at the same time. "The sonogram was inconclusive," she said. "The little dickens drew one leg up and hid the evidence."

Meg sobered, looked away briefly. "Would you hate me if I admitted I'm a little envious? Because the baby's coming, I mean, and because you already have Liam, and Travis loves you so much?"

"You know I couldn't hate you," Sierra answered gently, but there was a worried expression in her blue eyes. Long ago, Meg and Travis had dated briefly, and they were still very good friends. While Sierra surely knew neither of them would deceive her, ever, she might think she'd stolen Travis's affections and broken Meg's heart in the process. "Truth time. Do you still have feelings for Travis?"

"The same kind of feelings I have for Jesse and Keegan and Rance," Meg replied honestly. She drew a deep breath and puffed it out. "Truth time? Here's the whole enchilada. I fell hard for Brad O'Ballivan when I was in high school, and I don't think I'm over it."

"Is that a bad thing?"

Meg remembered the way Brad had looked as they stood in his kitchen, after the steak dinner on the patio. She'd seen sorrow, disappointment and a sense of betrayal in his eyes, and the set of his face and shoulders. "I'm not sure," she said. Then she stood, carried her empty cup and Sierra's to the sink. "I'd better get home. Ted's there alone, and he wasn't feeling well when I left to take Carly to school."

Sierra nodded, remaining in her chair, squirming a little and looking anxious.

"You're okay, right?" Meg asked, alarmed.

"Just a few twinges," Sierra said. "It's probably nothing."

Meg was glad she'd already set the cups down, because she'd have dropped them to the floor if she hadn't. *"Just a few twinges?"*

"Would you mind calling Travis?" Sierra asked. "And Mom?"

"Oh, my God," Meg said, grabbing her bag, scrabbling through it for her cell phone. "You've been sitting there listening to my tales of woe and all the time you've been *in labor?*"

"Not the whole time," Sierra said lamely. "I thought it was indigestion."

Meg speed-dialed Travis. "Come home," she said before he'd finished his hello. "Sierra's having the baby!"

"On my way," he replied, and hung up in her ear.

Next, she called Eve. "It's happening!" she blurted. "The baby—"

"For heaven's sake," Sierra protested good-naturedly, "you make it sound as though I'm giving birth on the kitchen floor."

"Margaret McKettrick," Eve instructed sternly, "calm yourself. We have a plan. Travis will take Sierra to the hospital, and I will pick Liam up after school. I assume you're with Sierra right now?"

"I'm with her," Meg said, wondering if she'd have to deliver her niece or nephew before help arrived. She'd watched calves, puppies and colts coming into the world, but *this* was definitely in another league.

"Did you call Travis?" Eve wanted to know.

"Yes," Meg watched Sierra anxiously as she spoke.

"My water just broke," Sierra said.

"Oh, my God," Meg ranted. "Her water just broke!"

"Margaret," Eve said, "get a grip—and a towel. I'll be there in five minutes."

Travis showed up in four flat. He paused to bend and kiss Sierra soundly on the mouth, then dashed off, returning momentarily with a suitcase, presumably packed with things his wife would need at the hospital.

Meg sat at the table, with her head between her knees, feeling woozy.

"I think she's hyperventilating," Sierra told Travis. "Do we have any paper bags?"

Just then, Eve breezed in through the back door. She tsk-tsked Meg, but naturally, Sierra was her main concern. As her younger daughter stood, with some help from Travis, Eve cupped Sierra's face between her hands and kissed her on the forehead.

"Don't worry about a thing," she ordered. "I'll see to Liam."

Sierra nodded, gave Meg one last worried glance and allowed Travis to steer her out the back door.

"Shouldn't we have called an ambulance or something?" Meg fretted.

"Oh, for heaven's sake," Eve replied. "You don't need an ambulance!"

"Not for *me,* Mother. For Sierra."

Eve soaked a cloth at the sink, wrung it out and slapped it onto the back of Meg's neck. "Breathe," she said.

Brad watched from a front window as Livie parked the Suburban, got out and headed for the barn. "Here we go," he told Willie, resigned. "She's on the hunt for Ransom again, and that means I'll have to go. You're going to have to stay behind, buddy."

Willie, curled up on a hooked rug in front of the living room fireplace, simply sighed and closed his eyes for a snooze, clearly unconcerned. Some of the advance people from the movie studio had already arrived in an RV, to scout the location, and the kid with the backward baseball cap was a dog-lover. If necessary, Brad would press him into service.

Brad had been up half the night going over the script, faxed by Phil, penning in the occasional dialogue change. For all his reluctance to get involved in the project, he liked the story, tentatively titled *The Showdown,* and he was looking forward to trying his hand at a little acting.

The truth was, though, he'd had to read and reread because his mind kept straying to Meg. He'd been so sure, right along, that they could make things work. But seeing Carly—a younger version of Meg, and most likely of the daughter they might have had—brought up a lot of conflicting feelings, ones he wasn't sure how to deal with.

It wasn't rational; he knew that. Meg's explanation was believable, even if it stung, and her reasons for keeping the secret from him made sense. Still, a part of him was deeply resentful, even enraged.

Livie was saddling Cinnamon when he reached the barn.

"Where do you think you're going?" he asked.

She gave him a look. "Three guesses, genius," she said pleasantly. "And the first two don't count."

"I guess you didn't hear about the blizzard that blew up in about five minutes when Meg and I were up in the hills trying to find that damn horse?"

"I heard about it," Livie said. She put her shoulder to Cinnamon's belly and pulled hard to tighten the cinch. "I just want to check on him, that's all. Just take a look."

Brad leaned one shoulder against the door frame, arms folded, letting his body language say he wasn't above blocking the door.

Livie's expression said *she* wasn't above riding right over him.

"I'll see if I can talk one of Meg's cousins into taking you up in the helicopter," Brad said.

"Oh, right," Livie mocked. "And scare Ransom to death with the noise."

"Livie, will you listen to reason? That horse has survived all this time without a lick of help from you. What's different now?"

"Will you stop calling him 'that horse'? His name is Ransom and he's a *legend,* thank you very much."

"Being a legend," Brad drawled, "isn't all it's cracked up to be."

Livie led Cinnamon toward him; he moved into the center of the doorway and stood his ground.

"What's different, Livie?" he repeated.

She sighed, seemed even smaller and more fragile than usual. "You wouldn't believe me if I told you."

"Give it a shot," Brad said.

"Dreams," Livie said. "I have these dreams—"

"Dreams."

"I knew you wouldn't—"

"Hold it," Brad interrupted. "I'm listening."

"Just get out of my way, please."

Brad shook his head, shifted so his feet were a little farther apart, kept his arms folded. "Not gonna happen."

"He talks to me," Livie said, her voice small and exasperated and full of the O'Ballivan grit that was so much a part of her nature.

"A horse talks to you." He tried not to sound skeptical, but didn't quite succeed.

"In dreams," Livie said, flushing.

"Like Mr. Ed, in that old TV show?"

Livie's temper flared in her eyes, then her cheekbones. "No," she said. "Not 'like Mr. Ed in that old TV show'!"

"How, then?"

"I just hear him, that's all. He doesn't move his lips, for pity's sake!"

"Okay."

"You believe me?"

"I believe that you believe it, Liv. You have a lot of deep feelings where animals are concerned—sometimes I wish you liked people half as much—and you've been worried about that—about Ransom for a long time. It makes sense that he'd show up in your dreams."

Livie let Cinnamon's reins dangle and set her hands on her hips. "What did you do, take an online shrink course or something? Jungian analysis in ten easy lessons? Next, you'll be saying Ransom is a symbol with unconscious sexual connotations!"

Brad suppressed an urge to roll his eyes. "Is that really so far beyond the realm of possibility?"

"Yes!"

"Why?"

"Because Ransom isn't the only animal I dream about,

that's why. And it isn't a recent phenomenon—it's been happening since I was little! Remember Simon, that old sheepdog we had when we were kids? He told me he was leaving—and three days later, he was hit by a car. I could go on, because there are a whole lot of other stories, but frankly, I don't have time. Ransom is in trouble."

Surprise was too mild a word for what Brad felt. Livie had always been crazy about animals, but she was stone practical, with a scientific turn of mind, not given to spooky stuff. And she'd never once confided that she got dream messages from four-legged friends.

"Why didn't you tell me? Did Big John know?"

"You'd have packed me off to a therapist. Big John had enough to worry about without Dr. Doolittle for a grand-daughter. Now—will you please move?"

"No," Brad said. "I won't move, please or otherwise. Not until you tell me what's so urgent about tracking down a wild stallion on top of a damn mountain!"

Tears glistened in Livie's eyes, and Brad felt a stab to his conscience.

Livie's struggle was visible, and painful to see, but she finally answered. "He's in pain. There's something wrong with his right foreleg."

"And you plan to do what when—and if—you find him? Shoot him with a tranquilizer gun? Livie, this is Stone Creek, Arizona, not the *Wild Kingdom*. And dream or no dream, that horse—" He raised both hands to forestall the impatience brewing in her face. "*Ransom* is not a charac-ter in a Disney movie. He's not going to let you walk up to him, examine his foreleg and give him a nice little shot. If you *did* get close, he'd probably stomp you down to bone fragments and a bloodstain!"

"He wouldn't," Livie said. "He knows I want to help him."

"Livie, suppose—just *suppose,* damn it—that you're wrong."

"I'm not wrong."

"Of *course* you're not wrong. You're a freaking O'Ballivan!" He paused, shoved a hand through his hair. Tried another tack. "There aren't that many hours of daylight left. You're not going up that mountain alone, little sister—not if I have to hog-tie you to keep you here."

"Then you can come with me."

"Oh, that's noble of you. I'd *love* to risk freezing to death in a freaking blizzard. Hell, I've got nothing *better* to do, besides nurse a wounded dog that *you* brought to me, and make a freaking *movie*—also your idea—"

Livie's mouth twitched at one corner. She fought the grin, but it came anyway. "Do you realize you've used the word 'freaking' three times in the last minute and a half? Have you considered switching to decaf?"

"Very funny," Brad said, but he couldn't help grinning back. He rested his hands on Livie's shoulders, squeezed lightly. "You're my little sister. I love you. If you insist on tracking a wild stallion all over the mountain, at least wait until morning. We'll saddle up at dawn."

Livie looked serious again. "You promise?"

"I promise."

"Okay," she said.

"Okay? That's it? You're giving up without a fight?"

"Don't be so suspicious. I said I'd wait until dawn, and I will."

Brad raised one eyebrow. "Shake on it?"

Livie put out a hand. "Shake," she said.

He had to be satisfied with that. In the O'Ballivan family, shaking hands on an agreement was like taking a blood oath—Big John had drilled that into them from childhood. "Since we're leaving so early, maybe you'd better spend the night here."

"I can do that," Livie said, turning to lead Cinnamon back to his stall. "But since I'm not going tonight, I might as well make my normal rounds first. I conned Dr. Summers into covering for me, but he wasn't too happy about it." Her eyes took on a mischievous twinkle as he approached, took over the process of unsaddling the horse. "How are things going with Meg?"

Brad didn't look at her. "Not all that well, actually."

"What's wrong?"

"I'm not sure I could put it into words."

Livie nudged him before pushing open the stall door to leave. "It's a long ride up the mountain," she said. "Plenty of time to talk."

"I might take you up on that," he answered.

"I'll just look in on Willie, then go make my rounds. See you later, alligator."

Brad's eyes burned. Like the handshake, "See you later, alligator" was a holdover from Big John. "In a while, crocodile," he answered on cue.

By the time he got back to the house, Livie had already examined Willie, climbed into the Suburban and driven off. A note stuck to the refrigerator door read, *Are you making supper, Mr. Movie Star? Or should I pick up a pizza?*

Brad chuckled and took a package of chicken out of the freezer.

The phone rang.

"Yea or nay on the double Hawaiian deluxe with extra ham, cheese and pineapple?" Livie asked.

"Forget the pizza," Brad replied. "I'm not eating anything you've handled. You stick your arm up cows' butts for a living, after all."

She laughed, said goodbye and hung up.

He started to replace the receiver, but Meg was still on his mind, so he punched in the digits. Funny, he reflected, how he remembered her number at the Triple M after all this time. He couldn't have recited the one he'd had in Nashville to save his life.

Voice mail picked up. "You've reached 555-7682," Meg said cheerily. "Leave a message and, if it's appropriate, I'll call you back."

Brad moved to disconnect, then put the receiver back to his ear. "It's Brad. I was just—a—calling to see how things are going with your dad and Carly—"

She came on the line, sounding a little breathless. "Brad?"

His heart did a slow backflip. "Yeah, it's me," he said.

"I hear you're making a movie in Stone Creek."

He closed his eyes. He'd blown it again—Meg should have heard the news from him, not via the local grapevine. "I thought maybe Carly could be an extra," he said.

"She'd love that, I'm sure," Meg said with crisp formality.

"Meg? The movie thing—"

"It's all right, Brad. I'm happy for you. Really."

"You sound thrilled."

"You could have mentioned it. Not exactly an everyday occurrence, especially in the wilds of northern Arizona."

"I wanted to talk about it in person, Meg."

"You know where I live, and clearly, you know my telephone number."

"I know where your G-spot is, too," he said.

He heard her draw in a breath. "Dirty pool, O'Ballivan."

"All's fair in lust and war, McKettrick."

"Is that what this is? Lust?"

"You tell me."

"I'm not the one who took a step back," she reminded him.

He knew what she was talking about, of course. He'd been pretty cool to her the night of the steak dinner. "Livie and I are riding up the mountain again tomorrow, to look for Ransom. Do you still want to go?"

She sighed. He hoped she was thawing out, but with Meg, it could go either way. Ice or fire. "I wish I could. Ted's being admitted to the hospital tomorrow morning, and I promised to take Carly to visit him as soon as school lets out for the day."

"She's having a pretty rough time," he said. "If there's anything I can do to help—"

"The T-shirt was a hit. So is having your autograph on all those CDs. Your kindness means a lot to her, Brad." A pause. "On a happier note, Sierra went into labor today. I'm expecting to be an aunt again at any moment."

"That is good news," Brad said, but he put one hand to his middle, as though he'd taken a fist to the stomach.

"Yeah," Meg said, and he knew by the catch in her voice that, somehow, she'd picked up on his reaction. "Well, anyway, congratulations on the movie, and thanks for getting in touch. Oh, and be careful on the mountain tomorrow."

The invisible fist moved from his solar plexus to his throat, squeezing hard. *Congratulations on the movie... thanks for getting in touch...so long, see you around.*

She'd hung up before he could get out a goodbye.

He thumbed the off button, leaned forward and rested his head against a cupboard door, eyes closed tight.

Willie nuzzled him in the thigh and gave a soft whine.

Two hours later, Livie returned, freshly showered and wearing a dress.

"Got a hot date?" Brad asked, trying to remember the last time he'd seen his sister in anything besides boots, ragbag jeans and one of Big John's old shirts.

She ignored the question and, with a flourish, pulled a bottle of wine from her tote bag and set it on the counter, sniffing the air appreciatively. "Fried chicken? Is there no end to your talents?"

"Not as far as I know," he joked.

Livie elbowed him. "We should have invited the twins to join us. It would be like old times, all of us sitting down together in this kitchen."

Not quite like old times, Brad thought, missing Big John with a sudden, piercing ache, as fresh as if he'd just gotten the call announcing his grandfather's death.

Livie was way too good at reading him. She snatched a cucumber slice from the salad and nibbled at it, leaning back against the counter and studying his face. "You really miss Big John, don't you?"

He nodded, not quite trusting himself to speak.

"He was so proud of you, Brad."

He swallowed. Averted his eyes. "Keep your fingers out of the salad," he said.

Livie laid a hand on his arm. "I know you think you disappointed him at practically every turn. That you should have been here, instead of in Nashville or on the road or wherever, and maybe all of that's true, but he *was* proud. And he was grateful, too, for everything you did."

"He'd raise hell about this movie," Brad said hoarsely.

"He'd brag to everybody who would let him bend their ear," Livie replied.

"Do you know what I'd give to be able to talk to Big John just one more time? To say I'm sorry I didn't visit— call more often?"

"A lot, I guess. But you can still talk to him. He'll hear you." She stood on tiptoe, kissed Brad lightly on the cheek. "Tell me you've already fed the horses, because I'd hate to have to swap out this getup for barn gear."

Brad laughed. "I've fed them," he said. He turned, smiled down into her upturned face. "I never would have taken you for a mystic, Doc. Do you talk to Big John? Or just wild stallions and sheepdogs?"

"All the time," Livie said, plundering a drawer for a corkscrew, which Brad immediately took from her. "I don't think he's really gone. Most of the time, it feels as if he's in the next room, not some far-off heaven—sometimes, I even catch the scent of his pipe tobacco."

Since Brad had taken over opening the cabernet, Livie got out a couple of wineglasses. Willie poked his nose at her knee, angling for attention.

"Yes," she told the dog. "I know you're there."

"Does he talk to you, too?" Brad asked, only half kidding.

"Sure," Livie replied airily. "He likes you. You're a little awkward, but Willie thinks you have real potential as a dog owner."

Grinning, Brad sloshed wine into Livie's glass, then his. Raised it in a toast. "To Big John," he said, "and King's Ransom, and Stone Creek's own Dr. Doolittle. And Willie."

"To the movie and Meg McKettrick," Livie added, and clinked her glass against Brad's.

Brad hesitated before he drank. "To Meg," he said finally.

During supper, they chatted about Livie's preliminary plans for the promised animal shelter—it would be state of the art, offering free spaying and neutering, inoculations, etc.

They cleaned up the kitchen together afterward, as they had done when they were kids, then took Willie out for a brief walk. He was still sore, though the pain medication helped, and couldn't make it far, but he managed.

Since he hadn't slept much the night before, Brad crashed in the downstairs guest room early, leaving Livie sitting at the kitchen table, absorbed in his copy of the script.

Hours later, sleep-grogged and blinking in the harsh light of the bedside lamp, he awakened to find Livie standing over him, fully dressed—this time in the customary jeans—and practically vibrating with anxiety.

He yawned and dragged himself upright against the headboard, "Liv, it's the middle of the night."

"Ransom's cornered," Livie blurted. "We have to get to him, and quick. Call a McKettrick and borrow that helicopter!"

Chapter 12

The whole thing was crazy.

It was two in the morning.

He'd have to swallow his pride to roust Jesse or Keegan at that hour, and ask for a monumental favor in the bargain. *My sister had this dream, involving a talking horse,* he imagined himself saying.

But the look of desperation in Livie's eyes made the difference.

"Here's a number," she said, shoving a bit of paper at him and handing him the cordless phone from the kitchen.

"Where did you get this?" Brad asked as Willie, curled at the foot of his bed, stood, made a tight circle and laid himself down again.

Livie answered from the doorway, plainly exasperated. "Jesse and I used to go out once in a while," she said. "Make the call and get dressed!"

She didn't give him a chance to suggest that *she* make

the request, since she and Jesse had evidently been an item at one time, but hurried out.

As soon as the door shut behind her, Brad sat up, reached for his jeans, which had been in a heap on the floor, and got into them while he thumbed Jesse's number.

McKettrick answered on the second ring, growling, "This had better be good."

Brad closed his eyes for a moment, used one hand to button his fly while keeping the receiver propped between his ear and his right shoulder. "It's Brad O'Ballivan," he said. "Sorry to wake you up, but there's an emergency and—" He paused only briefly, for the last words had to be forced out. "I need some help."

Barely forty-five minutes later, the McKettrickCo helicopter landed, running lights glaring like something out of *Close Encounters of the Third Kind,* in the field directly behind the ranch house. Jesse was at the controls.

"Hey, Liv," he said with a Jesse-grin once she'd scrambled into the small rear seat and put on a pair of earphones.

"Hey," Livie replied. There was no stiffness about either of them—the dating scenario must have ended affably, or not been serious in the first place.

Brad sat up front, next to Jesse, with a rifle between his knees, dreading the moment when he'd have to explain what this moonlight odyssey was all about.

But Jesse didn't ask for an explanation. All he said was, "Where to?"

"Horse Thief Canyon," Livie answered. "On the eastern rim."

Jesse nodded, cast one sidelong glance at Brad's rifle, and lifted the copter off the ground.

I might have to get one of these things, Brad thought, still sleep-jangled.

Within fifteen minutes, they were high over the mountain, spot-lighting the canyon, so named for being the place where Sam O'Ballivan and some of his Arizona Rangers had once cornered a band of horse rustlers.

"There he is!" Livie shouted, fairly blowing out Brad's eardrums. He leaned for a look and what he saw made his heart swoop to his boot heels.

Ransom gleamed in the glare of the searchlight, rearing and pawing the ground with his powerful forelegs. Behind him, against a rock face, were his mares—Brad counted three, but it was hard to tell how many others might be in the shadows—and before him, a pack of nearly a dozen wolves was closing in. They were hungry, focused on their cornered prey, and they paid no attention whatsoever to the copter roaring above their heads.

"Set this thing down!" Livie ordered. "Fast!"

Jesse worked the controls with one hand and hauled a second rifle out from under the pilot's seat with the other. Clearly, he'd spotted the wolves, too.

He landed the copter on what looked like a ledge, too narrow for Brad's comfort. The wait for the blades to slow seemed endless.

"Showtime," Jesse said, shoving open his door, rifle in hand. "Keep your heads down. The updraft will be pretty strong."

Brad nodded and pushed open the door, willing Livie to stay behind, knowing she wouldn't.

Just fifty yards away, Ransom and the wolf pack were still facing off. The mares screamed and snorted, frantic with fear, their rolling eyes shining white in the darkness.

With only the moon for light now, the scene was eerie.

The small hairs rose on the back of Brad's neck and one of the wolves turned and studied him with implacable amber eyes. His gray-white ruff shimmered in the silvery glow of cold, distant stars.

Some kind of weird connection sparked between man and beast. Brad was only vaguely aware of Jesse coming up behind him, of Livie already fiddling with her veterinary kit.

I'm a predator, the wolf told Brad. *This is what I do.*

Brad cocked the rifle. *I'm a predator, too,* he replied silently. *And you can't have these horses.*

The wolf pondered a moment, took a single stealthy step toward Ransom, the stallion bloody-legged and exhausted from holding off the pack.

Brad took aim. *Don't do it, Brother Wolf. This isn't a bluff.*

Tilting his massive head back, the wolf gave a chilling howl.

Ransom was stumbling a little by then, looking as though he'd go down. That, of course, was exactly what the pack was waiting for. Once the great steed was on the ground, they'd have him—and the mares. And the resultant carnage didn't bear considering.

Jesse stood at Brad's side, his own rifle ready. "I wouldn't have believed he was real," McKettrick said in a whisper, though whether he was referring to Ransom or the old wolf was anybody's guess, "if I hadn't seen him with my own eyes."

The wolf yowled again, the sound raising something primitive in Brad.

And then it was over.

The leader turned, moving back through the pack at a trot, and they rounded, one by one, with a lethal and hesitant grace, to follow.

Brad let out his breath, lowered his rifle. Jesse relaxed, too.

Livie, carrying her kit in one hand, headed straight for Ransom.

Brad moved to stop her, but Jesse put out his arm.

"Easy," he said. "This is no time to spook that horse."

It would be the supreme irony, Brad reflected grimly, if they had to shoot Ransom in the end, after going to all this trouble to save his hide. If the stallion made one aggressive move toward Livie, though, he'd do it.

"It's me, Olivia," Livie told the legendary wild stallion in a companionable tone. "I came as soon as I could."

Brad brought his rifle up quickly when Ransom butted Livie with his massive head, but Jesse forced the barrel down, murmuring, "Wait."

Ransom stood, lathered and shining with sweat and fresh blood, and allowed Livie to stroke his long neck, ruffle his mane. When she squatted to run her hands over his forelegs, he allowed that, too.

"I'll be damned," Jesse muttered.

The vision was surreal—Brad wasn't entirely convinced he wasn't dreaming at home in his bed.

"You're going to have to come in," Livie told the horse, "at least long enough for that leg to heal."

Unbelievably, Ransom nickered and tossed his head as though he were nodding in agreement.

"How the hell does she expect to drive a band of wild horses all the way down the mountain to Stone Creek Ranch?" Brad asked. He wasn't looking for an answer from Jesse—he was just thinking out loud.

Jesse whacked him on the shoulder. "You've been in the big city too long, O'Ballivan," he said. "You stay here, in case the wolves come back, and I'll go gather a roundup

crew. It'll be a few hours before we get here, though—
keep your eye out for the pack and pray for good weather.
About the last thing we need is another of those blizzards."

By that time, Livie had produced a syringe from her
kit, and was preparing to poke it through the hide on Ransom's neck.

Brad moved a step closer.

"Stay back," Livie said. "Ransom's calm enough, but
these mares are stressed out. I'd rather not find myself at
the center of an impromptu rodeo, if it's all the same to
you."

Jesse chuckled, handed Brad his rifle, and turned to
sprint back to the copter. Moments later, it was lifting off
again, veering southwest.

Brad stood unmoving for a long time, still not sure he
wasn't caught up in the aftermath of a nightmare, then
leaned his and Jesse's rifles against the trunk of a nearby
tree.

Ransom stood with his head down, dazed by the drug
Livie had administered minutes before. The mares, still
fitful but evidently aware that the worst danger had passed,
fanned out to graze on the dry grass.

In the distance, the old wolf howled with piteous fury.

Pinkish-gold light rimmed the eastern hills as Meg returned to the house, after feeding the horses, and the phone
was ringing.

She dived for it, in case it was Travis calling to say Sierra had had the baby.

In case it was Brad.

It was Eve.

"You're an aunt again," Meg's mother announced, with

brisk pride. "Sierra had a healthy baby boy at four-thirty this morning. I think they're going to call him Brody, for Travis's brother."

Joy fluttered inside Meg's heart, like something trying delicate wings, and tears smarted in her eyes. "She's okay? Sierra, I mean?"

"She's fine, by all reports," Eve answered. "Liam and I are heading for Flagstaff right after breakfast. He's beside himself."

After washing her hands at the kitchen sink, Meg poured herself a cup of hot coffee. By habit, she'd set it brewing before going out to the barn. Upstairs, she heard Ted's slow step as he moved along the corridor.

"Ted's checking in today," she said, keeping her voice down. "I'll stop by to see Sierra and the baby after I get him settled." She drew a breath, let it out softly. "Mother, Carly is not handling this well."

Eve sighed sadly. "I'm sure she isn't, the poor child," she said. "Why don't you keep her out of school for the day and let her come along with you and Ted?"

"I suggested that," Meg replied, as her father appeared on the back stairs, dressed, with a shaving kit in one hand.

Their gazes met.

"And?" Eve prompted.

"And Ted said he wants her to attend class and visit later, when school's out for the day."

Ted nodded. "Is that Eve?"

"Yes," Meg said.

He gestured for the phone, and Meg handed it to him.

"This is Ted," he told Meg's mother. While he explained that Carly needed to settle into as normal a life as possible, as soon as possible, Carly herself appeared on the stairs, looking glum and stubborn.

She wore jeans and the souvenir T-shirt Brad had given her, in spite of the fact that it reached almost to her knees. The expression in her eyes dared Meg to object to the outfit—or anything else in the known universe.

"Hungry?" Meg asked.

"No," Carly said.

"Too bad. In this house, we eat breakfast."

"I might puke."

"You might."

Ted cupped a hand over one end of the phone. "Carly," he said sternly, "you *will* eat."

Scowling, Carly swung a leg over the bench next to the table and plunked down, angrily bereft. Meg poured orange juice, carried the glass to the table, set it down in front of her sister.

It was a wonder the stuff didn't come to an instant boil, considering the heat of Carly's glare as she stared at it.

"This bites," she said.

"Okay, I'll pass the word," Ted told Eve. "See you later."

He hung up. "Eve's hoping you can have lunch with her and Liam after you visit Sierra and the baby."

Meg nodded, distracted.

"It bites," Carly repeated, watching Ted with thunderous eyes. "You're going to the *hospital,* and I have to go to that stupid school, where they'll probably put me in *kindergarten* or something. I'm *supposed* to be in seventh grade."

Meg had no idea how Carly had fared on the tests she'd taken the day before, but it seemed safe to say things probably wouldn't go as badly as all that.

She got a frown for her trouble.

"This time next week," Ted told his younger daughter,

"you'll probably be a sophomore at Harvard. Drink your orange juice."

Carly took a reluctant sip and eyeballed Meg's jeans, which were covered with bits of hay. "Don't you have like a *job* or something?"

"Yeah," Meg said, putting a pan on the stove to boil water for oatmeal. "I'm a ranch hand. The work's hard, the pay is lousy, there's no retirement plan and you have to shovel a lot of manure, but I love it."

Breakfast was a dismal affair, one Carly did her best to drag out, but, finally, the time came to leave.

Meg remained in the house for a few extra minutes while Ted and Carly got into the Blazer, giving them time to talk privately.

When she joined them, Carly was in tears, and Ted looked weary to the center of his soul.

Meg gave him a sympathetic look, pushed the button to roll up the garage door and backed out.

When they reached the school, Ted climbed laboriously out of the Blazer and stood on the sidewalk with Carly. They spoke earnestly, though Meg couldn't hear what they said, and Carly dashed at her cheeks with the back of one hand before turning to march staunchly through the colorful herd of kids toward the entrance.

Ted had trouble getting back into the car, but when Meg moved to get out and come around to help him, he shook his head.

"Don't," he said.

She nodded, thick-throated and close to tears herself.

When they reached the hospital in Flagstaff, Eve was waiting in the admittance office.

"I'll take over from here," she told Meg, standing up extra-straight as she watched a nurse ease Ted into a wait-

ing wheelchair. "You go upstairs and see your sister and
your new nephew. Room 502."

Meg hesitated, nodded. Then, surprising even herself,
she bent and kissed Ted on top of the head before walking
purposefully toward the nearest elevator.

Sierra glowed from the inside, as though she'd distilled
sunlight to a golden potion and swallowed it down. The
room was bedecked in flowers, splashes of watercolor
pink, blue and yellow shimmered all around.

"Aunt Meg!" Liam cried delightedly, zooming out of the
teary blur. "I've got a brand-new brother and his name is
Brody Travis Reid!"

With a choked laugh, Meg hugged the little boy, almost displacing his Harry Potter glasses in the process.
"Where *is* this Brody yahoo, anyhow?" she teased. "His
legend looms large in this here town, but so far, I haven't
seen hide nor hair of him."

"Silly," Liam said. "He's in the *nursery,* with all the
other babies!"

Meg ruffled his hair. Went to give Sierra a kiss on the
forehead.

"Congratulations, little sister," she said.

"He's so beautiful," Sierra whispered.

"Boys are supposed to be *handsome,* not beautiful,"
Liam protested, dragging a chair up on the other side of
Sierra's bed and standing in the seat so he could be eye to
eye with his mother. "Was I handsome?"

Sierra smiled, squeezed his small hand. "You're *still*
handsome," she said gently. "And Dad and I are counting
on you to be a really good big brother to Brody."

Liam turned to Meg, beaming. "Travis is going to adopt

me. I'll be Liam McKettrick Reid, and Mom's changing her name, too."

Meg lifted her eyebrows slightly.

"Somebody had to break the tradition," Sierra said. "I've already told Eve."

Sierra would be the first McKettrick woman to take her husband's last name in generations.

"Mom's okay with that?" Meg asked.

Sierra grinned. "Timing is everything," she said. "If you want to break disturbing news to her, be sure to give birth first."

Meg chuckled. "You are a brave woman," she told Sierra. Then, turning to her nephew, she held out a hand. "How about showing me that brother of yours, Liam McKettrick Reid?"

Jesse returned at midmorning, as promised, with a dozen mounted cowboys. To Brad, the bunch looked as though they'd ridden straight out of an old black-and-white movie, their clothes, gear and horses only taking on color as they drew within hailing distance.

Brad was bone-tired, and Livie, her doctoring completed for the time being, had fallen asleep under a tree, bundled in his coat as well as her own. He'd built a fire an hour or so before dawn, but he craved coffee something fierce, and he was chilled to his core.

Before bedding down in the wee small hours, Livie had cheerfully informed her brother that while he ought to keep watch for the wolf pack, he didn't need to worry that Ransom and the mares would run off. They knew, she assured him, that they were among friends.

He'd kept watch through what remained of the night,

pondering the undeniable proof that his sister *had* received an SOS from Ransom.

Now, with riders approaching, Livie wakened and got up off the ground, smiling and dusting dried pine needles and dirt off her jeans.

Jesse, Keegan and Rance were in the lead, ropes coiled around the horns of their saddles, rifles in their scabbards.

Rance nodded to Brad, dismounted and walked over to Ransom. He checked the animal's legs as deftly as Livie had.

"Think he can make it down the mountain to the ranch?" Rance asked.

Livie nodded. "If we take it slowly," she said. Her smile took in the three McKettricks and the men they'd rallied to help. "Thanks, everybody."

Most of the cowboys stared at Ransom as though they expected him to sprout wings, like Pegasus, and take to the blue-gold morning sky. One rode forward, leading mounts for Livie and Brad.

Livie took off Brad's coat and handed it to him, then swung up into the saddle with an ease he couldn't hope to emulate. He kicked dirt over the last embers of the camp-fire while Rance handed up Livie's veterinary kit.

The ride down the mountain would be long and hard, though thank God the weather had held. The sky was blue as Meg's eyes.

Brad took a deep breath, jabbed a foot into the stirrup and hauled himself onto the back of a pinto gelding. He was still pretty sore from the *last* trip up and down this mountain.

The cowboys went to work, starting Ransom and his mares along the trail with low whistles to urge them along.

Livie rode up beside Brad and grinned. "You look like hell," she said.

"Gosh, thanks," Brad grimaced, shifting in the saddle in a vain attempt to get comfortable.

She chuckled. "Think of it as getting into character for the movie."

Seeing Brody for the first time was the high point of Meg's day, but from there, it was all downhill.

Ted's tests were invasive, and he was drugged.

Liam was hyper with excitement, and didn't sit still for a second during lunch, despite Eve's grandmotherly reprimands. The food in the cafeteria tasted like wood shavings, and she got a call from the police in Indian Rock on her way home.

Carly had ditched school, and Wyatt Terp, the town marshal, had picked her up along Highway 17. She'd been trying to hitchhike to Flagstaff.

Meg sped to the police station, screeched to a stop in the parking lot and stormed inside.

Carly sat forlornly in a chair near Wyatt's desk, looking even younger than twelve.

"I just wanted to see my dad," she said in a small voice, taking all the bluster out of Meg's sails.

Meg pulled up a chair alongside Carly's and sat down, taking a few deep breaths to center herself. Wyatt smiled and busied himself in another part of the station house.

"You could have been kidnapped, or hit by a car, or a thousand other things," Meg said carefully.

"Dad and I thumbed it lots of times," Carly said defensively, "when our car broke down."

Meg closed her eyes for a moment. Waited for a sensible reply to occur to her. When that didn't happen, she opened them again.

"Will you take me to see him now?" Carly asked.

Meg sighed. "Depends," she said. "Are you under arrest, or just being held for questioning?"

Carly relaxed a little. "I'm not busted," she answered seriously. "But Marshal Terp says if he catches me hitchhiking again, I'll probably do hard time."

"You pull any more stupid tricks like this one, kiddo," Meg said, "and *I'll* give you all the 'hard time' you can handle."

Wyatt approached, doing his best to look like a stern lawman, but the effect was more Andy-of-Mayberry. "You can go, young lady," he told Carly, "but I'd better not see you in this office again unless you're selling Girl Scout cookies or 4-H raffle tickets or something. Got it?"

"Got it," Carly said meekly, ducking her head slightly.

Meg stood, motioned for her sister to head for the door.

Carly didn't move until the lawman raised an eyebrow at her.

"Is it the badge that makes her mind?" she whispered to Wyatt, once Carly was out of earshot. "And if so, do you happen to have a spare?"

He needed to see Meg.

It was seven-thirty that night before Ransom and his band were corralled at Stone Creek Ranch, and the McKettricks and their helpers had unsaddled all their horses, loaded them into trailers and driven off. Livie had greeted Willie, taken a hot shower and, bundled in one of Big John's ugly Indian-blanket bathrobes, gobbled down a bologna sandwich before climbing the stairs to her old room to sleep.

Brad was tired.

He was cold and he was hungry and he was saddle sore.

The only sensible thing to do was shower, eat and sleep like a dead man.

But he still needed to see Meg.

He settled for the shower and clean clothes.

Calling first would have been the polite thing to do, but he was past that. So he scrawled a note to Livie—*Feed the dog and the horses if I'm not back by morning*—and left.

The truck knew its way to the Triple M, which was a good thing, since he was in a daze.

Lights glowed warm and golden from Meg's windows, and his heart lifted at the sight, at the prospect of seeing her. The McKettricks, he recalled, tended to gather in kitchens. He parked the truck in the drive and walked around to the back of the house, knocked at the door.

Carly answered. She looked wan, as worn-out and used-up as Brad felt, but her face lit up when she saw him.

"I get to stay in seventh grade," she said. "According to my test scores, I'm gifted."

Brad rustled up a grin and resisted the urge to look past her, searching for Meg. "I could have told you that," he said as she stepped back to let him in.

"Meg's upstairs," Carly told him. "She has a sick headache and I'm supposed to leave her alone unless I'm bleeding or there's a national emergency."

Brad hid his disappointment. "Oh," he said, because nothing better came to him.

"I heard you were making a movie," Carly said. Clearly she was lonesome, needed somebody to talk to.

Brad could certainly identify. "Yeah," he answered, and this time the grin was a little easier to find.

"Can I be in it? I wouldn't have to have lines or anything. Just a costume."

"I'll see what I can do," Brad said. "My people will call your people."

Carly laughed, and the sound was good to hear.

He was about to excuse himself and leave when Meg appeared on the stairs wearing a cotton nightgown, with her hair all rumpled and shadows under her eyes.

"Rough day?" he asked, a feeling of bruised tenderness stealing up from his middle to his throat, like thick smoke from a smudge fire.

She tried to smile, pausing a moment on the stairs.

"Time for me to get lost," Carly said. "Can I use your computer, Meg?"

Meg nodded.

Carly left the room and Brad stood still, watching Meg.

"I guess I should have called first," he said.

"Sit down," Meg told him. "I'll make some coffee."

"I'll make the coffee," Brad replied. "*You* sit down."

For once, she didn't give him any back talk. She just padded over to the table and plunked into the big chair at the head of it.

"Did you find Ransom?" she asked, while Brad opened cupboard doors, scouting for a can of coffee.

"Yes," he said, pleased that she'd remembered, given everything else that was going on in her life. "He and the mares have the run of my best pasture." He told Meg the rest of the story, or most of it, leaving out the part about Livie's dreams, not because he was afraid of what she might think of his sister's strange talent, but because the tale was Livie's to tell or keep to herself.

Meg grinned as she listened, shaking her head. "Rance and Keegan and Jesse must have been in their element, driving wild horses down the mountain like they were back in the old West."

"Maybe," Brad agreed, leaning back against the counter as he waited for the coffee to brew. "As for me—if I never have to do that again, it'll be too soon."

Meg laughed, but her eyes misted over in the next moment. She'd looked away too late to keep him from seeing. "Sierra—my other sister—had a baby this morning. A boy. His name is Brody."

Brad ached inside. It had been hard for Meg to share that news, and it shouldn't have been. Given the way he'd shut her out after meeting Carly, he couldn't blame her for being wary.

He went to her, crouched beside her chair, took one of her hands in both of his. "I'm sorry about the other night, Meg. I was just—I don't know—a little rattled by Carly's age, and her resemblance to you."

"It's okay," Meg said, but a tear slipped down her cheek.

Brad brushed it away with the side of one thumb. "It isn't okay. I acted like a jerk."

She sniffled. Nodded. "A *major* jerk."

He chuckled, blinked a couple of times because his eyes burned. Rose to his full height again. "I was hoping to spend the night," he said. "Until I remembered Carly's living here now."

Meg bit her lip. "I have guest rooms," she told him.

She didn't want him to leave, then.

Brad's spirits rose a notch.

"But what about Willie, and your horses?"

"Livie's at the house," he said, moving away from her, getting mugs down out of a cupboard. If he'd stayed close, he'd have hauled her to her feet and laid a big sloppy one on her, complete with tongue, and with a twelve-year-old in practically the next room, that was out. "She'll take care of the livestock."

After that, they sat quietly at the venerable old McKettrick table and talked about ordinary things. It made him surprisingly happy, just being there with Meg, doing nothing in particular.

In fact, life seemed downright perfect to him.

Which just went to show what *he* knew.

Chapter 13

Brad blinked awake, sprawled on his back on the big leather couch in Meg's study, fully dressed and covered with an old quilt.

Carly stood looking down at him, a curious expression on her face, probably surprised that he hadn't slept with Meg.

"What time is it?" he asked, yawning.

"Six-thirty," Carly answered. She was wearing jeans and the T-shirt he'd given her, and it looked a little the worse for wear. "Have you decided if I get to be in your movie?"

Brad chuckled, yawned again. "I haven't heard from your agent," he teased.

She frowned. "I don't have an agent," she replied. "Is that a problem?"

"No," he relented, smiling. "I can promise you a walk-on. Beyond that, it's out of my hands. Deal?"

"Deal!" Carly beamed. But then her face fell. "I hope my dad makes it long enough to see me on the big screen," she said.

Brad's heart slipped, caught itself with a lurch that was almost painful. "We could show him the rushes," he said after swallowing once. "Right in his hospital room."

"What are rushes?"

"Film clips. They're not edited, and there's no music—not even sound, sometimes. But he'd see you."

Meg appeared in the doorway of the study, clad in chore clothes.

"I get to be in the movie," Carly informed her excitedly. "Even though I don't have an agent."

"That's great," Meg said softly, her gaze resting with tender gratitude on Brad. "Coffee's on, if anybody's interested."

Brad threw back the quilt, sat upright, pulled on his boots. "Somebody's interested, all right," he said. "I'll feed the horses if you'll make breakfast."

"Sounds fair," Meg answered, turning her attention back to Carly. "Nix on the T-shirt, Ms. Streep. You've worn it for three days in a row now—it goes in the laundry."

On her way to certain stardom, Carly apparently figured she could give ground on the T-shirt edict. "Okay," she said, and headed out of the room, ostensibly to go upstairs and change clothes.

"Carly got arrested yesterday," Meg announced, looking wan.

Brad stood, surprised. And not surprised. "What happened?"

"She decided to cut school and hitchhike to Flagstaff to see Ted in the hospital. Thank God, Wyatt happened to be heading up Highway 17 and spotted her from his squad car."

Brad approached Meg, took her elbows gently into his hands. "Having doubts about being an instant mother, McKettrick?" he asked quietly. She seemed uncommonly fragile, and knowing she'd been flattened by a headache the night before worried him.

"Yes," she said after gnawing at her lower lip for a couple of seconds. "I've always wanted a child, more than anything, but I didn't expect it to happen this way."

He drew her close, held her, buried his face in her hair and breathed in the flower-and-summer-grass scent of it. "I know you don't think of Ted as a father," he said close to her ear, "but a reunion with him this late in the game, especially with a terminal diagnosis hanging over his head, has to be a serious blow. Maybe you need to acknowledge that Carly isn't the only one with some grieving to do."

She tilted her head back, her blue eyes shining with tears. "Damn him," she whispered. "Damn him for coming back here to die! Where was he when I took my first steps—lost my front teeth—broke my leg at horseback riding camp—graduated from high school and college? Where was he when you—"

"When I broke your heart?" Brad finished for her.

"Well—" Meg paused to sniffle once. "Yeah."

"I'd do anything to make that up to you, Meg. Anything for a do over. But the world doesn't work that way. Maybe besides finding a place for Carly, where he knows she'll be loved and she'll be safe, Ted's looking for the same thing I am. A second chance with you."

She looked taken aback. "Maybe," she agreed. "But he sure took his sweet time putting in an appearance, and so did you."

Brad gave her another hug. They were on tricky ground, and he knew it. Carly could be heard clattering down the stairs at the back of the house, into the kitchen.

They needed privacy to carry the conversation any further.

"I'll go feed the horses," he reiterated. "You make breakfast." He kissed her forehead, not wanting to let her go. "Once you've dropped Carly off at school, you could drop in at my place."

He held his breath, awaiting her answer. Both of them knew what would happen if he and Meg were alone at Stone Creek Ranch.

"I'll let you know," she said at long last.

He hesitated, nodded once and left her to feed the horses.

Breakfast turned out to be toaster waffles and microwave bacon.

"Next time," Brad told Meg, after they'd exchanged a light kiss next to her Blazer, with Carly watching avidly from the passenger seat, "I'll cook and *you* feed the horses."

He sang old Johnny Cash favorites all the way home, at the top of his lungs, with the truck windows rolled down.

But the song died in his throat when he topped the rise and saw a sleek white limo waiting in the driveway. Some gut instinct, as primitive as what he'd felt facing down the leader of the wolf pack up at Horse Thief Canyon, told him this wasn't Phil, or even a bunch of movie executives on an outing.

The chauffer got out, opened the rear right-hand door of the limo as Brad pulled to a stop next to it, buzzing up the truck windows and frowning.

A pair of long, shapely legs swung into view.

Brad swore and slammed out of the truck to stand like a gunfighter, his hands on his hips.

"I'd be perfect for the female lead in this movie," Cynthia Donnigan said, tottering toward him on spiked heels that sank into the dirt. Her short, stretchy skirt rode up on her gym-toned thighs, and she didn't bother to adjust it.

He stared at her in amazement and disbelief, literally speechless.

Cynthia lowered her expensive sunglasses and batted her lashes—as fake as her breasts—and her collagen-enhanced lips puckered into a pout. "Aren't you glad to see me?" ·

Her hair, black as Ransom's coat, was arranged in artfully careless tufts stiff enough to do damage if she decided to head butt somebody.

"What do you think?" he growled.

Luck, Big John had often said, was never so bad that it couldn't get worse. At that moment, Meg's Blazer came over the rise, dust spiraling behind it.

"I think you're not very forgiving," Cynthia said, following his gaze and then zeroing in on his face with a smug little twist of her mouth. "Bygones are bygones, baby. I'm ideal for the part and you know it."

Brad took a step back as she teetered a step forward. "Not a chance," he said, aware of Meg coming to a stop behind him, but not getting out of the Blazer.

Cynthia smiled and did a waggle-fingered wave in Meg's direction. "I've checked into a resort in Sedona," she said sweetly. "I can wait until you come to your senses and agree that the part of the lawman's widow was written for me."

Brad turned, approached the Blazer and met Meg's

wide eyes through the glass of the driver's-side window. He opened the door and offered a hand to help her down.

"The second wife?" Meg asked, more mouthing the words than saying them.

Brad nodded shortly.

Meg peered around him as she got out of the Blazer. Then, with a big smile, she walked right up to Cynthia with her hand out. "I think I've seen you in several feminine hygiene product commercials," she said.

That made Brad chuckle to himself.

Cynthia simmered. "Hello," she responded, in a dangerous purr. "You must be the girl Brad left behind."

Meg had grown up rough-and-tumble, with a bunch of mischievous boy cousins, and served on the executive staff of a multinational corporation. She wasn't easy to intimidate. To Brad's relief—and amusement—she hooked an arm through his, smiled winningly and said, "It's sort of an on-again, off-again kind of thing with Brad and me. Right now, it's definitely on."

Cynthia blinked. She was strictly a B-grade celebrity, but as Brad's ex-wife and sole owner of an up-and-coming production company, she was used to deference of the Beverly Hills variety.

But this was Stone Creek, Arizona, not Beverly Hills.

And the word *deference* wasn't in Meg's vocabulary.

Temporarily stymied, Cynthia pushed her sunglasses back up her nose, minced back toward the waiting limo. The driver stood waiting, still holding her door open and staring off into space as though oblivious to everything going on in what was essentially the barnyard.

Brad followed. "If you manage to wangle your way into this movie," he said, "I'm out."

Cynthia plopped her scantily clad butt onto the leather

seat, but didn't draw her killer legs inside. "Read your contract, Brad," she said. "You signed with Starglow Productions. *My* company."

The shock that made his stomach go into a free fall must have shown in his face, because his ex-wife smiled.

"Didn't I tell you I changed the name of the company?" she asked. "No me, no movie, cowboy."

"No movie," Brad said, feeling sick. The whole county was excited about the project—they'd have talked about it for years to come. Carly and a lot of other people would be disappointed—not least of all, himself.

"Back to Sedona," Cynthia told the driver, with a lofty gesture of one manicured hand.

"Yes, ma'am," he replied. But he gave Brad a sympathetic glance before getting behind the wheel.

Brad stood still, furious not only with Cynthia, and with Phil, who had to have known who owned Starglow Productions, but with himself. He'd been too quick to sign on the dotted line, swayed by his own desire to play bigscreen cowboy, and by Livie's suggestion that he build an animal shelter with the proceeds. If he tried to back out of the deal now, Cynthia's lawyers would be all over him like fleas on an old hound dog, and he didn't even want to think of the potential publicity.

"So that's the second wife," Meg said, stepping up beside him and watching as the sleek car zipped away.

"That's her," he replied gloomily. "And I am royally, totally screwed."

She moved to stand in front of him, looking up into his face. "I was trying hard not to eavesdrop," she said, "but I couldn't help gathering that she wants to be in the movie."

"She *owns* the movie," Brad said.

"And this is so awful because—?"

"Because she's a first-class, card-carrying bitch. And because I can hardly stand to be in the same room with her, let alone on a movie set for three or four months."

Meg took his hand, gave him a gentle tug in the direction of the house. "Can't you break the contract?"

"Not without getting sued for everything I have, including this ranch, and bringing so many tabloid stringers to Stone Creek that they'll be swinging from the telephone poles."

"Then maybe you should just bite the proverbial bullet and make the movie."

"You haven't read the script," Brad said. "I have to kiss her. And there's a love scene—"

Meg's eyes twinkled. "You sound like a little boy, balking at being in the school play with a *girl*." She tugged him up the back steps, toward the kitchen door.

Willie met them on the other side, wagging cheerfully.

Brad let him out, scowling, and he and Meg waited on the porch while the dog attended to his duties.

"You have no idea what she's like," Brad said.

Meg gave him a light poke with her elbow. "I know you must have loved her once. After all, you married her."

"The truth is a lot less flattering than that," he replied, unable, for a long moment, to meet Meg's eyes. What he had to say was going to upset her, for several reasons, and there was no way to avoid it. "We hooked up after a party. Six weeks later, she called and told me she was pregnant, and the baby was mine. I married her, because she said she was going to get an abortion if I didn't. I went on tour—she wanted to go along and I refused. Frankly, I wasn't ready to present Cynthia to the world as my adored bride. She called the press in, gave them pictures of the 'wedding.'

And then, just to make sure I knew what it meant to cross her, she had the abortion anyway."

The pain was there in Meg's face—she had to be thinking that, had she told him about *their* baby, he'd have married her with the same singular lack of enthusiasm—but her words took him by surprise. "I'm sorry, Brad," she said softly. "You must have really wanted to be a dad."

He whistled for Willie, since speaking was beyond him for the moment, and the dog, obviously on the mend, made it up the porch steps with no help. "Yeah," he said.

"I have an idea," Meg said.

He glanced at her. "What?"

"We could rehearse your love scene. Just to be sure you get it right."

In spite of everything, he chuckled. The sound was raw and hurt his throat, but it was genuine. "Aren't you the least bit jealous?" he asked.

She looked honestly puzzled. "Of what?"

"I'm going to have to kiss Cynthia. Get naked with her on the silver screen. This doesn't bother you?"

"I'll cover my eyes during that part of the movie," she joked, with a little what-the-hell motion of her shoulders. Then her expression turned serious. "Of course, there's a fine line between hatred and passion. If you care for Cynthia, you need to tell me—now."

He laid his hands on her shoulders, remembered the satiny smoothness of her bare skin. "I care for *you,* Meg McKettrick," he said. "I tried hard—with Valerie, even with Cynthia—but it never worked. I was always thinking about you—reading about you in the business pages of newspapers, getting what news I could through my sisters, checking the McKettrickCo Web site. Whenever I read or heard your name, I got this sour ache in the pit of my stomach, because I was scared a wedding announcement would follow."

Meg stiffened slightly. "What would you have done if one had?"

"Stopped the wedding," he said. "Made a scene Indian Rock and Stone Creek would never forget." He smiled crookedly. "Kind of a sticky proposition, given that I could have been married at the time."

"Not to mention that my cousins would have thrown you bodily out of the church," Meg huffed, but there was a smile beginning in her eyes, already tugging at the corners of her mouth.

"I said it would have been an unforgettable scene," he reminded her, grinning. "I would have fought back, you see, and yelled your name, like Stanley yelling for Stella in *A Streetcar Named Desire*."

She pretended to punch him in the stomach. "You're impossible."

"I'm also horny. And a lot more—though I'm not sure you're ready to hear that part."

"Try me."

"Okay. I love you, Meg McKettrick. I always have. I always will."

"You're right. I wasn't ready."

"Then I guess rehearsing the love scene is out?"

She smiled, stood on tiptoe and kissed the cleft in his chin. "I didn't say that. Hardworking actors should know their scenes cold."

He bent his head, nibbled at her delectable mouth. "Oh, I'll know the scene," he breathed. "But there won't be anything 'cold' about it."

* * *

Meg hauled herself up onto her elbows, out of a sated sleep, glanced at the clock on the table next to Brad's bed and screamed.

"What?" Brad asked, bolting awake.

"Look at the time!" Meg wailed. "Carly will be out of school in fifteen minutes!"

Calmly, Brad reached for the telephone receiver, handed it to her. "Call the school and tell them you've been detained and you'll be there soon."

"Detained?"

"Would you rather say you've been in bed with me all afternoon?"

"No," she admitted, and dialed 411, asking to be connected to Indian Rock Middle School.

When she arrived at the school forty-five minutes later, Carly was waiting glumly in the principal's office. Her expression softened, though, when she saw that Brad had come along.

"Oh, great," she said. "Brad O'Ballivan shows up at my school, *in person,* and nobody's around to see but the geek-wads in detention. Who'd believe a word *they* said?"

Brad laughed. "Did I ever tell you I was one of those 'geek-wads' once upon a time, always in detention?"

"Get out," Carly said, intrigued.

"Don't get the idea that being in detention is cool," Meg warned.

Carly rolled her eyes.

The three of them made the drive to Flagstaff in Brad's truck. Carly chattered nonstop for the first few miles, pointing out the place where she'd been "busted" for trying to hitch a ride, but as they drew nearer to their destination, she grew more and more subdued.

It didn't help that Ted was worse than he'd been the day before. He looked shrunken, lying there in his bed with tubes and monitors attached to every part of his body.

Looking at her father, it seemed to Meg that he'd used up the last of his personal resources to fling himself over an invisible finish line—getting Carly to her for safekeeping. For the first time it was actually real to Meg: he *was* dying.

Brad gave her a nudge toward the bed, an unspoken reminder of what he'd said about her having grieving to do, just as Carly did.

"How about a milk shake in the cafeteria?" Meg heard Brad say to Carly.

In the next moment, the two of them were gone, and Meg was alone with the man who had abandoned her so long ago that she didn't even remember him.

"That young man," Ted said, "is in love with you."

"He left me, too," Meg said without meaning to expose the rawest nerve in her psyche. "It's a pattern. First you, then Brad."

"Do yourself a favor and don't superimpose your old man over him," Ted struggled to say. "And when Carly gets old enough, don't let her make that mistake, either. I don't have time to make it up to you, what I did and didn't do, but he does. You give him the chance."

Tears welled in Meg's eyes, thickened her throat. "I hate it that you're dying," she said.

Ted put out his left hand, an IV tube dangling from it. "Me, too," he ground out. "Come here, kid."

Meg let him pull her closer, lowered her forehead to rest against his.

She felt moisture in the gray stubble on his cheeks and didn't know if the tears were hers or her father's. Or both.

"If I could stay around a little longer, I'd find a way to prove that you're still my little girl and I've always loved you. Since I'm not going to get that chance, you'll have to take my word for it."

"It isn't fair," Meg protested, knowing the remark was childish.

"Not much is, in this life," Ted answered, as Meg raised her head so she could look into his face. "Know what I'd tell you if I'd been around all this time like a regular father, and had the right to say what's on my mind?"

Meg couldn't answer.

"I'd tell you not to let Brad O'Ballivan get away. Don't let your damnable McKettrick pride get in the way of what he's offering, Meg."

"He told me he loves me," she said.

"Do you believe him?"

"I don't know."

"All right, then, do you love him?"

Meg bit her lower lip, nodded.

"Have you told him?"

"Sort of," Meg said.

"Take it from me, kid," Ted countered, trying to smile. "'Sort of' ain't good enough." His faded eyes seemed to memorize Meg, take her in. "Get the nurse for me, will you? This pain medication isn't working."

Meg immediately rang for the nurse, and when help came, rushed to the elevators and punched the button for the cafeteria. By the time she got back with Carly and Brad, the room was full of people in scrubs.

Carly broke free and rushed to her dad's bedside, squirming through until she caught hold of his hand.

The medical team, in the midst of an emergency, would

have pushed Carly aside if Brad hadn't spoken in a voice of calm but unmistakable authority.

"Let her stay," he said.

"Dad?" Carly whispered desperately. "Dad, don't go, okay? Don't go!"

A nurse eased Carly back from the bedside, and the work continued, but it was too late, and everyone knew it.

The heartbeat monitor blipped, then flatlined.

Carly turned, sobbing, not into Meg's arms, but into Brad's.

He held her and drew Meg close against his side at the same time.

After that, there were papers to sign. Meg would have to call her mother later, but at the moment, she simply couldn't say the words.

Carly seemed dazed, allowing herself to be led out of the hospital, back to Brad's truck. She'd been inconsolable in Ted's hospital room, but now she was dry-eyed and the only sound she made was the occasional hiccup.

Brad didn't take them back to the Triple M, but to his own ranch. There, he called Eve, then Jesse. Vaguely, as if from a great distance, Meg heard him ask her cousin to make sure her horses got fed.

There were other calls, too, but Meg wasn't tracking. She simply sat at the kitchen table, watching numbly while Carly knelt on the floor, both arms around a sympathetic Willie, her face buried in his fur.

Olivia arrived—Brad must have summoned her—and brought a stack of pizza boxes with her. She set the boxes on the counter, washed her hands at the sink and immediately started setting out plates and silverware.

"I'm not hungry," Carly said.

"Me, either," Meg echoed.

"Humor me," Olivia said.

The pizza tasted like cardboard, but it filled a hole, if only a physical one, and Meg was grateful. Following her example, Carly ate, too.

"Are we staying here tonight?" Carly asked Brad, her eyes enormous and hollow.

Olivia answered for him. "Yes," she said.

"Who are you?"

"I'm Livie—Brad's sister."

"The veterinarian?"

Olivia nodded.

"My dad died today."

Olivia's expressive eyes filled with tears. "I know."

Meg swallowed, but didn't speak. Next to her, Brad took her hand briefly, gave it a squeeze.

"Do you like being an animal doctor?" Carly asked. She'd said hardly a word to Meg or even Brad since they'd left the hospital, but for some reason, she was reaching out to Olivia O'Ballivan.

"I love it," Olivia said. "It's hard sometimes, though. When I try really hard to help an animal, and they don't get better."

"I kept thinking my dad would get well, but he didn't."

"Our dad died, too," Olivia said after a glance in Brad's direction. "He was struck by lightning during a roundup. I kept thinking there must have been a mistake—that he was just down in Phoenix at a cattle auction, or looking for strays up on the mountain."

Meg felt a quick tension in Brad, a singular alertness, gone again as soon as it came. Her guess was he hadn't known his sister, a child when the accident happened, had secretly believed their father would come home.

"Does it ever stop hurting?" Carly asked, her voice small and fragile.

Meg squeezed her eyes shut. *Does it ever stop hurting?* she wondered.

"You'll never forget your dad, if that's what you mean," Olivia said. "But it gets easier. Brad and our sisters and I, we were lucky. We had our grandfather, Big John. Like you've got Meg."

Brad pushed his chair back, left the table. Stood with his back to them all, as if gazing out the darkened window over the sink.

"Big John passed away, too," Olivia explained quietly. "But we were all grown up by then. He was there when it counted, and now we've got each other."

Carly turned imploring eyes on Meg. "You won't die, too? You won't die and leave me all alone?"

Meg got up, went to Carly, gathered her into her arms. "I'll be here," she promised. *"I'll be here."*

Carly clung to her for a long time, then, typically, pulled away. "Where am I going to sleep?" she asked.

"I thought maybe you'd like to stay in my room," Olivia said. "It has twin beds. You can have the one by the window, if you'd like."

"You're going to stay, too?"

"For tonight," Olivia answered.

Carly looked relieved. Maybe, for a child, it was a matter of safety in numbers—herself, Meg, Brad, Olivia and Willie, all huddled in the same house, somehow keeping the uncertain darkness at bay. "I think I'd like to sleep now," she said. "Can Willie come, too?"

"He'll need to go outside first, I think," Olivia said.

Brad took Willie out, without a word, returned and

watched as the old dog climbed the stairs, Carly leading the way, Olivia bringing up the rear.

"Thanks," Meg said when she and Brad were alone. "You've been wonderful."

Brad began clearing the table, disposing of pizza boxes. Meg caught his arm. "Brad, what—?"

"My grandfather," he said. "I just got to missing him. Regretting a lot of things."

She nodded. Waited.

"I'm sorry, Meg," he told her. "That your dad's gone, and you didn't get a chance to know him. That you've got a rough time ahead with Carly. And most of all, I'm sorry there's nothing I can do to make this better."

"You could hold me," Meg said.

He pulled her into an easy, gentle embrace. Kissed her forehead. "I could hold you," he confirmed.

She wanted to ask if he'd meant it, when—was it only a few hours ago?—he'd said he loved her. The problem was, she knew if he took the words back, or qualified them somehow, she wouldn't be able to bear it. Not now, while she was mourning the father she'd lost years ago.

They stood like that for a while, then, by tacit agreement, finished tidying up the kitchen. Before they started up the backstairs, Brad switched out the lights, and Meg stood waiting for him, blinded, not knowing her way around the house, but unafraid. As long as Brad was there, no gloom would have been deep enough to swallow her.

In his room upstairs, they undressed, got into bed together, lay enfolded in each other's arms.

I love you, Meg thought with stark clarity.

They didn't make love.

They didn't talk.

But Meg felt a bittersweet gratification just the same,

a deep shift somewhere inside herself, where spirit and body met.

On the edge of sleep, just before she tumbled helplessly over the precipice, Angus crossed her mind, along with a whisper-thin wondering.

Where had he gone?

Chapter 14

The snows came early that year, to the annoyance of the movie people, and Brad was away from the ranch a lot, filming scenes in a studio in Flagstaff. He'd grudgingly admitted that Cynthia had been right—she was perfect for the part of Sarah Jane Stone—and while Meg visited the set once or twice, she stayed away when the love scenes were on the schedule.

She had a lot of other things on her mind, as it happened. She and Carly were bonding, slowly but surely, but the process was rocky. With the help of a counselor, they felt their way toward each other—backed off—tried again.

When the day came for Carly's promised scene—she played a nameless character in calico and a bonnet who brought Brad a glass of punch at a party and solemnly offered it. She'd endlessly practiced her single line—a "you're welcome, mister" to his "thank you"—telling

Meg very seriously that there were no small parts, only small actors.

The movie part gave Carly something to hold on to in the dark days after Ted's passing, and Meg was eternally grateful for that. Both she and Carly spent a lot of time at Brad's house, even when he wasn't around, looking after Willie and gradually becoming a part of the place itself.

Ransom and his mares occupied the main pasture at Stone Creek Ranch, and the job of driving hay out to them usually fell to Olivia and Meg, with Carly riding in the back of the truck, seated on the bales. During that time, Meg and Olivia became good friends.

In the spring, when there would be fresh grass in the high country, and no snow to impede their mobility, Ransom and the mares would be turned loose.

"You'll miss him," Meg said once, watching Olivia as she stood in the pickup bed, tossing bales of grass hay to the ground after Carly cut the twine that held them together.

Olivia swallowed visibly and nodded, admiring the stallion as he stood, head turned toward the mountain, sniffing the air for the scents of spring and freedom. On warmer days, he was especially restless, prancing back and forth along the farthest fence, tail high, mane flying in the breeze.

Meg knew there had been many opportunities to sell Ransom for staggering amounts of money, but neither Olivia nor Brad had even considered the idea. In their minds, Ransom wasn't theirs to sell—he belonged to himself, to the high country, to legend. With his wounds healed, he'd have been able to soar over any fence, but he seemed to know the time wasn't right. There in the O'Ballivans' pasture, he had plenty of feed and easily accessible water, hard to find in winter, especially up in the red peaks and canyons, and he'd be at a disadvantage with the wolves. Still, there was a palpable, restless air of yearning about him that bruised Meg's heart.

It would be a sad and wonderful day when the far gate was opened.

Olivia cheered herself, along with Meg and Carly, with the fact that Brad had decided to make the ranch a haven for displaced mules, donkeys and horses, including unwanted Thoroughbreds who hadn't made the grade as racers, studs or broodmares. At the first sign of spring, the adoptees would begin arriving, courtesy of the Bureau of Land Management and various animal-rescue groups.

In the meantime, the ranch, like the larger world, seemed to Meg to be hibernating, practically in suspended animation. Like Ransom, she longed for spring.

It was after one of their visits to Brad's, while they were attending to their own horses on the Triple M, that Carly brought up a subject Meg had been troubled by, but hadn't wanted to raise.

"Where do you suppose Angus is?" the child asked. "I haven't seen him around in a couple of months."

"Hard to know," Meg said carefully.

"Maybe he's busy on the other side," Carly suggested. "You know, showing my dad around and stuff."

"Could be," Meg allowed. Until his last visit—the night he'd been so anxious for a look at the McKettrick family Bible—Meg had seen and spoken to her illustrious ancestor almost every day of her life. She hadn't had so much as a glimpse of him since then, and while there had been countless times she'd wished Angus would stay where he belonged, so she could be a normal person, she missed him.

Surely he wouldn't have simply stopped visiting her

without even saying goodbye. It appeared, though, that that was exactly what he'd done.

"I wish he'd come," Carly said somewhat wistfully. "I want to ask him if he's seen my dad."

Meg slipped an arm around her sister, held her close against her side for a second or two. "I'm sure your—our—dad is fine," she said softly.

Carly smiled, but sadness lingered in her eyes. "For a while, I hoped Dad would come back, the way Angus did. But I guess he's busy or something."

"Probably," Meg agreed. It went without saying that the Angus phenomenon was rare, but there were times when she wondered if that was really true. How many children, prattling about their imaginary playmates, were actually seeing someone real?

They started back toward the house, two sisters, walking close.

Inside, they both washed up—Meg at the kitchen sink, Carly in the downstairs powder room—and began preparing supper. After the meal, salad and a tamale pie from a recently acquired cookbook geared to the culinarily challenged, Meg cleared the table and loaded the dishwasher while Carly settled down to her homework.

Like most kids, she had a way of asking penetrating questions with no preamble. "Are you going to marry Brad O'Ballivan?" she inquired now, looking up from her math text. "We spend a lot of time at his place, and I know you sleep over when I'm visiting Eve. Or he comes here."

Things were good between Brad and Meg, probably because he was so busy with the movie that they rarely saw each other. When they *were* together, they took every opportunity to make love.

"He hasn't asked," Meg said lightly. "And you're in

some pretty personal territory, here. Have I mentioned lately that you're twelve?"

"I might be twelve," Carly replied, "but I'm not stupid."

"You're definitely not stupid," Meg agreed good-naturedly, but on the inside, she was dancing to a different tune. Her period, always as regular as the orbit of the moon, was two weeks late. She'd bought a home pregnancy test at a drugstore in Flagstaff, not wanting word of the purchase to get around Indian Rock as it would have if she'd made the purchase locally, but she hadn't worked up the nerve to use it yet.

As much as she'd wanted a child, she almost hoped the results would be negative. She knew what would happen if the plus sign came up, instead of the minus. She'd tell Brad, he'd insist on marrying her, just as he'd done with both Valerie and Cynthia, and for the rest of her days, she'd wonder if he'd proposed out of honor, or because he actually loved her.

On the other hand, she wouldn't dare keep the knowledge from him, not after what had happened before, when they were teenagers. He'd never forgive her if something went wrong; even the truest, deepest kind of love between a man and a woman couldn't survive if there was no trust.

All of which left Meg in a state of suspecting she was carrying Brad's child, not knowing for sure, and being afraid to find out.

Carly, whose intuition seemed uncanny at times, blindsided her again. "I saw the pregnancy-test kit," she announced.

Meg, in the process of wiping out the sink, froze.

"I didn't mean to snoop," Carly said quickly. By turns, she was rebellious and paranoid, convinced on some level that living on the Triple M as a part of the McKettrick family was an interval of sorts, not a permanent arrangement. In her experience, everything was temporary. "I ran out of toothpaste, and I went into your bathroom to borrow some, and I saw the kit."

Sighing, Meg went to the table and sat down next to Carly, searching for words.

"Are you mad at me?" Carly asked.

"No," Meg said. "And I wouldn't send you away even if I was, Carly. You need to get clear on that."

"Okay," Carly said, but she didn't sound convinced. Meg guessed it would take time, maybe a very long time, for her little sister to feel secure. Her face brightened. "It would be so cool if you had a baby!" she spouted.

"Yes," Meg agreed, smiling. "It would."

"So what's the problem with finding out for sure?"

"Brad's really busy right now. I guess I'm looking for a chance to tell him."

Just then, as if by the hand of Providence, a rig drove up outside, a door slammed.

Carly rushed to the window, gave a yip of excitement. "He's here!" she crowed. "And Willie's with him!"

Meg closed her eyes. So much for procrastination.

Carly hurried to open the back door, and Brad and the dog blew in with a chilly wind.

"Here," Brad said, handing Carly a flash drive. "It's your big scene, complete with dialogue and music."

Carly grabbed the stick and fled to the study, fairly skipping and Willie, now almost wholly recovered from his injuries, dashed after her, barking happily.

Meg was conscious, in those moments, of everything that was at stake. The child and even the dog would suffer if the conversation she and Brad were about to have went sour.

"Sit down," she said, turning to watch Brad as he shed his heavy coat and hung it from one of the pegs next to the door.

"Sounds serious," Brad mused. "Carly get into trouble at school again?"

"No," Meg answered, after swallowing hard.

Brad frowned and joined her at the table, sitting astraddle the bench while she occupied the chair at the end. "Meg, what's the trouble?" he asked worriedly.

"I bought a kit—" she began, immediately faltering.

His forehead crinkled. "A kit?" The light went on. "A *kit!*"

"I think I might be pregnant, Brad."

A smile spread across his face, shone in his eyes, giving her hope. But then he went solemn again. "You don't sound very happy about it," he said, looking wary. "When did you do the test?"

"That's just it. I haven't done it yet. Because I'm afraid."

"Afraid? Why?"

"Things have been so good between us, and—"

Gently, he took her hand. Turned it over to trace patterns on her palm with the pad of his thumb. "Go on," he said, his voice hoarse, obviously steeling himself against who knew what.

"I know you'll marry me," Meg forced herself to say. "If the test is positive, I mean. And I'll always wonder if you feel trapped, the way you did with Cynthia."

Brad considered her words, still caressing her palm. "All right," he said presently. "Then I guess we ought to get married *before* you take the pregnancy test. Because either way, Meg, I want you to be my wife. Baby or no baby."

She studied him. "Maybe we should live together for a while. See how it goes."

"No way, McKettrick," Brad replied instantly. "I know lots of good people share a house without benefit of a wedding these days, but when it comes down to it, I'm an old-fashioned guy."

"You'd really do that? Marry me without knowing the results of the test? What if it's negative?"

"Then we'd keep working on it." Brad grinned.

Meg bit her lower lip, thinking hard.

Finally, she stood and said, "Wait here."

But she only got as far as the middle of the back stairway before she returned.

"The McKettrick women don't change their names when they get married," she reminded him, though they both knew Sierra had already broken that tradition, and happily so.

"Call yourself whatever you want," Brad replied. "For a year. At the end of that time, if you're convinced we can make it, then you'll go by O'Ballivan. Deal?"

Meg pondered the question. "Deal," she said at long last.

She went upstairs, slipped into her bathroom and leaned against the closed door, her heart pounding. Her reflection in the long mirror over the double sink stared back at her.

"Pee on the stick, McKettrick," she told herself, "and get it over with."

Five minutes later, she was staring at the little plastic stick, filled with mixed emotion. There was happiness, but trepidation, too. *What-ifs* hammered at her from every side.

A light knock sounded at the door, and Brad came in.

"The suspense," he said, "is killing me."

Meg showed him the stick.

And his whoop of joy echoed off every wall in that venerable old house.

* * *

"I think I have a future in show business," Carly confided to Brad later that night when she came into the kitchen to say good-night. She'd watched her scene on the study TV at least fourteen times.

"I think you have a future in the eighth grade," Meg responded, smiling.

"What if I end up on the cutting-room floor?" Carly fretted. Clearly, she'd been doing some online research into the moviemaking process.

"I'll see that you don't," Brad promised. "Go to bed, Carly. A movie star needs her beauty sleep."

Carly nodded, then went upstairs, flash drive in hand. Willie, who had been following her all evening, sighed despondently and lay down at Brad's feet, muzzle resting on his forepaws.

Brad leaned down to stroke the dog's smooth, graying back. "Looks like Carly's already got one devoted fan," he remarked.

Meg chuckled. "More than one," she said. "I certainly qualify, and so do you. Eve spoils her, and Rance's and Keegan's girls think of her as the family celebrity."

Brad grinned. "Carly's a pro," he said. "But you're wise to steer her away from show business, at least for the time being. It's hard enough for adults to handle, and kids have it even worse."

The topics of the baby and marriage pulsed in the air between them, but they skirted them, went on talking about other things. Brad was comfortable with that—there would be time enough to make plans.

"According to her teachers," Meg said, "Carly has a near-genius affinity for computers, or anything technical. Last week she actually got the clock on the DVD player to stop blinking twelves. This, I might add, is a skill that has eluded presidents."

"Lots of things elude presidents," Brad replied, finishing his coffee. "We're wrapping up the movie next week," he added. "The indoor scenes, at least. We'll have to do the stagecoach robbery and all the rest next spring. Think you could pencil a wedding into your schedule?"

Meg's cheeks colored attractively, causing Brad to wonder what *other* parts of her were turning pink. She hesitated, then nodded, but as she looked at him, her gaze switched to something just beyond his left shoulder.

Brad turned to look, but there was nothing there.

"I hate leaving you," he said, turning back, frowning a little. "But I've got an early call in the morning." Neither of them were comfortable sleeping together with Carly around, but that would change after they were married.

"I understand," Meg said.

"Do you, Meg?" he asked very quietly. "I love you. I want to marry you, and I would have, even if the test had been negative."

She said them then, the words he'd been waiting for. Before that, she'd spoken them only in the throes of passion.

"I love you right back, Brad O'Ballivan."

He stood, drew her to her feet and kissed her. It was a lingering kiss, gentle but thorough.

"But there's still one thing I haven't told you," she choked out, when their mouths parted.

Brad braced himself. Waited, his mind scrambling over possibilities—there was another man out there somewhere after all, one with some emotional claim on her, or more she hadn't told him about the first pregnancy, or the miscarriage...

"Ever since I was a little girl," she said, "I've been see-ing Angus McKettrick. In fact, he's here right now."

Brad recalled the glance she'd thrown over his shoul-der a few minutes before, the odd expression in her eyes. First Livie, with her Dr. Doolittle act—now Meg claimed she could see the family patriarch, who had been dead for over a century.

He thrust out a sigh.

She waited, gnawing at her lip, her eyes wide and hope-ful.

"If you say so," he said at last, "I believe you."

Joy suffused her face. "Really?"

"Really," he said, though the truth was more like: *I'm trying to believe you.* As with Livie, he would believe if it killed him, despite all the rational arguments crowd-ing his mind.

She stood on tiptoe and kissed him. "I'd insist that you stay, since we're engaged," she whispered, "but Angus is even more old-fashioned than you are."

He laughed, said good-night and looked down at Willie.

The dog was standing, wagging his tail and grinning, looking up at someone who wasn't there.

There were indeed, Brad thought, as he and Willie made the lonely drive back to Stone Creek Ranch in his truck, more things in heaven and earth than this world dreams of.

"Where have you been?" Meg demanded, torn between relief at seeing Angus again, and complete exasperation.

"You always knew I wouldn't be around forever," Angus said. He looked older than he had the last time she'd seen him, even careworn, but somehow serene, too. "Things are winding down, girl. I figured you needed to start get-ting used to my being gone."

Meg blinked, surprised by the stab of pain she felt at the prospect of Angus's leaving for good. On the other hand, she *had* always known the last parting would come.

"I'm going to have a baby," she said, struggling not to cry. "I'll need you. The baby and Carly will need you."

Angus seldom touched her, but now he cupped one hand under her chin. His skin felt warm, not cold, and solid, not ethereal. "No," he said gruffly. "You only need yourselves and each other. Things are going to be fine from here on out, Meg. You'll see."

She swallowed, wanting to cling to him, knowing it wouldn't be right. He had a life to live, somewhere else, beyond some unseen border. There were others there, waiting for him.

"Why did you come?" she asked. "In the first place, I mean?"

"You needed me," he said simply.

"I did," she confirmed. For all the nannies and "aunts and uncles," she'd been a lost soul as a child, especially after Sierra was kidnapped and Eve fell apart in so many ways. She'd never blamed her mother, never harbored any resentment for the inevitable neglect she'd suffered, but she knew now that, without Angus, she would have been bereft.

He was carrying a hat in his left hand, and now he put it on, the gesture somehow final. "You say goodbye to Carly for me," he said. "And tell her that her pa's just fine where he is."

Meg nodded, unable to speak.

Angus leaned in, planted a light, awkward kiss on Meg's forehead. "When you get to the end of the trail," he said, "and that's a long ways off, I promise, I'll be there to say welcome."

Still, no words would come. Not even ones of farewell. So Meg merely nodded again.

Angus turned his back and, in the blink of an eye, he was gone.

She cried that night, for sorrow, for joy and for a thousand other reasons, but when the morning came, she knew Angus had been right.

She didn't need him anymore.

The wedding was small and simple, with only family and a few friends present. Meg still considered the marriage provisional, and went on calling herself Meg McKettrick, although she and Carly moved in at Stone Creek Ranch right away. All the horses came with them, but Meg still paid regular visits to the Triple M, always hoping, on some level, for just one more glimpse of Angus.

It didn't happen, of course.

So she sorted old photos and journals when she was there, and with some help from Sierra, catalogued them into something resembling archives. Eve, tired of hotel living, planned on moving back in. A grandmother, she maintained, with Eve-logic, ought to live in the country. She ought to bake pies and cookies and shelter the children of the family under broad, sturdy branches, like an old oak tree.

Meg smiled every time she pictured her rich, sophisticated, well-traveled mother in an apron and sensible shoes, but she had to admit Eve had pulled off a spectacular country-style Christmas. There had been a massive tree, covered in lights and heirloom ornaments, bulging stockings for Carly and Liam and little Brody, and a complete turkey dinner, only partly catered.

She'd already taken over the master bedroom, and she'd

brought her two champion jumpers from the stables in San Antonio, and installed them in the barn. She rode every chance she got, often with Brad and Carly and sometimes with Jesse, Rance and Keegan.

Meg, being pregnant and out of practice when it came to horseback riding, usually watched from a perch on the pasture fence. She didn't believe in being overly cautious—it wasn't the McKettrick way—but this baby was precious to her, and to Brad. She wasn't taking any chances.

Dusting off an old photograph of Holt and Lorelei, Meg stepped back to admire the way it looked on the study mantle. She heard her mother at the back of the house.

"Meg? Are you here?"

"In the study," Meg called back.

Eve tracked her down. "Feeling nostalgic?" she asked, eyeing the picture.

Meg sighed, sat down in a high-backed leather chair, facing the fireplace. "Maybe it's part of the pregnancy. Hormones, or something."

Eve, always practical, threw off her coat, draping it over the back of the sofa, marched to the fireplace and started a crackling, cheerful blaze. She let Meg's words hang, all that time, finally turning to study her daughter.

"Are you happy, Meg? With Brad, I mean?"

When it came to happiness, she and Brad were constantly charting fresh territory. Learning new things about each other, stumbling over surprises both profound and prosaic. For all of that, there was a sense of fragility to the relationship.

"I'm happy," she said.

"But?" Eve prompted. She stood with her back to the fireplace, looking very ungrandmotherly in her tailored slacks and silk sweater.

"It feels—well—too good to be true," Meg admitted.

Eve crossed to drag a chair closer to Meg's and sit beside her. "You're holding back a part of yourself, aren't you? From Brad, from the marriage?"

"I suppose I am," Meg said. "It's sort of like the first day we were allowed to swim in the pond, late in the spring, when Jesse and Rance and Keegan and I were kids. The water was always freezing. I'd stick a toe in and stand shivering on the bank while the boys cannonballed into the water, howling and whooping and trying to splash me. Finally, more out of shame than courage, I'd jump in." She shuddered. "I still remember that icy shock—it always knocked the wind out of me for a few minutes."

Eve smiled, probably remembering similar swimming fests from her own childhood, with another set of McKettrick cousins. "But then you got used to the temperature and had as much fun as the boys did."

Meg nodded.

"It's not smart to hold yourself apart from the shocks of life, Meg—the good ones or the bad. They're all part of the mix, and paradoxically, shying away from them only makes things harder."

Meg was quiet for a long time. Then she said quietly, "Angus is gone."

Eve waited.

"I miss him," Meg confessed. "When I was a teenager, especially, I used to wish he'd leave me alone. Now that he's gone—well—every day, the memories seem less and less real."

Eve took her hand, squeezed. "Sometimes," she said very softly, "just at twilight, I think I see them—Angus and his four sturdy, handsome sons—riding single-file along the creek bank. Just a glimpse, a heartbeat really, and then they're gone. It's odd, because they don't look like ghosts. Just men on horseback, going about their ordinary business. I could almost convince myself that, for a fraction of a moment, a curtain had opened between their time and ours."

"Rance told me the same thing once," Meg said. "He used different words, but he saw the riders, traveling one behind the other beside the creek, and he knew who they were."

The two women sat in thoughtful silence for a while.

"It's a strange thing, being a McKettrick," Meg finally said.

"You're an O'Ballivan now," Eve surprised her by saying. "And your baby will be an O'Ballivan, too."

Meg looked hard at her mother, startled. Eve had been miffed when Sierra took Travis's last name, and made a few remarks about tradition not being what it once was.

"What about the McKettrick way?" she asked.

"The McKettrick way," Eve said, giving Meg's hand another squeeze, "is living at full throttle, holding nothing back. It's taking life—and change—as they come. Anyway, lots of women keep their last names these days— taking their husbands' is the novelty now." She paused, studying Meg with loving, intelligent eyes. "It's what's standing in your way," she said decisively. "You're afraid that if you're not Meg McKettrick anymore, you'll lose some part of your identity, and have to get to know yourself as a new person."

Meg realized that she *was* a new person—though of course still herself in the most fundamental ways. She was a wife now, a mother-figure as well as a sister to Carly. When the baby came, there would be yet another new level to who she was.

"I've been hiding behind the McKettrick name," she mused, more to herself than Eve.

"It's a fine name," Eve said. "We take a lot of pride in it—maybe too much, sometimes."

"Would *you* take your husband's name, if you remarried?" Meg ventured.

Eve thought about her answer before shaking her head from side to side. "No," she said. "I don't think so. I've been a McKettrick for so long, I wouldn't know how to be anything else."

Meg smiled. "And you don't want me to follow in your footsteps?"

"I want you to be *happy*. Don't stand on the bank shivering, Meg. *Jump in. Get wet.*"

"Were *you* happy, Mom?" The reply to that question seemed terribly important; Meg held her breath to hear it.

"Most of the time, yes," Eve said. "When Hank took Sierra and vanished, I was shattered. I don't think I could have gone on if it hadn't been for you. Though I realize it probably didn't seem that way to you, that you were my main reason for living, you and the hope of getting Sierra back. I'm so sorry, Meg, for coming apart at the seams the way I did. For not being there for you."

"I've never resented that, Mom. As young as I was, I knew you loved me, and that the things that were happening didn't change that for a moment. Besides, I had Angus."

The clock on the mantelpiece ticked ponderously, marking off the hours, the minutes, the seconds, as it had been doing for over a hundred years. It had ticked and tocked through the lives of Holt and Lorelei and their children, and the generations to follow.

The sound reminded Meg of something she'd always known, at least unconsciously. Life seemed long, but it was finite, too. One day, some future McKettrick would sit listening to that same clock, and Meg herself would be a memory. An ancestor in a photo.

"Gotta go pick Carly up at school," she said, standing up.

Time to find Brad, she added silently, *and introduce him to his wife.*

"Hello," I'll say, as if we're meeting for the first time. "My name is Meg O'Ballivan."

Chapter 15

That late March day was blustery and cold, but there was a fresh, piney tinge to the air. Brad, Meg and Carly stood watching from a short distance as Olivia squared her shoulders, walked to the far gate, sprung the latch and opened the way for Ransom to go.

A part of Meg hoped he'd choose to stay, but it wasn't to be.

Ransom approached the path to freedom cautiously at first, the mares straggling behind him, still shaggy with their winter coats.

When the great stallion drew abreast of Olivia, he paused, nickered and tossed his magnificent head once, as if to bid her goodbye. Tears slipped down Olivia's cheeks, and she made no attempt to wipe them away. She'd arrived during breakfast that morning and said Ransom had told her it was time.

Meg, who had after all seen a ghost from childhood, didn't question her sister-in-law's ability to communicate with animals. Even Brad, quietly skeptical about such things, couldn't write it all off to coincidence.

Carly, her own face wet, leaned into Brad a little. Meg sniffled, trying to be brave and philosophical.

He put one arm around her shoulders and one around Carly's. Glancing up at him, Meg didn't see the sorrow she and Carly and Olivia were feeling, but an expression of almost transported wonder and awe.

Ransom walked through the gate, turned a little way beyond and reared onto his hind legs, a startlingly beautiful sight against the early-spring sky, summoning his mares with a loud whinny.

"I guess being in a couple of movie scenes went to his head," Brad joked, a rasp in his voice. "He thinks he's Flicka." The filming was over now, and things were settling down on the ranch, and around town. Local attention had turned to the new animal shelter, now under construction just off Main Street.

Meg's throat was so clogged with emotion, she couldn't speak. She rested her head against Brad's shoulder and watched, riveted, as Ransom shot off across the meadow, headed back up the mountain.

The mares followed, tails high.

Olivia watched them out of sight. Then, with a visible sigh and another squaring of her shoulders, she slowly closed the gate.

Meg started toward her, but Brad caught hold of her hand and held her back.

Olivia passed them by as if they were invisible, climbed

agilely over the inside fence, and moved toward her perennially dusty Suburban.

"She'll be all right," Brad assured Meg quietly, watching his sister go.

Together, Brad, Carly and Meg returned to the house, saying little.

Life went on. Willie needed to go out. The phone was ringing. Business as usual, Meg thought, quietly happy, despite her sadness over the departure of Ransom and the mares. She knew, as Brad did, and certainly Olivia, that they might never see those horses again.

"I don't suppose I could stay home from school, just for today?" Carly ventured, as Brad answered the phone and Meg started a fresh pot of coffee.

Outside, the toot of a horn announced the arrival of the school bus, and Brad cocked a thumb in that direction and gave Carly a mock stern look.

She sighed dramatically, still angling for an Oscar, as Brad had once observed, but grabbed up her backpack and left the house.

"No, Phil," Brad said into the telephone receiver, "I'm *still* not doing that gig in Vegas. I don't *care* how good the buzz is about the movie—"

Meg smiled.

Brad rolled his eyes, listening. "I am so not over the way you stuck me with Cynthia for a leading lady," he went on. "You owe me for that one, big-time."

When the call was over, though, Brad found his guitar and settled into a chair in the living room, looking out over the land, playing soft thoughtful chords.

Meg knew, without being told, that he was writing a new

song. She loved listening to him, loved being his wife. While he was still adamant about not doing concert tours, they'd been drawing up plans for weeks for a recording studio to be constructed out behind the house. Brad O'Ballivan was filled with music, and he had to have some outlet for it.

He didn't seem to long for the old life, though. First and foremost, he was a family man. He and Meg had legally adopted Carly, though he was still Brad to her, and Ted would always be Dad. He looked forward to the baby's birth as much as Meg did, and had even gone so far as to have the first sonogram framed.

Their son, McKettrick "Mac" O'Ballivan, was strong and sturdy within Meg's womb. He was due on the Fourth of July.

Meg paused by Brad's chair, bent to kiss the top of his head.

He looked up at her, grinned and went on strumming and murmuring lyrics.

When a knock came at the front door, Willie growled halfheartedly but didn't get up from his favorite lounging place, the thick rug in front of the fire.

Meg went to answer, and felt a strange shock of recognition as she gazed into the face of a stranger, somewhere in his midthirties.

His hair was dark, and so were his eyes, and yet he bore a striking resemblance to Jesse. Dressed casually in clean, good-quality Western clothes, he took off his hat and smiled, and only then did Meg remember Angus's prediction.

One of them's about to land on your doorstep, he'd said.

"Meg McKettrick?" the man asked, showing white teeth as he smiled.

"Meg O'Ballivan," she clarified. Brad was standing behind her now, clearly curious.

"My name is Logan Creed," said the cowboy. "And I believe you and I are kissin' cousins."

* * * * *

Michelle Major grew up in Ohio but dreamed of living in the mountains. Soon after graduating with a degree in journalism, she pointed her car west and settled in Colorado. Her life and house are filled with one great husband, two beautiful kids, a few furry pets and several well-behaved reptiles. She's grateful to have found her passion writing stories with happy endings. Michelle loves to hear from her readers at michellemajor.com.

Books by Michelle Major

Harlequin Special Edition

Crimson, Colorado

Anything for His Baby
A Baby and a Betrothal
Always the Best Man
Christmas on Crimson Mountain
Romancing the Wallflower
Sleigh Bells in Crimson
Coming Home to Crimson

HQN

The Magnolia Sisters

A Magnolia Reunion
The Magnolia Sisters
The Road to Magnolia
The Merriest Magnolia

Visit the Author Profile page
at Harlequin.com for more titles.

A BABY AND A
BETROTHAL

Michelle Major

To the Special Edition readers.
You are the best ever and I feel blessed
to be part of your world!

Chapter 1

It was pretty much a given that a first date was a disaster when getting ready for it had been the best part of the evening.

Katie Garrity picked at the pale pink polish on her fingernails as she tried to look interested in the man sitting across from her. Owning a bakery was tough on her hands, so she'd tried to make them look more feminine tonight. She'd blown out her hair, applied makeup and even worn a dress and heels. All to look datable, the kind of woman a man would want to marry and have babies with. Her stomach squeezed at the time and effort she'd wasted. Or maybe it was her ovaries clenching.

Her date tapped his fingers on the table and her gaze snapped to his. "I have a couple of friends who are on gluten-free diets," she said, hoping she was responding to the question he'd asked. "I've been working on some recipes that would appeal to them."

"I'm talking about more than gluten-free." Her date shook his head. "I mean a full overhaul to a raw-foods diet. You would not believe how fast your colon cleans out when—"

"Got it," Katie interrupted, looking over his shoulder for the waitress. The man, Mike, the project manager from nearby Aspen, had already given her too many details on what happened to his digestive system after a few bites of bread.

Why had she agreed to this date in the first place?

Because one of her customers had offered to set her up, and Katie wanted a date. A date that might lead to more, might give her the future she so desperately craved but couldn't seem to manage on her own.

She knew almost everyone in her hometown of Crimson, Colorado, but her popularity hadn't helped her love life in recent years. Men might be addicted to the pastries she created in her bakery, Life is Sweet, but that was where their interest in her ended.

"You should think about changing your shop to a raw-foods restaurant. The one in Aspen is doing quite well."

Katie focused on Mike, her eyes narrowing. "Are you suggesting I close my bakery? The one I inherited from my grandmother and has been in my family for three generations?" She had nothing against vegetables, but this was too much.

"Sugar could be considered a drug," Mike continued, oblivious to the fact that steam was about to start shooting from her ears. "It's like you're running a meth lab."

She felt her mouth drop open. "Okay, we're done here." She stood, pulled her wallet out of her purse and threw a few bills on the table. "Thank you for an enlightening evening. Have a safe drive back to Aspen."

Mike blinked, glanced at his watch then up at her. "Should I call you?"

"I'll be busy," she answered through gritted teeth. "Baking in my 'meth lab.'"

She turned for the bar. Although they'd met for dinner at the brewery that had opened in downtown Crimson a few months ago, Mike had insisted they both order water while droning on about the contaminants in microbrewed beer. She needed a good dose of contaminants right about now.

The doors to the brewery's patio were open, letting in fresh mountain air on this early-summer night. The days were warm in Crimson in June, but because of the altitude the temperatures dropped at night. Still, there was a crowd out front, and Katie was glad for it. Crimson was a quaint, historic town nestled at nine thousand feet deep in the Rocky Mountains, with streets lined with Victorian-era houses. Crimson attracted a fair number of visitors, and anything that brought more people into downtown was good for all the local businesses, including her bakery.

Turning back to the bar, her gaze snagged on a set of broad shoulders hunched over the polished wood. Katie felt her ovaries go on high alert. *Down, girls*, she admonished silently.

She walked closer, ordered a pale ale from the bartender and nudged the shoulder next to her. "Hey, Noah. When did you get to town?"

"Katie-bug." Noah Crawford's deep voice washed over her. Then he smiled, turning her insides to mush. Of course, she'd had this response to Noah since high school, so she was used to functioning as a glob of goo. "I got in a few days ago to see my mom. What are you doing out tonight?"

"I had a date," she mumbled, taking a drink of the beer the bartender set in front of her.

"A date?" Noah's cobalt blue eyes widened a fraction. He normally had a good six inches on her, but while sitting on the bar stool while she stood, they were the same height.

"Yes, Noah, a *date*." She grabbed a handful of nuts from the bowl on the bar and popped a few in her mouth. "It's when a man and a woman go out together in public. It usually involves more than alcohol and meaningless sex, so you might not be familiar with the term."

"Ouch." He shifted toward her, turning on the bar stool so his denim-clad knee grazed her hip. She felt the connection all the way up her body and gripped her beer glass harder, gulping down half the amber liquid.

"Did I do something to you, Bug? Because I thought we were friends. Hell, you've been one of my best friends since we were sixteen. Lately… I'm not the most observant guy, but it seems like you kind of hate me."

She took a breath through her mouth, trying to ignore the way Noah's scent—the smell of pine and spice—washed over her. "We're still friends, Noah," she whispered. "But stop calling me Bug. That was a nickname for a kid. I'm not a kid anymore."

"I know that, *Katie*." His tone was teasing and he poked her shoulder gently. "How was the date?"

"Stupid." She glanced at him out of the corner of her eye, not trusting herself to look straight at him and keep her emotions hidden. One beer and she was tipsy. She signaled the bartender for another.

Yes, she and Noah were friends, but she'd always wanted more. Noah had never acknowledged her silly infatuation. She wasn't sure he'd even noticed.

"Stupid, huh?" She felt rather than saw him stiffen. "Do I need to kick his butt? Was he out of line?"

"Nothing like that. Just boring."

"So why'd you go out with him in the first place?" The bartender brought refills for both of them. Katie watched Noah's fingers grip the pint glass. His hands were big and callused from the work he did as a division chief for the United States Forest Service. He spent his days outside, and she knew he was in great shape. She did *not* sneak a glance at the muscles of his tanned forearm as he raised the glass to his mouth. Nope, that would get her nowhere except more frustrated than she already was.

"I'm going to have a baby." She took a sip of beer as Noah choked and spit half of his beer across the bar. "I should say I want to have a baby."

"*Going* to or *want* to?" Noah pulled on the sleeve of her lightweight sweater, spinning her to face him. "There's a big difference."

She rolled her eyes. "Want to. Would I be in a bar drinking if I was pregnant now?"

"Good point." He lifted the hem of his olive green T-shirt to wipe his mouth just as she handed him a napkin. His lips quirked as he took it from her. His dark blond hair was longer than normal, curling a little at the nape of his neck. The top was messed as though he'd been running his hands through it. Which she knew he did when he was stressed. "Aren't these things supposed to happen naturally?"

"Easy for you to say." She took another drink, the beer making her stomach tingly and her tongue too loose. "You smile and panties all through the Rocky Mountains spontaneously combust."

He tilted back his head and laughed then flashed her

a wide grin. A glass shattered nearby, and Katie turned to see a young woman staring slack-jawed at Noah. "See what I mean?"

He winked at the woman then turned his attention back to Katie. "Are your panties combusting?" He leaned in closer, his mouth almost grazing her jaw.

Katie resisted the urge to fan herself. "My panties are immune to you."

"That's why we can be friends," he said, straightening again.

Katie felt a different kind of clenching than she had earlier. This time it was her heart.

"Seriously, though, why would you agree to a date with a loser?"

"I didn't know he was a loser when I agreed. I'm at the bakery by four every morning and in bed most nights by nine. My social life consists of pleasantries exchanged with customers and the occasional girls' night out."

"Have one of your girlfriends set you up."

"I've asked. They're looking." She propped her elbows on the bar and dropped her head into her hands. "Everyone is looking. It's a little embarrassing. People are coming out of the woodwork with men for me to date. I feel like a charity case."

"It's not that." His hand curled around the back of her neck, massaging the tight muscles there. It shamed her how good even such an innocent touch felt. How it ignited the rest of her body. "Locals in Crimson love you, just like they loved your grandma when she ran the bakery. You help everyone, Bug. It's time to let them return the favor."

She started to correct his use of the nickname he'd given her so long ago when he added, "You deserve to be happy."

Something in his tone made her head snap up. Through

the haze of her slight buzz, she studied him. Fine lines bracketed his blue eyes, and although they were still brilliant, she realized now they also seemed tired. The shadow of stubble across his annoyingly chiseled jaw looked not careless but as if he'd been too busy or stressed to shave.

"What's going on, Noah? Why are you in town?"

"I told you, to visit my mom."

She'd seen that look in his eyes before. A decade ago, the year his father died of cancer. "Because…"

He crossed his arms over his chest, the soft cotton of his T-shirt stretching around his biceps. He was wound tight enough to break in half. "She has a brain tumor." The words came out on a harsh breath, and she could tell how much it cost him to say them out loud. A muscle throbbed in his jaw.

"Oh, no. I'm sorry." She closed her eyes for a moment then met his guarded gaze.

For all her mixed emotions toward Noah, she loved him. Not just romantically, but deep in her soul, and she hated to see him hurting. Katie knew better than most how difficult his dad's illness had been, the toll it had taken on the entire Crawford family and Noah in particular. She reached out and wrapped her fingers around his wrists, tugging until she could take his hands in hers. Despite the beating her hands took in the bakery, they looked delicate holding his. "What can I do?"

"It's okay." He shook his head but didn't pull away. "It's called a meningioma. Based on the results of the MRI, it's benign. Apparently she'd been having symptoms for a while and finally went to Denver for an MRI. She didn't call Emily or me until she had the results so we wouldn't worry."

"That sounds like your mom." Meg Crawford was one

of the strongest women Katie had ever met. She'd seen her husband, Noah's father, Jacob, through stage-four pancreatic cancer with grace and optimism. No matter how bad things got, Meg's attitude had never wavered. "Is Emily back in town, too?" Noah's younger sister lived on the East Coast with her attorney husband and young son.

"I picked up her and Davey in Denver earlier today."

Katie had never met Emily's four-year-old son. "How long will the two of you be here? What's the treatment? Your mom's prognosis?"

"Slow down there, Bug." A hint of a smile crossed his face. "I mean Katie."

"You get a free pass tonight. Call me whatever you want." She squeezed his hand.

"I'll take her to Denver early next week for a craniotomy. They'll biopsy the tumor to confirm that it's benign. She'll have follow-up cognitive testing. The first couple of weeks are when she'll need the most help, but it'll be at least six until she's back to normal. If all goes well, it's just a matter of regular MRIs going forward."

"She'll recover completely? No long-term side effects?"

"That's what her doctor is saying now, although there are a lot of variables. The brain is complex. But she's... We're hopeful."

"She's going to be fine, Noah. Your mom is strong."

"So was my dad."

"Do you two want another round?" The bartender spoke before Katie could answer.

"Not for me." She drew her hands away from Noah's, suddenly aware of how intimate they looked sitting together. She caught the jealous glare of the woman who'd dropped her drink earlier. That woman was Noah's type, big bust and small waist—a girl who looked as if she knew how to party. Opposite of Katie in every way.

Noah followed her gaze and the woman smiled.

"Your next conquest?" Katie couldn't help asking.

"Not tonight." He stood and took his wallet from the back pocket of his faded jeans, tossing a few bills on the bar. "I'll walk you home."

"You don't have to—"

"I *want* to." He shrugged. "Sitting here drinking is doing me no good. I... I don't want to be alone right now, you know?"

She nodded. "Want to watch a movie?"

"*Elf*?" he asked, his expression boyishly hopeful.

"It's June, Noah," she said with a laugh. The two of them shared a love for all things Will Ferrell.

"Never too early for some holiday cheer."

"*Elf* it is, then."

He flashed a grateful smile and chucked her on the shoulder. "What would I do without you, Bug?"

Katie ignored the butterflies that skittered across her stomach at his words. Noah was a friend, and no matter what her heart wanted, she knew he'd never be anything more.

Chapter 2

As they walked along the street that led away from downtown, Noah couldn't think of anyone he would have been happier to see tonight than Katie. His yellow Lab, Tater, clearly felt the same way. The dog stuck close to Katie, nudging her legs every few steps. He'd adopted Tater after some hikers found the tiny puppy sick and shivering near a trailhead outside of Boulder almost five years ago. Katie had been the one to name the dog when Noah had brought the pup to Crimson for Christmas that year, saying she looked like a golden tater tot. She was still his go-to dog sitter when he traveled to DC for meetings or conferences.

Now Katie laughed as Tater trotted in front of them, flipping the tennis ball she carried out of her mouth then rushing forward to catch it again. He was relieved the tension between them had disappeared. His work for the United States Forest Service kept him busy and normally he was in the Roosevelt National Forest, about two hours east of Crimson near Boulder. He tried to get back to his hometown on a regular basis to visit his mom, but Katie recently made excuses as to why she couldn't hang out like they used to in high school and college.

Although he wasn't in town often, he loved Crimson. Tonight the sky above the mountain was awash in shades of purple and pink, soft clouds drifting over the still-snow-capped peak. At least he'd be able to enjoy the view this summer. It had been too long since he'd spent any time in the forests in this part of the state, so he tried to focus on the only positive in this whole situation with his mom's illness.

As if reading his mind, she asked, "What are you doing about your job?"

"I've been transferred temporarily to White River. I'll be running the division office out of Crimson for the summer."

"Oh." Her step faltered, and he glanced at her. "That will make your mom happy."

"But not you?"

Her smile didn't meet her eyes. "I'm swamped at the bakery right now and helping to coordinate the bake-off for the Founder's Day Festival."

"Plus you have to make time for dating all the men being offered up." A horn honked and he waved to one of the guys he'd been friends with in high school as a big black truck drove by.

"No need to make it sound like they're lambs being led to the slaughter."

"Marriage and fatherhood…" He gave a mock shiver and was rewarded with a hard punch to his shoulder. "I'm joking. Any guy would be lucky to have you."

She huffed out a breath and increased her pace, flipping

her long dark hair behind her shoulder. Now it was Noah's step that faltered. The thought of Katie Garrity belonging to another man made a sick pit open in his stomach. He wasn't lying when he said any guy would be lucky. Katie was the kindest, most nurturing person he knew.

Now, as he watched her hips sway in her jeans, he realized she was also gorgeous. The pale yellow sweater she wore hugged her curves and its demure V-neck highlighted her creamy skin. For so long she'd been like a sister to him, but the way his body was reacting to her all of a sudden made his thoughts turn in a totally different direction. He shook his head, trying to put brakes on the lust that rocketed through him. This was Katie-bug.

She wanted more than he was willing to give.

Deserved more, and he'd do well to remember that.

"Are you staying at your mom's farm?" She turned, her brows furrowing as she took in his expression.

He quickly schooled his features and took a few steps to catch up to her. "No. Tonight I'm using the garage apartment at Logan and Olivia's place. I have to spend a few days out on the trail starting tomorrow to get caught up on things in this section of the forest. There will be no nights away for me once Mom has the surgery. When I get back from this survey trip, I'll move out to the farm but..."

"You haven't stayed a night at the farm since your father died."

There were good and bad things about someone knowing you so well.

"Every time I'm there it reminds me of how much I failed him when he was sick."

"You didn't—"

"Don't make excuses. I couldn't handle watching him

die. I spent as much time away from home as possible our senior year."

"You were a kid." They turned down the tree-lined street where Katie lived. Noah had been to the house only once since she'd inherited it from her grandmother. That spoke poorly of him, he knew. He'd been a lousy son and was quickly realizing he was also a lousy friend.

"Bull. Emily had just turned sixteen when he was diagnosed. She was there, helping Mom with his care every step of the way."

"You're here now." Katie turned down the front walk of a cute wood-shingled bungalow and Noah stopped. He barely recognized her grandmother's old house.

Katie glanced back at him over her shoulder and seemed pleased by his surprise. "I made some changes so it would feel more like mine."

The house was painted a soft gray, with dark red shutters and a new covered front porch that held a grouping of Adirondack chairs and a porch swing painted to match the maroon trim. "I like it. It fits you."

A blush rose on her cheeks. "Thanks. I hope Gram would approve."

"In her eyes you could do no wrong." He followed her up the steps and waited as she unlocked the front door.

"I miss her," she said on a sigh then crossed the threshold into the house. She pointed toward the cozy family room off the front hall. "The DVDs are in the TV cabinet. Will you set it up while I get snacks together?"

Noah felt his remaining tension melt away. There was something about this house and this woman that put him at ease. Always had.

She made hot chocolate to go with the Christmas theme of the movie and brought in a plate of the bakery's famous

chocolate-chip cookies. They watched the movie in companionable silence. It was nice to forget about his life for
a couple of hours. "I can't even count the number of your
grandma's cookies I ate that last year of high school." On
the screen, Will Ferrell as Buddy the Elf was working his
magic in the movie's department-store Santa display.

Katie gave a small laugh. "Every time you and Tori had
a fight, you'd end up here or at the bakery."

Noah flinched at the name of his high school girlfriend.
The girl he'd expected to spend the rest of his life with
until she broke his heart the weekend before graduation.
"It made her even madder. Since the two of you were such
good friends, she felt like you belonged to her."

"I'd get in trouble for taking your side. Tori and I lost
touch after she left for college." Katie used her finger to
dunk a marshmallow in her mug of hot chocolate. "I've
heard her interior-design business is successful. Someone
said she was working on a project in Aspen this summer."

"Huh." That was all Noah could think to answer. He'd
purposely put his ex-girlfriend as far out of his mind as
possible for the past decade. Now, watching Katie lick
the tip of her finger, he could barely even remember his
own name. He concentrated on the television, where Santa's sleigh was flying over the rooftops of New York City.

When the movie ended, Katie flipped off the television.
His whole body was humming with desire, inappropri-
ately directed at the woman next to him, but he couldn't
seem to stop it. He didn't move, continued to watch the
dark screen that hung on the wall above the antique pine
cabinet where the DVD player sat. Clearly misunderstanding his stillness—maybe believing it had something to do
with memories of Tori or thoughts of his mother—Katie

scooted closer and placed her fingers on his arm. That simple touch set him on fire.

"If there's anything you need, Noah," she said into the quiet, "I'm here for you."

He turned, studying her face as though he was seeing her for the first time. The smooth skin, pert nose and big melted-chocolate eyes. Her bottom lip was fuller than the top, and there was a faint, faded scar at one edge from where she'd fallen out of bed as a girl. That was what she'd told him when he'd asked about it years ago, but now he wanted to know more. He wanted to explore every inch of her body and discover each mark that made her unique.

As if sensing his thoughts, she inhaled sharply. His gaze crashed into hers, and her eyes reflected the same flame of desire he felt. Had it always been there and he'd been too blind to notice it? Now he couldn't see anything else.

But this was Katie, and her friendship meant something to him. More than any of his casual flings. She mattered, and despite his raging need for her, Noah didn't want to mess this up. Which was how it worked with him—as soon as a woman wanted more than he was capable of giving, he bailed.

He couldn't do that with Katie, but would he be able to offer her anything more?

He lifted his hand, tracing his thumb across her bottom lip. "Katie," he whispered, "I want to kiss you right now."

Her eyes widened a fraction and he expected her to jump up or slap away his hand. To be the voice of reason when he couldn't.

Instead she leaned forward, her eyes drifting shut as he moved his hand over her face then wound his fingers through her mass of thick hair. His own eyes closed, anticipating the softness of her lips on his. They flew open again when she nipped at the corner of his mouth then traced her tongue along the seam of his lips.

Although he didn't think it was possible, his need for her skyrocketed even more. Where the hell had Katie Garrity, who claimed not to have time for a social life, learned to kiss like this? He pulled her against him, deepened the kiss further and fell back against the couch, taking her with him.

His hands ran down her sweater before hiking up the hem so he could touch her skin. He smoothed his callused palms up her back until he felt the clasp of her bra strap under his fingers. With one quick movement, he unhooked the clasp.

He felt Katie giggle against his mouth. His hands stilled as she lifted herself on her elbows, amusement mingling with the desire in her eyes. "Somehow, I knew you'd be good at that."

"At unhooking a bra?"

She nodded, her tone teasing. "Loads of experience, I imagine."

To his embarrassment, Katie didn't have to imagine. Noah made no secret of the fact that he loved women. He'd had more than his share of no-commitment flings and one-night stands, many of which Katie had witnessed, at least from a distance. Now he felt a niggling sense of shame that he traded quantity for quality in his relationships with the opposite sex. Once again, the thought that Katie deserved better than him filled his mind.

He shifted and she sat up, straddling his hips in a way that made it hard to do the right thing. "Maybe we shouldn't—"

She pressed her hand over his mouth. "I want to know

what else you're good at, Noah." Her voice caught on his name, and the fingertips touching his lips trembled.

Before he had time to form another halfhearted protest, Katie yanked up her sweater and whipped it over her head, taking her unfastened bra along with it. She held her arms over her breasts.

"You are beautiful," he said softly, amazed that he hadn't noticed it before. "Drop your hands, Katie."

She did as he asked, revealing herself to him. He covered her with his hands, running his thumbs across her nipples and hearing her sharp intake of breath as he did.

He leaned forward and pressed his mouth to her puckered skin as she pulled off his T-shirt. He shucked it off and drew her to him once again, flipping her onto her back then easing his weight onto her. "The bedroom," he managed on a ragged breath.

"Here, Noah," she said against his mouth. "Now."

Katie watched as Noah dropped to his knees next to the couch and tugged on the waistband of her jeans, undoing the button and pulling the fabric, along with her underpants, down her hips. She wasn't sure where she'd got her courage in the past several minutes. Stripping off her sweater as Noah watched? That was totally unlike her.

But when Noah had said he wanted to kiss her, something in Katie's world shifted. It was all she could ever remember wanting, and there was no way she was going to let this moment pass her by, no matter how out of her element she felt. She knew if she revealed her doubts and insecurities, Noah would stop. The women she'd watched him choose throughout the years were experienced and worldly, able to keep up with him and his desires. Katie found that what she lacked in experience, she made up for in the magnitude of wanting him. It made her bold, and she wasn't about to let this night end now.

She bit down on her bottom lip as his jeans and boxers dropped to the floor. She hadn't seen his bare chest since the summer after college and Noah had filled out every bit of the promise his younger body had held. He was solid muscle, broad shoulders tapering to a lean waist and strong legs. She tried to avoid looking too closely at certain parts of him—big parts of him—afraid she'd lose her nerve after all.

A tiny voice inside her head warned her this was a mistake. Noah had been drinking and he was an emotional wreck between worry over his mother and memories of his father. The thought that she might be taking advantage of him slid through her mind and she fervently pushed it away. If anyone was destined to be hurt in this situation, it was Katie. Yet she couldn't stop.

He pulled a wallet from the back pocket of his jeans and took out a condom before tossing the wallet onto her coffee table. He sheathed himself as he bent toward her again. "You're going to hurt that lip biting it so hard," he said, drawing her attention back to his face.

"Give me something better to do with my mouth," she told him, amazed at her own brazenness.

His answering smile was wicked and he kissed her again, his hand sliding along her hip then across her thighs. She loved his hands on her, warm and rough. He seemed to know exactly how much pressure she wanted, how to make her body respond as though she'd been made for him. His fingers brushed her core and she squirmed then let herself sink into the sensation he evoked. She moaned, gasped then shifted, arching off the sofa as his rhythm increased.

"Not enough room," she said on a gasp, flinging her hand toward the edge of the sofa.

"You're so ready, Katie." Noah kicked at the coffee table with one leg, shoving it out of the way then rolling off the couch, pulling her with him onto the soft wool rug as he went. They fell in a tangle of limbs and he eased her onto her back once more, cradling her face in his big hands as he whispered her name. "I want you so much."

"Yes, Noah. Now." She grabbed on tight to his back, loving the feel of his smooth skin and muscles under her hands. He slid into her and for a moment it was uncomfortable. It had been an embarrassingly long time since she'd been with a man. Then it felt good and right. Perfect like nothing she could have ever imagined. Noah groaned, kissed her again then took her nipple between his fingers. It was enough to send her over the edge. She broke apart, crying out his name as he shuddered and buried his face into the crook of her neck.

A long time later, when their breathing had slowed and she could feel the sweat between them cooling, he placed a gentle kiss against her pulse point then lifted his head.

Katie was suddenly—nakedly—aware of what they'd done, what she'd instigated. How this could change their friendship. How this changed *everything*.

"I guess practice *does* make perfect," she said softly, trying to show with humor that she was casual and cool.

"*You* make it perfect," Noah answered, smoothing her hair away from her face.

Her eyes filled with tears before she blinked them away. How was she supposed to keep cool when he said things like that? When he looked at her with something more than desire, deeper than friendship in his gaze? He might as well just open up the journal she'd kept for years and read all her secret thoughts.

He reached up and grabbed the light throw that hung over the back of the couch. He wrapped it around them both, turning on his side and pulling her in close. "But the floor? I should be ashamed of myself taking you like this. You should be worshipped—"

"I feel pretty worshipped right now," she said, running her mouth across his collarbone. "I like being with you on the floor."

"Then you'll love being with me in bed," he answered. He stood, lifting her into his arms as he did, and carried her down the hall to her bedroom.

Chapter 3

Katie blinked awake, turning her head to look at the clock on her nightstand. 3:30 a.m. She woke up every morning at the same time, even on her day off. Her internal clock was so used to the extreme hours of a baker, they had become natural to her.

But today something was different. She wasn't alone in bed, she thought, shifting toward where Noah slept beside her. Except he wasn't there. The empty pillow was cool to the touch. It had been only a couple of hours since he'd made love to her a second time, then tucked her into his chest, where she'd fallen asleep.

She sat up and thumped her hand against her forehead. That was exactly the kind of thinking that would get her into trouble. Noah hadn't *made love* to her. They'd *had sex*. An important distinction and one she needed to remember. She knew how he operated, had heard enough gossip around town and witnessed a few tearful outbursts by women he'd loved then left behind.

Still, she hadn't thought he would be quite so insensitive when it came to her. Love 'em and leave 'em was one thing, but they were supposed to be friends. She climbed out of bed, pulling on a robe as she padded across the hardwood floor. Her limbs felt heavy and a little sore. She found herself holding her breath as she made her way through the dark, quiet house. Maybe Noah hadn't been able to sleep and had come out to the kitchen. Maybe he hadn't rushed from her bed the moment he could make an easy escape.

The rest of her house was as empty as her bedroom. He'd put the coffee table back and straightened the cushions on the couch. Without the aches from her body and the lingering scent of him on her, Katie wouldn't quite have believed this night had happened. She'd imagined being in his arms so many times, but nothing had prepared her for the real thing or the pit of disappointment lodged deep in her gut at how the morning after dawned.

She glanced at the glowing display on the microwave clock and turned back for her bedroom. There was no time for prolonged sadness or a free fall into self-pity. It was Friday morning and she had the ingredients for her cherry streusel coffee cake waiting at the bakery.

She had a life to live, and if Noah didn't want to be a part of it, she had to believe it was his loss. She only wished that knowledge could make her heart hurt a little less.

When Noah climbed out of his Jeep four days later, he was hot, sore and needed a shower.

It was a perfect early-summer day in Colorado, clear blue skies and a soft breeze. The weather had been great on the trail, too, and normally Noah would have relished the time in the forest. As he'd climbed the ranks of the United States Forest Service, more of his time was spent in meetings and conference rooms than outside. Since he'd be town-bound once his mom had her surgery and started treatment, he'd taken the opportunity to check out a trail restoration project on the far side of Crimson Pass. He didn't want to think about the other reasons he might have disappeared into the woods for a few days—like worry over his mom's health or what had happened between him and Katie the night before he'd left.

Because if he'd wanted to escape his thoughts, he should have known better than to try to do it with the silence of the pristine forest surrounding him. It was as if the rustling of the breeze through the tall fir trees amplified every thought and feeling he had. Most of them had been about Katie. The tilt of her head as she smiled at him, the way her lips parted when he was buried inside her, the soft sounds she'd made. He'd been consumed by visions of her, catching the sweet smell of vanilla beneath the pine-scented air around his tent.

He knew he should have talked to her before he left. Hell, he had the start of two different notes wadded up in the glove compartment of the Jeep. But he hadn't got more than a few words past *Dear Katie* either time. She was worth more than pat lines and unconvincing excuses as to why he couldn't stay. As much as he wanted her, he should have never given in to his desire. Katie wanted more than he would ever be able to give her.

Maybe he'd left like a coward because he wanted to prove to both of them that, despite his best intentions, he couldn't change who he was. She wasn't a one-night stand, although that was how he'd treated her. Regret had been his faithful companion during his time on the mountain.

Katie had always seen more in him than most people, and the worry of ruining their friendship weighed heavily. He owed her an explanation, and that was the first thing on his agenda this morning. After getting cleaned up.

"Do you smell as bad as you look?" a voice called from behind him.

He turned to see his friend Logan Travers coming down the back steps of the house he shared with his wife, Olivia. It was midmorning, and Logan held a stainless-steel coffee mug and a roll of paper—no doubt construction plans for one of his current renovation projects.

"Probably." Noah hefted his backpack from the Jeep's cargo area. Tater jumped out and trotted over to Logan, rolling onto her back so that Logan could access her soft belly.

Shifting the plans under his arm, Logan bent and scratched. "You made someone very happy taking off like that."

Noah's gaze snapped to Logan before realizing that his friend was talking about the dog. "She loves being out on the trail."

"A perfect match for you."

Noah didn't like the idea that the only female he could make happy was of the canine variety. "Thanks for letting me use the garage apartment." He took the rest of his supplies from the backseat and set them near the Jeep's rear tire. He'd need to air everything out once he got to his mom's house. "I'm going to pack up later and head out to the farm. Emily will want to skin me alive for showing up at the last minute."

Logan straightened, ignoring the thump of Tater's tail against his ankle. "The surgery is tomorrow."

Noah gave a curt nod in response.

"I've cleared my schedule so if you need company in the waiting room I can be there."

"No need." Noah tried to make his tone light, to ignore the emotions that roared through him when he thought of his mother's scheduled five-hour surgery. "There won't be much to do except…"

"Wait?" Logan offered.

"Right." He slung the backpack onto one shoulder. "I appreciate the offer, but I'm sure you have better things to do than hang out at the hospital all day."

"We're friends, Noah. Josh and Jake feel the same way," he said, including his two brothers. "Not just when it's time to watch the game or grab a beer. If you need anything, we're here for you."

"Got it." Noah turned away, then back again. It was difficult enough to think about being there, let alone with his friends, who knew him as the laid-back, fun-loving forest ranger, an identity he'd cultivated to keep people in his life at a safe distance. A place where they couldn't hurt him and he wouldn't disappoint anyone. But he was quickly realizing that being alone wasn't all it was cracked up to be when life got complicated. "I'll call tomorrow and update you on her condition. If you want to swing by at some point, that would be great."

Logan reached out and squeezed his shoulder. "Will do, man."

He waited for his friend to offer some platitude about how everything would be okay, the clichéd phrases of support he'd grown to resent during his dad's illness. But Logan only bent to pet Tater behind her ears before turning for his big truck parked in the garage.

Noah headed for the steps leading up to the garage apartment, letting out a shaky breath as he did. He'd like to run back to the forest, to hide out and avoid everything that was coming. But his mom needed him. He owed it to her, and he'd made a promise to his father over ten years ago to take care of the family. He hadn't been called on to do much more than change an occasional lightbulb or fix a faucet drain until now. This summer would change that, and during his few days away he'd realized who he wanted by his side as he managed through all of it.

He walked into Life is Sweet forty-five minutes later and inhaled the rich scent of pastries and coffee. The morning crowd was gone, but the café tables arranged on one side of the bakery were still half-full with couples and families.

Crimson was the quirky, down-home cousin to nearby Aspen and benefited from its proximity to the glitzy resort town when it came to tourism. That and the fact that the town was nestled in one of the most picturesque valleys in the state. He knew the bakery was popular not only with locals, but also with people visiting the area thanks to great reviews on Yelp.

His gaze snagged on Katie, bent over a display of individually wrapped cookies and brownies near the front counter. Today she wore a denim skirt that just grazed her knees, turquoise clogs that gave her an extra inch of height and a soft white cotton T-shirt with a floral apron tied around her waist. He wanted nothing more than to run his hand up the soft skin of her thighs but didn't think she'd appreciate that in the middle of her shop or after how he'd left her.

Her hair was tied back in a messy knot, a few loose tendrils escaping. The scent of her shampoo reached him as he approached, making him want her all the more.

"Hey, gorgeous," he whispered, trailing one finger down her neck.

"What the—" She whipped around and grabbed his finger, pinning it back at an angle that made him wince.

"It's me, Bug," he said through a grimace.

"I know who it is," she said, lessening the pressure on his hand only slightly. "Your free pass is over, Noah. Don't call me Bug. Or gorgeous." She leaned closer. "I'm not interested in your bogus lines. What you did was lousy. We were friends and now…" Her voice broke on the last word and she dropped his hand, turning back to the cookies. "Lelia's taking orders today." She nodded her head toward the young woman at the register. "If you want something, talk to her."

"What I *want* is to talk to you." He reached out, but she moved away, stepping behind the counter, her arms now crossed over her chest. He knew he'd messed up leaving the way he had but didn't think Katie would be this angry. There was nothing of the sweetness he usually saw in her. The woman in front of him was all temper, and 100 percent of it was directed at him. "Let me explain."

"I know you, Noah. Better than anyone. You don't have to explain anything to me. I should have seen it coming." She waved a hand in front of her face, bright spots of color flaming her cheeks. "Lesson learned."

"It wasn't like that." He moved closer, crowding her, ignoring the stares of the two other women working behind the counter and the sidelong glances from familiar customers. "Being with you—"

"Stop," she said on a hiss of breath. "I'm not doing this here."

"I'm not leaving until you talk to me."

* * *

Katie huffed out a breath but grabbed his arm and pulled him, none too gently, through the swinging door that led to the bakery's industrial kitchen. She'd prepared herself for this conversation for the past four days. Actually, she'd wondered if Noah would even try to talk to her or if he'd just pretend nothing had happened between them. Maybe that would have been better because prepared in theory was one thing, but having him in front of her was another.

Her heart and pride might be bruised by the way he'd walked away, but her body tingled all over, sparks zinging across her stomach at the way he'd touched her—at least until she'd almost broken his finger. She had to keep this short, or else she'd be back to melting on the floor in front of him.

Once the door swung shut again, she released him and moved to the far side of the stainless-steel work counter that dominated the center of the room.

Suddenly Noah looked nervous. Which didn't seem possible because he was never nervous, especially not with women. "I'm sorry," he said simply, as if that was all he had to offer her.

"Okay," she answered and began to rearrange mixing bowls and serving utensils around on the counter, needing to keep her hands busy.

"Okay?"

"Fine, Noah. You're sorry and you don't want me to be mad at you." An oversize pair of tongs clattered to the floor. She bent to retrieve them then pointed the tongs in his direction. "You've apologized. I've accepted. You can go now."

"What if I don't want to go?"

"You sure weren't in a hurry to stick around the other

night." She tossed the tongs into the sink across from the island. "How long after I fell asleep did you sneak out? Ten minutes?"

Her eyes narrowed when he didn't answer. "Five?" she said, her voice an angry squeak.

"I didn't sneak out," he insisted. "You have to get up early and I didn't want to wake you." He leaned forward, pressing his palms on the counter's surface, his dark T-shirt pulling tight over his chest as he did. "You knew I was heading out on the trail for a few days."

Her mouth went dry, and she cursed her stupid reaction to Noah Crawford. His hair was still damp at the nape of his neck and she could smell the mix of soap and spice from his recent shower. He'd got more sun while in the woods, his skin a perfect bronze, and there was a small cut along one of his cheeks, like a branch had scraped him. Despite her anger, she wanted to reach out and touch him, to soothe the tension she could see in his shoulders. She had to get him out of her bakery before her resolve crumbled like one of her flaky piecrusts.

"I get it. But I was disappointed in you…" He flinched when she said the word *disappointed*, but she continued. "Mainly, I'm furious with myself." She lowered her arms to her sides, forced herself to meet his blue eyes. "I know who you are, how you treat women. I shouldn't have expected it would be any different with me."

He shook his head. "You are different—"

"Don't." She held up one hand. "We've been friends too long for you to lie to me. It was one night and it was good."

One of his brows shot up.

"Great," she amended. "It was great and probably just what I needed to bolster my confidence."

"Your confidence?"

"My confidence," she repeated, suddenly seeing how to smooth over what had happened between them without admitting her true feelings. "It had been...a while since I'd been with a man. Truthfully, I was kind of nervous about how things would go...in the bedroom." She forced a bright smile. "But now I feel much better."

"Are you saying I was a rehearsal?"

"For the real thing." She nodded. "Exactly."

"That didn't seem real to you?" His gaze had gone steely, but Katie didn't let that stop her.

"What's real to me is wanting a husband and a family." She bit down on her lip. "Great sex isn't enough."

"And that's all I'm good for?"

"You don't want anything else." She fisted her hands, digging her fingernails into the fleshy part of her palms. "Right?"

He didn't answer, just continued to stare. So many emotions flashed through his gaze.

"This is a difficult time for you. I went to see your mom yesterday."

"I talked to her on the way here," he answered on a tired breath. His shoulders slumped as if he carried a huge weight on them. "She told me."

"She's worried about you and Emily. About the toll this will take on both of you."

Noah scrubbed one hand over his face. "Did you meet Emily's son?"

"Davey?" Katie nodded. "I did."

"Then you know Em's got her hands full."

"You both will after tomorrow."

"We'll get through it. I'm sorry, Katie," he said again. "Disappointing the people I care about is something I can't seem to help."

"I'm fine. Really." She stepped around the counter. "I need to get back out front. There will be enough talk as it is."

"Mom's cooking lasagna tonight. She insisted on a family dinner before her surgery." He lifted his hand as if to touch her then dropped it again. "Would you join us? She thinks of you as part of the family."

"I can't." She offered a small smile. "I have a date tonight."

She saw him stiffen, but he returned her smile. "You really do deserve a good guy." He shut his eyes for a moment, and when he opened them again his mask was firmly back in place. This was the Noah he showed to the outside world, the guy Katie didn't particularly like—all backslapping and fake laughter.

As if on cue, he gently chucked her shoulder. "If this one gives you any trouble, he'll have to deal with me." He turned and walked out to the front of her shop, leaving her alone in the kitchen that had been her second home since she was a girl.

Katie stood there for several minutes, trying to regain her composure. She was too old for girlish fantasies. She'd held tight to her secret crush on Noah for years, and it had got her nowhere except alone. She *did* deserve a good man, and no matter how much she wanted to believe Noah could be that man, he clearly wasn't interested.

It was time she moved on with her life.

Chapter 4

"Do you want another glass of milk?" Noah's mother was halfway out of her chair before she'd finished the question. "More salad?"

"Mom, sit down." Noah leaned back in his chair, trying to tamp down the restlessness that had been clawing at him since he'd moved his duffel bag into his old room at the top of the stairs. "You shouldn't have gone to so much trouble, especially the night before your surgery. You need to rest."

His mother waved away his concerns. "I'll have plenty of time to rest during my recovery. I want to take care of the two of you..." His mom's voice broke off as she swiped at her eyes. "To thank you for putting your lives on hold for me. I'm so sorry to put this burden on either of you."

A roaring pain filled Noah's chest. His mother, Meg Crawford, was the strongest person he knew. She'd been the foundation of his family for Noah's whole life. Her love and devotion to Noah's late father, Jacob, was the stuff of legend around town. She'd been at her husband's side through the diagnosis of pancreatic cancer and for the next year as they'd tried every available treatment until the disease finally claimed him. She'd been the best example of how to care for someone Noah could have asked for. As difficult as it was to be back in this house, he owed his mother so much more than he could ever repay in one summer.

He glanced at his sister, whose gaze remained fixed on the young boy sitting quietly next to her at the table. Something had been going on with Emily since she'd returned to Crimson with her son. Normally she would have rushed in to assure their mother that everything was going to be fine. That was Em's role. She was the upbeat, positive Crawford, but there was a change in her that Noah didn't understand.

He cleared his throat. "We want to be here, Mom. It's no trouble. *You* are no trouble." That sounded lame but it was the best he could do without breaking down and crying like a baby. The surgeon had reassured them of the outcome of tomorrow's surgery, but so many things could go wrong. "It's all going to be fine," he said, forcing a smile as he spoke the words. "Right, Em?"

Emily started as if he'd pinched her under the table, a trick he'd perfected at family dinners and during Sunday church services when they were growing up. She focused her gaze, her eyes the same blue color their father's had been, first on Noah then on her mother. "Of course. You're going to get through this, Mom. We're all going to get through it together. And we're happy to spend a summer in Colorado. Henry's family will be in Nantucket by now. The beach is great, except for all that sand. Right,

Davey?" She ruffled her son's hair then drew back quickly as he pulled away.

"Can I play now, Mommy?" Davey, Emily's four-year-old son, stared at his plate. He looked like his father, Noah thought. He'd only met his brother-in-law, Henry Whitaker, the weekend of Emily's wedding in Boston four years ago, but he knew Davey got his thick dark hair from his father. The boy's eyes, however, were just like Emily's. And his smile... Come to think of it, Noah hadn't seen Davey smile once since they'd arrived in Colorado.

Emily's own smile was brittle as she answered, "You've barely touched your meatballs, sweetie. Grandma made them from scratch."

"Don't like meatballs," Davey mumbled, his dark eyes shifting to Noah's mom then back to his plate. He sucked the collar of his T-shirt into his mouth before Emily tugged it down again.

"Not everyone likes meatballs," Meg told him gently. Noah couldn't think of one person who didn't like his mother's homemade meatballs and sauce but didn't bother mentioning that. "I think it would be fine if you went to play, Davey. If you're hungry later, I'll make you a bowl of cereal or a cheese sandwich."

Before Emily could object, the boy scrambled off his chair and out of the room.

"He can't live on only cereal, cheese and bread," Emily said with a weary sigh. She picked up the uneaten spaghetti and passed it to Noah. "No sense in this going to waste."

Noah wasn't going to argue.

"When you were a girl, there was a month where you ate nothing but chicken nuggets and grapes. Kids go through stages, Emily."

"It's not a stage, Mom, and you know it. You know——"

Noah paused, the fork almost to his mouth, as Emily looked at him then clamped shut her mouth. "What does she know?" He put the fork on the plate and pushed away the food. "What the hell am I missing here? Is Davey homesick?"

Emily gave a choked laugh. "No."

"Then what gives?" Noah shook his head. "I haven't seen you since last summer but he's changed. At least from what I remember. Is everything okay with you and Henry?"

"Nothing is okay, Noah."

Emily's face was like glass, placid and expressionless. Dread uncurled in Noah's gut. His sister was always animated. Whatever had caused her to adopt this artificial serenity must be bad.

"Davey started having developmental delays in the past year—sensory difficulties, trouble socializing and some verbal issues." Meg reached out for Emily's hand but she shook off their mother's touch, much like her son had done to her minutes earlier. "I wanted to get him into a doctor, figure out exactly what's going on and start helping him. Early intervention is essential if we're dealing with…well, with whatever it is. But Henry forbade it."

Noah took a deep breath and asked, "Why?" He was pretty sure he wouldn't like the answer.

Emily folded the napkin Davey had left on his seat. "He said Davey was acting out on purpose. He started punishing him, yelling at him constantly and trying to force him to be…like other kids." She shook her head. "But he's not, Noah. You can see that, right?" Her tone became desperate, as if it was essential that he understand her son.

"I can see that you love Davey, Em. You're a great

mother. But where does that leave your marriage? You also loved Henry, didn't you?"

"I don't know how I feel," Emily said. "You have no idea what would have happened if I'd stayed. Henry is going to run for Congress next year. The Whitakers are like the Kennedys without the sex scandals. They're perfect and they expect perfection from everyone around them. Davey was... Henry couldn't handle the changes in him. I had to get him away from there. To protect him. Our divorce was finalized a month ago."

"Why haven't you come home before now?" Noah looked at his mother. "Did you know?"

Meg shook her head. "Not until a few weeks ago."

"And neither one of you had the inclination to tell me?"

The two women he cared about most in the world shared a guilty look. "We knew you had a lot going on, that it was going to be difficult for you to stay here for the summer," his mom answered after a moment. "Neither of us wanted to add any more stress to your life. We were trying to protect you, Noah."

He shot up from the table at those words and paced to the kitchen counter, gripping the cool granite until his fingertips went numb. "I'm supposed to protect you," he said quietly. He turned and looked first at his mom then his little sister. "Dad told me to take care of you both."

"Noah." His mother's tone was so tender it just about brought him to his knees. "Your father didn't mean—"

He cut her off with a wave of his hand. "Don't tell me what he meant. He said the words to *me*." It was the last conversation he'd had with his father and he remembered everything about it in vivid detail. Hospice workers were helping to care for his dad in the house and a hospital bed had been set up in the main-floor office. His memories of those last days were the reason he'd spent so little time in his parents' house since then. Everything about this place, the smells, a shaft of light shining through the kitchen window, reminded him of his dad's death. He thought he'd hid his aversion to home with valid excuses—his work, travel, visiting friends. But it was clear now that Katie hadn't been the only one to understand his cowardice.

"I'm here," he told them both. "Now and for the long haul. Don't hide anything from me. Don't try to *protect* me. I don't need it. If we're going to get through this it has to be together."

His mom stood and walked toward him, her eyes never wavering from his. The urge to bolt was strong but he remained where he was, took her in his arms when she was close enough and held her tight. "Together," she whispered.

He looked at his sister across the room. "Come on over," he said, crooking a finger at her. "You know you want to."

With a sound between a laugh and a sob, Emily ran across the room and Noah opened up his embrace to include her, too. He'd made a lot of mistakes in his life, but he was at least smart enough to try to learn from them. His first lesson was sticking when things got tough. Nothing like starting with the hard stuff.

"I want you to tell me more about Davey," he said against Emily's honey-colored hair. "What he needs, how to help him."

He felt her nod, and then her shoulders began to shake with unshed tears. His mother's crying was softer, but he heard that, too.

Noah tightened his hug on the two of them. "We can get through anything together," he said, lifting his gaze to the ceiling and hoping that was true.

* * *

"I had a good time tonight."

Katie glanced at the man sitting in the driver's seat next to her and smiled. "I did, too. Thank you for dinner."

"It was smart to choose a restaurant outside of town. We got a little privacy that way. Everyone seems to know you around here." Matt Davis, the assistant principal and swim-team coach at the local high school, returned her smile as he opened the SUV's door. "I'll walk you to your door."

"You don't have to—" she began, but he was already out of the Explorer.

He was a nice guy, she thought, and their date had been fun—easy conversation and a few laughs. Matt was relatively new to Crimson. He was a California transplant and a rock-climbing buddy of her friend Olivia's husband, Logan Travers. It was Olivia who'd given Matt her number. He was cute in a boy-next-door kind of way, medium height and build with light brown hair and vivid green eyes. He'd been a semiprofessional athlete in his early twenties and had trained briefly at her father's facility near San Diego. Now he seemed safe and dependable, although he'd made a few jokes during dinner that made her think he didn't take life too seriously.

She liked him, a lot more than her carb-police date from Aspen last week. And if her stomach didn't swoop and dip the way it did when she looked at Noah, it was probably for the best. Katie didn't want head-over-heels passion. She was looking for a man she could build a life with, and although this was only a first date, Matt Davis had definite potential.

He opened her door and she stepped out onto the sidewalk in front of her house. Bonus points for being a gentleman. She'd left on the front porch light and stopped when they came to the bottom of the steps, just outside the golden glow cast by the Craftsman-inspired fixture. She could hear the sounds of her neighborhood, a dog barking in the distance and music playing from the rental house at the end of the block.

For a moment she debated inviting Matt in for a drink, not that she had any intention of taking this date too far, but it had been nice. *He* had been nice. Something stopped her, though, and she didn't dwell too long on the thought that Noah had been the last man in her house or why she might not want to let go of her memories of that night.

"Thank you again," she said, holding out her hand. That was appropriate, right? Didn't want to give him the wrong impression of the kind of girl she was.

He shook it, amusement lighting his eyes. He really did have nice eyes. There was that word again. *Nice.* "I hope we can do it again sometime," he said, still holding her hand.

A dog whined from nearby. A whine Katie recognized, and she went stiff, glancing over her shoulder toward the darkness that enveloped her house.

Misunderstanding her body language, Matt pulled away. "If you're not—"

"I'd love to," she said on a rush of air. "See you again, that is."

He brightened at her words, placed his hands gently on her shoulders. "I'll call you, then." He leaned closer and Katie's eyes shut automatically then popped open again when the crash of a garbage can reverberated from her side yard.

Matt jumped back, releasing her once more.

"Probably just a bear," she said, her eyes narrowing

at the darkness. "They can be *annoying* sometimes." Her voice pitched louder on the word *annoying*.

"Do you want me to take a look?" Matt asked at the same time he stepped back. It took a while to get used to the wildlife that meandered into mountain towns, especially for those who'd moved to Colorado from the city. Besides, Katie had no intention of allowing him to discover exactly what—or who—was lurking in her side yard.

"It's fine." She crossed her arms over her chest. "I keep the regular can in the garage. There's nothing he can mess with over there. I'd better go in, though. Early morning at the bakery."

Matt kept his wary gaze on the side of her house. "I had a great time, Katie. I'll call you soon. You should get in the house." He flashed a smile but waited for her to climb the steps before turning to his Explorer.

Katie waved as he drove away. She stood there a minute longer until his taillights disappeared around the corner. Blowing out a frustrated breath, she tapped one foot against the wood planks of the porch. "You can come out now," she called into the darkness. A few seconds later, Tater trotted onto the porch, tail wagging. Katie bent and scratched the dog's ears. Tater immediately flipped onto her back.

"Slut," Katie whispered as she ran her fingers through the Lab's soft fur. She didn't want to think about how much she had in common with Tater, since Katie's instinct was to beg for loving every time she thought about Noah. Even at her angriest she wanted him, which made her more pathetic than she was willing to admit.

She commanded herself to *woman up* as Noah hopped onto her porch and leaned against the wood rail.

"Are you afraid to come any closer?" she asked, straightening. Tater flipped to her feet and headed into the box spruce bushes that ran along the front of the house.

"Should I be?" His voice was low and her body—stupid, traitorous body—immediately reacted. The darkness of the night lent a sort of intimacy to their exchange that Katie tried her best to ignore.

She forced herself not to look at him standing in the shadows. She was stronger than she had been a week ago, committed to moving on from her silly girlhood crush. The fact that the object of that crush had just crashed a very promising first date was irrelevant. "What are you doing here, Noah?"

"Protecting you."

She huffed out a laugh. "From a really nice guy who might actually be interested in me?" She turned for the house, opening the screen door. "Excuse me if I forget to thank you."

Her fingers had just touched the door handle when Noah was beside her, reaching out to grab her wrist. "I'm sorry," he whispered, releasing her when she tugged away from his grasp. "I *did* want to make sure you were okay."

"Why wouldn't I be?"

"I don't know." He raked his fingers through his blond hair, leaving the ends sticking out all over. It should have made him look silly, but to Katie it was a reminder of running her own hands through his hair when he'd held her. "I've been a lousy friend, and this isn't my place. I've told you I can't give you what you want. We both know that. But…you're *alone* here, Katie."

Her lungs shut down for a second as sharp pain lanced through her at his words. Then she gasped and his gaze met hers, a mix of tenderness and sympathy that had her blinking back sudden tears. He knew, she realized. Her biggest fear, the one nobody recognized because she kept it so hidden. As busy as she was, as much as everyone in this community needed her, at the end of the day Katie was alone. Alone and afraid that if she didn't make herself useful, they'd toss her aside. It was irrational, she knew, but she couldn't seem to stop herself from believing it. Without the bakery and her volunteering and offers to help wherever it was needed, where would she be? Who would want her—who would love her—if she didn't have something to give them?

Could Noah possibly understand? And if he did, how could she ever look at him again?

He paced to the edge of the porch and back. "When was the last time you saw your parents?"

Her mouth dropped open and she clapped it shut again. "Two summers ago. They had a layover in Denver. Dad had just finished an Ironman in Europe."

"They didn't come to Crimson?"

She shook her head. "He wanted to get back to his business. His coaching business has exploded in the past few years. He still races but spends more time training other elite athletes." He continued to watch her, so she added, "Mom and Dad haven't been here since my grandma's funeral."

"So no one in your family has seen the changes you've made to the bakery? How successful you've made it."

"It was successful when Gram ran it."

"Not to the level it is now. Do your parents have any idea?"

"They wanted me to sell the shop and the house after Gram died. Mom never liked me working at the bakery. You know that." She smoothed a hand across her stomach. "She didn't think it was good for me to be near all that sugary temptation. She was afraid I'd get fat again."

"You weren't fat."

She almost smiled, but the memory of so many years of being ashamed about her weight and having every mouthful of food analyzed by her mother drained any wistful humor she felt about the past. "You don't remember when I first moved to Crimson. By the time you started dating Tori in high school, I was halfway to the goal weight my parents set for me."

"I remember you just fine." Noah shrugged. "I just never saw you like that."

Katie suppressed a sigh. Was it any wonder she'd fallen in love with him back then? She bit down on her lip, forcing herself to keep the walls so newly erected around her heart in place. "You never saw me at all."

As if he needed that reminder, Noah thought, as Katie's words hung in the air between them. He should walk away right now. It had been a stupid, impulsive idea to show up at her house when he knew she had a date. He had no business intruding on her life.

"I'm a jackass, Katie-bug," he said with a laugh then cringed when she didn't correct him. "But I wasn't lying when I said I wanted you to be happy. I came here because... I guess it doesn't matter why. I want to be a better friend if you'll let me." He shut his eyes for a moment, clenched his fists then focused on her. "Even if that means vetting your dates for you."

She arched one eyebrow, a look so out of place and yet so perfect on her he had to fight not to reach for her again.

"Matt Davis is a good guy."

Her eyes narrowed. "How do you know my date's name?"

"I asked around." He shrugged. "I'm sorry if I cut your night short. I'm sorry I keep doing things that make me have to apologize to you." He flashed a smile. "Good night, Katie."

He stepped around her onto the porch steps.

"Noah?"

He turned. His name on her tongue was soft. The same tenderness that had annoyed him earlier from his mother now made him want to melt against Katie. To beg her not to give up on him.

"I'll be praying for your mom tomorrow." She wrapped her arms tight around herself as if she was also trying to hold herself back. "And you."

He gave a quick jerk of his head in response then took off into the night. He couldn't stand there and let her watch his eyes fill with tears. Her kindness slayed him, made him want and wish for things that weren't going to be. Even now, as he moved down the quiet street, Tater's breathing soft at his side, he wanted to run. The feelings that had bubbled to the surface at his mom's house earlier were still churning inside of him. It was part of what had driven him to Katie tonight.

After his mom and Emily had gone to bed, the farm-house had been so quiet that Noah's mind had gone into overdrive. Thinking and remembering. Two pastimes he'd tried like hell to avoid the past decade. His job kept him moving and he surrounded himself with friends—and women—during his downtime. Noah was always up for a good time as long as there were no strings attached. It was what had affected his friendship with Katie. Like his mom, she wanted more from him. She knew the serious stuff, the demons that haunted him, and it had been easier to keep her at arm's length than to see himself fail at living up to her expectations.

But he couldn't run any longer. He was tethered to this town and to the women in his life by an unbreakable, invisible thread. He wasn't sure whether he had it in him to become what each of them needed, but it was past time he tried.

Chapter 5

The next morning dawned far too early. Noah moved on autopilot as he drove his mother along with Emily and Davey toward Denver. His mom tuned the radio to her favorite station, all of them silent as music filled the SUV. He expected Emily to initiate some sort of conversation, but when he glanced at her in the rearview mirror, all her attention was focused on Davey watching a movie on his iPad. Normally the winding drive down into the city calmed Noah, but he hardly noticed the scenery. His mom worked quietly on her knitting until they arrived at the hospital.

She'd already had her pre-op visit and filled out most of the paperwork, so it was only a short wait at registration before she was admitted. They stayed with her until she was moved to the OR, emotion lodging in Noah's throat as she kissed his cheek.

"I love you, Mom," he called as they wheeled her through the double doors.

She waved, her smile cheery as she disappeared.

He felt Emily sag against him and wrapped one arm around her shoulders. "She's going to be fine."

His sister's response was to punch him lightly in the stomach. "I know you're as scared as I am. Don't act like you aren't."

He sighed and closed his eyes, allowing his fear to wash through him for just a moment, testing how it felt, how much of it he could handle. When the feelings rose up and threatened to choke him, he forced them down again. "I'm acting like I believe she's going to make it through this, Em. I can't stomach the alternative right now."

"That's fair," she answered softly. "We *will* get through this."

"I need to go potty," Davey announced. The boy stood just a foot away from them, his arms straight at his sides, his gaze fixed on the linoleum squares of the hospital's tiled floor.

"Let's go, then, little man." She glanced at Noah with a halfhearted smile.

"I'll be in the waiting room." He watched his sister guide Davey around the corner toward the restrooms, and then he turned and made his way down the hall to the surgical waiting area.

A man stood as he approached. "What are you doing here?" Noah asked.

Jason Crenshaw shrugged. "Where else would I be?" He stepped forward and gave Noah a quick hug. "Meg is the closest thing to a mom I had. You're like a brother to me. Of course I'm here."

Jase had been Noah's best friend since they started second grade, assigned to sit next to each other alphabetically. Noah hated to admit how many tests he'd passed by looking over his friend's shoulder. Jase had been smart, motivated and intent on doing the right thing all the time—a perfect teacher's pet and the exact opposite of Noah. But the two had forged an unlikely bond that had seen them through both good times and bad.

Like Katie, Jase saw past his good-old-boy act. Unlike Katie, most of the time he let Noah get away with it. Although Jase hadn't been athletic as a kid, he'd grown into his body and now stood an inch taller than Noah's own six foot two. Whenever Noah was in town, he and Jase would find time for some type of extreme outdoor activity—rock climbing in the summer and fall or backcountry snowboarding in the winter. With Jase's dark hair and glasses covering his hazel eyes, they didn't look like family, but Jase had always felt like a brother to Noah.

But he'd purposely kept his communication with Jase to texts and voice mails this trip. Jase had been raised by an alcoholic single father and had spent many afternoons, most weekends and even one extended stay with Noah's family when his dad had finally ended up doing jail time after too many DUIs. Noah knew their close relationship should have made him reach out to Jase, but instead the idea of sharing his pain with his friend had been too much.

Now he realized he'd probably hurt Jase by not including him—another fence to mend during his time in Crimson.

"I'm sorry I haven't—"

"No apologies," Jase interrupted. "You get to deal with this however works for you. But I'm going to be here one way or another."

Noah bit the inside of his cheek and nodded. "I'm glad."

"How's your mom holding up?" Jase asked as Noah sat in the chair next to him. The waiting room was almost empty at this early hour, only an older man in a far corner reading the newspaper. That should be his father, Noah thought with a sense of bitterness. His dad should be here now, and the old loss tugged at him again.

"She's a trouper, like always. She's happy to have Emily and me under her roof again, even if it's for such an awful reason."

"Emily's here, too?"

Noah glanced up at his friend's sharp tone. "She came in last week with her son."

"What about her husband? The politician, right?"

"I hear you're the local politician now." Both men looked at Emily, who walked up to where they sat, Davey following close at her heels but still not touching her.

Jase scrambled to his feet. "Hey, Em." He shoved his hand forward and ended up poking Emily in the stomach as she leaned in to hug him.

Noah hid a smile as his sister grunted, rubbed at her belly and stepped back.

"Sorry about that," Jase mumbled, reaching one of his long arms to pat her awkwardly on the shoulder. "It's good to see you, but I'm sorry this is the reason for your visit." He continued to thump her shoulder until Emily finally pulled his arm away.

Noah cringed for his buddy. Jase's crush on Emily was well-known to everyone but Noah's sister. She'd never seen him as anything but one of Noah's annoying friends.

He thought about Katie and how feelings could change in an instant. Still, he couldn't imagine his lively, sophisticated sister with a hometown boy like Jase. Emily had always wanted more than Crimson could offer, even more so after their father died. But life didn't always pan out the way a person expected. The gauzy circles under his sister's eyes were a testament to that.

"It's nice of you to be here, Jason," Emily said in a tone Noah imagined her using at fancy society dinners where she'd lived with Henry in Boston. "And congratulations on your success in Crimson. I'm sure you'll make a great mayor."

Color rose to Jase's neck. "The campaign's just started, but I'm cautiously optimistic."

Emily glanced at Noah. "We know that feeling."

"Is this your son?" Jase crouched down to eye level with Davey. Noah saw Emily's eyes widen and wondered what he'd missed. "What's your name, buddy?"

"Davey, say hello to Mr. Crenshaw." Her voice was wooden as she threw Noah a helpless look. Davey continued to hide behind her legs.

"Hey, Jase," Noah said quickly. "Tell me more about your plans for the campaign. Maybe I can help while I'm home."

Jase glanced up at Noah then straightened. Emily took the opportunity to duck away, leading Davey over to the far side of the waiting area and taking out a LEGO box from the shopping bag slung over her shoulder.

"She really doesn't like me," Jase muttered. "Something about me literally repels her. Always has."

"It's not like that." Noah placed a hand on his friend's back. "She's dealing with a lot right now."

Jase's gaze turned immediately concerned. "Like what? Is she okay? Is that East Coast prick treating her right?"

Noah squeezed shut his eyes for a moment. This was the last conversation he wanted to have right now, and he couldn't share Emily's story with Jase anyway. It wasn't his to tell.

He looked at Jase again, ready to offer an excuse and change the subject, when something made him glance down the hospital's hall. Katie walked toward him, balancing a large picnic basket in her arms. She wore a pale blue sundress and a yellow cardigan sweater over it. A well-worn pair of ankle-high boots covered her feet, and the few inches of pale skin between the top of the leather and the hem of her dress were the sexiest thing he'd ever seen. Her hair was swept up, tiny wisps framing her face. He caught her eye and she gave him a sweet, almost apologetic smile.

He stepped forward, heart racing, to greet her.

"Sorry I wasn't here earlier," she said, lifting the basket. "I wanted to bring—"

Before she could finish, he grabbed the picnic basket from her hands, set it on the ground and wrapped his arms tight around her. He buried his face in her hair, smelling the sugar-and-vanilla scent that was uniquely hers. With Katie in his arms, a sense of peace flooded through him. Suddenly he had hope—for his mom and for himself. Everything else melted away, from his sister's hollowed eyes to Jase's unwanted concern. He'd deal with everything. But all that seemed to matter at the moment was that Katie hadn't given up on him.

Katie tried to keep her heart guarded as the warmth of Noah's big body seeped through her thin sweater and dress. She hadn't even been sure she should come to the hospital today after how their last conversation had ended.

But she'd known his family forever and she wasn't the type of person to desert a friend in need, even if it took a toll on her emotions. Who was she kidding? She couldn't possibly have stayed away. People in need were Katie's specialty. She'd gone extra early to the bakery this morning to make fresh scones and sandwiches for later. Food was love in her world, and she was always ready to offer her heart on a plate—or in a picnic basket.

But Noah dropped the food to the floor as if it didn't matter. Right now, he was holding on to her as though she was his rock in the middle of a stormy sea. Funny that for years she'd wanted to be that person for Noah, but he'd been unwilling to look at life as anything but a continual party. Now that she'd decided to give up on her unrequited love for him, he wanted her for something more.

For how long? she couldn't help but wonder. Even as his breath against her neck made her stomach dip and dive, she could already see the ending. His mom would make it through the surgery—there was no question in Katie's mind about that. And as soon as Meg recovered fully, Noah would go back to his party-boy ways and leave Katie and Crimson behind once again.

She knew he was friends with many of the women he'd dated over the years. In his heart, he loved women—all women—he just couldn't commit to one. When things got serious, he'd move on. Yet Katie'd always been amazed at the warmth between him and most of his former flames. It was impossible to remain angry with Noah for long. He couldn't help who he was. But Katie had to keep the truth about him fresh in her mind so she wouldn't make what was happening between them into something more than it was.

When she caught both Jase and Emily staring at them, she pulled away, quickly picking up the picnic basket and holding it in front of her like a shield. "Is everything okay?" she asked, thinking maybe there was a reason for his uncharacteristic display of affection toward her. "Have you heard something?"

He glanced at the clock hanging above the elevator doors across the hall and shook his head. "It's too early. The doctor estimated close to five hours for the surgery." His blue eyes were intense as he looked back at her. "Thank you for coming. It means…a lot to me."

She swallowed, her throat dry. Why did she ever think she could keep her heart out of the equation with this man? As much as she wanted to support Noah and his family, this was dangerous territory for her. "I wanted to bring by some food. There's breakfast and lunch in here."

"Katie, I—"

"By breakfast, I hope you mean something you baked this morning." Jase Crenshaw stood and moved forward, as if he could sense how hard this was for Katie. Jase was one of the nicest guys she knew, and at this moment, Katie appreciated the rescue.

"Cranberry-orange-and-cinnamon scones," she answered with a smile, beginning to lift the cover off the basket.

"Thanks." Noah quickly took it from her and handed it to his friend. "Here you go, Jase. Give us a minute."

Jase took the basket and Katie clenched her palms together in front of her stomach, feeling exposed without something separating her from Noah. She gave a small wave to Emily, who nodded but stayed with her son on the floor in one corner of the waiting room.

Jase peeked in the basket. "Looks and smells delicious, Katie."

"There are paper plates and napkins on the bottom." She took a step around Noah but he grabbed her wrist.

"A minute," he said again to Jase, who lifted his brows but turned away with the basket of food.

As if realizing he was holding on to her in a way that seemed almost proprietary, Noah released her arm. "You didn't have to bring the food."

She flashed a bright smile. "Have you eaten anything today?"

He looked at her for a long moment before shaking his head.

"You have to keep up your strength for your mom. She's going to need you."

"I need…" he began then shook his head. "You're right, as usual."

"Josh and Logan are planning on coming down later. They don't want you and Emily waiting here alone."

"Logan told me, but they don't have to do that."

"They're your friends, Noah. They want to be here." She gestured to where Jase stood with Emily. "I'm glad Jase is with you. He cares about your family a lot."

Noah continued to watch her, as if anticipating her next words.

"I only wanted to drop off the food. I have some things for the bakery I need to pick up in Denver and—"

"Stay."

Her lips parted as he breathed out the one word, as if she could catch the air whispering from his lungs. "You don't—"

"I don't want your food, Katie." He stopped, ran one hand through his thick blond hair. "It was sweet and generous of you to bring the basket of stuff. I'm sure it will help while we're waiting. But I want… I need…" His gaze slammed into hers and she almost took a step back at the intensity in his blue eyes before he blinked and shuttered his emotions once more. "Just stay," he whispered.

"Okay," she answered and could almost feel the tension ease out of him. His shoulders relaxed and he flashed her his most charming smile.

He put his arm around her shoulders and led her toward the chairs where he and Jase had been sitting. It was as if he thought she might make a run for it if he didn't hold on to her.

She couldn't have walked away if she wanted to, not when he was finally giving her a glimpse into the soul she knew he kept hidden behind his devil-may-care mask. Even if she ended up with her heart crushed, this was where she belonged right now. It wouldn't change her future, she told herself fiercely. This momentary vulnerability didn't make Noah a long-term type of guy. But if he would take what she was able to give him right now, that would be enough. She'd move on with her life when this was finished, find a nice man and live as happily ever after as she could manage. Right now she was going to follow her heart.

And her heart had always belonged to Noah.

Chapter 6

By the time the doctor came out almost four hours later, the waiting room was filled with Noah's friends. Jase was still there, helping Emily's son to build an elaborate LEGO structure on the floor. Logan and Josh Travers had arrived an hour earlier. Josh was sprawled on one of the small couches in the waiting room while Logan paced the hallway. Each time a hospital staff member walked through the doors to the OR, all conversations and movement in the waiting room stopped. So far there'd been no word on Meg.

Katie had expected Noah to leave her in order to hang out with his friends. His normal role was the jokester of the group, and she figured he had plenty of steam to let off during these hours of waiting. Instead, he'd stayed by her side or kept her near him when he got up to pace the hall. Even now, he sat silently staring at the ceiling, and while none of his friends had left, they'd given up on pulling him into any sort of conversation.

Katie shrugged her shoulders at the questioning glance Jase threw her from across the room. She'd never seen Noah so quiet, and unfortunately, Katie wasn't the type to fill the silence with light conversation. As she shifted in her chair, Noah's hand took her wrist in a vise-like grip.

"Where are you going?" he asked, his voice hoarse. His fingers gentled, his thumb tracing a circle over the pulse point on the inside of her wrist.

"Nowhere." She moved again. "My foot fell asleep from crossing my legs too long."

"Give it to me." Noah smoothed his palm down her dress and over her thigh, inching up the fabric between his fingers.

"Stop," Katie squeaked. She swatted away his hand, color rising in her cheeks as everyone in the waiting room turned. "Noah, what are you doing?"

He looked baffled. "Give me your foot. I'll massage it until it's back to normal."

She swallowed. "In the middle of the hospital? Are you crazy?"

To her surprise, he seemed to ponder the question seriously. "I don't know, Bug. But I can tell you sitting here without a damn thing to do is testing my sanity."

"Noah," she whispered, reaching up to place her hand against the rough stubble darkening his jawline. Their friends were still watching, but she didn't care. "We'll hear something soon."

As if she'd conjured him, an older man in blue scrubs came through the double doors that led to the operating rooms. Noah jumped to his feet and both he and Emily rushed forward.

"How is she?" Noah asked as Emily added, "When can we see her?"

"Your mother is a strong woman," the doctor told them. He glanced at the crowd of people gathering behind the two, but didn't comment. "The surgery was a success. We did an initial scan in the OR and it appears we were able to remove all of the tumor without impacting any of her nerve centers. We'll do a biopsy and will have to rescan once the swelling goes down. Plus she'll still need a course of radiation to make sure it's totally gone." He paused, took a breath, scrubbing his fingers over his eyes. "But it's a positive outcome. The best we could have hoped for."

As a cheer went up from the assembled group, Katie watched Noah's shoulders rise and fall in a shuddering breath. Logan and Josh patted him on the back and high-fived each other.

Emily started to cry, wiping furiously at her cheeks even as she laughed. "I cry at everything these days."

Katie noticed Jase take a step forward then stop himself.

"Can we see her?" Emily asked again, her voice more controlled.

The doctor glanced from Emily to where Davey still sat on the carpet with his LEGO bricks. "Yes. They're moving her up to the Neuro ICU now. Come with me and the nurses will take you. But no children allowed."

"I'll stay with him," Jase offered immediately. He folded his long legs down to the carpet. "We can't stop in the middle of the construction project anyway." He picked up a handful of colored blocks.

Emily looked as if she wanted to argue, but Noah took her hand. "Just for a few minutes," he said, "so we can see that she's really okay."

She turned to Jase, almost reluctantly. "Thank you," she whispered and followed Noah and the doctor toward the double doors.

Katie watched, knowing she should get her things and leave before they got back. Although it felt wrong, she loved being here for Noah when he needed her. But his mom had made it through surgery, and she'd served her purpose. She had people covering at the bakery all day, but it wouldn't hurt to check in.

She saw Noah say something to the doctor then turn back as the physician and Emily disappeared through the double doors. He walked toward her, his expression unreadable until he took her face in his hands. The look in his eyes was at once tender and fierce, as if he couldn't quite figure out his own feelings.

Katie opened her mouth to speak, but he pressed his lips to hers. The kiss was gentle yet possessive, and there was no confusion in it. He pulled back after a moment and whispered, "Thank you for getting me through today."

As he walked away, a strange silence descended on the waiting room. Katie felt the stares from Josh, Logan and Jase. She shook her head, pressing her fingers to her lips and not making eye contact with any of them. "I don't want to talk about it," she said, then gathered her purse and the picnic basket and hurried toward the elevator.

Katie glanced at the clock on the wall behind the bakery's counter as a demanding knock sounded on the door. They'd been closed for almost an hour, and she was alone in the empty shop.

The urge to ignore the group of women she could see gathered on the sidewalk in front of the bakery was strong, but it would only postpone the inevitable. In truth, she was surprised it had taken them this long to descend.

She turned the lock on the door and opened it, plastering a smile on her face. "Why do I feel like I'm being visited by *Macbeth*'s Three Witches?" she asked as she stepped back to allow the women to enter.

Sara Travers, Josh's wife, was the first to enter. "Nice reference. Going classic with Shakespeare. I like it." Sara not only helped Josh run a guest ranch outside of town, but she was a Hollywood actress who was enjoying a resurgence in her career in the past few years.

Natalie Donovan followed her. Another Crimson native, Natalie and she had forged a true friendship in the past few years, despite not having been close growing up. Until she reconnected with her high school sweetheart, Liam Donovan, Natalie had been a divorced mom raising her son by herself. Katie had helped with babysitting nine-year-old Austin on a regular basis but didn't see him as often now that Natalie and Liam were married and Nat wasn't working so many hours and juggling multiple jobs.

"Do you have brownies?" Natalie asked as she threw Katie a "what were you thinking?" glance. "We're going to need chocolate for this conversation."

"I left a plate on top of the display counter." Katie had anticipated this visit.

The last woman in their trio was Millie Travers, who had married the eldest Travers brother, Jake, earlier this year. "Olivia says not to pay attention to Natalie," she told Katie, giving her a quick hug after she shut the door. "She's been having morning sickness all day long, otherwise she would be here."

"Poor thing," Katie murmured as she followed Millie to the table where Natalie had set the brownie plate. "I'll text her later and see if I can bring her anything."

She didn't pretend to wonder why her friends had come today. "It wasn't my fault," she told them, focusing on

Sara and Millie, who were more likely to be sympathetic than Natalie.

Of course, it was Nat who answered. "Right. His mouth just ran into yours."

"It wasn't like that," Katie murmured, sinking into a chair. She pointed a finger at Natalie. "And I won't share my sweets if you're mean."

With an exaggerated eye roll, Natalie snagged a brownie off the plate. "I'm never mean."

Millie snorted as Sara filled water glasses from the pitcher on the counter. "It was probably just a strange reaction to stress. You and Noah have always been just friends, but today had to be hard on him."

"I saw plenty of people dealing with stress when I worked at the nursing home." Natalie broke off a piece of brownie. "They didn't start making out with their friends in the hallway."

Katie gasped. "We weren't making out. It was… I don't know what it was."

"A reaction to stress," Millie said firmly.

"A mistake?" Sara's tone was gentle.

"A kiss from the guy you've been in love with since high school." Natalie didn't form her response as a question, and while the other women stared, she sucked a bit of chocolate off her finger then pointed at Millie and Sara. "You two may be newer to town, but you can't ignore our girl's feelings for the ever-gorgeous man-boy Noah."

Man-boy. Katie almost snorted at that description but didn't bother to deny Natalie's assessment. It was pathetic that so many people knew about her crush on Noah when he'd always been oblivious. Even if he had been interested in settling down, Noah was way out of her league, another fact she'd pushed aside when he'd wrapped his arms around her. Now she could imagine the reaction from the locals. Noah was well-known for dating gorgeous, wild women. There was no shortage of those on the outskirts of a fancy ski town like Aspen. Katie didn't fit that bill. "I'm an idiot," she muttered, dropping her head into her hands.

"Josh said Noah kissed you." Sara placed four waters on the table and sat in the last empty chair. "The way he described the scene, I would have loved to be there."

"How did he describe it?" Katie asked, trying not to cringe as she lifted her gaze to meet Sara's.

"Well…" Sara answered with a smile. "He said it was 'pretty crazy,' and Josh has seen plenty of crazy, so that's a big deal for him. I don't think any of the guys saw it coming."

"Join the club," Katie said. "They probably think I'm a slut."

All three of her friends laughed. "You are the least slutty woman in Crimson," Millie told her.

"Only on the outside." Sometimes Katie hated her sainted reputation. The pressure to live up to what people thought about her could be enough to drive her crazy. "If you knew what I was thinking and feeling on the inside…"

Natalie wiggled her eyebrows. "Which is?"

"That I'd like to get Noah into the bedroom." She reached for a brownie and added, "Again."

"Again?" three voices chorused.

Katie ignored the heat rising in her cheeks, both from revealing the secret to her friends and from the memory of Noah's hands all over her body. "We didn't plan it the first time, and I know it was a mistake based on his reaction."

"Let me guess." Natalie pushed back in her chair. "He freaked out."

"Took off into the woods for several days," Katie said with a nod. "He couldn't handle it."

"I don't know him well," Sara said, "but it doesn't seem like Noah does long-term relationships."

"Noah's idea of *long term* is a second date," Natalie confirmed.

Millie placed a gentle hand on Katie's wrist. "And you're ready to settle down with the right guy. That's the whole reason for Project Set Up Katie."

"I'm a project? That's depressing."

"Not if it gets you the future you want," Sara argued.

"Unless what you want has changed," Natalie suggested. "Because I thought you were moving on from how you feel about Noah. You know he's not the type of guy to settle down. You want hot sex, I bet he can serve that up on a silver platter. Nothing more, Katie."

"I get it," she agreed then paused. "But if you saw how he looked at the hospital, how alone he was… He needs more in his life than a string of one-night stands. He needs…"

"You?" Sara asked.

Before she could answer, Natalie sat forward. "No. He needs to grow up and take responsibility for his own stuff. You've been available to him for years, and he suddenly realizes you're there just when his mom is sick and he's back in Crimson for the summer. Too much of a coincidence for my taste."

"But if she cares about him, maybe this is the opportunity they've needed." Millie absently brushed the brownie crumbs into her palm. "Maybe she's what Noah needs."

"Of course she is," Natalie agreed. "Any guy would be lucky to have our Katie. But he doesn't deserve her."

"Stop talking like I'm not here." Katie stood abruptly

and grabbed the empty brownie plate. "I know all about Noah. I know he's not a long-term bet, but I do care about him. I can't turn that off. It doesn't matter anyway. He has me on such a pedestal, he couldn't handle something real between us."

"Does that mean more kissing and stuff?" Sara asked with a wink.

"Or does it mean no more dates with other men?" Millie asked. "Because Olivia had high hopes for Matt Davis."

"Matt is a great guy." Katie walked behind the counter and set the plate in the sink. "I told him I'd go out with him again."

"And Noah?"

She shook her head. "No more kissing and stuff. You're right. I want something more. Something Noah is unwilling and unable to give me."

Millie looked as if she wanted to argue, but Natalie spoke first. "I'm glad that's settled. Which one of the guys is nominated to straighten out Noah?"

"I'll handle Noah." Katie flipped off the lights behind the counter and checked to make sure all of the baked goods were put away for the night.

Millie stood and gave Katie a tight hug. "Speaking of needing you," she said with a hopeful smile, "any chance you're free on Saturday to keep Brooke for the night? Jake and I are supposed to go to Denver. Sara and Josh have a family reunion arriving to the ranch, and with Olivia not feeling well…"

"I'd love to watch her. We'll have a girls' night."

"Are you still able to help with the brunch at the ranch on Sunday morning?" Sara asked.

"Sure," Katie answered automatically. "I'll bring Brookie with me to deliver everything. She'll love it."

"Thanks, sweetie." Millie gave her another hug. "What would we do without you?"

"I hope you'll never have to find out." She grabbed an envelope off the counter. "Can I give these to you?" she asked Sara. "They're the Life is Sweet donations for the Founder's Day Festival." Sara was chairing the silent-auction portion of the event.

"Gift cards for the bakery?" Natalie looked interested. "Perhaps a year's worth of brownies delivered to my door?"

Katie laughed. "A couple of gift certificates for merchandise," she explained. "Also a private baking lesson for a group of up to six friends." She pointed to Natalie. "In case you ever want to learn to make your own brownies."

Nat mock shuddered. "I pride myself on helping to keep you in business."

"But Katie *gives* you the brownies half the time," Millie pointed out with a smile.

"Only half the time," Natalie said.

"Thanks for these." Sara hugged Katie. "We can always count on you."

The statement was true and normally comforting. Today it gave her an empty feeling in the pit of her stomach. She didn't say this to her friends, though. She was the even-keeled, dependable one in their group. They didn't need another reason to worry about her. Katie hated the feeling of being any kind of burden, especially emotional, on someone else.

Satisfied she wasn't headed down a dark and crazy path with Noah, the three women said goodbye and headed out into the late-afternoon sunshine.

Katie finished checking things in the shop then stood staring at the baked goods tucked away in the refrigerated display cabinet. For the first time in as long as she could remember, she had the almost uncontrollable urge to open up the glass and stuff as many cookies in her mouth as would fit.

She took a couple of deep breaths, but the smell of sugar and vanilla that permeated the air of the bakery didn't help suppress her craving. She quickly locked up the store and started walking away from Crimson's town center, where Life is Sweet was located. There was a bike path along the edge of town, next to the bubbling Crimson Creek, and she made her way to the crushed gravel path. It would take her longer to get home on this route, but she counted on the familiar sound of the water to help smooth her tumbling emotions.

When she and her parents had first moved to Crimson, her dad was still competing in Ironman triathlons and other distance sporting events. Katie had felt as out of her element in the small mountain town as she did in her own family. The only thing her mother had ever been dedicated to in life was Katie's father. Monica Garrity didn't have much use for her family's small bakery or her sweet, unassuming mother who ran it. But she'd liked the convenience of being able to leave Katie with her grandma so she could travel with Katie's father, Mike, as he competed and trained.

Neither of her parents could accept the fact that Katie hadn't inherited either their natural athleticism or their need for adrenaline. Katie had eaten to stuff down the feelings she had of being unworthy to even be a part of her immediate family, although she hadn't known that was why she was doing it back then. All she'd understood was being in her grandma's kitchen, both at Gram's house and in the bakery, felt like where she belonged.

But when her weight had become too much of an issue

for her mother to ignore, Monica had threatened to ban Katie from Life is Sweet so she wouldn't be tempted to overindulge. Katie had quickly learned to limit her weakness for bingeing on baked goods and had found that it made her a better apprentice baker. When she wasn't constantly shoving food in her mouth, she actually appreciated the flavors more. Katie's time in the bakery had always bothered her mother, but once she lost the extra weight there wasn't much of an argument Monica could give to keep her away.

Although the scale and mirror might not reflect it, Katie still felt like the same chubby girl she'd been so many years ago. She'd traded stuffing her own face for giving her baked goods away to friends and for charity events, like the Founder's Day silent auction. But when her emotions threatened to get out of hand, food was always the first place she turned for comfort.

Add that to the growing list of reasons to stay clear of Noah. She liked being in control of her emotions. Mostly. Sometimes the pressure of always being stable, friendly and ready to lend a helping hand was too much. She'd chosen this, as clearly as she'd decided to take the bike trail back to her house. Straying from her path now would be very messy. And Katie wasn't one for mess.

Chapter 7

Noah spent two nights at the hospital with his mother before she finally sent him away.

"I love you, Noah," Meg said from where she was propped up against several pillows, flipping through a gardening magazine. "But you're making me nervous with all that pacing." As was her habit at home, she woke early in the hospital. Much of the normal color had returned to her face and they'd removed the bandage from her head. The angry red of the scar from her surgery was beginning to fade to a lighter pink color already.

"I'm not pacing," he countered and forced himself to stop moving back and forth across her small room.

"And you smell," she added, folding back the page of an article she wanted to keep. One of his trivial but vivid memories from childhood was the stack of magazines always piled in the corner of his mother's bedroom, all with folded pages she'd never look at again. She'd saved them for years, from magazines she looked at during road trips and throughout the endless hours she spent on the sidelines of the various sports he played as a kid. The morning after his father's funeral, she'd emptied out her entire bedroom, packing up his dad's clothes to donate and loading stack after stack of magazines into the back of the pickup truck to be recycled. He remembered watching in numb silence, too swept up in his own sorrow to either stop her or offer to help.

It was odd to watch her with a magazine again.

He started to argue about his need for a shower then lifted his T-shirt and took a whiff. She was right. "I'll drive up to the farm, shower and come back. Tater is fine out at Crimson Ranch, but I don't want you to be alone here for too long."

"That's at least five hours round-trip. It's too much. Emily texted a few minutes ago. She and Davey are on their way. She got a hotel room in Denver for the night." His mother let the magazine fall to her chest and sighed. "I'm worried about her, Noah."

"She's fine," he answered, although he didn't believe that was true. "You need to focus on yourself."

Meg waved away his concern. "All the scans are clear. The doctor is happy with my progress. I'm going to be discharged in a few days. There will be plenty of time for your hovering once I'm back home."

"I'm not hovering." Except he was. Hovering and pacing. He couldn't seem to stop himself.

"I'm not going to die, Noah." His mother flashed a wry smile. "Not yet, anyway."

"Don't joke about that," he snapped automatically then forced himself to take a breath. "I'm sorry. I know you're going to be fine. You have to be fine."

"I think you're avoiding going back to Crimson."

He laughed, although it sounded hollow to his own ears. "That's crazy. I just don't want to leave you."

"Emily told me about the kiss."

"Emily should worry about her own problems."

"A minute ago you said she was fine."

He scrubbed a hand over his face. "If it means we don't have to talk about me, I've changed my mind."

"Katie is a good friend," his mother said, unwilling to be distracted. "She cares for you."

"But I'm too messed up to deserve her," he interrupted.

"I didn't say that."

"You're thinking it." He turned toward her then sank down on the edge of the hospital bed. "I'm thinking it. Everyone must be."

"You're my son, Noah." She nudged his hip with her foot. "I think you deserve everything you want in life."

"Thanks, Mom." He shifted closer and took her hand in his, running his fingers along the hospital bracelet that circled her wrist. His mother's hands had never been delicate. Her nails were short and rounded, the top of her palm callused from work on the farm. Maybe that was the reason women with ornately manicured nails and dainty hands always made him suspicious. Katie had strong hands, too, he realized. Still feminine, but not delicate thanks to her hours in the bakery.

"The question is, do you *want* Katie?"

"If you'd asked me that two weeks ago, I would have said you were crazy for even asking me. She was Tori's best friend all through high school. I never thought of her that way. In the years since then…"

"You're my son," his mother repeated. "But you have horrible taste in women."

"I haven't brought a woman home in years."

"No one since Tori," she agreed.

"So how do you know anything about my taste in women?"

"It's a small town. For that matter, it's a small state when it comes to gossip. I still have friends in Boulder. I hear things."

"You've been keeping tabs on me?"

She shrugged. "Worrying is what mothers do. Your father's death—"

"Has nothing to do with the women I date."

"My surgeon asked me to dinner," she said quietly, picking up the magazine again.

"Are you kidding?" Noah shot off the bed and stalked to the edge of the room, something close to panic creeping up his throat at the thought of his mom with a man who wasn't his father. "That's got to be a breach of the doctor-patient relationship. I'll file a complaint with the hospital. I'll kick his—"

"I'd like to go out with him, Noah."

His righteous indignation fled as quickly as it had come. "Why would you want to do that?" He tried and failed to keep his voice steady.

"It's been more than ten years since your dad died." Unlike his own, Meg's voice was gentle. "He was my whole world, and for a while I wished I'd died right along with him. If it hadn't been for you and Emily, I'm not sure I could have kept going." She placed the magazine on the rolling cart on the far side of the bed. "But I haven't been with a man in all this time."

Noah grimaced. "Mom, I can't have this conversation with you."

"Get your mind out of the gutter," she said with uncharacteristic impatience.

As difficult as this was for him, Noah realized it was just as hard for his mom. He owed her more than he was giving right now. This was why he was here, he reminded himself. To support her.

"I'm sorry." He walked back to the bed, pulled up a chair and sat across from her. "You want to go on a date with the doctor? I'm okay with that. Emily will be, too."

"Sweetie, I appreciate that, but it's not the point. Each of us was deeply affected by losing your father. I've spent too many years with a ghost as my only company. Emily just wanted to get away however she could. And you—"

"I tried, Mom." He interrupted her before she could delve too far into his demons. That was the last thing he needed right now. "I was going to ask Tori to marry me. I wanted to be with her forever." He shrugged, rubbed his hands along his thighs. "Before she cheated on me, that is. Maybe my reluctance to get into another serious relationship has more to do with finding my girlfriend with her naked legs wrapped—" He stopped, stood again. "I can't have this conversation, either."

Meg laughed. "I may be your mother, but I'm a grown woman. I know what teenage couples do in the back of a car."

He turned, narrowed his eyes. "How did you know I found them in the back of a car?"

"Small town," she repeated. "Don't let your father's death or what happened with Tori stop you from believing in love or your capacity for it."

"I think my track record speaks for itself."

She sighed. "I can't stop you from believing the worst

about yourself. But it's not how I see you. I don't think it's how Katie sees you, either."

"She should. I haven't done right by her."

"You can't change the past." His mother leaned back against the pillow, closed her eyes. "But you can choose how to move forward."

He thought about that for a moment then leaned forward and placed a soft kiss on her forehead. "Have you always been this smart?"

"Yes." She cracked open one eye. "Take a shower, Noah. Take Tater for a hike. Talk to Katie. I'll be fine here and I'll call if I need anything."

"I'll come back—"

"Tomorrow," she finished for him.

"Tomorrow," he agreed. "I love you, Mom."

"You too, sweetie."

He walked to the door then looked over his shoulder. "And your new Dr. Love better treat you right. I meant what I said about kicking his butt otherwise."

With his mother's smile in his mind, he walked out of the hospital to head toward the mountains.

"Have dinner with me?"

Katie whirled around from where she was stapling a flyer for the Founder's Day Festival onto the community bulletin board outside the bakery.

Noah crossed his hands in front of his face and ducked. "Maybe you want to put down the weapon before you answer."

She lowered the arm that held the staple gun. "How's your mom?" she asked, ignoring his question.

Some of the stress had eased from his face. In fact, he looked much better than he had when she'd last seen him in the hospital. Almost perfect, damn him. He wore his Forest Service uniform, and the gray button-down shirt stretched across his muscled chest while the olive-colored pants fit his long, toned legs perfectly. Okay, she needed to not think about his body. At all.

"She's good," he answered, one side of his mouth kicking up as if he could read her mind's wayward thoughts. "Healing up nicely and itching to be out of the hospital and back home. She's due to be released on Friday."

"You've been staying at the hospital?"

He gave a quick nod. "She finally got sick of me and sent me home. I need to get caught up on some paperwork at the office and thought I'd pick up a dozen cookies to take in with me."

"Lelia's working the counter," Katie told him. "She can help you. I want to hand out a few more flyers along Main Street."

"Mind if I keep you company?"

Mind if I plaster myself across your body?

"Sure." She handed him half the stack of papers in her hand. "You take this side of the street. I'll do the other and meet you on the corner."

Before he could argue, she dashed across the street, narrowly avoiding being hit by a minivan with Kansas license plates pulling out of a parking space. She heard Noah shout her name but didn't look back, ducking into the outdoor-equipment store in the middle of the block. She made a few minutes of small talk with the shop's owner then proceeded to the next storefront. She took her time, part of her hoping Noah would give out all of his flyers and leave for the Forest Service headquarters near the edge of town.

Instead he was waiting for her at the corner, leaning back against a light post with his head tilted up to the sun.

He wore his usual wraparound sunglasses and the ends of his golden hair curled at the nape of his neck. How long would she have to tell herself she'd got over him before her body believed it was true?

"Getting hit by a car is a little extreme as a way to avoid talking to me," he said as she approached.

"I didn't plan that part of it," she answered, taking the remaining flyers he handed to her. His finger brushed her wrist and she pulled back, sucking in a breath. This had to stop or he was going to drive her crazy. "What do you want, Noah?"

"You didn't answer my question about dinner." He smiled at her, a grin she recognized from years of experience. It was the devil-may-care smile he gave to women in bars, at parties or in general as he easily charmed his way into their hearts and beds. It wasn't going to work on Katie, even if her toes curled in automatic response to it.

"No."

She moved around him, looked both ways on the street and stepped off the curb.

It was only seconds before he caught up with her. "You don't mean that."

"I do."

"You can't."

"And why is that?" she asked, glancing at him out of the corner of her eye.

He was staring at her and wiggled his brows. "Because you want me."

"Wow." She shook her head, almost tripped over her own two feet. "Your ego never fails to astound."

"I want you even more." He leaned closer, his breath tickling the hair that had fallen out of her long braid. "It was too good between us. I haven't been able to stop thinking about you. The way you touched me…the sounds you made when I—"

"Stop!" She turned and pushed him away, hating the way her body had caught fire at his words. "I can't do this anymore." She crushed the flyers to her chest, as if she could ease the panic in her heart.

"So what if I want you?" She poked at his chest with one finger. "Every woman you've ever been with—and don't forget I know many of them—still wants you. You've got skills." Her eyes narrowed as she glared at him. "Unfair, maddening skills. But you're…you're…a man-boy."

"Man-boy?" His body went rigid. "What the hell does that mean?"

"We've been over this. You want a good time. I want a future. I'm not going to deny that I'm attracted to you. Eighty-year-old women and babies are attracted to you. But I want more. The only way I'm going to get it is to move on. How am I supposed to do that if I hop back into bed with you?"

"I asked you to dinner, Katie. A date. I'm not looking for friends with benefits. I could find that anywhere."

She gasped, and he cringed in response. He ran one hand through his hair, blew out a breath. "Let's start over. I'm messing this up and that wasn't part of my plan." He took off his sunglasses and the intensity of his piercing blue eyes captured her. She couldn't have moved if she'd wanted to. "Would you please have dinner with me, Katie Garrity? A real date." He smiled, but this time it was hesitant and a little hopeful.

The catch in her heart made her sure of her answer. "No," she whispered.

Noah's head snapped back as if she'd struck him. She expected him to stalk away. Noah liked his women agreeable and easy. And Katie wanted to be, not just because of her feelings for him but because she liked making people happy. She was agreeable to a fault, but somewhere inside, her instinct for self-preservation wouldn't allow her to succumb to Noah's charms. She'd promised herself she was moving on, and that was what she was going to do.

But he didn't move. He didn't speak, just continued to stare at her as if she was a puzzle he wanted to solve.

"I'm going out with Matt again," she offered into the silence. Katie hated awkward silences. "You and I are friends, Noah. That's how it's been for years and it's worked just fine."

"Has it?" He reached out and rubbed a loose strand of her hair between two fingers. She shivered. "I'm not sure—"

"Well, isn't this cozy," a voice said from behind Noah.

His hand dropped at the same time Katie felt her stomach pitch and roll.

He flipped his sunglasses down before turning away from her. "Hey, Tori," he said to the woman glaring at the two of them. "Welcome back to Crimson."

Noah wanted to see his ex-girlfriend at this moment like he wanted to be stuck on the side of a mountain in a lightning storm.

The analogy seemed to fit as he could almost feel the tension radiating between the two women. He didn't understand that at all. Katie had been Tori's shadow and best friend throughout high school. Yes, she'd taken his side in the breakup. But since he'd caught Tori in the act with one of his football buddies, Noah wasn't sure how she could fault Katie for not being more sympathetic. As far as he knew, the two hadn't spoken in all these years.

Now he wished he would have questioned that more. Hell, there was a lot more he wished he'd paid attention to over the years. Katie had just always been there, consistent like the sun rising, and he'd never thought about the possibility of that changing. Or how he'd feel if she wasn't a part of his life.

He wasn't going to give up on her, even if he knew he should. His mom was right—Noah may have not done his best in life up until now, but there was no better time to change his future. Of course, he needed to convince Katie of that before it was too late. He'd seen the way Matt Davis had looked at her the night of their date. But as far as Noah was concerned, Katie was his and always would be.

"How long are you in town?" Katie asked, her voice shaky. Noah saw her dart a glance between Tori and him. She couldn't possibly think he still had feelings for his old girlfriend.

"At least a month," Tori answered, bitterness blazing in her eyes as she glared at Katie. Noah had to resist the urge to step between the two of them. If memory served, Tori could be vicious when she wanted to. "I'm redesigning a residence in Aspen. My client is wealthy enough to want me on-site for the whole project. I'm visiting my parents while I'm here." She leaned forward and placed a hand on Noah's arm. "I've been thinking about both your mother and you. There are so many reminders of our time together here."

As Katie let out a snort, Tori's eyes narrowed further. "Let's grab a drink sometime while we're both in town. There's so much I'd like to explain to you about that night, Noah. Details you've never heard."

He shook out of her grasp, noticing that Tori's fingers were long, the nails bright red and perfectly manicured. "I saw enough detail to last me a lifetime, Tori. Let's leave the past where it belongs."

She bit down on her lip, the corner of her mouth dipping into a pout he used to find irresistible. Now it made her seem as if she was trying too hard. "If that's what you want, but I'd still be interested in that drink."

He felt Katie shift behind him. He wasn't about to let her get away. "I'm busy these days, Tori. But maybe we can work something out."

Her smile was immediate. "Why don't we—"

"I'll catch you later." Without waiting for a response, he turned and jogged to catch up to Katie. "What's the matter?"

"Nothing," she said on a hiss of breath. "But I think you just proved my point. It hadn't been a minute since I said 'no' and you were making a date with your ex."

They were back in front of the bakery. He took Katie's arm as she reached for the door. "I could care less about Tori, and you know it. I wanted to get away from her without making a scene. I didn't make a date. A *date* is where I pick up a woman at her house and buy her dinner. A date is what I want with *you*."

She looked so lost standing there, as if his simple request to take her to dinner was tearing her up inside. This wasn't what he wanted for Katie. He wanted a chance to make her happy, not to cause her more pain.

"I don't trust—"

"Katie?" A petite woman with shoulder-length brown hair poked her head out of the storefront. "Marian Jones is on the phone. She forgot to order a cake for her husband's retirement party and needs something by tomorrow."

"I'm coming, Lelia." She closed her eyes for a moment, and when she opened them again, her expression was carefully blank. "I've got to go, Noah. We're friends and it works. Let's not jeopardize that."

He started to speak but she held up a hand. "Tell your mom I'll be over to see her as soon as she gets back home." She stood on tiptoe, leaned forward and kissed his cheek. Her mouth was sweet, and he wanted to turn his face and claim it. But he didn't move and a second later she disappeared into the bakery. He pressed his fingertips to the skin where her lips had been, as if he could still feel their softness. That kiss had felt like goodbye, and no matter how much he wanted to, Noah didn't know how to change that.

Chapter 8

The sun was warm on her back when Katie climbed the steps of the Crawford family farmhouse the following week. Emily appeared a moment later, wearing a faded T-shirt and sweatpants and still managing to look more sophisticated than Katie did on her best day. If it wasn't for the shadow of sadness in Emily's ice-blue eyes, Katie might be jealous of the other woman.

Emily had been only a year behind them in school, but Noah's sister never had much use for anyone in Crimson. Even before Jacob Crawford had got sick, it was clear Emily was destined for a bigger future than this town could give her. Once her father had died, it seemed to Katie that Noah's sister had become more frenetic in her quest to get out of town.

But now she was back, just like Noah, and it bothered Katie to see how out of place Emily looked. Katie could relate to that feeling.

The smile Emily gave Katie was genuine, if drawn. "Come on in." She stepped back to allow Katie room to enter. The Crawfords had done quite a bit of renovations to the property when Noah and Emily were kids. Most of the first floor was covered in shiplap siding that had been painted warm gray. A colorful rug sat on top of slate tile floors, making the entry seem both modern and as if it would have fit the decade the house was originally built.

"Noah's not here right now. He's—"

"In Boulder," Katie finished, then nervously scraped at a bit of dried frosting near the hem of her shirt. She'd been working crazy hours at the bakery and was wearing the same clothes as yesterday. "He mentioned heading down for a meeting." Actually, she hadn't spoken to Noah since they'd run into his ex-girlfriend. She'd wanted to visit Meg but hadn't been able to deal with him again so soon. The older woman who answered the phones for the Forest Service office in town stopped in almost every day for a muffin and coffee, and it hadn't been difficult to get her to share Noah's schedule for the week.

One of Emily's delicate brows arched. "And you picked today to come out to the house?"

"Well, I thought…it seemed…" Katie could feel color heating her cheeks as she stumbled over an explanation. "Yes," she said finally. "I'm here today."

Emily looked at her another moment. "Most women fall at Noah's feet without him even lifting a finger."

"I've borne witness to that phenomenon more than once," Katie agreed.

"He needs more of a challenge than that."

"I'm not trying to challenge him."

"But you do." Emily nodded. "It's good for him."

"We're just friends, Em."

Katie had been here a few times over the years and always thought the house displayed not only Meg's design taste but the love of the family that lived here. Now it seemed almost too quiet.

"I watched him kiss you."

Katie shrugged. "He was…worried about your mom. It was an emotional response, and I happened to be there."

"I don't think my brother has ever had a truly emotional response to anything. He isn't built like that."

"Not true." Katie wasn't sure why she needed to defend Noah but couldn't seem to stop herself. "He cares too much, and it scares him. That's why and when he makes some of his more brilliantly stupid decisions. If he could learn to deal with what he feels…" She stopped, frowned at the knowing look Emily gave her.

"If someone could help him with that…" Emily flashed a hopeful smile.

Katie shook her head. "I can't be that person."

"Can't or won't?"

"Same outcome. I didn't come here for this. I care about Noah and your whole family, but Noah and I are only friends. How is your mom doing?" she asked, needing to steer the conversation to a safer topic. "If this isn't a good time—"

"She's feeling good and will be happy to see you." Emily started toward the back of the house. "Noah moved her bed down into Dad's office on the first floor. We thought it would be easier not to have to deal with steps." She looked over her shoulder. "According to Mom, he'll be moving it back upstairs by the end of the week. Home from the hospital three days and she wants everything back to normal."

They paused outside a closed door. Emily straightened her shoulders and reached for the handle.

"How are you, Em?"

The other woman turned, her hand still on the door-knob. "What has Noah told you?" Her expression had turned wary.

"Not a lot. He respects your privacy. I'm asking you."

"Things are peachy." Emily pushed her hair away from her face. "My marriage is over. I have no job and no prospects since I left college to pursue my dream of becoming a trophy wife." She smiled, but her voice dripped sarcasm. "I'm back in a town I couldn't wait to leave behind, friendless, penniless and living with my mother. I'm now fighting my ex-husband to get our son the treatment he needs for problems I barely understand. So, yeah, 'peachy' about sums it up."

"Emily, I'm sorry—"

"Don't." When Katie reached for her, Emily shook off the touch. "If there's one thing I can't take right now it's pity. I'm sure this whole town is talking about how the girl who was too good for Crimson has come crawling back with her tail between her legs."

"I don't think that's true and I certainly don't pity you. I remember how much you helped with your father's care. You're strong. You'll get through this."

Emily met her gaze, her blue eyes sparkling with bitterness and unshed tears. "You don't know me at all."

"Maybe not," Katie agreed, "but I'd like to. I'm helping with the committee for the Founder's Day Festival— more than I'd planned because my friend Olivia, who was chairing the celebration this year, is having a tough go with morning sickness. It's her first baby."

"Olivia Wilder?" Emily asked. "The wife of the mayor who skipped out of town?"

"She divorced him and married the youngest of the Travers brothers—Logan."

Emily shook her head. "The one with the twin who died? I thought he was trouble."

"People change. Logan came back to town for his brother's wedding and met Olivia. They're good for each other. He has a thriving construction business and she runs the community center now and took over the festival as an offshoot of her work there. Most of the plans are in place and it's going to be a lot of fun."

"That's quite a reinvention for both of them."

"The people in Crimson are more forgiving than you think, Emily. It's a great town, actually. If you got involved—"

"Don't push it, Katie. I'm happy for you to help Noah, but I don't need saving."

Emily's words stung, but Katie pressed on. She'd bet a pan of brownies that Noah's sister needed more help than she would admit. "I'm only trying to include you while you're in town."

"I'll think about it," Emily said then sighed. "I appreciate the offer." She opened the door then held out a hand. "Give me your cell phone and I'll put in my number. Text me the time of the next meeting and we'll see."

"Katie, is that you?"

Handing off her cell to Emily, Katie smiled and entered the room. "I'm sorry I haven't been by sooner, Mrs. Crawford. You look wonderful."

Noah's mother smiled and put aside the book she held in her hands. "No apologies. I understand how busy you are with the bakery." She waved Katie forward. "Your grandmother would be so proud of you, sweetheart. I'm proud of you."

Tears stung the backs of Katie's eyes. It had been a long time since anyone had given her that kind of praise. One problem with being a fixture in town for so long was the expectation she'd do well with the bakery, plus help out wherever needed. Her grandma had held the role and Katie'd taken it over without question. Only recently, since she'd decided she wanted something of a life for herself besides her business, did she wonder if there was more to her than the dependable girl next door everyone in Crimson saw. Hearing Meg say that her grandmother would be proud made the long hours and sacrifice worth it. Gram had been the most important person in her life, and there was nothing Katie wouldn't sacrifice to live up to her legacy.

"From what I hear, you're the one who deserves the praise," she said as she took the seat next to the head of the bed. "Your recovery has been amazing so far. I know both Noah and Emily are thrilled you're doing so well."

Meg waved away her words. "They worry too much. Noah especially, although he'd never admit it. Now tell me what you brought me."

Katie bit back a laugh. "What makes you think I brought you something?"

"Because 'life is sweet' isn't simply the name of your shop. It's what you do—you make life sweeter for the people around you."

Katie's heart swelled at the words, and she reached into the cloth shopping bag she'd carried in with her. "Cinnamon rolls," she said with a wink.

"My favorite," Meg whispered and took the box, opening it and licking her lips. "How do you remember everyone's preferences?"

"You're not just anyone, Mrs. Crawford."

"Call me Meg." She lifted the box as Emily walked up to the bed and handed Katie her phone. "She brought cinnamon rolls."

As Emily leaned forward to breathe in the scent, a deep voice called from the doorway, "You're planning to share those. Right, Mom?"

Katie's phone clattered to the tile floor and she heard a crack as the screen shattered. "Damn," she muttered, bending forward to retrieve it. Noah's long fingers wrapped around hers as she picked up the phone. "I've got it." As soon as she said the words, he released her. "I thought you were in Boulder today."

He quirked one brow at her statement. "Checking up on me?"

"Katie is my guest today, Noah," Meg said. "And you owe her a new phone."

"It's fine," Katie said quickly. "My fault."

"It was clearly Noah's fault," Emily said.

"Because I came home?" he asked, his voice incredulous.

"You made her drop the phone," Emily insisted.

Katie shifted in her chair, focusing her gaze on Emily and Meg. "He didn't."

"I'm sorry, Katie," Noah offered after a moment. "I'll gladly buy you a new phone if you'll make eye contact with me."

Katie sucked in a breath, shocked that he'd call her out publicly in front of his mom and sister.

Her eyes snapped to his, but before she could speak, Meg said, "Noah, would you please put on a pot of water for tea?"

"Emily can do that." He kept his blue gaze on Katie, who fingered the cracks on the screen of her phone. A dozen hairline fissures radiated out from the center. Splintered just like her heart felt since Noah had returned to Crimson.

"I'm going to check on Davey." Emily hitched a thumb toward Noah. "Save one of those for me. Don't let Noah eat them all."

"I may not let him have one if he doesn't do what I ask." Meg lifted a brow at her son. Katie kept her head down.

"Fine," he mumbled and followed Emily out of the room.

"I should go," Katie said when they were alone.

"You just got here," Meg argued.

Katie stood, dropped her ruined phone into her purse. "I really only came to drop off the cinnamon rolls to you. I came because…"

"Because you thought Noah was in Boulder today." Meg slowly shut the white cardboard box that held the cinnamon rolls. "He's my son and I love him. That doesn't mean I'm unaware of how he operates."

"He didn't mean for my phone to break."

"He wouldn't mean to break your heart, either."

Katie swallowed, nodded. "But he could."

"Or he could make it whole."

"I can't take that chance." She dropped a kiss on Meg's cheek, unwilling to consider the possibility of trusting Noah with her heart. "I'll be by to see you again. I hope you'll be well enough to attend some of the Founder's Day Festival events. I'd like Emily to help out with the committee."

Meg nodded. "That would be good for her. You're good for this family, Katie. For Noah. I hope you know that."

Katie didn't know how to answer, so she flashed a smile she hoped didn't look as forced as it felt. "Take care, Meg."

She slipped from the room and down the hall. She could hear Noah banging cabinet doors shut and china rattling in the kitchen as she sneaked by as quietly as she could.

Her foot hit the first step of the porch when the front door slammed. "Is this what it's come to?" Noah's voice rang out in the silence of midafternoon. "We go from friends to lovers to you running away from me? I'm used to being the person disappointing everyone around me. Now I understand how they've felt on the receiving end of it all these years."

He'd meant to rile her—because misery loved company, and Noah was miserable and angry right now. The anger was mostly self-directed. He'd finished his meetings early in Boulder and left before lunch to beat rush-hour traffic coming out of the city. When he'd pulled up to his mom's house and seen Katie's Subaru parked in front, a flash of pleasure and anticipation had surged through him. He couldn't think of a better way to spend the afternoon than on the front porch of the farmhouse with a cold beer in his hand and Katie on the porch swing next to him.

Except it was obvious she not only hadn't expected his return but was upset by it. Katie, who had always been ready with a smile and a hug, didn't want to see him and tried to sneak out to avoid him.

Oh, yeah. He was pissed. But as he watched her stiffen while strands of hair blew around her shoulders in the summer breeze, he wondered if he'd gone too far.

All Noah wanted to do was get closer, but the only thing he seemed to manage when he opened his mouth was push her further away.

"I came to see your mom." Katie turned, her fingers

gripping the painted railing. "This has nothing to do with you."

"I don't believe you."

Her eyes narrowed. "Have you had that drink with Tori?"

He shook his head. "I won't if it upsets you."

"It's none of my business."

"It matters what you think, whether it's your business or not. You said it yourself—we're friends." And more, even if she wouldn't admit it and he barely understood his changing feelings about their relationship. He felt alive with Katie, his body electric in its response to her. Her blue cotton T-shirt hugged the curves of her breasts and her slim waist, and he knew how her skin felt underneath it. That was the thing making him so crazy. It was knowing her in a way no one else did. People in town saw her as the dependable, caring baker they could count on in any situation. But he wanted more of the passionate woman who had nipped and teased him, responsive to every kiss and touch. He wanted to close the distance between them and place his mouth on her throat, where a tiny patch of dried icing stuck to her skin. The idea of sucking it off, imagining the sugar on his tongue mixed with her unique taste made him grow hard.

"Friends," she repeated, drawing him back to the moment.

"If that's all you'll give me." He cleared his throat, doing multiplication facts in his head to keep his heated thoughts in check.

She tilted her head, pulled her hair over one shoulder as if deciding whether she could trust him. He knew the answer to that but wasn't about to share it with her.

"I need your help," she said after a moment.

"Anything." He stepped forward. "What is it? Founder's Day? The bakery? Something at your house?"

"Slow down, Noah," she said with a small smile.

Something in him fizzed and popped at the sight of that smile. He ran one hand through his hair, needing to pull it together.

"I'd like you to teach me to swim."

His brain tried to compute that request. "You know how to swim. I've seen you at the hot springs."

She shook her head. "In open water. I haven't been to the reservoir since I freaked out during the triathlon my dad signed me up for when I was twelve."

"Why now?" He braced himself for her answer, confident he wasn't going to like it.

"Matt invited me out on his boat for the Fourth of July. A group of his friends is going to Hidden Canyon."

He bit back the irritating urge to growl at the mention of the other man's name. "He's a swim coach, right? Why not have him teach you?"

"What if I panic again? My stomach feels sick just thinking about going in the water. I don't want him to see me like that."

"But it's okay if I see you like that?"

"We're *just* friends," she said softly.

"You want me to help you overcome your fear so you can go out with another guy?"

She looked at him for a moment then shook her head. "Never mind. I'll deal with it on my own." She turned and headed toward her car, dust from the gravel driveway swirling behind her.

"Katie, wait." When she didn't stop, Noah cursed and ran after her, his hand slamming against the driver's-side door as she reached for the handle. "I'll help you. Of course I'll take you swimming."

"Forget it. I shouldn't have asked you. It's stupid anyway. It's not as if I'm going to hide who I am from him forever. I don't even own a bathing suit."

"Let me help you with this." He crouched down so they were at eye level. "Please."

She met his gaze then pressed a hand to her eyes. "I feel like I'm going to throw up."

"You won't throw up." He took her hand in his, gently peeling it away from her face. "We can get you through this."

Her gaze turned hopeful. "I want to be the fun girl. The one who can hang out with a guy's friends. The one you call for a good time."

Noah kept a smile plastered on his face, although the thought of some other guy having a "good time" with Katie just about sliced him open. "I have one condition."

She rolled her eyes. "Seriously?"

He nodded. "Your bathing suit needs to be one piece. The one you wear on July Fourth, anyway. With me, I'd recommend a string bikini."

"Right," she said, choking out a laugh. "Can you see me in a string bikini?"

"I'm picturing it right now," Noah whispered then groaned when she bit down on her bottom lip. "Definitely a string bikini with me."

"But only you?"

He shrugged, tried to look nonchalant. "I'm thinking of you. Everyone goes cliff jumping at Hidden Canyon Reservoir over the Fourth. You don't want to lose your top in front of all those partyers."

"Oh, no." She slapped her hand back over her eyes. "I forgot about the cliff jumping."

"You don't have to—"

"And get left on shore serving snacks when they return?" She shook her head. "I'm tired of being the town's mother hen. I'm going to jump off the highest rock out there." She swallowed, hitched a breath. "Or the second-highest."

"That's a girl." Noah couldn't help himself. He reached out a finger and touched the bit of icing dried to her skin. "I can get time off next Tuesday. It's supposed to be warm. We can go then when it won't be crowded."

"Okay. Thank you." She fingered the base of her throat. "I'm covered in frosting. What a mess."

"You're beautiful," he answered.

She swayed closer and for an instant he thought she might kiss him. Damn, he wanted her to. Instead she blinked and pulled back.

"I'll see you next week."

Removing his hand from her door, he balled it into a fist at his side as she got in her car and drove away. He tried to tell himself this was progress, although helping her win the affection of another man was hardly a step in the right direction. But it would allow him more time with her, which had to count for something.

Katie didn't need to become more adventurous or change in any way as far as Noah was concerned. She was perfect exactly the way she was. He only wished it hadn't taken him so long to realize it.

Chapter 9

"Are you sure you want to do this?" Jase asked him two days later.

"Absolutely. Hand me that microphone stand." Noah was in the park at the center of town. It was a block wide with picnic tables and a covered patio area on one side and an open expanse of grass and a playground on the other. He was helping Jase set up the temporary stage for the concert that would take place tonight. The Founder's Day committee had organized it as a teaser for the big festival, to get both locals and tourists vacationing in the area excited about the upcoming event.

"Thanks, man. I know you're juggling a lot between your mom and work. It means a ton that you'd come out to help."

Noah didn't answer, just lifted an amplifier into place.

"Katie's more involved with the committee this year."

"Emily might have mentioned that," Noah admitted. He saw Jase shake his head. "But that's not why I'm here."

His friend laughed. "Uh-huh."

"It's not the *only* reason I'm here," Noah amended. "I hate being in that house."

Jase continued setting up the stage but asked, "Is everything okay with your mom?"

"Yes. She's amazing. As always. Made me promise I'd move the bed back upstairs tomorrow. She has a date next week with one of her doctors."

"She's led a pretty solitary life since your dad died."

"I didn't realize that until I came back to stay. Don't get me wrong, it's been good to see her and Emily. Em and I were close as kids, you know? Really close. I thought I understood her. Since she's come back I can't figure out what the hell she thinks about anything. She's so overwhelmed with Davey and her divorce but won't open up."

"Some things take time."

"I guess Katie's asked her to help with the baking competition—coordinating judges or something like that."

"Maybe that will help." Jase turned to him, unlooping a microphone cord as he spoke. "Is that why you hate being in the house—because of Emily and her son?"

"No," Noah answered quickly. "Not at all. I like the kid, actually. He's quirky but in an interesting way. Tater adores him." Noah ran a hand through his hair. "If I was anyplace else with them, maybe it would be different. It's that house. The memories there. How I failed my father. All the mistakes I made."

"I doubt your mother sees it that way."

"She's my mom. Of course she'll support me no matter what."

"That's no guarantee," Jase said softly.

"Damn. I'm sorry."

"It's old news. Just don't take her love for granted."

Now Noah felt like an even bigger jerk. Jase's mother had deserted her family when Jase was only eight. He'd grown up with only an alcoholic father to parent him.

"I get it, and I love my mom and Em. But I can't stand being reminded of how much I wasn't around when Dad needed me."

"You're here now."

"Funny," Noah said with a chuckle. "That's exactly what Katie said."

"She's smart." Jase unrolled a colorful Oriental rug across the wood of the stage floor.

"Smart enough to be done with me." Noah blew out a breath. "I can't let that happen, Jase."

"Why now?" his friend asked. "Katie's been a part of your life forever. She's put up with you for years and suddenly you realize she was worth looking at all this time."

"Yes." Noah helped straighten the rug then leaned back on his heels. "I mean no. I don't understand it. All I know is now that I've seen her—really seen her—I can't give her up."

"She's coming to the concert with Matt Davis."

"You know that for sure?" Noah let out a string of curses. "I thought since she was on the committee she'd be here working."

"Making her easy pickings for you?"

"Why are you giving me a hard time? You've got to be on my side."

"I *am* on your side." Jase jumped off the stage onto the grass. "You think you failed your father and that belief has haunted you for over a decade. If you hurt Katie, it's going to be just as bad. For both of you. Don't go down that path."

"But I need her," Noah whispered. "I want her even if I don't deserve her."

"Be careful and be sure." Jase glanced to the pavilion end of the park, where people were gathered in front of the barbecue food truck parked near the sidewalk. "We have a few more things to unload before everyone heads this way."

Noah nodded. "Put me to work. Whatever my motivations for being here, I'm definitely cheap labor."

"Bless you for that." Jase smiled and led the way to his truck.

Noah worked without a break for the next two hours. He helped set up the four-piece bluegrass band's instruments and moved trash and recycling cans around the perimeter of the lawn. He saw quite a few people he knew and found it was good to catch up with most of them. The universal sentiment seemed to be that he was the golden child for coming back to Crimson to help take care of his mom. He tried to downplay it as much as he could since his first instinct was to clarify how much he had to make up for from his father's illness. By the time the concert started, he was wrung out emotionally and ready to retreat to the back of the stage to watch the show. It was out of character since he never walked away from a party. Being around other people was the best way he knew to avoid dealing with his own thoughts. But tonight he craved a little solitude.

As he moved through the crowd, he saw Katie along with Matt Davis and another couple laying a blanket across the grass. The same picnic basket she'd brought to the hospital was tucked under her arm. She wore a lemon yellow shirt with thin straps and a pair of tight jeans and platform-heeled sandals. She looked fresh and beautiful, like sunshine come to life.

He slapped his hand against his forehead as Matt draped

a sweater over her shoulders. No matter how warm it got during the day, the temperature in the mountains almost always cooled by at least fifteen degrees in the evening.

Noah hated the idea of another man touching her, even in such an innocent way, but he couldn't stop it. All he could do was stick it out, something he'd never excelled at, and hope that she would understand his feelings were real.

"Stop staring at me." Katie planted her feet on the grass and crossed her arms over her chest as she glared at Noah. Feeling his gaze on her was making it hard to remember she was on a date with another man this evening.

He sat alone behind the stage, his face obscured by shadows. "How's the date going?" he asked gently, not bothering to get up or face her. Darkness had fallen completely over the town, and the music coming from the stage was loud and boisterous.

The four-piece bluegrass band had driven over from Breckenridge to play this concert. Their songs ranged from slow ballads to livelier tunes like the one they were playing now. If she tilted her head, Katie could see the crowd in front of the stage, many of them on their feet dancing and swaying to the beat. The lights strung across the green gave the whole scene a warm glow.

But the heat she'd felt had been from Noah's gaze on her. She'd seen him when her group had first settled on the grass but had expected him to join Jase and his other friends once the concert started. Instead, he'd remained alone—something Noah never did.

"The date would be going a lot better if I wasn't being watched." She took a step forward, wanting to see him. She couldn't explain the reason. "Why are you back here by yourself anyway? Jase is out there with Josh, Sara and a whole group of your friends."

"I'm not in the mood for a big group tonight." He stood, turned to face the stage but didn't step out of the shadows. "You weren't dancing."

"Matt isn't much of a dancer."

"But you love it. Do you want me to ask you to dance, Bug?"

Oh, yes. Her body ached for him to twirl her into his arms. "No," she said through clenched teeth. "Why are you watching me?"

"Because you're beautiful," he answered simply.

Katie felt a current race through her, as if her whole body was electric. She tingled from head to toe, a sensation she seemed to feel only with Noah. It was dangerous, exciting and she should hate it. Instead, it drew her to him and away from her plan, her date and her idea of what life should look like.

"I'm trying to move on."

"I should let you go?"

She sighed. "You never had me in the first place."

"Didn't I?" He moved suddenly, reaching for her. He took hold of her arm, pulled her in front of him. He wrapped his arms around her, pressed her back to his chest. His breath tickled her ear as he spoke against her skin. "Because when I see you with him, all I can think is *mine*."

"I'm not," she argued, but her voice was breathless and she loved the feel of his body against hers. The band started a slower song, the guitar and fiddle playing a mournful tune as the singer sang words of longing for a lost love. Goose bumps rose along Katie's bare arms as Noah pressed a kiss on her shoulder.

"You need your sweater," he whispered, wrapping his

arms more tightly around her, enveloping her in his heat. He swayed with her, almost dancing but more intimate. Just the two of them, moving together.

God, she was a slut. No, that wasn't true. She only wanted to be when it came to Noah. Her willpower faded along with the chill she felt from the cool night air as he turned her in his arms and kissed her. His mouth molded to hers and every ounce of intelligence she possessed disappeared. She didn't care that it was wrong or that she would be hurt in the end. All that mattered was this moment and the man making her senseless with his touch.

"This is wrong," she whispered, pulling away as far as he'd let her. "You don't want me."

He laughed, the sound vibrating against her skin as he ran his lips over her jaw. "I want you so much, Katie."

The sound of applause from the front of the stage brought her back to reality. "No." She took two steps away, trying to get her breath, her emotions and her heart under control. "Not the way I'm looking for. You've said so yourself."

"Maybe I can change. For you."

She wanted to trust him, but what if it didn't work out? Katie knew what it was like to be rejected by the people you cared about most in the world. She'd spent most of her adult life overcoming the pain of not being the person her parents wanted her to be. With Noah it could be even more heartbreaking.

"We won't know unless you give me a chance."

She'd loved him almost half her life, but it was easier to love in secret than risk him seeing all the things she'd hidden about herself from the world. Her doubts, her fears, her moments of anger and pettiness.

Noah had the same perfect image of her as most people in town. The one she'd cultivated through the years, but which now weighed her down with its limits. That was why she was trying to start fresh with someone like Matt—a man who had no preconceived notions about her. She could be anyone she wanted with him—wild, impetuous, or selfish when it suited her. Although nothing about him brought out her wild side like Noah did.

She wanted someone to see her as real, more than the supportive friend or generous local shop owner. Yet Katie didn't know who she was without those labels. What if she peeled back her layers for Noah and he didn't like the person she was underneath?

That would do more than break her heart. It would crush her soul.

"I've got to go," she said. "Matt and the others will be waiting for me."

"Katie…" Noah's voice was strained, as if he was holding back so much of what he wanted to say.

"I don't want to ruin our friendship," she told him. "It's too important to me."

She turned and fled, unable to look at him for one more second without launching herself into his arms.

The next several days Katie spent in the kitchen at the bakery, tweaking the new recipe for her parents' superfood bar and finishing up orders for several events taking place in Aspen over the weekend.

She had just enough time to deliver a final round of cupcakes before hurrying back to Crimson for a Founder's Day Festival committee meeting. As much as she wanted to help out Olivia, what Katie really needed was to take a nap. As she drove along the highway that ran between the two towns, her eyes drifted shut for one brief moment—or so it felt—and she almost swerved across the median. Between her work on the festival, late nights at the bakery and losing sleep over thoughts about Noah, Katie was exhausted. Maybe she should pull back a bit.

Fighting back a yawn, she got out of her car and climbed the steps to the community center, planning to tell Olivia exactly that before the meeting.

Her friend was waiting for her near the receptionist desk in the lobby.

"Katie, you're a lifesaver," Olivia said as she approached. She looked pale and more fragile than ever leaning against the wall behind the desk. "I don't know what we'd do without you stepping in on the committee."

"I wanted to talk to you about that." Katie hugged her purse close to her body. She never said no or reneged on a commitment, so the thought of letting Olivia down almost made her physically nauseous.

"Can it wait?" Logan came around the corner at that moment and Katie took a step back. Logan was big, with the broad, strong body of a man who made his living doing physical labor all day. He could be intimidating, but Olivia's presence had softened him a great deal since his return to Crimson. Now the expression on his face was downright scary.

"I've got time," Olivia said gently, laying a hand on his arm.

"You need to get to the hospital."

"The hospital?" Katie stepped forward, swallowing around the worry that crept into her throat. "Is everything okay with the baby?"

"Yes," Olivia answered at the same time Logan said, "We don't know."

Olivia waved away his concern. "It's a routine appointment. My doctor wants me to go in for a blood test and some monitoring they can't do in his office."

"Plus IV fluids," Logan added.

"She thinks I'm dehydrated." She smiled, but it looked strained. "The morning sickness isn't getting better."

Logan took her hand. "And it lasts all day."

"But it isn't an emergency." Olivia stepped forward, swayed and leaned into her husband. "Really, Katie. I'm tired and weak. It's not life threatening."

Logan glowered. "Not yet."

"You two go on." Katie gave Olivia a quick hug and patted Logan awkwardly on the shoulder.

"But if you need something—"

"It can wait." Katie felt embarrassment wash through her. She was worried about needing a nap when Olivia could be in the middle of a real crisis. "I'll drop off dinner to your house so that it's there when you get home."

"You're doing so much already," Olivia said, pursing her lips.

"But we'd appreciate it." Logan shrugged when his wife threw him a disapproving look. "What? You need to eat something besides crackers and I know she's a great cook." He turned to Katie. "I'm parked on the next block. Would you stay with her while I pull up my truck?"

"Of course."

He gave Olivia a quick, tender kiss on the top of her head and jogged toward the front door.

"He worries too much," Olivia said when the door shut behind him.

"He loves you." Katie linked her arm in her friend's. "Does Millie know you're going to the hospital?"

"Please don't say anything," Olivia answered, shaking her head. "I promise I'll text if we find anything serious."

She squeezed Katie's hand. "I love this baby so much already. I know it's wrong to become attached so early in the pregnancy. So many things can go wrong, and I'm not exactly a spring chicken."

"Don't be silly." Olivia was in her early thirties and Logan a couple of years younger than Katie. Although an unlikely couple, they were actually perfect for each other. "Have the tests and I'm sure the news will be good."

"Of course. You're right."

They walked out of the community center just as Logan pulled to the curb. He jumped out of the truck and came around to open Olivia's door for her. The love in his eyes as he looked at his wife made Katie's heart ache.

"Thanks, Katie," they both said as Olivia climbed into the truck.

Katie waited until they'd disappeared down the block then turned back toward the community center. Tori Woodward stood on the sidewalk in front of her.

Katie smothered a groan. The last thing she needed today was a run-in with her former friend. "Hey, Tori." She went to step around the other woman. Tori, as always, looked Aspen chic in a pair of designer jeans with elaborate stitching on the pockets, a silk blouse and strappy sandals. Katie glanced at her own utilitarian clogs, part of her standard work uniform. The pair she wore today were bright purple, shiny like a bowling ball and totally clunky in front of Tori's delicate sandals. "I've got a Founder's Day Festival meeting right now. Good to see you."

Tori moved, blocking Katie's way again. "Of course you do, Saint Katie. I see you're still using the same martyr routine to ingratiate yourself with people. Does anyone have a clue as to who you really are?"

Katie's head snapped back at Tori's words. "This is who I am," she said, wishing her voice sounded more sure.

"Right. You're also the person who would ruin her supposed best friend's chance at love."

Katie swallowed. It would be simple to think Tori was talking about present day and the change in Katie's relationship with Noah, but she knew that wasn't the case. "You're the one who cheated, Tori. You made that choice."

"Noah would have never found out if you hadn't given him that note."

"The note he received wasn't signed."

"Don't play dumb," Tori said with a snort. She lifted her Prada sunglasses onto the top of her head, her green eyes boring into Katie's. "You were the only person who knew about my fling with Adam."

"You can't know that for sure. And if you were so committed to Noah, you wouldn't have fooled around with someone else."

"I was eighteen and stupid, I'll grant you that. Mainly stupid to trust you with my secret. You had a crush on Noah even then. It killed you that he was in love with me."

"I was happy for you," Katie argued, shaking her head. She felt her breathing start to come faster, bile rising in her throat. "But it wasn't fair to him."

"He wasn't himself that year," Tori shot back. "When his dad got sick, Noah couldn't focus on anything else."

"He was going to ask you to marry him."

"Exactly," Tori practically hissed. "I would have said yes. We were going to be happy together. Noah was my first, you know." She shook her head, gave a bitter laugh. "Of course you knew—you were my best friend. I thought you understood I needed to make sure he was the one."

"I never understood why you needed to sleep with another guy." Katie crossed her arms over her chest. "It was wrong, just like it was wrong of you to ask me to cover it up."

"So why didn't you just tell him instead of letting him find out the way he did?"

Katie almost blurted out the truth. How she couldn't stand to be the one who hurt Noah, had been afraid Tori would turn it back on her. Katie and Tori had become friends freshman year of high school, when Tori's family moved to Crimson—her father had worked in one of the exclusive hotels in Aspen, and Tori acted as if that made her better than the local kids around Crimson. She'd been a snob, yes, but she'd also been beautiful, gregarious and so confident.

It had felt as if a spotlight suddenly shone on her when Tori chose her as a friend. Now it seemed clear Tori had liked Katie because her low self-esteem made her easy to manipulate. It was her mother all over again. Tori made small digs about Katie's weight or lack of style, and like a puppy eager to please, Katie would do more to make herself indispensable so Tori wouldn't drop her.

"You don't know it was me who left the note."

"All this time, and you're still denying it? You haven't even admitted it to him. What's Noah going to think when he finds out his perfect Katie-bug was the one to break his heart?"

Katie swallowed around the panic lodged in her throat. Yes, Tori had cheated, but Katie remembered how angry Noah had been at the anonymous note that had led him to find his girlfriend with another guy. "Why are you doing this? Do you want him back? Is that why you're here?"

Tori closed her eyes for a moment, as if she was debating her answer. "No. I'm way past wanting to be the wife of a forest ranger." She tapped one long nail against her glossy mouth. "Although I wouldn't mind a roll in the sheets for old times' sake. If Noah had mad skills in the bedroom back then, I can only imagine how he's improved over the years."

Katie felt herself stiffen. When Tori's gaze narrowed, she realized she'd walked right into a trap.

"You've had sex with him."

"I didn't mean—"

"That's why I'm going to tell him." Tori leaned closer. "You betrayed me, and no one gets away with that."

"It was ten years ago."

"Doesn't matter. In this town I'm the one who crushed Noah Crawford's already broken heart and you're the angel who picked up the pieces. But we were both responsible for his pain. I'm tired of everyone looking at me like I'm some sort of Jezebel."

"No one thinks—"

"Noah does. His friends do. Hell, my own mother reminds me every Christmas about the one that got away. Maybe I deserve it, but I'm not the only one."

Tori had started dating Noah sophomore year of high school, and Katie thought he'd always loved her more than she deserved. When Tori alienated most of her girlfriends besides Katie, she'd become more dependent on Noah's attention. But she'd always wanted Katie to tag along, almost as a buffer or proof to Noah that she wasn't the mean girl other people made her out to be. Katie knew she was, and as her feelings for Noah had grown, it became more difficult for her to watch the way Tori strung him along.

Maybe she'd taken advantage of the knowledge she had to break them up. But she'd believed it was the right thing to do. He'd been wrecked that summer, and holding tight to his relationship with his self-centered, shallow girlfriend wasn't going to make his grief over his father's death any easier.

But would Noah understand her motivations and why she'd never revealed that it was she who'd typed that note?

"Don't do this," she whispered. "I was a good friend to you and that note wouldn't have changed the outcome of your relationship with Noah."

The other woman pursed her glossy lips. "I won't say anything," she said after a moment.

Katie started to breathe a sigh of relief but Tori added, "Yet. But I'm here the whole summer. And I may change my mind. You'll never know. Any day, any moment I may decide to throw you under the bus the way you did me."

Katie shook her head. "I'll deny it. You have no proof."

"You won't," Tori answered confidently. "If he confronts you, I know you won't lie. The little *bug* doesn't have it in her."

Oh, that nickname. Noah had started calling her Bug after he heard Katie's mother chastise her for something she'd eaten at the bakery. Katie had been so embarrassed, feeling fat and sloppy. But Noah had put his arm around her shoulders and whispered that she was no bigger than a little bug, and next to his height and bulk, she'd actually felt petite.

Over the years it had become a reminder of their "buddy" relationship. Hearing Tori speak the word made her want to run home and inhale a pan of brownies in one sitting.

"I'm going to my meeting," she said after a moment. "I'm sorry you're still angry. But you need to figure out where that animosity should really be directed. It isn't at me."

"Don't be so sure." Tori adjusted her sunglasses back on her face then walked away, her sandals clicking on the sidewalk as she went.

Katie fisted her hand then pushed it against her stomach, trying to ward off the pain and dread pooling there. All she wanted was to eat and sleep right now, but she turned and started back into the community center. She had responsibilities, people depending on her, and no matter what she wanted for herself, she couldn't stand to let them down.

Chapter 10

Noah drummed his thumbs against the steering wheel, glancing every mile marker at Katie's profile.

It was a great day for swimming, unseasonably warm for late June with the sun shining from a sky so blue it looked like the backdrop on one of Sara's movie sets. He'd borrowed a small fishing boat from Crimson Ranch so he could take Katie to the far side of the reservoir where the water might be a degree or two warmer than near the mouth of the mountain stream that fed it.

The day was perfect, other than the fact that Katie had barely said two words since he'd picked her up an hour ago.

"We're almost there," he said and adjusted the radio to a satellite station with better reception this far into the mountains.

Hidden Valley Reservoir lay on the far side of the pass past Aspen. The dirt road that wound into the hills above the valley was maintained but still rutted in places.

"Okay" was her only response.

"You nervous?" He placed one hand on her leg, squeezing softly in the place above her knee where he knew she was ticklish. Immediately she flinched away from him and he pulled his arm away from her.

"A little." She continued to look out the window for a few minutes, then added, "I'm tired. Sorry I'm bad company."

"You're never bad company, Bug."

"Noah," she said, her tone harsh.

"Sorry. It's a habit. I won't call you that." He focused more closely on the road as they passed an SUV coming from the other direction. "I mean it in a good way, you know? I always have."

"I don't like it," she snapped.

"Are you sure you want to do this?" He wasn't sure what was going on, but if swimming took her off her game this much, was it really worth it?

"If you want to turn around, go ahead." She pressed her fingers to her temples. "I'm not sure what's wrong with my mood today, but I understand if you don't want to be with me."

As he came to the opening in the trees that signaled the entrance to the state park where the reservoir was located, he pulled off onto the shoulder of the gravel road. "Listen to me," he said, moving his seat belt aside so he could face her. "I don't give a damn about your mood. Happy, sad, pissy for no reason. It happens and I'll take them all. We're friends, Katie. You've seen me at my worst. The more I think about it, I've never seen you anything but kind, generous and ready to please whoever you're with. I can take one afternoon of a bad mood without turning tail. Give me a little credit."

She looked at him as if she wanted to argue, then shocked him when she asked, "Do you think you would have been happy married to Tori?"

He felt his mouth drop open, clamped it shut again. "Where the hell did that question come from?"

"It's weird seeing her back in town for an extended period of time. It makes me wonder—"

"Don't." Noah lifted his hand to cut her off. "I'm not interested in reuniting with my old girlfriend, if that's what you want to know."

She shook her head. "That's not it. But if things had gone differently that summer, you'd have asked her to marry you."

"I was a different person back then. Young and in so much pain." He pressed his head against the seat back, looked out the front window to the endless blue sky above the treetops. "I had no business thinking of spending my life with anyone. In the end, Tori and I chose very different directions for our lives. Who knows if that would have made a marriage too difficult?"

"Maybe it was good that you broke up? I mean, in the long run?"

He let out a bark of laughter, surprised at the bitterness he felt after all these years. "I sure as hell can't say I'm glad things happened the way they did. But I don't regret not having Tori as my wife."

Memories of the pain of that summer, the sting of her betrayal when he was already so low flooded through him. The thought that people knew about what she was doing, and no one had the guts to actually talk to him about it. A stupid, cowardly note left under his windshield wiper.

As his body tensed, he felt Katie's fingers slide up his

arm. "Thank you for answering the question. I know you don't like to talk about that part of your past."

"Did it help you?" He inclined his head so he could look at her, watched her bite down on her bottom lip as she thought about her answer.

"Yes," she said after a moment. "It did."

He grabbed her hand, kissed the inside of her palm then pulled back onto the road again. "Then it was worth it." He squeezed her fingers before placing her hand back in her lap. "And bad mood or not, we're doing this. You have nothing to be afraid of with me, Katie."

Her chest rose and fell as she stared at him. "You have no idea, Noah."

"Katie."

"We're going to do this. I'm going to do this." The way she looked at him, her brown eyes soft and luminous in the bright daylight, made his breath catch.

She must be talking about swimming, but he thought— and hoped—her words might have more meaning.

Best not to push her too far too fast. So he nodded and finished the drive to the reservoir.

Who would have guessed the hardest part of going swimming with Noah would be stripping down to her bathing suit in front of him?

"Turn around." They'd launched the small boat he'd borrowed into the water and now it was tethered to the small dock down the hill from the state park's gravel parking lot. Katie stood next to the back of the truck, clutching a beach towel to her chest.

"I've seen you naked, Katie." Noah grinned at her, looking every bit the modern-day rake she knew him to be. "I think I can handle a bikini."

"I did *not* wear a bikini. And it was dark that night at my house. Broad daylight is different." She reached for the wet suit he held in his hand. "Give that to me and turn around. I don't need you watching while I encase myself like a sausage."

"The water's not bad today," he said with a laugh, holding out his arms wide. "You won't need that."

"Easy for you to say." Noah wore a pair of low-slung board shorts, Keen sandals and a T-shirt with the Colorado state flag on the front. He looked like a high-mountain surf bum. Cold air and water had never bothered him, and his work for the Forest Service only seemed to make him more impervious to the elements.

He frowned as he studied her. "You're already shivering. It must be close to ninety degrees today. What's going on?"

"Nerves." She squeezed the edges of the towel tighter. "My teeth are chattering."

Noah took a step closer to her, placing his palms over the tops of her arms, his skin warm against hers. "You don't have to do this. If Matt or any other guy cares that you don't like boating or swimming, they're not worth it. This is who you are."

She shook her head. "It's not who I *want* to be. It probably seems like nothing because you aren't afraid of anything. But I'm sick of being scared and living life on the sidelines."

He bent until they were at eye level and flipped his sunglasses off his head, his brilliant blue eyes intense. "There are plenty of things I'm afraid of, and you don't live life on the sidelines. Not being the adrenaline junkies your parents are doesn't make you less of a person, Katie-bug. You have friends who care about you, a thriving business, and you're an important part of this community."

"Because I have no life so I'm always available," she muttered, although she had to admit his words soothed her a bit.

"Will boating on the Fourth of July give you a life?"

"The start of one, maybe." She shook her head. "Matt knew my parents out in California—that's where he went to college and he trained with my dad for an Ironman a few years ago."

"I thought Logan and Olivia introduced you."

"They did. My parents told Matt we wouldn't have much in common since I'm such a homebody." She tried to make her voice light. "My own parents think I'm a homebody."

Noah's eyes narrowed. "Your parents are wrong."

"I'd like to prove to myself that I'm more than who they think I am."

He placed a soft kiss on the top of her head. "I'll wait for you down by the boat. We're going swimming today."

As he turned away, Katie placed the towel on top of his truck and squeezed into the wet suit. The thick black material covered the entire upper half of her body but cut off at midthigh. Zipping it up, Katie glanced at her reflection in the passenger-side window then groaned. She looked like a cross between a rubber inner tube and a baby seal. The wet suit fit like a second skin, and while it was more coverage than her bathing suit, it still showed more of her figure than she was used to.

It was good she was doing this with Noah before she went boating with Matt and his friends. She could boost her confidence not only in the water but out of it. She made her way down to the dock and forced herself to lower the towel to her side as Noah looked up. The wet suit might be tight, but it was basically modest. She had nothing to be embarrassed about in front of him.

Nothing at all, she realized as his eyes widened in appreciation at her approach. "Damn," he said when she hopped onto the dock. "I've never seen anyone make a wet suit look sexy."

She waved away his compliment, but butterflies zipped across her belly at his words.

"Seriously, Katie." He helped her step into the boat. "Sexy. As. Hell."

"Stop." She placed the tips of her fingers in his and jumped onto one of the captain's chairs near the front then down onto the floor. Noah gave her a tug, and she landed against his chest as his arms came around her. "Just friends, Noah."

His smile was teasing. "There are many types of friends."

"We're the type who don't call each other sexy," she answered but didn't pull away.

He placed his mouth against her ear. "If you say so." His breath tickled the sensitive skin. "Still nervous?"

She heard the smile in his voice and moved away, lowering herself into one of the leather chairs. "I'm in a boat," she whispered. "On a lake."

"A reservoir, to be specific."

"I'm going swimming, and you're trying to distract me so I won't be so scared."

He tucked a lock of her hair behind her ear. "Is it working?"

"I'm not cold. That's a start."

He took the seat behind the steering wheel and reached past her to open the glove compartment. He took out a faded baseball cap. "Put this on and tighten it."

"Won't it blow off?"

It was one of his favorites and it felt strangely intimate to adjust it on her head.

"Should be fine and it'll keep your hair from tangling in the wind."

"You have a lot of experience with the long-hair issue on the water?"

Without answering, he leaned over the side of the boat to unfasten the rope looped on one of the dock's pillars. A minute later he'd motored them away from the shore and toward the mountains rising up on the far side of the water. The reservoir was calm, almost placid, and they passed only a couple of smaller fishing boats with old men casting from the sides. Over the holiday weekend, the state park would be crowded with tents and RVs in the campground on the high ridge. Over a dozen boats would dot the water, with people tubing, water-skiing and wakeboarding along the waves.

Colorado might be a landlocked state, but enough outdoor enthusiasts lived in and near the mountains to make the best of the sprinkling of man-made lakes and reservoirs throughout the high country. As popular as these areas were during the summer, Katie had managed to avoid going out on the water since she'd had her bad experience as a girl. To call it a near drowning might be exaggerating, but it had felt that way to her.

Her fear of open water was irrational, but until now she'd had no reason to confront it. She concentrated on breathing as the boat sped across the water.

Noah's hand landed on hers a moment later, and he tried to pry her fingers loose from the seat. "You're safe," he called over the hum of the motor.

She shrugged out of his grasp. "You should keep both

hands on the steering wheel," she yelled back. "And eyes on the road. I mean the water."

He laughed, his voice carrying over the noise.

She recited the ingredients for favorite recipes in her head, focusing on the familiar to distract her from how far away the dock was now. She knew Hidden Canyon Reservoir was nearly seven miles long, making it one of the larger bodies of water in the state. It wasn't as wide as Lake Dillon in nearby Summit County, a fact that comforted her a bit. She could see from edge to edge, and she watched cars drive along the state highway that bordered the park, counting the seconds between them as she tried not to hyperventilate.

After what seemed like an eternity, Noah slowed the boat and she could hear waves slapping against the aluminum side. Aluminum. Ugh. She was basically floating in a soda-pop can. The thought did not reassure her.

"We're in the middle," she said, her breath hitching. "How deep is it here?"

Noah checked the depth finder mounted near the boat's dashboard. "About eighty-five feet."

Katie swallowed.

"Water temperature is seventy-two degrees. That's like a hot tub for this time of year."

"What are those things?" She pointed to the black dots moving across the square screen.

"Fish. It tells you their depth so you know how to set the down riggers. Josh mainly uses the boat to take groups of guests fishing." He glanced at her then grinned. "The big schools of trout stick to the ten-to twelve-foot range. They won't be nibbling your toes, if that has you worried."

Katie dug her fingernails deeper into the seat cushion. "Everything has me worried." She straightened her shoulders and stood. "If I'm going to do this…" She began to step onto the side of the boat.

"Hold up, Little Mermaid." Noah grabbed her around the waist. "Don't dive in quite yet. This isn't the swimming lesson I had in mind."

Katie frowned. "Then why are we here?"

He killed the engine. "I want you to have a chance to get used to the water."

"I'd like to get this over with and get the heck off the water."

"Do you know anything about Hidden Valley?"

"It's big and black and terrifies me?"

He swiveled her chair until she faced him. "The Hidden Valley dam was one of the first to be built in this area, back in the early 1940s, under the Roosevelt administration. There's a hydroelectric power plant at the base of the dam that, along with some of the other facilities in the area, provides electricity for almost fifty thousand homes. So it's more than just a recreation area."

"Why do you know so much?"

He shrugged. "Colorado history interests me, especially how the areas that are surrounded by national forest were developed. People think of it as just another body of water, but there's more to it than that."

"My dad used to come up here after a big storm, when the water was choppy, to swim. It was the closest he could get to conditions in the ocean when he was training for the Ironman."

"But a ton colder."

"He liked that," she answered. "Thought it made him stronger. Wanted it to make me stronger."

"Is this where you had the bad experience?"

"No. My freak-out was in Lake Dillon. It was the summer they decided I was getting too fat and needed to train for a junior triathlon. I was twelve, and I'd developed early, you know?"

His eyes stayed on her face. "I can imagine," he said gently.

"My mom always had a boyish figure, ninety pounds soaking wet. I was a mutant Amazon compared to her and my dad." She tried to smile. "It's not good when the pre-teen daughter wears a bigger jeans size than her father."

"You're a woman," Noah argued. "You're supposed to have curves."

"The only curves my dad approved of were muscles. I didn't have those." She shrugged. "They were helping organize the event, and I'd been swimming and running and biking all summer long. I wanted to make them proud. But I'd only trained at the high school pool. I didn't realize how different open water would be. There were so many kids, all of them more prepared and in shape than me. When the race bell sounded, my group ran for the water. But as soon as I dived in, I freaked out. I had goggles but couldn't see in front of me. Other kids were swimming into me, over me. I kept going. I could hear my dad shouting from the shore and I wanted to finish. But the farther I swam, the more fear took over. I tried to stand and catch my breath, but I was out too far and I couldn't touch. Then the next wave of swimmers came and there were too many kids around me. I couldn't keep going."

She looked into the black water and the scene came back to her again. Panic rose in her chest at the memories of trying to lift her head and being knocked to the side. Taking in big gulps of water that left her choking and struggling to tread water. She realized she was almost hyperventilating when Noah placed his hands on her knees. "Breathe, sweetheart," he whispered. "I promise I'm going to take care of you today."

"I had to signal for the rescue dinghy. They hauled me onto it—it took two men to lift me out of the water. I threw up into the bottom of the boat. It felt like everyone was disappointed. I had to watch the rest of the swimmers before they brought me to shore." She shook her head. "My dad couldn't look at me. He was a world-class athlete and his daughter couldn't even swim a quarter mile."

"You panicked. It happens. Adrenaline can sometimes have a strange effect."

"My dad got the opportunity to help establish the training center in California shortly after school started in the fall." She picked at the skin on one of her fingers. "Mom suggested it would be better for me to stay with Gram."

"I thought you chose to stay in Crimson."

Katie saw the confusion on his face. Of course that was what he thought; it was the way she'd told the story. "It was less embarrassing than saying my parents had ditched me here. Of course, Gram was wonderful. I loved living with her." She leaned over toward the edge of the boat and dipped her fingers in the cool water. It was translucent in her hands, the shallow puddle in her palm as clear as if it had come from a faucet. Not scary at all.

"I remember you visited your parents during the summer and over winter break each year."

Katie shrugged. "At first it was awkward. We all knew the reason they left me behind, but no one wanted to talk about it. Then I started baking for them—energy bars to use at the training center. My dad really got into it—he's fascinated with the perfect fuel for the body. It's the one thing that still keeps me connected to them."

Noah looked toward the mountains. "Katie, you don't—"

"I'm not going to let one incident from my childhood define me. That day in the water was a turning point for me, and not in a good way. I need to move past it, as silly as it might seem."

"It doesn't seem silly." Noah's voice was gruff. "Let's go swimming."

Chapter 11

She humbled him with her bravery.

Noah turned off the motor as the boat drifted toward the small inlet near the cliffs on the western side of the reservoir. As they neared the bank, he tugged his T-shirt over his head and jumped into the water, his shoes squishing in the sandy bottom. He pulled the boat close to a fallen tree and tied the rope to one of the dead branches.

"You can stand here."

Katie stared at him for a moment before her brows shot down over her eyes. "This was a terrible idea. I can't get in the water with you looking like that..." She flicked her fingers at him. "And I look like a sausage." She smoothed her hands over the black material, and not for the first time, Noah wished he was touching her.

"You're the cutest sausage I've ever seen."

She snorted in response, making him grin. "I feel ridiculous." She stood, arms crossed over her chest. "It's stupid to be afraid of getting in water that's only as high as my knees."

"Don't say that. Nothing about you is stupid." He leaned down, splashed some of the cold lake water onto his chest and arms. He was overheated, and not only because of the warming temperature and sun beating down. Katie had weathered so much rejection from her parents, but she kept moving forward. He never would have guessed the full truth of why she'd lived with her grandma, and it made him feel like even more of a failure as a friend.

He couldn't imagine being deserted by his parents—because that would have never happened in his family. Noah was the one who'd separated himself during his father's illness, pulling away by degrees when the pain of staying became too intense.

Katie thought he had no fear, but that was far from the truth. He was afraid of everything that made him feel. He'd tried to insulate himself from the pain of possibly losing someone else he cared about. The fact that she trusted him gave him hope that he could change, that it wasn't too late. For either of them.

"You're stalling." He motioned her forward. "Get in the water."

She squeezed shut her eyes for a second. "I'm stalling," she admitted and inched closer to the port side of the boat. Flipping one leg over, she balanced on the ledge. Her knuckles turned white as she clenched the metal edge.

"It's shallow. You're safe." He wanted her to believe him, and not just in this moment. He may have failed in lots of areas, but he was determined to keep her safe. Not many people took Noah seriously and with good reason. Sure, he was good at his job and had plenty of responsibility with the Forest Service, but in none of his relationships with coworkers, friends or his family did people trust him with anything deeply emotional. Katie had, and it went a long way to fill some of the emptiness inside him.

He had lost time to make up for with her. Beginning now. He walked through the water and stopped at the side of the boat. His first impulse was to tease or splash her— something to lighten the mood and break through her nerves. But this was serious, and he wanted to respect that.

"Take my hand," he told her instead. "I've got you."

A knot of tension loosened in his chest when she placed her fingers in his. She hopped down, landing in the water with a splash.

"It's cold," she said, sucking in a breath.

"You'll get used to it."

She was gripping his fingers so tight he could see the tips turning bright pink. Katie holding him like a lifeline was the best sensation he'd had in ages.

"What now?" she asked, her body stiff.

"We walk out a little farther. Only as deep as you can handle."

"I'm such a wimp," she said with a groan.

"You're doing this, Katie. That makes you a badass."

She smiled. "I've never once been described as a bad anything."

"Stick with me," he assured her and was rewarded with a soft laugh.

A moment later the water was at her waist. She stopped and closed her eyes. He could almost see her steeling herself on the inside, fighting whatever demons were left over from that long-ago fear. The cold water lapped at his hips. A benefit, he thought, since the vulnerability in her expression was having the inconvenient reaction of turning him on. He had to get a hold on himself where Katie was concerned.

Slowly he let go of her hand. Her eyes snapped open as he backed away.

"Where are you going? You can't leave me."

"Come with me," he said, sliding his fingers through the ripples on the reservoir's surface. He moved deeper into the water.

She gave her head a short shake.

"You can do this," he told her, sinking under the water. Damn, it really was cold. He resurfaced, pushed the water from his face and grinned when he saw she'd stepped out far enough for the waves to brush the underside of her breasts. Too bad the wet suit covered them up so efficiently. He leaned back and gave several hard kicks until he was out far enough not to touch the bottom.

"Swim, Katie," he called to her.

She glanced behind her at the grassy shoreline then put her arms out straight and dived forward. As soon as her face hit the water, she reared up, sputtering and coughing, wet hair draped forward over her eyes and cheeks. She swiped at it, looking both scared and angry, making his heart lurch.

"I'll come back in," he said loud enough to be heard over her panting breath. "We'll start slower."

"No." She held up a hand. "Give me a minute." She slicked her hair away from her face. Droplets of water glistened on the tips of her eyelashes. He couldn't tell if they were lake water or tears but continued to tread water and wait.

"You don't have to put your head in."

"Yes, I do."

Her lips were moving, as if she was giving herself

a silent lecture. Then she pushed off again, slower this time. He eased out a little farther as she swam for him. He shouldn't have been surprised that once she started her form was perfect. If she'd been taught to swim by her father, he would have made sure of that. Within a few strokes she was next to him.

She lifted her face out of the water and looked around. "I did it," she whispered. Her teeth were chattering but she grinned. "I sw-swam."

"Just like the Little Mermaid," he agreed, taking her hand and pulling her into him. Her arms wrapped around his neck as her legs went around his waist. Again he was grateful for the cold water. "How are you doing?"

"Freaking out. But in a good way this time." She hugged him then gently kissed his cheek. "Thank you, Noah."

He forced himself not to shift his head and take her mouth with his, not to take advantage of their position and her emotions. He was her friend today and grateful for the chance to support her. With an effort of will almost beyond him, he pushed her away. "Race you back to shore."

She splashed water in his face at the same time she yelled, "Go!"

He laughed, wiped his eyes then followed her through the water.

"I want to swim more," Katie told Noah an hour later.

"You've got to get in the boat, honey." Noah leaned over the front of the boat to where she was treading water in a different, deeper inlet. "Your lips are blue."

Katie pressed her fingers to her mouth and realized she couldn't feel her lips. She swam to the back and put her foot onto the step that hung from the edge, hoisting herself out of the water. Noah had taken her to several different parts of the park so she could gain confidence swimming in new areas. She'd stripped out of the wet suit for this last dip, since she wouldn't have it to cover her on the Fourth of July. There was too much adrenaline charging through her to be embarrassed by Noah seeing her in a bathing suit.

He took her arm to steady her as she stepped on the boat then cursed. "Your skin is like ice. Hell, you're probably halfway to hypothermia. I should have never let you stay in the water so long."

"I'm fi-ne," she told him, but her teeth were chattering so hard it was difficult to speak.

"You need to dry off." He wrapped a towel around her shoulders and she sank into one of the captain's chairs. Katie didn't care that she was freezing. She'd done it. She'd conquered her fear of the water. It felt like the first step toward something new and exciting in her life.

"Tha-at was so-o fu-un."

"Stop trying to talk." Noah picked up another towel to dry her hair. "You're shaking so hard you'll chip a tooth."

He covered her head with the towel, scrubbing it over her hair. His touch felt so good all Katie could think was the old advice of reheating someone with hypothermia by skin-to-skin contact. Just the thought of pressing herself to the broad expanse of Noah's chest warmed her a few degrees. She giggled, the sound coming out more like a hiccup with her teeth still chattering.

"What's so funny?" Noah used the edge of the towel to smooth the hair away from her face.

She shook her head, but couldn't seem to stop grinning. "I'm happy."

He dropped to his knees in front of her. "I'm proud of you, Katie. I'd like to think your dad would be proud, too, but he's an insensitive jerk."

She arched one eyebrow.

"And I'm learning not to be," he added. He leaned closer, his mouth almost brushing hers as the boat dipped and swayed on the water. "Which is why I'm not going to kiss you now," he whispered.

"You're not?" She wasn't sure whether to be relieved or disappointed.

Disappointed, her body cried. She expected her brain to register relief, but it shut off as she stared into Noah's familiar blue eyes.

He gave a small shake of his head. "I want you," he said softly. "You know I do. But you have to choose. I can't make any promises, and my track record isn't the greatest."

She gave an involuntary snort and he smiled. "Right." He traced one finger along the seam of her lips. She must have defrosted, because his touch made her whole body tingle. "You've got your new plan for life, and I don't fit into that. I'm going to try to do the right thing and respect that."

No, she wanted to shout. *Kiss me. Be with me.* But she didn't say those things. Swimming was one thing, but taking an emotional risk was a different level of courage. One she didn't yet possess.

"I brought lunch," she said, trying not to sound as lame as she felt.

Something passed through Noah's gaze, but he pulled away and stood. "Are you warming up?"

Not as much as she'd like. But with the towel wrapped around her shoulders, she nodded and pulled the insulated tote bag from under the dash. Taking out two sandwiches wrapped in wax paper, she handed one to Noah. "Chicken salad," she told him.

"My favorite. What are you having?"

"Same thing—it was easier to make two. I also have fruit, chips and homemade lemonade."

She glanced at him when he didn't move. He stood in the center of the boat staring at the wrapped sandwich resting in his hand.

"What's wrong?"

He glanced at her, his brows furrowed. "Chicken salad is my favorite, but you don't like it."

"That's not true." She pulled out the bag of potato chips from the tote. "Exactly."

He shook his head, sank down on the seat across from her. "Is this your grandma's recipe?"

"Of course." She pretended to search the bottom of the tote. "I know I packed forks for the fruit."

"Then you definitely don't like it. I remember from when she made it in high school."

"I don't *dislike* it. Why are you making a big deal over the sandwich?"

"Because you're starting a new life." He tugged the tote bag out of her grasp. "Or so you tell me. You've got to start making what you want a priority, even if it's in your choice of sandwich fillings." He placed the bag on the floor and, before she could stop him, grabbed her sandwich out of her hand. "And I bet…" He unwrapped the wax paper. "I knew it. You used the heels."

Katie felt more exposed than if she was prancing around in a string bikini. "Who cares? We don't use them at the bakery. Why waste food?"

He lifted one corner of his sandwich. "Then why not use them on mine, too? I'm not picky."

"Because…" She grabbed the chip bag, tore it open with such force that a few chips flew out and landed in her lap. She stared at them, hating the embarrassment coursing through her. "It's habit. I use the ends of the bread for myself. Maybe I like the ends."

"No one likes the ends." Noah picked up the chips scattered across her thighs, his fingers golden against her paler skin. "You think I don't notice things, and most of the time you're right. But we've been friends for over ten years, Bug. I know how you put the needs of everyone around you in front of your own."

"You make it sound like a bad thing," she muttered, brushing her palms across her legs. Her stomach rolled, as if she was eleven years old again and her mother had caught her taking extra cookies from the jar on her grandma's counter.

Noah sighed, caught her hands in his and held them until her gaze lifted to his. "It's not, but I want to make sure you make yourself a priority." His smile was tender. "You may not think I can take care of you, but the guy you choose should put you first. You're perfect the way you are."

She wanted to believe those words were true. But she'd had a lifetime of the people around her proving they weren't. She hadn't been enough for her own parents. And as much love as Gram had given her, Katie had never been sure if it was unconditional. From the moment her mom and dad left her in Crimson, she'd made herself indispensable, working after school, weekends and summer vacation in the bakery. She'd learned the art of baking and made herself a valuable part of the business. Of course she loved it. But what if she hadn't? What if she'd rebelled or turned her back on her grandmother's legacy? What if she didn't help whenever someone needed her now? If she wasn't giving them her best, would people leave her behind just like her parents had?

Noah would never understand the deep roots of her fear of rejection. Even though he'd been through a lot with his family, he'd always had their unwavering love and support. She forced a laugh, tugged away from his grip and grabbed the sandwich from his lap. "You win," she said lightly. "No more bread ends for me."

He studied her a moment then unwrapped his sandwich. "I hope that's true," he said. "If you need somewhere to donate all those ends, my stomach volunteers." He took a bite and gave a little moan of pleasure. "Especially if the ends come with your chicken salad between them."

She appreciated that he let go of the topic. The rest of the afternoon saw them back to their normal camaraderie. She stifled a yawn as he docked the boat an hour later.

"Worn-out?" he asked, hopping onto the wood planks and tying a rope to one of the poles.

"Exhausted," she admitted. "I've been tired in general lately." She gathered her sunscreen and tote bag and stood. "I hope I'm not getting sick. There's too much to do before the Founder's Day Festival for that."

He reached out a hand and steadied her as she climbed onto the dock. "That's what I'm talking about. You work too hard, doing your part and everyone else's."

"Olivia is pregnant," she argued, exasperated they were back on this subject. "It's not like she dumped her responsibilities on me for no good reason."

"All I'm saying is you matter, too."

"Point taken." She dropped her sandals to the ground and shoved her feet in them, starting toward his truck before he could lecture her any longer. His words were especially irritating because they were true. She was pushing herself too hard, taking on more special orders at the bakery just as the summer tourist season was heating up.

With the extra work for the festival, she was spread way too thin. It grated on her nerves to have Noah point it out. People praised her overzealous work ethic. They didn't chastise her for it.

Noah caught up to her as she reached the back of the truck. "Don't be mad. I only want you to take care of yourself."

The concern in his eyes was real. She knew that. He'd only said out loud what she'd been thinking the past week. "Maybe I'll put Lelia in charge of some of the smaller orders. She trained at a bakery in San Francisco, so she knows her way around the kitchen." Katie had never shared any significant chunk of responsibility at Life is Sweet since her grandma's death. But she couldn't keep going at this pace.

"Good idea," he said and opened her door for her.

"Do you need help with the boat? I didn't mean to run off and leave you with all the work."

"I've got it." He patted the passenger seat. "You probably swam a couple miles today. You deserve a rest."

The truck's interior was warm from the sun beating through the front window. Katie's eyes started to drift shut, but she managed to stay awake while Noah maneuvered the boat onto the trailer. By the time they headed back toward town, her eyelids were so heavy it was hard to fight off her need for a nap.

"Close them," Noah said softly.

With a sigh she did and immediately drifted asleep.

She woke in her own bed, the light spilling through the curtains indicating early evening. She vaguely remembered them arriving at her house and Noah carrying her to her bedroom. Rubbing her eyes, she climbed from the bed. She needed to find the new cell phone she'd got to replace hers and check messages in case anything had come up with the bakery or the festival. She found the cooler bag, her purse and her phone sitting in a neat pile on the kitchen counter. Next to them was a plate covered in plastic wrap with a note on top.

"I'm not the only one with favorites. Thanks for a great day. N."

She unwrapped the plate to find a peanut-butter-and-banana sandwich. He'd even cut off the crusts. She quickly took a bite, savoring the chewy peanut butter and sweet banana slices. So Noah remembered her favorite sandwich?

She knew it wasn't a big deal—they'd been friends long enough that he should remember that kind of detail about her. As she chewed, she tried—and failed—to convince herself that she'd be able to remain friends with Noah while trying to fall in love with another man.

Where did that leave their friendship? Katie didn't want to think about the answer. Maybe it would get easier once his mom was fully recovered and he wasn't around all the time?

She only hoped that was the case. Otherwise, she was in big trouble.

Chapter 12

By the time Noah checked in with the Forest Service ranger station and returned the boat to Crimson Ranch, it was almost dinnertime. When someone was sick or in trouble in Crimson, food poured forth from the community like manna from heaven. Right now there were enough lasagnas, casseroles and soups in his mother's freezer to last them another three months. He and Emily took turns defrosting food for dinner each night while his mom wrote thank-you notes for the meals, flowers and miscellaneous bits of support she'd received.

The house was empty when he walked in, however, and his mom's Toyota SUV that Emily had been driving wasn't in the garage. He hoped this meant pizza or some kind of carryout for dinner. A person could only handle so much lasagna.

His mother spent most of her afternoons reading or doing crossword puzzles on the screened-in back patio, but when he didn't find her there, Noah quickly climbed the steps to the second floor. She'd been doing great since she'd returned from the hospital, almost back to her regular self as far as Noah could tell. He also understood how quickly something could change. The pancreatic cancer that claimed his father had been sudden and ruthless, only a matter of months between the initial diagnosis and his dad's death.

"Mom, where are you?" Noah shouted as he sprinted down the hall to the master bedroom. The door was closed, and he burst through then stopped as his mother's gaze met his in the mirror over the dresser.

"What's the matter?" She whirled around, took a step toward him. "Are you okay?"

He held up one hand as he tried to catch his breath and still his pounding heart. "Of course I'm okay. It's you I'm worried about."

"Me?"

He nodded. "Why are you dressed like that?" She wore a long, flowing skirt with a gauzy tunic pulled over it. A bright beaded necklace circled her neck, a gift from his father for her fortieth birthday, shortly before his dad had got sick. Her head was covered in a silk turban, covering the scar that ran from her temple to her ear. He'd got so used to seeing her with a simple knit cap or a baseball hat, he couldn't quite make sense of her looking so glamorous. She was even wearing makeup, something he hadn't seen his ever-practical mother do in years. Suddenly his skin felt itchy. He glanced at his watch. "Where's Emily? It's her turn to make dinner."

"I'm sorry, sweetie. Did I forget to tell you?"

"Tell me what?" he said through clenched teeth.

Her smile was wide. "I have a date tonight." She spun

in a circle, and Noah's mouth dropped open. His mother was twirling as if she was a teenage girl or princess-movie character. "I have to admit I'm a little nervous." She turned again toward the mirror, patted her head. "I wish my hair would grow back faster. I may have more wrinkles than I used to, but I always had good hair."

Noah felt as though his head was about to start spinning, as if he was some demon-possessed horror-movie cliché. "Where's Em?"

"She drove to Aspen to meet a friend from back East who's vacationing there. Davey went with her. It's a big step for both of them. Other than helping Katie with a few things for Founder's Day and grocery runs, your sister has barely left the farm since she got here."

"Mom, you've been home less than a week. Don't you think you should take it easy?"

"I feel great, like something in me is coming back to life. Does that sound silly?"

It would have a few weeks ago, but after spending time with Katie, especially the way it made him feel to be the one to help her overcome her fear of the water today, his mother's words struck a deep chord inside him. All of them had been wounded by his father's death and they'd each stopped living in their own personal ways. He realized now that Tori's betrayal, so soon after his father had died, had made him wall off his emotions. He might act like casual flings and random hookups were all he wanted in a relationship, but that was a lie he couldn't maintain any longer.

Seeing his mother go out with another man might be difficult, but he'd never deny her the chance to feel alive again. She deserved whatever—or whoever—could make her happiest.

Meg opened a tube of lipstick, dotted another layer

onto her lips. He walked up behind her, wrapped her in a hug and kissed her cheek. The scent of the perfume she'd been wearing for years, flowery and delicate, washed over him. He couldn't remember smelling it since his father's death. She'd put away too much of herself as part of her grief. "You don't need makeup to look beautiful, Mom. You know Dad would have wanted this. For you to be happy again."

"I loved him," his mother whispered, her eyes shining with tears.

"I know."

"He was proud of you, Noah."

His arms stiffened, and he tried to pull away, but she held on to his wrists. "I know you don't believe it, but he already saw the man you were going to become. Don't ever doubt that."

"I don't doubt his vision, but my ability to live up to it."

"If you could only—"

The doorbell rang, interrupting her. "I think that's for you," Noah said with a smile and released her.

She dropped the lipstick onto the dresser and smoothed her fingers under her eyes. "I can't believe I'm nervous. It's just dinner." She gave Noah a quick hug. "Come down with me and meet John."

He followed her down the stairs and opened the front door while she gathered her purse. It was odd to see her doctor standing on the other side, not wearing a white lab coat or scrubs. Tonight the man wore a collared shirt and thin cargo pants, both carrying the logo of a well-known fly-fishing company.

"Dr. Moore," Noah said, but didn't move from the doorway. He'd never got into the "man of the house" role since his father died but felt suddenly protective of his mother.

"Please call me John." The older man smiled, almost nervously, and tilted his head to try to look around Noah. "Is Meg ready?"

"Almost." Noah stepped onto the porch. "Where are you *kids* headed tonight?" Tater ambled up to them, sniffed at the doctor, who scratched her behind the ears.

"There's a new restaurant that opened recently off the highway between here and Aspen. The owner is one of my patients."

Meg walked up behind Noah, and the doctor's eyes lit with appreciation. "You look wonderful," the man said softly then glanced at Noah, one brow raised.

Noah gave him a small nod. "Have her home at a reasonable hour. She still needs rest."

"Noah," his mother said on a laughing breath. "He's a doctor. You don't have to lecture him."

But John only nodded. "I'll take care of her," he assured Noah, as if he knew Noah's words were about more than her physical well-being.

"Have a good time, then."

She kissed his cheek, and then she and John headed for the Audi SUV parked in front of the house. It was another perfect summer night, the air holding just a hint of a breeze and the sky beginning to turn varied shades of pink and orange. Noah watched them drive away as Tater pushed her head against his legs. "I'm not the only one who's been left without dinner, huh, girl?" She nudged him again and he went back into the house and scooped kibble into her bowl.

As the dog crunched, Noah looked around the empty kitchen. He could heat up leftovers from the fridge, but he was no longer in the mood for dinner. Normally Noah craved solitude when he wasn't out with friends. It was part of what he loved about his job with the Forest Service, the ability to lose himself in the quiet of the woods. Despite being social, a piece of him needed occasional alone time to recharge. It was one more excuse he'd made for not engaging in serious relationships. He didn't want a woman to encroach on his private time. "Determined to be single," Katie had called him. While that determination had once felt like a privilege, now he realized the price he paid for it was being lonely.

It didn't sit well, and he took out his phone to start texting. Suddenly the last thing he wanted in his life was more time by himself.

"Why are we out here on the most crowded day of the year?" Liam Donovan growled as he slowed to steer his MasterCraft speedboat around another group of smaller boats on Hidden Canyon Reservoir over the holiday weekend.

Noah pulled the brim of his ball cap lower on his head as he scanned the boats dotted around the water.

"Because Noah is stalking Katie," Liam's wife, Natalie, answered with a grin.

Noah shot her a glare.

"And Noah taught me to wakeboard." Natalie's nine-year-old son, Austin, munched on a piece of red licorice, practically bouncing up and down on the seat next to Noah.

"You did great, kid." Noah ruffled the boy's dark hair.

"I could have taught you to wakeboard," Liam said, turning to look at his stepson.

Austin shrugged. "He's better than you."

"Ouch," Liam muttered.

Natalie reached over and rubbed his shoulders. "You have many other skills, dear husband."

Noah's gaze flicked to his friends. Natalie and Liam had been a couple in high school then spent close to ten years hating each other. When Liam had returned to Crimson at the end of last year, he'd been the consummate example of the phrase "money can't buy happiness." Liam was a hugely successful entrepreneur and had recently headquartered his newest company in Crimson. But reuniting with Natalie had made the biggest change in him. Liam finally realized there was more to life than business. Noah had to admit he envied his friend. To rediscover that kind of love was a gift, he now realized.

"There she is." Noah stood, pressing his palms to the edge of the boat. She wore a two-piece bathing suit, which practically killed him, and her thick hair was tied back in a ponytail. The sight of her did strange things inside Noah's chest, so he tried to focus on what he could control. "They've got a whole group on that boat. Might be too many. Not sure if it's legal."

"Want me to call them in?" Liam asked with a laugh. "Or do you remember how many guys we used to pile on my boat in high school?"

Noah snorted. "We were lucky we didn't sink that thing." He gestured toward the red-and-silver powerboat floating near the far end of the reservoir. It was at least twenty-six feet, the bright colors and sleek lines making it look as if it belonged in Southern California instead of a mountain lake high in the Rockies. "How close can you get without them spotting us?"

Natalie looked at Austin. "Don't listen to either of them. You will never do the stupid things these guys did." She pointed two fingers at her eyes then turned them toward Noah. "I'm not sure I like what's going on here. Why are we spying on Katie? She's on a date."

"You know how she feels about water. I want to make sure she's comfortable."

"You're not looking to sabotage her?" Natalie narrowed her eyes. He didn't blame Natalie for doubting him. But even if he and Katie were only friends, Noah wanted to be the best damn friend he could.

"No one deserves happiness more than Katie," he answered, sinking back into his seat as Liam inched closer to the cliffs where Matt's boat was anchored. "I want to make sure she gets it."

"With Matt?" Natalie asked. "Because she likes Matt, Noah. It could turn into something more if given the chance."

"Nat, enough with the third degree," Liam said gently.

Noah rubbed the back of his neck, where a dull ache had been bothering him since the morning.

Austin handed him a long band of licorice. "You need this more than me."

"Thanks." He took the licorice and bit off one end, meeting Natalie's wary gaze. "I'm not going to mess it up for her. Promise."

"Okay," she said after a moment. "But that still doesn't explain why we're here."

Noah didn't understand it himself. A part of him hoped that Katie would see them on the water and realize she belonged with him instead. He squinted as they got closer, trying to identify the people on Matt's boat. He could see the woman who worked with Katie at the bakery—Lelia, he'd heard her called. There were three other guys with them, all lean and rangy, friends of Matt's, he assumed.

The truth was he liked the feeling he'd had when he and Katie spent their day on the reservoir. *He* wanted to be the one to help her if she got scared, to bolster her confidence and make her see she was more than she believed. Now she laughed at something Matt said, throwing back her head and exposing her delicate throat as that long tumble of dark hair cascaded over her shoulders. Noah felt his pulse leap at the sight and wanted nothing more than to lay Matt Davis out on the ground.

"We should go," he said suddenly. "Nat, you're right. It's stupid that I'm spying on her this way. Katie can take care of herself."

"No way," Austin whined. "Liam, you promised we could go cliff jumping."

"You promised *what*?" Natalie choked out.

Out of the corner of his eye, Noah saw someone throw an oversize rubber inner tube into the water off the back of Matt's boat. Ignoring Liam and Natalie, he turned his full attention across the water. Katie was fastening a life vest across her chest as Matt adjusted one on Lelia's tiny frame.

Katie smiled at something one of the other guys said, but her hands were balled tight at her sides. "You don't have to prove anything to them," he whispered, willing his words to carry to her.

Instead, she and Lelia climbed onto the colorful tube, stomachs down, and Matt pushed them out behind the boat. Noah glanced at the sky—perfectly blue and the air was almost still. The temperature was forecast to hit over ninety today, so conditions were perfect for tubing. Hell, he'd had a great time in the water an hour earlier helping Austin learn how to balance on the wakeboard.

He knew Katie was more confident now, but he hadn't expected her to volunteer for something like this. He hoped Matt took it easy on the two women. Depending on the boat's driver, tubing could be fun or it could be a crazy ride.

As Matt's boat sped off toward the open middle of the reservoir, Natalie came to stand next to him. "Is Katie tubing?" she asked incredulously.

"Yeah."

"You took her swimming last week, right?"

He gave a brief nod, cursing under his breath as the tube disappeared around a bend in the lake.

"She's not afraid anymore?"

"She's good," he said, more for his own benefit than Natalie's. "She can handle this."

His stomach lurched as the boat came back into view. "If that idiot will slow the hell down. He's going way too fast."

"Can we go to the cliffs now?" Austin asked.

"In a minute," Natalie said automatically. Noah heard her breath catch as the inner tube hit another boat's wake and popped into the air a few feet. Both women held on and Matt headed toward the center of the reservoir then spun the boat in a wide arc. The tube skidded across the water, bumping through the waves as slack filled the line before it jerked tight again.

"They're heading for us," Natalie murmured.

Noah shook his head and glanced past the front of Liam's boat. "He's taking them to the edge of the reservoir." The concrete dam front loomed on the other side of the cliff face. It was where the water from the mouth of the Hidden Creek River flowed into the dam. A rope and buoys floated fifty yards in front of the dam, alerting boaters and swimmers that the area was off-limits. It made that stretch of water almost empty compared to the popularity of the rest of the lake on a weekend holiday.

"Liam, head toward the dam." As his friend hit the throttle, both he and Natalie dropped into seats.

Austin leaned forward around Noah. "Is that Miss Katie?" he asked, pointing at the inner tube skimming through the water.

Natalie's smile looked forced as she turned to her son. "Sure is, bud. She's quite the daredevil, isn't she?"

Noah glanced at the boy and saw his eyes widen. "That's way faster than you went on the wakeboard, Noah."

"That's faster than anyone should be driving with the reservoir so crowded." As if his words were an omen, a small Jet Ski took a sharp turn then stalled out, stopping directly in the path of Matt's boat. Noah cursed as the boat swerved one way then the other. He could see the men in back laughing and pumping their fists as if egging on Matt's reckless driving. The tube hit the boat's wake and ricocheted into the air before slamming back down. It immediately flew up again and this time one of the women came off, bouncing across the water like a skipped stone. Lelia hit the water and popped back up thanks to her life vest, brushing her hair out of her face.

Noah's vision turned red as he saw Matt bump knuckles with one of his friends on the boat. But he didn't slow down, instead making another wide turn then a sharper one, sending the tube airborne and Katie soaring through the air along with it.

"Katie," Natalie yelled. "Liam, get to her now."

But unlike Lelia, Katie didn't pop up out of the water. Instead, her life vest immediately surfaced. Empty.

"Where is she?" Natalie screamed.

"Stop," Noah yelled and stripped off his shirt, diving in toward the place where the yellow life vest bobbed empty in the water.

Chapter 13

For a few moments, Katie didn't register anything but the sensation of flying through the air. Then she hit the water with a force that tore the air from her lungs. Her arms already burned from holding on to the handles of the inner tube, so she pumped her legs, finally surfacing with a choked breath.

When she began to sink again, she patted her chest and realized with a start that the life vest had ripped off when she landed. Panic seized her as a wave splashed over her head. She focused on treading water, squinting against the sun's reflection on the lake. Surely Matt would be coming for her any second, but it was hard to see anything beyond the waves from various boat wakes swelling around her. Her heart squeezed and she struggled to rein in her hysteria. A flash of yellow caught her gaze as the water receded for a moment.

Her life vest.

Make it to the life vest.

Her arms felt like lead weights as she lifted one then the other out of the water. *You can do this*, she told herself, but the voice in her head sounded like Noah's. Coaxing her, calming her and making her believe she could overcome the fear that had been a part of her for so long. She could almost hear his voice calling to her.

Then he was in front of her, appearing over the crest of a wave, her life jacket in his hand. "Grab on," he said and she reached for it. Reached for him.

His arms went around her waist. "I've got you, sweetheart," he said against her hair, his voice thick with emotion. "Damn, you scared me."

She opened her mouth, but no sound came out. Fear and panic still lapped at the corners of her mind, just like the water rising and falling around her.

"Focus on me," he said and she did. On his blue eyes, even brighter against his sun-kissed skin, on the scruff on his jaw. His thumb brushed across her cheek, the slight pressure making her wince. "You already have a bruise forming. Just a minute more and Liam will have the boat here."

"What are you—" Water splashed into her face and she coughed again.

"Katie, are you okay?" She looked up as she heard Natalie yelling to her.

Her brain wouldn't register why her friend was peering down at her from the side of a shiny blue-and-silver speedboat.

"Where's Lelia?"

"She's fine."

"What about Matt and the boat?"

She felt Noah stiffen, his lips thinning into a tight line. "Let's get you to safety. Then we'll deal with Matt Davis."

"My arms…" she whispered. "I don't think I can pull myself out of the water."

"I'll help you." He swam them toward the back of the boat, where Liam had slung a plastic ladder next to the engine.

"Pull her up," Noah commanded, positioning Katie in front of the ladder. "Step up as he lifts you, Bug," he whispered in her ear.

Gritting her teeth against the pain, she took hold of the metal railing. With his hands on her hips, Noah held her out of the water while Liam gripped under her arms and hauled her onto the boat. She stumbled and Natalie grabbed her around the waist, helping her to one of the seats near the front of the boat as she wrapped a towel around Katie's shoulders.

"Are you okay?" Natalie repeated her earlier question.

Embarrassment washed over her. After all her preparation, she'd needed to be rescued from the water yet again. "I'm fine," she mumbled, but they all knew it was a lie.

Apparently Austin believed her because a wide grin broke across his face. "That was so cool, Miss Katie. You must have caught six feet of air." He stood on tiptoes and reached his hand above him to indicate how high the inner tube had flown. "Then you slammed down on the water."

She could return his smile now that she was safely on the boat. So many parts of her body ached, but the reality was she'd made it.

"You hit so hard your life vest came off," he all but shouted. "Wait until I tell my friends that story. They won't believe it from the cupcake lady."

"Austin, enough." Natalie's tone was firm but gentle.

"Sorry." He looked at Katie, sheepish. "No offense."

"None taken." She ran two fingers over her cheek. It hurt but not as badly now. "I was wearing one of the larger life vests because Lelia's so tiny she needed the woman's size. I thought I'd tightened it enough, but it must have slipped over my head on impact."

"Impact," Noah growled, sounding disgusted. "What the hell was he thinking taking you on that kind of ride?"

"Don't make this a big deal, Noah." Katie lifted her chin. "I mean it."

He opened his mouth to respond, but at that moment Matt's boat came closer. The guys on the boat were cheering with shouts of "Awesome, Katie," "Sweet dismount" and "You nailed it."

"You want to swim over and we'll get you back in the boat?" Matt called. Lelia stood next to him, grinning from ear to ear. It made Katie feel like an even bigger wimp.

She sucked in a breath as Noah snapped, "You're an ass—"

"We're heading to shore," Liam said, cutting off Noah midsentence. "We'll meet you over there."

Matt nodded, still smiling as Liam motored away.

Natalie reached out to take Katie's hand. "You're sure you—"

"Please don't say anything," Katie said, glancing from Natalie to Noah. "None of them knew I was nervous on the water."

"It doesn't matter," Noah yelled over the roar of the engine. "He shouldn't have been driving that fast."

Katie agreed, but she wasn't going to fuel Noah's anger by admitting it.

The ride across the reservoir to the grassy shore below the parking lot and picnic area lasted only a few minutes.

In that time, Katie took stock of what had happened. She blamed herself for letting Matt and his friends convince her to get on the tube in the first place. She liked Matt, but the more time she spent with him, the more she realized he was an adrenaline junkie like her father. As much as she wanted to fit in with him and his friends, someone like Lelia had much more in common with them. Most of the talk on the boat today had centered around the best spots around Crimson for mountain biking and rock climbing, both sports Lelia had been eager to try. Other than another inner-tube ride, Katie could think of nothing she'd want to do less.

"I need a bathroom break," Natalie said as they pulled into a space between two smaller boats.

Noah hopped into the water, hauling the boat to shore with the rope Liam tossed him. As muscles bunched in his arms and across his shoulders, Katie's mouth went dry and she dropped her head into her hands. She was pathetic.

Austin jumped into the water, too, leaving Natalie and her alone in the boat.

"Why were you guys out there?" she asked, lifting her gaze. "Liam normally hates crowds. A holiday weekend on the lake can't be his idea of a good time."

"Noah was worried about you."

"Why? Didn't he think I could handle it?"

"From what I could tell, it's because he cares about you." Natalie shook her head, one side of her mouth curving. "I've never seen him like that. He had us motoring all over the lake to find you." She held up a hand when Katie would have argued. "Not because he didn't think you could handle yourself. He wanted to look after you. Like a friend, but it was more. A lot more."

Katie sighed, looked at Noah standing on the bank talking to Liam and Austin. "This was the summer I was going to get over him, Nat. There's no future there."

"Are you sure? People change. Sometimes they only need to open their eyes to what's in front of them." She gave Katie's shoulder a squeeze. "I think the combination of seeing you with another guy then hurtling across the lake may have done that for our buddy Noah."

Katie thought about that. Yes, she'd vowed to move past her feelings for him. She wanted more from life than he was willing to give her, and the frustration at her unrequited love was beginning to take a toll on their friendship. But what if Natalie was right? Had she given up too soon? Or was he only interested in her because suddenly she was out of reach?

She glanced up as Matt's boat pulled in at the end of the line of boats docked below the picnic area. One of his friends was driving now, and Matt climbed off the front to beach the boat and tether it to a tree stump. She closed her eyes so she wouldn't be tempted to compare him to Noah. Matt was handsome, but her body didn't react to him like it had to Noah moments ago.

"That won't end well."

Katie blinked at Natalie's words. As Matt finished knotting the rope, Noah was stalking toward him, every muscle in his body radiating anger.

She scrambled forward, holding the towel around her waist as she threw her legs over the side of the boat. She made her way up the shoreline, picking her way over the rocks that dug into her bare feet.

"You're a reckless idiot," Noah yelled, pushing Matt in the chest.

The other man, several inches shorter than Noah, stumbled back, the easy smile disappearing from his face. "What the hell was that for?" He took two steps toward Noah.

"For putting those women in danger. You were driving like an idiot with them on the tube behind you."

"Who are you, the coast guard?" Matt came forward until his chest almost touched Noah's. "We were having fun, Grandpa."

Noah's head snapped back as if Matt had actually hit him. In his circle of friends, Noah was the life of the party. Katie knew he cultivated and protected that image like a coveted prize.

"Fun?" Noah all but spit the word in Matt's face. "You almost killed Katie."

Matt's expression registered shock then anger. "She was having a good time."

"She's afraid of the water," Noah ground out.

Katie was right behind them but stopped as the group took in Noah's words. Again embarrassment rolled through her. "I'm fine," she said tightly, unwilling to look at Matt's friends on the boat. She kept her gaze fixed on him and Noah.

"Is that true?" Matt backed up from Noah a few steps. "Why didn't you say anything?"

"It's not…" She trailed off. How could she deny something so much a part of her, even if she didn't want it to be? "I was having fun."

Noah cursed under his breath. "Are you joking?" He turned fully toward her, blocking Matt's view with his body. "That was the opposite of fun for you."

"I wanted to get on that inner tube, Noah. No one forced me."

"He shouldn't have been driving like that."

"I'm sorry," Matt said behind him. "Katie, you should have signaled me to slow down."

"I thought it was great," Lelia called from the boat.

Katie narrowed her eyes at the woman.

"Sorry," Lelia muttered. "But I did."

"You're enough," Noah whispered, pitching his voice low enough that she was the only one who could hear him. "Just the way you are, Katie. You don't need to try this hard."

His words cut across her, turned her insides to liquid and fire. All she'd wanted in life was to be enough for someone. Without having to try. She'd *always* had to try, as if she was inherently lacking as a person. She'd told herself she was turning over a new leaf, but it felt as if she'd traded one mask for a different guise. She'd wanted to move off the sidelines so badly that she'd pitched herself headfirst into becoming someone she was never meant to be.

"Okay," Matt said, stepping around Noah. "Now we know that you're not one for adventure." His voice was kind, but there was a note of disappointment in it she couldn't miss. He held out a hand to her. "Let's have lunch. Then you can keep the boat steady while the rest of us cliff jump."

On the boat, Lelia clapped her hands.

Noah snorted and bent so he was looking into her eyes, his gaze intense. "You're not going back out there with him," he said softly.

She bit down on her lip, glanced at Matt. "I came with them, Noah. I don't want anyone to think that ride rattled me."

"Who cares what they think?" he shot back.

"I do."

He straightened and turned on his heel. "Liam, I'm done

for the day. I'll catch you back in town," he called and stomped off, heading up the hill.

Matt rubbed his hand along her upper arm. "Damn, that was intense. Makes me want a beer." When she only stared, he dropped his hand. "You brought lunch, right?"

She nodded. "In the cooler on the boat."

"Great." He chucked her on the shoulder. "That was a massive crash," he said with a boyish grin.

Katie looked between Matt's boat to where Liam's was tethered five feet away. Natalie raised her eyebrows, her silent question clear to Katie.

"I'm not going back on the boat with you." She spoke the words out loud and saw Natalie nod in approval.

Matt shrugged. "Suit yourself. Can we still keep the food?"

"Sure."

"Katie, do you want me to come with you?" Lelia spoke from the deck of the boat.

"No, you stay." She smiled. "Have fun and take tomorrow off. I'll see you at the bakery on Tuesday."

The young woman squealed with delight. "Really? Tomorrow off? You're the best boss ever."

The best boss, the best friend, the best committee chair. As long as it meant putting other people's needs in front of her own, Katie was a veritable expert.

But what about what she wanted? If she had to admit the truth, she was so unused to taking care of her own needs, she barely registered having any. Her eyes drifted to the parking lot above the reservoir.

"Take these," Natalie said behind her, and Katie whirled, unaware of her friend's approach. Natalie handed her a pair of slip-on sandals. "They'll make getting up the hill a lot easier."

Katie dropped the shoes to the ground and slipped her feet into them. "I'm sorry this day was so much trouble for you guys." She hitched her head toward Liam and Austin, who were busy tying a lure to the end of a fishing pole.

"This has been a great day," Natalie told her with a smile. "You have no idea how much I enjoyed watching Noah Crawford make a fool of himself over a woman." She winked. "Especially when that woman was you."

"He didn't—"

Natalie interrupted her with a wave of one hand. "Go on, before you miss him. Austin isn't going to leave the boat until we take him to the cliffs."

"Thanks, Nat." Katie gave her friend a quick hug and turned.

"And, Katie?"

She glanced over her shoulder.

"That landing will go down in history. It was epic."

Epic. That word had never been linked to her before, and Katie found that, despite the aches and pains that went with it, she kind of liked being epic. Even if it was an epic fail. With a laugh, she headed for the top of the hill.

Chapter 14

Noah sat in the parking lot, trying to get a handle on himself. His truck had been parked in the sun all day, and the temperature inside was almost stifling. He welcomed the heavy air and the bead of sweat that rolled between his shoulder blades. He hit the automatic door lock, as if that would keep him from dashing back down the hill to pluck Katie out of the boat with Matt and his adult-frat-boy friends.

It was none of his business. The rational part of him knew that, but logic had disappeared the moment Noah thought Katie was in danger. Hearing her downplay the incident to Matt left Noah feeling like an overprotective geezer. Hell, he and Liam had done way more danger-ous things over the years—on the water, on the slopes. The group mentality dumbed down their common sense to preteen-boy levels. But never Katie. Even over summer breaks, she'd been the responsible one, always making sure her friends got home safe. Maybe that was why he'd overlooked her for so long. He'd been so intent on acting out as a way to numb the regret and sadness he felt over his father's death. Katie, with her stability and sweetness, had been practically invisible to him.

Now she was all he could see. All he could feel. He wanted to share every tiny thing that happened in his day, to make up for lost time in discovering all the hidden-away pieces of her. But he was a bad bet, and he didn't blame her for rejecting him. It was payback long overdue. If nothing else, he'd take it like a man.

With a heavy sigh, he turned the key in the ignition as a knock sounded on the passenger-side window. Katie stared in at him, peering through the glass.

He rolled down the window then wiped the back of his hand across his forehead.

"I just wanted to say thank you." Her chest rose and fell as if she was having trouble catching her breath. He could barely tear his gaze away from the slight swell of her breasts peeking out from the low V-neck of the bathing-suit top. "For rescuing me. For being there when I needed you."

"You didn't need me," he answered, shaking his head. "You would have been fine. You were swimming toward the life vest when I got to you. I overreacted, and I'm sorry." He laughed, but the sound was bitter. "Again. I know you can take care of yourself."

"And everyone else in town while I'm at it?" she said, humor in her voice.

His gaze snapped to hers. "I hate that you wore a bikini today."

She looked down at herself then back at him, her eyes suddenly dancing. "It's a tankini and about an inch of skin is showing between the top and bottom."

"It's an access thing," he said irritably but couldn't help his smile as she laughed so hard she snorted. He'd bet Matt Davis never made her snort, and the feeling of accomplishment was ridiculous. But the thought of another man having access to Katie's body, to the vibrant passion he knew she hid under her placid, sweet surface, made his temper flare again. "What is this, Katie? What are you doing up here when the *fun* is down on the lake?"

She straightened her shoulders, as if steadying herself or drawing courage. "Unlock the car, Noah," she whispered.

Something had changed in her tone, and his pulse leaped in response. He flicked the button for the lock but didn't watch as she climbed in next to him. He kept his eyes straight out the front of the truck, but he was all too aware of her. Even after a dip in the reservoir, Katie smelled delicious. This time the scent of vanilla was mixed with suntan lotion. The combination made him immediately hard.

He put his hands on the steering wheel, not trusting himself to resist reaching for her.

"You told me to choose," she said softly. "I choose you."

He felt dizzy, as if every one of his secret desires was being handed to him on a platter and he didn't know which to select first. He turned to her now, his hands still on the wheel. He didn't want to ruin this moment, to push her too far. More than anything, he didn't want to hurt her by being his usual self.

"Say it again." He kept his voice calm, his expression neutral, but Katie smiled.

She folded her legs underneath her on the leather seat and leaned over the console. Cupping his face with her hands, she swayed closer until her lips were almost grazing his and he sucked in her breath each time he inhaled. It was sweeter than he'd ever imagined. Her eyes held his as she spoke against his mouth. "I choose us." She brushed her lips against his, gentle and almost tentative, as if she expected him to push her away.

That was the last thing on Noah's mind. He took hold of her waist and hauled her fully onto his lap, pressing her to his bare chest. His hands moved up and down her back as he deepened the kiss, sweeping his tongue into her mouth, groaning as she met his passion. Her nails dug into the muscles under his shoulder blades and he welcomed the sensation, which only heightened his own pleasure in the moment. This was what he'd wanted—for so much longer than he'd realized.

A loud wolf whistle split the air and someone banged hard on the hood of his truck. "Get a room," whoever it was called as the sound of laughter spilled into the truck.

Katie still clung to him, giggling against his throat. He tipped up her chin, her lips wet and swollen from his kisses. He wanted to take her, right here in the cab of his truck, in broad daylight. He felt like a teenager again, light and carefree, his only concern the fastest way to get her naked.

The thought made him grin. "I'm going to take you home now." His grin widened as she frowned. "I'm coming in with you. I'm going to stay with you, Katie. All night long."

"Oh." She breathed out the one syllable, then climbed back into the passenger seat. After fastening her seat belt, she slunk down low, her face cradled in her hands.

"What are you doing?" he asked as he drove out of the parking lot and onto the county highway toward town.

She lifted her head once they were on the open road. "People saw us…you know…making out. What if they recognized me? Or you? Or the two of us together?"

"I don't care who knows it's you and me." He reached for her hand, tugged it away from her face and laced their fingers together. "I want everyone to know you're mine, Katie. Because you are now. I'll kiss you all over the damn town if that's what it takes. In fact, there are lots of things I can think of for us to try." Then, her hand in his, he proceeded to tell her all the wicked things he wanted to do to her and with her—in Crimson, in the forest, in every room of her house.

It was the longest hour of his life.

By the time Noah parked the truck crooked against the curb in front of her house, Katie felt dizzy with need. All the way home, he'd whispered the details of what he wanted to do to her as his thumb traced a light circle on the back of her hand, and it was driving her crazy.

They laughed as they raced up the front walk. She'd locked her door when she'd left this morning since there were so many nonlocals in town for the holiday, but her purse was still stuffed into a cubby on Matt's boat.

"My hide-a-key," she said on a gasp, bending to lift the rock from under the bushes where the key was hidden. Then gasping again as Noah whirled her around, his mouth crashing into hers. They stayed there for several minutes, kissing deep and long. He was making good on his promise of claiming her in front of the whole town, and Katie wondered if any of her elderly neighbors were watching this public display.

Noah picked her up as he climbed the steps, and she automatically wrapped her legs around his lean hips. One of his hands inched up her back. "Give me the key," he said against her mouth, and she pressed it into his palm.

She wasn't sure how he was going to manage to hold

on to her and open the front door, but a moment later the lock turned.

"You have mad skills," she said on a laugh.

He drew back enough to look into her eyes, his grin wicked. "You have no idea."

As well as she knew him, he might be right. The first time with Noah had been amazing, but this felt completely new. He'd chosen her. They'd chosen each other, and it made all the difference. She'd tried to convince herself that what was between them was only physical, but now she didn't bother to guard her heart. It was pointless anyway. Noah had her heart, and he had from the first. No matter what happened down the road, this was her moment to revel in all she felt for him.

He kicked shut the door then moved toward her bedroom. Bending to rip away the quilt and sheets, he dropped her on the bed with so much force she bounced once and her breath, already uneven, whooshed out of her lungs. "Tell me you have protection," he whispered as he followed her onto the bed. His hands were on her stomach, inching up her swim top. He pressed his mouth to her belly button then skimmed his tongue along her rib cage.

"I… Yes…oh, yes…" she whispered.

"Oh, yes, in general?" he asked and she heard the smile in his voice. "Or, yes, you have protection?"

"In the nightstand."

"Good. Now lift your arms."

She raised them over her head and he pulled her bathing suit up and off, leaning over her to open the nightstand drawer.

He sat back again, gazing down at her. "Has anyone told you today how beautiful you are?"

Normally Katie would feel shy at being so exposed, but

the intensity in his gaze gave her confidence. She tapped a finger to her chin, pretending to ponder the question. "One of Matt's friends told me I was the hottest muffin maker he'd ever met. Does that count?"

Noah growled low in his throat. "I'm going to kill that guy." He planted his hands on either side of her head and lowered himself over her. His chest hair tickled her bare skin, and heat pooled low in her body. "You are the most beautiful thing I've ever seen," he whispered. He slanted his lips over hers, but when she tried to deepen the kiss, he broke away, his mouth trailing to her jaw then down her throat and finally to her breast. "So beautiful," he said again, then took one nipple into his mouth.

She arched off the bed with a moan. He continued to lick and suck at her breasts, driving her wild, as he tugged the bathing-suit bottom over her hips. Her hands splayed across his lower back, kneading the muscles there. She wanted to feel all of him, to stay like this and never let reality back into their lives. Nothing had ever felt so good, she thought, but still she wanted more. Reaching between them, she unsnapped the waistband of his board shorts, pushing at them.

He released her for just a moment, stripped off the shorts and his T-shirt then tore open the foil wrapper. He settled himself between her legs, moving just enough that the pressure made her breath catch.

"Yes, Noah. Please." She didn't care if she was begging. She needed him so much. He kissed her deeply as he rocked against her but lifted his head as he thrust into her. Their gazes locked and it seemed to heighten the pleasure, to increase the intimacy until Katie felt a tear drop from the edge of her eye onto the pillow.

Noah pressed his lips to her skin and she twined her

legs more tightly around him. A groan ripped from his throat that sent shivers through her. Pressure built inside her until it finally burst, a bright shower of golden light engulfing her, soothing all the parts inflamed by their passion. Noah shuddered, burying his face against her neck and crying out her name.

It was the most beautiful thing she'd ever heard.

They lay like that for several minutes, the heat of his body cocooning her in warmth. He smoothed the hair back from her face, threading his fingers through it as he spread it across the sheets. The kisses he gave her now were gentle, tiny touches of light on her skin. She didn't dare move, afraid to break the spell and have him leave her as he had the last time.

"All night," he said, as if reading her thoughts. He gently sucked her earlobe into his mouth and she squirmed underneath him. "Right now if you keep moving like that."

As she laughed, he rose from the bed, padded to the bathroom then returned a few minutes later. Katie still lay where she was, staring at the ceiling, although she'd pulled the sheets and quilt up over herself.

He lifted the covers and climbed in next to her, dropping a kiss to her mouth just as she stifled a yawn.

"Sorry," she said automatically. "I'm always tired lately."

"It's the time on the lake," he said, turning on his side and tucking her in tight against his chest. "Swimming is tiring enough, but the daredevil stunt from today would exhaust anyone."

She yawned again. "Natalie told me it was *epic*."

"All I know is it almost gave me an epic heart attack." He pressed his mouth to her bare shoulder. "How's your body holding up after that crazy ride?"

She shrugged. "My cheek hurts and my arms are sore. I have another bruise on my chin. It'll hurt worse tomorrow, I know. But I'm okay."

"Just okay?"

"Tired," she added and he nipped at her neck. "And blissfully satisfied. And happy. Mainly happy."

"Me too. Go to sleep now, Bug."

"Are you—"

"I'll be here when you wake up. I keep a change of clothes in the truck for when Jase and I go for a run or to the gym after work. I'm not going anywhere. Promise."

She wasn't sure whether it was the words that made her trust him or the conviction with which he said them. Perhaps it was the overwhelming exhaustion she felt. The constant fatigue, even with her busy schedule, was starting to concern her. She'd worked long hours for years, but the past few weeks had been difficult to handle. As she drifted off, she decided she'd make an appointment with her family doctor next week. She wouldn't tell Noah, though. No need to give him something extra to worry about after what had just happened with his mom.

But right now a nap was exactly what she needed. She fell asleep, happy to be enveloped in Noah's embrace.

Chapter 15

Noah registered Katie's surprise as she walked into the kitchen hours later.

"You're still here." Her voice was scratchy with sleep and she wore a tattered floral robe that was so worn it was practically see-through.

"I promised," he told her, tamping down the annoyance that flared at the thought she hadn't believed he would stay.

"I'm glad," she said, walking forward to kiss him. All thoughts of annoyance fled as he buried his face in her hair. She smelled like sleep, vanilla and like him. A wave of primal satisfaction rolled through him and somewhere deep in his gut the word *mine* reverberated.

She was his.

"Why are you always sniffing me?" She pulled back, looping a long strand of hair between her fingers and pulling it to her nose. "Do I need a shower?"

"No. You smell fantastic. You always do. You smell like…"

Home.

His chest constricted at the word. It was true, even if he hadn't realized it before now. Katie had always felt like home to him.

"You smell like the bakery," he answered instead.

"Mixed with a healthy dose of lake water." She grimaced. "The bruise on my cheek is darkening."

"Matt is an idiot."

She smiled, reached around him for the glass of water he'd set down. "I would have said the same thing about you a few weeks ago," she answered, taking a drink.

"I'm a slow learner." He tugged on the tie looped around the front of the robe. "How is it possible that an article of clothing your grandma would have worn can be such a turn-on to me?"

"This was Gram's robe."

"I feel like a sick pervert." His fingers worked to loosen the tie.

She swatted at his hand. "Stop," she said with a giggle. "I'm not wearing anything underneath."

"Doubly perverted."

She pushed away from him. "Before you go too far, I'm starving. Let me make us something to eat."

"Done." He inched the fabric off her chest and kissed the swell of her breast.

She moaned a little, but glanced around her empty kitchen. "How?"

The doorbell rang. "Delivery," he said against her skin.

"No one delivers on the holiday. All the restaurants are too busy."

The doorbell rang again.

"I pulled some strings at the brewery."

Reluctantly he stepped away from her. "You should put on some clothes, or the food's going to be cold before we get to it."

"Sweet-potato fries?" she asked, rubbing her stomach.

"Of course. They're your favorite."

She grinned. "I owe you, then." She quickly pulled the robe apart to flash her breasts at him. "Later."

"Forget the food," Noah growled, lunging for her.

She jumped away, running for her bedroom. "Answer the door, Noah," she called over her shoulder.

He set out containers of food, glancing up as she returned. She'd traded the robe for a tank top and black sweatpants. Her hair tumbled down in waves around her shoulders. When she moved, he could see a purple lace bra strap peeking through. Had she always worn lacy lingerie? What a fool he'd been all these years. He had so much time to make up.

"I can't believe how hungry I am," she said, taking plates from the cabinet.

They sat down to eat the burgers and fries. Noah lit the candle that sat in the middle of the table then dimmed the kitchen lights.

"Romantic," Katie murmured, her voice a little breathless. He had to agree. As casual as it was, this was indeed the most romantic dinner he'd ever had.

"But this isn't a date," he told her firmly. "I'm going to take you out for a real date with reservations at the best restaurant in Aspen."

"I don't care about that," she said, shaking her head. "Tonight is perfect."

"Agreed, but you deserve the five-star treatment, and I want to be the guy to give it to you."

Katie went suddenly still.

"What's wrong?"

"Nothing. We're missing the big fireworks display. I hope you didn't have plans to take your mom and sister?"

He shook his head. "Mom has a date tonight." At her questioning gaze, he shrugged. "Her surgeon. Second time out with him this week. She really likes him."

"And you're okay with that?"

"I am," Noah said, releasing a breath. "Dad would want her to be happy, so I want the same thing."

She came around the table and plopped onto his lap, snagging one of his fries in the process. "You're a good man, Noah Crawford." She kissed him on the cheek then popped the bright orange fry into her mouth.

"Do you really believe that or are you just angling for my food?"

"Both."

He kissed her then glanced at his watch. "I've got a surprise for you."

She angled her head. "Is it a good surprise?"

"I hope so." He lifted her to her feet. "I'll get the dishes cleaned up while you put on a sweater. We have about ten minutes."

"Where are we going?" She smoothed a hand over her tank top. "Should I change clothes or at least brush my hair?"

"Neither. It's a private party tonight. Trust me."

He said the words lightly, but something tender unfurled in his chest when she nodded and disappeared toward her bedroom. It had been a long time since anyone he cared about really trusted him. Sure, his mom said she depended on him, but even after her illness she'd been almost as self-sufficient as usual.

He put the plates in the dishwasher and repacked the empty boxes in the paper sack. By the time Katie came out, he was pacing the front of the house, anxious in a way he hadn't been since he was a teenager.

"I'm ready," she said, having buttoned a thick sweater over her tank top and traded the sweats for a faded pair of jeans.

"Great," he said, embarrassed when his voice caught. "Great," he repeated, clearing his throat.

She came toward him. "Are you nervous?" She sounded amused.

"Of course not." He wiped his palms on his shorts then took her hand. "I just want you to like what I have planned."

Katie had never seen Noah like this, especially not with her. He was always confident and sure of himself. He took very little in life seriously, and never his relationships with women—not since Tori had broken his heart.

An image of Tori flashed through Katie's mind. What would Noah think if his ex-girlfriend made good on her threat to expose Katie's part in their breakup?

Maybe it wasn't a big deal. It had been so long ago and Katie hadn't been the one to cheat or to break his heart. Surely he'd understand that? In fact, she should just tell him herself so she could explain why she'd done it. She'd wanted to protect him. Tori might accuse Katie of wanting him for herself, but that wasn't true. She'd never believed Noah could belong to her.

Now he did.

He held her hand as he led her through the front door, squeezing gently on her fingers. She'd tell him tomorrow.

A little voice inside her called her a coward, but she ignored it. She wasn't going to ruin this night.

"Where are we going?"

He led her around the side of the house and stopped. "Up," he answered with a boyish grin.

A ladder had been propped against the gutter where the roof of the front porch sloped up to meet the house's roofline.

"I checked and we have a view of the mountain from your roof. Fireworks start in five minutes."

"I'd never thought of that," she said softly.

"Start climbing, sweetheart."

She grabbed the sides of the ladder, her arms still sore from hanging on to the inner tube earlier. But she was using them only for balance, so she began to make her way slowly up the metal rungs.

"If you need a break, feel free to stop for a minute." Noah's voice drifted up to her. "I'm okay if we miss the fireworks since I've got a better view from down here."

She glanced down to where he was grinning up at her. Careful not to lose her balance, Katie wiggled her hips a bit and was rewarded by his rich laughter. She understood Noah's popularity with the ladies, but he made her feel as if she was the only woman in the world who mattered. It was as if every part of her was desirable and he couldn't get enough. She also knew his affections could change in an instant, especially if she started to take what was between them too seriously. Once again, she reminded herself to simply enjoy the moment.

She hitched herself onto the roof then waited for Noah to join her. Her neighborhood was dark and mainly quiet. From a few blocks away, she could hear the soft sounds of classic rock playing and smell hamburgers on the grill—

someone must be having an outdoor barbecue. To the east of her house was downtown Crimson, lights glowing from the Fourth of July party the town hosted. To the west was Crimson Mountain, its top just visible in the darkness, a ridge that split the sky. The night was clear and stars dotted the sky over the valley. She hugged her arms around her waist as Noah's head appeared over the side of the house.

"This is great," she told him as he planted a foot onto the roof.

"We're not there yet." He pointed toward the high edge of the roof. "Can you make it a little farther?"

The truth was she felt nervous being up this high. Her roofline wasn't steep and she had no problem getting traction on the tiles with her gym shoes. Still, Katie wasn't one to go scaling roofs. But with Noah studying her, his blue eyes almost indigo in the dark, she wanted to be. She felt safe with him and that gave her courage.

"Lead on," she told him. "It's my turn for the view."

He laughed and began to scramble up the center of the roof toward her chimney. She followed, keeping her palms on the shingles as she did. When she got to the top, she glanced up to see a blanket spread over the tip of the roof and a cooler attached to the chimney by a bungee cord wrapped around the bricks.

"When did you do all this?" she asked, easing onto the blanket and dusting off her hands.

"While you were napping. You've always slept like the dead, so I figured I wouldn't wake you." He took out a pint of ice cream from the cooler, peeled back the lid and handed her a spoon.

"How—"

"I paid the delivery guy extra to swing by the store for dessert. I hope raspberry chip is still your favorite flavor."

She took the ice cream and dug in her spoon. Ice cream was her go-to dessert because it didn't involve any work on her part or elicit comparisons to her own baking. "You've been paying more attention than I thought," she said around a mouthful.

He leaned in and kissed her, licking a bit of ice cream from the corner of her lips. "Glad you noticed." Reaching into his pocket, he took out his phone and typed in the passcode. "I bookmarked the website for the radio station that's broadcasting the music for the fireworks. It should be starting any second."

There was a hiss in the distance. Then the sky lit up in front of the mountain.

Katie let out a breath. "It's amazing from here."

A crack split the night, and golden lights sprinkled down from the sky, followed quickly by a whistle and another pop as a colorful spray of red, white and blue filled the air. Noah inched closer to her, tucking her into his side as they watched. The mountain was a majestic backdrop for the lights and sounds of the Fourth of July fireworks. He balanced the phone on his knee and she listened to the choreographed music swell then soften as the night continued to glow.

Katie kept her eyes on the display but felt Noah nuzzling her neck after a few minutes. Despite the coolness of the air, her body automatically heated. She squirmed as he sucked her earlobe into his mouth. "You aren't watching."

"You're too distracting," he whispered against her ear.

"If you don't stop that," she said, ducking her head, "I'm going to lose my balance and fall off the roof."

"I'll hold you." As if to prove his point, he drew her closer against him. But with one more kiss to her temple, he turned and watched the rest of the display.

Katie couldn't remember ever being so happy. For many years, she'd worked the Life is Sweet booth at the town's annual July Fourth party. She'd watched couples stroll by, arm in arm, and always felt a tug of envy. Especially when her friends fell in love and she was surrounded by so much togetherness while she was always alone.

"I normally watch the fireworks as I'm packing up the booth," she said softly during a lull in the display. "I'm glad that a couple of the college kids working for me this summer wanted the extra money to run the event. You haven't been back to Crimson over the Fourth for several years."

"I'm usually on duty over the holiday," Noah told her. "Lots of extra help needed with so many campers in the forest this weekend."

She tipped her head to look at him. "Why not this year?"

"I had more important people to watch over."

Katie smiled, then kissed him just as the big finale began. They both turned toward the shimmering ribbons of light. She felt the boom and pop of hundreds of bursts of color reverberate through her, even from miles away. Or maybe it was just her heart beating as the walls that guarded it came crumbling down.

Chapter 16

On Monday morning Katie stumbled out of a stall in the community center's bathroom, only to find Emily Whitaker waiting for her. She grabbed the wad of paper towels the other woman handed her, dabbing at her eyes before wiping her mouth.

Even with the problems Emily was dealing with from her divorce and her son's issues, she still looked every inch the society wife, from her demure striped skirt to the crisp button-down and strand of pearls she wore.

It made Katie feel all the more tired and rumpled, especially since Emily had just listened to her throwing up most of the bagel she'd had for breakfast.

"Don't get too close," she warned as she stepped to the sink to wash her hands and splash cold water on her face. She glanced at herself in the mirror and grimaced. Under the bathroom's fluorescent lights, her skin looked even pastier, the dark circles under her eyes more pronounced.

"I thought I was just tired from being swamped at the bakery and the extra work for the festival. I guess I've caught some kind of a bug."

Emily balanced one thin hip on the corner of the sink. "You're pregnant."

Katie's hand stilled on the handle of the towel dispenser. She turned to Emily, water dripping off her face. "No, I'm not."

Emily rolled her pale blue eyes. "Are you sure? Noah was lecturing me on how I need to do more for the festival because you're exhausted." She handed another paper towel to Katie. "I've seen how much you eat during the committee meetings."

"I don't..." Katie broke off. She had been extra hungry lately, but she blamed it on needing fuel to keep up with all of her commitments.

"And..." Emily waved a hand toward Katie's blouse. "No offense, but I don't remember you being quite so... well-endowed."

Katie glanced down at her chest, her eyes widening at the cleavage on display. She quickly fastened another button on her chambray shirt. "Maybe it's a new bra."

"Is it a new bra?"

"I... That doesn't mean..." She inhaled, her lungs suddenly constricting. "No, it's not new. Why are you in here anyway? Can't a girl puke in peace?"

"I was using the restroom and wanted to make sure you're okay." She leaned forward. "Are you, Katie?"

Katie placed her hands on the cool porcelain of the white sink, ignoring the slight tremble of her arms. She did the math in her head and moaned. "This can't be happening. We used protection," she mumbled, her stomach rolling once again.

"Nothing is foolproof," Emily said. "Is it safe to assume the baby is Noah's?"

"Of course. If there is a baby." Katie glanced up at Emily in the mirror. "I need to take a pregnancy test. Nothing is certain until then."

"Noah's going to be a father." Emily tapped a finger on her chin, one corner of her mouth lifting. "At least I won't be the most messed-up person in the family anymore."

At this comment Katie straightened and turned to Emily. "Noah isn't messed up." She hugged her arms to her stomach. "And my baby…" She paused, let the implications of those two words sink in. *My baby.* "If there is a baby," she clarified, "that's not messed up, either. Noah will make a wonderful father." There was that stomach rolling again.

Emily arched one eyebrow.

"But don't say anything," Katie added quickly. "To anyone."

"You're not going to tell Noah?"

"There's nothing to tell until I take the test and talk to my doctor." She bit down on her lip. "I don't want… Things are so new between us, you know? I don't want to freak him out if this is just me getting regular sick. It's the first morning I've thrown up, so it could be nothing."

"He cares about you."

"But he's not… We're not…" She brushed away a tear from the corner of her eye. "I told him I wanted a family. What if he thinks this is a trap? I don't know if he's ready for this. How can he be?"

"Are you?" Emily's voice was gentle.

Katie breathed through the panic that constricted her lungs, and the next instant it was gone. She took a few more breaths, put her hand on her chest and found her heartbeat returning to its regular rhythm. "Yes." She nodded once, suddenly sure of this one thing. "Yes, I'm ready. If I'm pregnant, I'll love that baby with my whole heart. I'll give him or her the best life I know how to create."

Emily's normally cool expression warmed as pink colored her cheeks. She took two steps toward Katie and wrapped her in a hug. "Congratulations, then. Being a mom is the best and hardest job in the world."

Katie opened her mouth to tell Emily that nothing was certain yet, then stopped herself. Her fingers drifted to her belly and she *knew*. "I'm going to be a mom," she whispered and looked at Emily with a new understanding. "Watching your son struggle has to be the hardest part." She didn't ask a question, but stated the obvious fact.

"More than leaving my marriage and my life or crawling back to Crimson after I'd sworn never to return." Emily bit down on her lip. "To me, Davey is perfect, but no one in Boston saw him that way. If I could take away what he has to go through, the challenges that his life might hold, I'd do it in a millisecond. But I wouldn't change him. I love him for the boy he is, not who he might have been if things were different."

"He's lucky to have you."

"And my brother is lucky to have you, Katie. You might be the best thing that ever happened to him."

Both women turned when the door to the restroom slammed shut. Katie took three steps forward to peer around the entrance to the community center's main hallway. No one was there, but something had made the door move. She opened it and looked both ways down the hall, but it was empty.

As Emily came up behind her, both women stepped out of the restroom.

"Weird," Emily murmured.

"You don't think someone was eavesdropping?" Katie asked, her voice a nervous croak.

"I think the only people here this early are on the festival committee, and I'm sure any of those women would have announced themselves."

Katie glanced at her watch. "The meeting was scheduled to start ten minutes ago. I need to get in there."

"Do you want me to handle it?"

Katie glanced at Emily.

"Not the festival," she quickly clarified. "But today's meeting. If you give me your notes, I can go over things with everyone. Organizing volunteers is one of my few useful skills."

Katie hesitated. She didn't like to depend on other people. It made her feel as if she wasn't pulling her own weight, weak and useless, even though she understood that was just the leftover dysfunction from her childhood. "That would be great," she said after a moment. "Jase will be there, too, and he can answer any questions that come up from the subcommittee chairs."

"Of course." Emily's smile was wry. "Perfect Jase can handle anything."

"He's not—"

"Never mind," the other woman interrupted. "All hands on deck and whatnot."

"Thank you." Katie took the binder from her tote bag and handed it to Emily. "I'm heading to the pharmacy—"

"You might want to—"

Katie held up a hand. "To the pharmacy over in Aspen where no one will recognize me. Then to my doctor if the test is positive. You promise you won't tell Noah?"

"Promise."

With another quick hug, Katie walked out of the community center into the morning light. This day was going to change her life, of that much she was certain. She just hoped the change wouldn't cost her Noah.

Three days before the Founder's Day Festival, Noah turned his truck off the Forest Service access road and headed for town. He'd been up most of the night, investigating reports of teenagers partying near one of the campsites above a popular hiking trail. The local emergency dispatcher had received an anonymous call about possible vandalism and a bonfire. The vandalism was bad, but a fire could potentially be catastrophic to the area.

Noah had had plans with Katie last night, like he had almost every evening since July Fourth. They took turns at her place or she'd come to dinner at his mom's. With Katie at his side, he'd even managed through a family barbecue with John Moore, who was quickly becoming his mother's steady boyfriend.

It had been strange to see another man in his parents' kitchen, gamely helping his mom chop vegetables for a salad and making beer runs to the garage refrigerator. Logan and Olivia had been there now that she was feeling better, along with Jake and Millie. Jake and John had done some shoptalk about the hospital, but Noah had to admit the older doctor was comfortable with all of them. And his mother had radiated happiness.

Noah understood that feeling, barely able to keep the goofy grin off his face every time he looked at Katie. He loved her. Was madly *in* love with her. He hadn't told her yet, but he planned to later tonight. As promised, he'd made a reservation at a five-star restaurant in Aspen. His relationship with Katie had been casual for too long. He'd taken her for granted and was determined that she understood how much he'd changed.

Something was off with her, and he worried it had to do with not trusting his feelings for her. She was quieter, sometimes staring off into space as if she was a thousand miles away. When he asked her about it, she claimed she was tired but it felt…different. He'd walked in on Emily and her arguing in the kitchen of his mom's house, both women startling when he came into the room. They'd said it was simply a disagreement about the Founder's Day Festival, but he didn't believe them. That night Katie had clung to him as they made love, holding on as though she thought he might slip away at any moment.

She didn't trust that he wasn't going to leave her. He needed to tell her how he felt so she could relax. The idea of talking about his emotions made him prickly all over, but he was in love with Katie. He hadn't felt like this for so long—his whole life, maybe—and he was ready to risk opening himself up again.

He took a quick shower then picked up a bouquet of flowers on his way through downtown. He couldn't resist a visit to the bakery before heading to his office. One night away and he needed to see her face before he started his day. He laughed, wondering what his friends would think if they could see him now. He didn't care. He finally understood why some of his buddies looked so content as their women led them around on a string. Nothing mattered more than wrapping his arms around Katie.

The bakery was crowded with both locals and summer tourists, the two young women behind the counter hustling to fill orders. Katie wasn't part of the action, which surprised him. Normally she was front and center with customers during peak hours. He waved to a few people he knew, then walked to the edge of the display cabinet.

"She in back?" he asked Lelia.

"Um... I think so," the woman muttered, not meeting Noah's gaze as she bent to select a pastry from the cabinet. "But she's kind of busy this morning. Do you want me to tell her you stopped by?"

"I'll tell her myself," he said, holding up the bouquet. "No one is too busy for flowers, right?"

He opened the door to the bakery's kitchen quietly. If he could manage it, he wanted to sneak up on Katie, wrap his arms around her and hear her squeal of surprise before she melted into him.

But it was Noah who was in for the surprise, because Katie wasn't alone. She and Tori stood at the far counter, in front of the deep stainless-steel sink. Katie was shaking her head, clearly distraught, as Tori spoke. Noah started to move forward, anger gripping him that his ex-girlfriend wouldn't leave Katie alone. He froze in place when he heard her hiss the words *pregnant* and *liar*.

Katie's gaze slammed into his. So many emotions flashed through her brown eyes—love, guilt and regret. He shook his head as if denying it would ward off the truth of the scene unfolding in front of him.

Tori turned after a moment, her eyes widening at the sight of him. "This isn't exactly what I'd planned," she said, visibly swallowing. "But I guess the secret's out now. Or is about to be. How much did you hear, Noah?"

"Enough," he said through clenched teeth, keeping his eyes on Tori. He'd thought she was perfect when they were together, but now her expensive sun-kissed highlights and flawless makeup made her appear to be trying too hard. And like before, what she was trying to do was ruin his life.

She gave the barest nod, took a step toward him. "Then you know I wasn't the only one guilty of hurting you that night."

"You were having sex with one of my friends."

"It was stupid," she agreed. "A meaningless fling before you asked me to marry you. You were going to propose to me before graduation."

"But I didn't."

"Because of the anonymous note," she all but spit. "Now you know who wrote it. Your precious, oh-so-perfect Katie-bug. You think she cared about you, but she only wanted to break us up so she could have you all to herself."

He saw Katie close her eyes and shake her head.

"Now you're stuck with her," Tori continued. "But she still won't tell you the truth." She whirled on Katie. "Was this all part of some master twisted plan?"

"Of course not," Katie answered, her voice shaking. "I didn't mean… This isn't…" She seemed to shrink in on herself, crossing her arms over her stomach as she spoke. A baby was growing in her stomach. His baby. Noah's knees went weak at the thought.

"Get out of here, Tori." He pointed to the door. "This is none of your business anymore."

"I understand." Tori's voice turned to the whine he remembered so well. "But she isn't—"

"Get out," Noah yelled, flipping his arm wide, sending several baking sheets drying on the counter crashing to the floor as he did. Katie jumped at the noise and Tori suddenly looked unsure of herself. Noah wasn't known for his temper. Even when he'd discovered Tori cheating, he'd simply compartmentalized his feelings and walked away. But now, in this moment, he could barely contain the emotions that rattled through him. It felt as if a virus had infected his body and was eating away at his heart even as it still beat in his chest. The pain was almost unbearable.

"I just want you to know I'm not the only one who deceived you," Tori said then stalked through the door to the front of the shop.

Lelia poked her head in a moment later. "Everything okay?"

"We're fine," Katie said in a shaky voice at the same time Noah growled, "Get out."

When they were alone, Katie spoke in a whisper. "I'm sorry, Noah." He felt her step toward him but kept his eyes on the ground. "I never meant—"

"Don't." He held up one hand. He could not bear it if she touched him right now. All that need for her had warped, and turned ugly in the space of a few moments. He hardly trusted himself to speak, but if she touched him he'd be a goner for sure.

"Are you pregnant?" he choked out, the words heavy in his throat. Bile and panic rose up, warred in his chest.

"Yes."

"And the baby is mine?"

He heard her gasp before answering, "Yes."

He'd wanted to hurt her with the words, for her to experience a tiny bit of the pain he felt. But even though he knew he had, it didn't give him any relief from his own tumbling emotions. This was why he'd walled himself off for so long. This gut-wrenching pain, the same thing he'd felt when his parents had finally told him about his father's illness. When it had been too late.

"How far along?"

"About seven weeks." He heard her begin to clean up the fallen baking sheets. "It must have been the first time we were together."

"We used protection."

She gave a small laugh. "That's what I told your sister but it's not—"

He whirled and grabbed her arms, hauling her off the floor, the metal baking sheets clattering to the tile floor. "What do you mean when you told my sister?" He brought his face inches from hers. "Emily knows about the baby? You told my *sister* before you bothered to share the news with *me*? Who else knows?"

Her eyes widened. "No one knows. It wasn't like that, Noah. She heard me getting sick one morning and she guessed."

"When was this?" He gripped her harder, forced himself not to shake her.

"Last week. At the community center."

He released her as suddenly as he'd taken hold of her. His head pounding, he stalked to the edge of the kitchen then back toward her. "Why does Tori know?"

"She overheard Emily and me talking. I didn't realize until she came here today with her threats."

"And the note?" he asked, remembering the other piece of venom that had spewed from Tori's glossy lips.

She nodded, squeezed her eyes shut then opened them again. "I left it for you."

"Why not tell me?"

"I don't know. I was afraid you'd blame me. Kill the messenger and all that. It was stupid."

"And at no time in the past eight years did you think to mention it?" His voice was steady even as his body shook with rage.

"I should have said something. I wanted to." She dragged in a breath. "I just didn't trust…"

"Me." He spoke the word on an angry breath.

"I can only tell you I'm sorry. I regret it so much."

"Because it was wrong or because I found out?" When she opened her mouth, he shook his head. "It doesn't matter now. *That* doesn't matter." He glanced toward the counter, saw a sheet of muffin tins half filled with batter. That must have been what she was working on when Tori had interrupted her. He could see ripe blueberries floating in the yellow mixture and wondered if he'd ever be able to stomach another blueberry muffin. "You're *pregnant*." A thought struck him and he scrubbed one hand over his face. "God, Katie, you were pregnant when you fell off the inner tube. When we climbed to the top of your roof."

"I didn't *know*." Her expression was miserable, and earlier this morning he would have done anything to ease her pain. The longer he stood here now, the less he felt. She'd brought him back to life, but he should have known it wouldn't last.

"I should have been with you, Katie. When you took the test. At the doctor. I deserved to know."

"I was going to tell you," she said, her voice pleading with him to believe her. "Tonight at dinner. I wanted it to be special."

"As special as my sister knowing a week before I did?" He knew he was being unfair because he'd planned to tell her how he felt during that same dinner. To say the words *I love you* and really mean them. Now he was bitterly grateful he hadn't revealed his feelings earlier. He'd feel even more the fool that she hadn't trusted him. "This wasn't the plan, Katie. Hell, I don't know how to be a father."

Her face paled at his words, but she straightened her shoulders. "I want this baby, Noah. I know it wasn't part of the plan, but it's a blessing. I want to be a mother. I want *our* baby."

"I want the baby, too, Katie. Don't put words in my mouth like I'm suggesting anything else. But I need time to get used to the idea. Time you should have given me."

"I know—" she began, but he held up a hand to stop her.

"I can tell you one thing I know for damn sure." He was made of rock, no feeling left anywhere inside him. "I want this baby," he repeated, hating the hope that flared in her eyes at his words. Hating her for giving him hope that someone could finally believe in him. "But I *don't* want you."

Chapter 17

Katie stumbled back as if Noah had struck her. But the physical pain would be nothing compared to the heartache that ripped through her at his words.

She deserved it. She never should have waited to tell him. Despite what he believed, her own fear had held her back. The fear he wouldn't want her or the baby. That he would feel obligated to stay with her.

This was worse.

"I love you, Noah," she whispered, unable to offer him anything else. "I never meant to hurt you."

"It's not enough," he answered, but what she heard was that *she* wasn't enough. Because Katie had never been enough, and she couldn't bake or volunteer or smooth over this hurt. She had nothing to give him right now but her love, and *she wasn't enough*.

"I can't…" He pushed his hand through his hair. He looked as broken as she felt. But still strong and so handsome in his uniform. She wanted to hold on to that strength but could feel the invisible wall between them. She knew what that meant. She'd seen the way his father's death and Tori's betrayal had ripped him apart. Watched as he'd shut himself off, pretended nothing was wrong and moved on.

He'd be moving on from her.

"I want to be involved." He said the words with emotion, but his eyes were ice-cold. "When is your next doctor's appointment?"

"Three weeks."

He narrowed his eyes as if he didn't believe her.

"He wants to do some early blood work. Everything is fine with the pregnancy, Noah. I don't see the doctor regularly until closer to the due date."

He gave a brief nod. "Text me the date and time. I'll be there."

He turned and stalked out of the kitchen. Katie's legs finally gave way and she sank to the floor. He wanted the baby but not her. She'd lost the love of her life *and* her best friend. She wasn't sure which was worse. Even as her feelings for Noah had ebbed and flowed over the years, he'd always been a constant in her life. Now she was alone, but also tethered to him by the life she carried inside her. How could she raise a child with a man who hated her?

A keening sound reverberated through the room and she realized it had come from her throat. She didn't look up as Lelia came into the kitchen, couldn't register the words the other woman spoke. The only thing that filled her mind was the hurt and anger on Noah's face.

Later, maybe minutes or maybe hours, an arm slid around her shoulders.

"Let's go, honey." Natalie helped her to her feet.

"I can't go out there," she said, hitching her head toward the front of the bakery.

"Olivia's parked in the alley out back."

"Nat, I messed up so badly." She bit back a sob, her legs beginning to crumple once more.

"Shhh," her friend crooned. "Let's get you to the car. One step at a time."

Katie, who was always so reluctant to lean on anyone, held tight to Natalie and let herself be led out into the bright sunlight of another Colorado summer morning.

Natalie opened the back door of the Subaru wagon and Katie dropped into the seat. Her arms wouldn't work, so Natalie strapped the seat belt across her. She met Olivia's sympathetic gaze from the driver's seat.

"Katie, what happened? Are you okay?"

She shook her head once then sucked back a sob.

"We're going to take her home," Natalie told Olivia as she climbed into the car and shut the door. "We'll get her something to drink—maybe whiskey—and sort this out."

"It's not even noon," Olivia whispered to Natalie. She looked at Katie in the rearview mirror as she pulled out of the alley. "How about a nice cup of tea?"

Natalie groaned. "She needs something strong for whatever this is."

"Can't." To Katie's own ears, her voice was a hoarse croak.

Natalie waved away her concern. "We won't tell."

"I'm pregnant."

Olivia hit the brakes suddenly and the car lurched forward, the seat belt cutting into Katie's chest. She wished it would slice all the way through so she could reach in and pull out her aching heart.

Neither of her friends spoke, but she saw them exchange a glance across the front seat.

"Tea, then," Olivia said gently. "Or orange juice. OJ was my go-to drink in my first trimester."

"I liked milk shakes." Natalie shifted in her seat to glance at Katie. "Want us to stop for ice cream? We can make whatever kind of milk shake you want."

The casual conversation seemed to lift Katie out of the fog threatening to engulf her. "I have vanilla ice cream at home. And strawberries."

"Strawberry milk shakes all around," Natalie answered with a smile.

She should have said something more, explained the circumstances. Although maybe it was obvious. Both women knew how babies were made, after all. Besides, she needed more time to pull herself together, to clean up the emotional wreckage around her heart.

She managed to get from the car to her door without assistance. She kept Natalie's words in her mind—*one step at a time*. Moving still proved difficult, and once she'd made it through the front door her strength waned again. She collapsed on the couch, tucking her knees to her chest to make a tight ball as Olivia covered her with a blanket.

As she closed her eyes she heard the soft sound of her two friends talking in the kitchen then the whir of the blender. A few minutes later she started as something cool brushed her forehead. She sat up straighter, took the glass from Natalie and sipped. She was so cold on the inside that the milk shake almost seemed warm in comparison. But it was soothing, both to her stomach and her emotions.

"Our babies will be friends," Olivia said as she gave Katie a gentle smile.

"I didn't mean for this to happen."

Natalie reached over to pat her arm then took a slurping drink of milk shake. "You don't need to explain to us."

"I want you to understand. It was an accident..." Katie glanced between the two of them. "But I want this baby. I *love* this baby already."

"Of course you do."

Natalie made a face. "And Noah?"

"It's no secret I love him, too." Katie circled a drop of condensation with her finger. "But he wants nothing to do with me."

"That can't be true." Natalie shook her head. "I saw how he acted on the Fourth of July. He loves you, honey."

"I've known for a week," Katie muttered. "I was afraid to tell him, but Emily heard me getting sick and guessed. His ex-girlfriend was listening as Emily and I talked. Tori came to the bakery today and threatened to reveal another secret I kept from him. That was bad enough but the pregnancy on top of it... He's never going to forgive me."

"He'll come around," Olivia said. "I mean, you were *going* to tell him soon."

"You don't understand. When Noah's dad got sick, he was the last one to know. He'd had a tough senior year and his parents were worried about how the news of the cancer would affect him. They told Emily right away. By the time Noah found out, his dad only had a few months to live."

"An unfortunate coincidence," Natalie agreed. "But not insurmountable."

"It is for Noah. And for me, too, in a different way. I spent most of my childhood feeling like an obligation to my parents. Having me held them back from how they wanted to live. I'm not going to be an unwanted burden for Noah. He made it clear that this wasn't his plan. If he wants to be part of the baby's life, I'll welcome that. I won't ask him for anything more."

"And if he decides he wants more?" Olivia asked, placing her glass on the coffee table. "Today was a shock. He'll recover from it and move forward. He cares about you. Those feelings aren't wiped away in an instant."

"He cared about me like a *friend*. Maybe it could have developed into something more if we'd had time. I don't know." She gave a strangled laugh. "I've loved him for over half my life. I tried to deny it, tried to turn off my feelings when I knew he didn't return them. I *want* to be loved like that in return. Not because I'm having a baby or I'm helpful or easy to be with. I want to be loved in an everything sort of way." She pointed to each of her friends. "What you have with Logan and Liam. A whole heart-and-soul kind of love. I deserve that."

"You do, Katie," Olivia said.

"Without a doubt," Natalie agreed.

She shrugged. "I'm not sure Noah understands how to love like that." She took a final drink of milk shake. "I thought he could, but if you'd seen how he looked at me today... There was nothing in his eyes. No emotion. He completely shut down, shut me out."

"We're here for you no matter what happens." Natalie patted Katie's knee.

She felt color rise to her cheeks. "Thank you for rescuing me from my meltdown. Sorry if I took you away from something important."

"Nothing is more important than friends," Olivia said.

"I can take Austin this weekend." Katie turned to Natalie. "To thank you, as payback. If you and Liam——"

Natalie immediately held up a hand. "Girl, you better shut your mouth before I lose my temper."

"About what?"

"You don't need to *pay me back* for being your friend."

"I just thought..." Katie began.

"You do far too much for other people..." Olivia added, "For this whole town. But you don't owe anyone."

"That's what Noah told me."

Natalie snorted. "He might be acting like an idiot now, but on that point I agree with him. You have a place here, Katie. It's wonderful how you help everyone, but that isn't why we care about you. We're your friends. We'll love you no matter what."

"No matter what," Katie repeated. It was what she'd wanted her whole life, never let herself believe she deserved. "I like the sound of that." She glanced at the clock on the mantel above the fireplace. "I need to get back to the bakery. There's so much going on and everyone must be wondering where I am."

"You don't have to—"

"I want to go back," Katie interrupted Natalie. "The bakery is also part of me, just like helping out in the community. I like contributing."

"Just so you know, you don't always have to be the one on the front lines," Natalie told her.

"I'm feeling better," Olivia added. "I can take back some of the Founder's Day Festival responsibilities. I feel horrible that we expected you to take over so I could deal with my pregnancy when you were having the same problems."

"I'm fine." When Natalie rolled her eyes, Katie slapped her gently on the arm. "I mean it. I've been to the doctor and everything looks normal." She pointed at Olivia. "You had a serious scare. It's different."

"The spotting has stopped." Olivia pursed her lips. "But Logan is still squawking about bed rest."

Katie smiled at the image of bad-boy Logan Travers squawking about anything. "Most of the work is done," she said. "The subcommittee chairs have things under control. I'll talk to Jase about extra help, but it's not going to be you."

"I can switch around some of my shifts at the nursing home to be available," Natalie offered. Katie thought it was funny that although Liam Donovan was one of the richest men in Colorado, Natalie continued working as a nurse at a local retirement center and nursing home. And that Liam respected her choice.

Having a baby would definitely affect the hours she put in at the bakery, and she wondered how she'd balance everything. The thought made the milk shake start to gurgle uncomfortably in her stomach, so she tried to push the worries away. *One step at a time.*

"Thank you both," she said again, standing and folding the blanket from her lap. "I'm not sure how I would have pulled out of my meltdown without help."

"You're not alone," Olivia said gently.

"For the first time in a long while, you've made me believe that." She bent to give each of the women a hug.

"Give Noah some breathing room," Natalie advised, picking up the empty glasses from the coffee table. "The men around Crimson aren't quick on the uptake, but they eventually do the right thing. Noah cares about you, Katie."

She nodded, feeling the prick of tears behind her eyes. She still didn't believe he loved her enough to make things right between them. And she couldn't take having him in her life simply because he felt obligated to do the "right thing." She finally realized that as much as she loved him, something so one-sided wasn't enough anymore.

"Let's clean up your kitchen," Olivia said. "Then I'll drive you back to the bakery if you're sure you're up for it."

Thirty minutes later, she walked into Life is Sweet with a small pit of embarrassment widening in her stomach. Luckily, the café portion of the store was almost empty and only two customers waited near the front counter. Of course, it had been busier when first Tori then Noah had stormed out, and she didn't relish the thought of being a hot gossip topic around town.

She stepped behind the counter, absently wiping a crumb from the glass top as she did. Lelia and another young woman, Suzanne, stopped what they were doing to turn to her.

"Everything okay?" Lelia asked.

Katie thought about lying, glossing over what had happened, but answered, "No. Not by a long shot. But it will be eventually. I don't know what you heard from the back earlier, but I'm sorry for the drama. You shouldn't have to deal with that at work."

"Are you kidding?" Suzanne, a petite dark-haired college student who was a Crimson native, answered. "I'd give up my share of the tips to watch Noah Crawford stalk through the bakery every day. He's kind of old but still hot as—"

She stopped speaking when Lelia elbowed her in the ribs. "All we could hear from the front was when the baking pans fell. None of the conversation. Not much, anyway. Promise."

Katie looked at Suzanne, who nodded in agreement then turned to take the order of a couple who'd just walked into the store.

A bit of tension released from her shoulders. She didn't want anyone knowing about the pregnancy until she was ready to share the news. That thought in mind, she asked Lelia to follow her into the back.

When she went through the large swinging doors, she stopped short. The entire kitchen was spotless and a batch of perfect muffins sat cooling on the stainless-steel counter.

"I know the kitchen is your domain," Lelia said quickly. "But we had a lull and I didn't want you to come back to a mess. I hope you don't mind."

Katie shook her head, emotion surging at the small gesture. Or was it pregnancy hormones? She'd learn a lot about herself over the next nine months. "I appreciate it," she told Lelia, "and that's part of why I want to speak to you." She stepped closer to the counter, running her fingers across the cool surface. "I'm pregnant."

Lelia drew in a shocked breath. Okay, maybe the argument earlier really hadn't been heard out front. "That's why Noah was so angry?"

Katie nodded.

"Because it's not his?" Lelia continued, her tone dejected and a little bitter.

"What?" Katie blinked several times. "No. The baby is Noah's. Who else? I haven't been with—"

She broke off, noticed the way Lelia relaxed and a smile split her face. "Congratulations, then," the other woman said. "You'll be a wonderful mom."

"Who did you think...? Matt?"

Lelia's gaze dropped to the ground.

"I've noticed that he's picked you up after work the past couple of days," Katie said carefully. "Does that mean—"

"I feel awful about it." Lelia covered her face with her hands. "Stealing my boss's boyfriend."

"He's not—"

"But I really like him. We have so much in common and…"

"I'm happy for you, Lelia. Matt is a great guy but not for me. If you like him, I support you, especially because you're a great addition to our town."

Lelia lowered her hands. "You mean it? You're not mad?"

"Not at all. In fact, the reason I told you my news is because with a baby to plan for, I'm going to need to make some changes at the bakery. Delegate responsibility. I was hoping you'd agree to become my first official manager?"

"Really?" Lelia practically bounced up and down. "You mean that?"

"I do. We'll increase your hours and you can start learning the business side of the bakery. I think we'll make a great team."

"That's amazing." Lelia reached forward to hug Katie. "I can't wait to share this with Matt. I was so worried you were going to fire me for not telling you about us right away."

Pain pinched Katie's heart as she thought of the price she'd paid for waiting to tell Noah her news. "I wouldn't do that. Give me a few weeks to come up with a new job description. I have to get through Founder's Day and we have two big orders of wedding cupcakes for that same weekend."

"Of course. I better get back out front." She began to leave then turned. "Is Noah not happy about the baby?" she asked softly.

"It's complicated" was the only answer Katie could give without emotions getting the best of her again.

Chapter 18

"Remember the good old days when life wasn't so complicated?" Noah asked Jase as he helped load hay bales into the back of Jase's truck early on the first morning of the festival.

Jase hefted another hay bale then wiped his gloved hand across his forehead. "Life has always been complicated. You were just too checked out of it to notice."

"I wasn't exactly checked out," Noah argued but realized Jase was right. Before this summer, he'd been living life without ever getting too involved. He was good at his job, but when things got too complicated or bureaucratic, he'd slip away into the woods to recharge. Instead of stepping up when he finally learned about his father's cancer, he'd let his anger and hurt over being the last one to know spoil the last days he had with his dad. He'd avoided anything in life that made him uncomfortable, using the excuse that he wanted to keep things light and fun.

Even with Katie… No, she was different. Wasn't she? He'd tried with her, put himself out there—at least in his mind—and she'd let him down. The pain was a killer, a reminder of why it was better to stick to the superficial.

"So what happened?"

"Nothing," Noah muttered and threw a hay bale, harder than necessary, onto the flatbed.

"Right." Jase put his hands on his hips and gave Noah his best attorney stare. "Because a few days ago you were burping unicorns and now you look like you're ready to breathe fire on anyone who crosses you."

Noah stood for a moment, thought about how to answer and finally settled on the truth. "Katie is pregnant."

"Whoa." Jase took a step back then reached forward and slapped Noah on the back. "Congratulations, man. That's awesome."

"Are you kidding? This is the opposite of awesome."

"Why? You obviously love her. She's been crazy about you for as long as anyone can remember. The two of you and a baby—it's the perfect family."

There was so much wrong with Jase's words, Noah didn't know where to begin. "What do you mean 'for as long as anyone can remember'? Katie and I only started seeing each other this summer."

Jase looked genuinely confused. "If 'seeing each other' is code for 'getting naked' then yeah. That part might be new but you've been friends for years."

"Friends. That's it."

"Because you're an idiot," Jase agreed. "You were busy bedding the wrong women while the right girl was waiting patiently the whole time."

"No." Noah's world started to spin again and he wondered if things would ever get back to normal. If he'd even recognize normal. "I was her friend."

Jase arched a brow and stared.

"Do you do that in the courtroom?" Noah asked, adjusting the collar of his T-shirt, which suddenly felt too tight. "Because it's annoying as hell."

"I'm not a trial lawyer," Jase said calmly. "Don't change the subject. If Katie is pregnant, why haven't I seen you two together? Why do you look miserable?"

"She didn't tell me."

"What does that mean?" Jase shook his head. "She's already had the baby and hidden it from you?"

"Don't be an ass," Noah mumbled. "It took her a week to tell me and that was only because I heard her arguing with Tori about it. Emily had found out and somehow Tori was eavesdropping when they discussed it." He moved his shoulders as if that should explain everything, but Jase continued to stare. "It was like my parents all over again. I can't deal with that. Not from Katie."

"Oh, boo-hoo," Jase mock cried. For a man known for his levelheadedness, he looked as angry as Noah had ever seen him. "You can't deal? What's the matter? Is your ego bruised?"

No, my heart, Noah wanted to answer but remained silent.

"Let me make sure I understand." Jase all but spit the words. "You can't deal, so you've deserted Katie to manage with the whole situation on her own."

Noah shook his head. "It's not like that. I told her I want to be there for the baby. I'll be at all the doctor appointments."

"How generous."

"What do you want from me?" Noah scrubbed a hand

over his jaw. He'd forgotten to shave for the past several days, felt lucky he'd remembered to brush his teeth.

"I want you to grow the hell up." Jake pointed a finger in Noah's face. "Did you ever think she was afraid to tell you because of how you'd react? Remember, this girl has been by your side every time things got serious. And no offense, man, but you don't handle serious so well."

"That's not true."

Jase held up a hand, ticking off points as he spoke. "What happened when you found out your dad had cancer? You barely spoke to him the last two months of his life. You missed your chance to say goodbye."

Noah clapped a hand to his chest, the painful memory threatening to suffocate him.

"Then your girlfriend cheated and that was awful but—"

"Katie was the one who sent the anonymous note."

"More power to her," Jase said. "You were better off without Tori. But how did you deal with that? You dated the longest string of flash-in-the-pan women you could find. All with Katie watching from the sidelines. As I remember it, you made her run interference more than once when things went sideways."

Noah winced. "She was willing to help."

"Because she *loves* you. She saw the worst of your behavior and loved you anyway. Believed you were better despite yourself. Of course she'd be afraid to tell you. You've given her no reason to trust you. Her parents were as selfish as people get, and still she turned out good and kind. But lacking in self-confidence, a fact that—no offense— you've used to your advantage all these years. Now that she needs you, you turn on her." Jase lifted his hands, palms up. "Before you start calling me an ass, take a long look in the mirror. I wouldn't be surprised if you started braying at your reflection."

Noah felt his mouth drop open and snapped it shut again. As he did it was as though the blinders he'd worn for all these years were stripped away. He'd been a fool. He was still a fool. And worse. He'd hurt the one person who mattered most to him, all because he was too scared to do anything else.

"Are you sure you're not a trial lawyer?" he asked Jase, shaking his head. "Because any jury who heard that closing argument would convict me without a second thought."

"It's not too late." Jase took a breath, spoke more softly. "Unlike in the courtroom, in life you get a second chance."

"If she'll give it to me." Noah's stomach rolled at the thought that he might have blown it for good. How would he survive without Katie and their baby as a part of his life? Without the chance to prove how much he loved her?

Jake flipped him the keys to the truck. "Only one way to find out."

If it was possible to be asleep while working nonstop, that was what Katie was doing the morning of the Founder's Day Festival. It was sunny and warm, already close to eighty degrees, which meant it would be downright hot by the time the events began at noon. She'd been at the county fairgrounds since sunup, managing the volunteers who assembled booths and directed vendors.

She'd thrown up twice behind the beer tent, but luckily it didn't seem as if anyone except Emily noticed her nausea. The other woman clearly wanted to talk to her, but Katie had managed to stay busy and unavailable. From the sympathetic looks Emily shot her across the food-judging tent, Katie guessed Noah had talked to her. She'd seen his mother earlier, as well. Now that she was feeling better, Meg was helping to judge the baking contests. She couldn't tell what Meg knew, but was avoiding her just in case.

She wasn't ready to talk to anyone about her pregnancy.

Other than Natalie and Olivia, none of her friends knew. Each day Katie fell more in love with the life growing inside her, but she was unsure of the future. She also wasn't ready to admit how bad Noah's rejection hurt. Eventually the pain would dull. She'd had enough experience with heartache over the years to believe that. At the same time, this was different because no matter how Noah felt, they were tied together forever.

"You look awful," a voice said at her shoulder.

Katie spun around to find Emily and Meg standing behind her.

"What she means," Meg tried to clarify, "is that you seem tired."

"I meant she looks like death warmed over," Emily said then dodged a maternal slap.

"Can we help you with something, sweetie?" Meg's voice was kind, her eyes a little hopeful. "You could go home for a few hours, put your feet up and have a snack."

Katie shook her head. "I'm fine and I promised to organize the food contests myself. Edna Sharpe and Karen Solanes are both vying for a blue ribbon in the fruit-pie category this year, and they've been fighting and accusing each other of cheating all week. I have to be here to mediate so things don't get out of hand."

Meg sniffed. "Edna's crust is always too crumbly. She doesn't have a chance against Karen's strawberry rhubarb."

"Even so..." Katie shook her head.

"We're worried about you," Meg said then leaned in

to wrap her arms around Katie. "I'm also excited for you and Noah."

Katie stiffened for a moment then let herself relax into Meg's motherly embrace. Katie hadn't told her own parents yet but didn't expect them to be rejoicing at the news of becoming grandparents.

"He'll come around," Meg whispered. "It takes Noah a while to process things…" Emily barked out a laugh at that assessment and Meg leaned back to shoot her daughter a glare before returning her gaze to Katie. "But he cares about you and he'll do the right thing."

Katie forced herself to nod, too afraid to speak and break down completely. There was that phrase again. But she didn't want to only be "the right thing." "I have to get through this weekend," she said after a deep breath.

"We can help," Meg offered again.

"I need to be here."

"Why?" Emily asked, one eyebrow raised.

"Because…" Katie started, not sure how to explain her reasoning.

Because she didn't want people to think she was weak and incompetent, the way she'd felt most of her childhood. Because she needed them to remember this weekend and her good reputation when the news eventually leaked that she was single and pregnant.

"Because I can't stand to be alone right now." The words slipped out before she could stop them.

"I'm going to kill my son," Meg said, shaking her head.

"This isn't Noah's fault," Katie answered quickly. "Don't be angry with him. He needs you right now."

"*You* need him." Meg gave her another hug then stepped back. "And to rest. Promise you'll take a break later. I'll handle Edna and Karen if things get out of hand."

The walkie-talkie clipped to Katie's belt chirped. Jase had given it to her this morning so they could communicate from opposite ends of the fairgrounds. At the same time, an older woman called to Katie from the far side of the tent. Katie pressed her fingers to her temples. Busy was difficult enough, but she couldn't very well clone herself to be two places at one time.

"You take care of things in here," Emily told her. "I'll go see what Jase wants."

"Thank you."

"I'll go with you, Katie." Meg straightened her shoulders. "Just to keep those women in line."

Once again, Katie was reminded that she wasn't alone. That she was part of a community that would support and care for her, even if her own parents never had.

Although she had Meg and Emily's help, she was pulled in a half dozen different directions over the next couple of hours. Her other friends arrived to pitch in, as well, but still everyone seemed to clamor for her attention. Her stomach continued to feel queasy, so she skipped the doughnuts and apples set out for volunteers.

By the time they were ready to open the ticket gates, she felt almost dizzy with exhaustion. Come to think of it, she felt dizzy, period. She was standing near the table that displayed the pies for one of the first tasting events. Her eyes drifted closed for a moment then snapped open as she felt herself sway.

The last thing she saw before she went down was Noah stalking toward her.

The first thing Noah saw as he entered the food tent was Katie drop from sight. Pushing people out of his way and vaulting over the corner of the table, he sank to the ground next to her.

"Katie, sweetheart." He lifted her head off the ground then took a breath as she opened her eyes, blinking up at him.

"Sorry," she whispered.

"No apologies." He smoothed a strand of hair off her pale face. "Are you hurt?"

She shook her head. "Didn't have a chance to eat. I'm fine."

"Katie, what is going on?" Edna Sharpe elbowed several onlookers to stand over the two of them. "You need to get up now, girl. The judging is about to start."

He followed Katie's gaze to where people were streaming into the tent, filling up the rows of chairs lined across the center. But when she started to stand, he scooped her into his arms. "She's not judging anything, Edna." He glared at the older woman, who glared right back at him. "I'm taking her home."

"You can't." Edna's voice hit a note that would make a dog wince. "We need her for the judging. She's the expert baker. She always judges the finalists."

"Not this year," Noah growled. "She needs rest more than you need her."

"It's fine," Katie whispered. "You can let me go, Noah."

He looked into her eyes. "No way, Bug. I'm never letting you go again."

Her eyes went wide as he leaned down and pressed a gentle kiss to her mouth. God, it felt so damn good to hold her again. How had he ever thought he could live without her?

He turned back to Edna and the group of volunteers who'd crowded around them. "You all should be ashamed of yourselves. She's been working too long, too hard, and none of you care as long as you're getting what you need from her." He caught his mother's gaze and she gave him an encouraging nod. "We should all be ashamed. Katie doesn't owe you anything. She helps because she's an amazing person. The best."

This got a round of head nods, so he continued, "But she does too much for others and we know it. We take advantage of her goodness and her generous heart. But she's more than earned her place in this community, and it's time she stop trying so hard. Time we stop expecting more of her than we do ourselves."

He gazed down at her, tried to show her all the things he'd never been able to say out loud, hoping she would understand. But when he saw tears cloud her vision, he knew he had to give her more. She deserved more and he'd come here to find her and prove he was willing to give it.

"It's time I show you how much you mean to me." He swallowed, took a steadying breath. "How much I love you."

He heard a resounding chorus of *awww*s from the people gathered under the tent. A bead of sweat trickled between his shoulder blades as he searched Katie's face for a reaction. She bit down on her lip and looked away.

"You don't have to say that," she whispered.

He knew what she was thinking, that he was doing this for the baby. And it was because once he'd wrapped his mind around the idea of being a father, he'd wanted the baby almost as much as he wanted Katie.

"I *need* to," he told her. "I should have said it a long time ago. I should have been brave enough to see what was right in front of me all this time." He gathered her tighter in his arms, adjusted his hold so he could tip her chin up to look at him. "I love you, Katie. I'm in love with you. As Buddy the Elf would say, 'I think you're really beautiful and I feel really warm when I'm around you and my tongue swells up.'"

She laughed at his lame joke and hope glimmered to life inside him, bright like a July Fourth sparkler.

"I love you, too, Noah." She lifted her head, brushed her soft lips across his.

"You're the key to all of this, Katie. I want you. I want a family. I want to spend the rest of our lives making you happy. I will never let anyone take advantage of you again."

"I didn't mean to take advantage," Edna said quickly, wiping at her eyes, her voice a plaintive whine. "But she's always been the one to manage everything."

"And we appreciate it," Noah's mother said, stepping forward. "But as much as we rely on Katie, Noah's right. She needs to put herself first for once." She draped an arm around Edna. "We'll manage this year on our own. You take her out of here, Noah."

He could have kissed his mother but settled for a grateful smile.

She nodded and gave him a little push. "Go on, now. Text me later to check in."

"I'll make you some chicken noodle soup," Edna called as he turned away.

He glanced over his shoulder. "She hates chicken noodle soup."

Katie gasped and he felt her shake her head against his shirt.

"What?" Edna put her hands on her hips. "I've been making her chicken noodle soup for years."

"Well, she doesn't like it. Try tomato basil next time."

"I really don't—" Katie began, but he stopped her argument with another kiss.

"We're going home," he said again. After a moment she nodded and buried her face in his shoulder with a small sigh. The shudder that went through her body as she melted fully into him propelled him forward, through the crowd and toward the fairgrounds parking lot.

Tater jumped up from where she was lying in the shade of the canvas tent as he strode by.

"Noah…" Katie said his name but he shook his head.

"Don't talk until we're at your house. I need a few minutes to recover from the shock of you hitting the ground back there."

"I just need to eat something."

"We'll take care of that, too." He got them both settled in the car and lifted her fingers to his lips. "We'll take care of everything that comes our way, sweetheart. Together."

"I love you so much," she whispered. "I'm sorry I gave you a reason to doubt that."

He shook his head. "I'm the one who should apologize. I've made so many mistakes over the years, Katie, and you've been the one to help me pick up the pieces from most of them. But things are going to change. I'm going to change. I'm going to be the man you saw in me when no one else did. I love you, sweetheart, for everything you are and for who I am when I'm with you."

He shifted in his seat, reached down to the outside pocket of his cargo pants and pulled out a black box. "This isn't exactly how I'd planned it, but I can't wait."

Her eyes widened and he smiled, not bothering to hide the slight tremble in his fingers as he opened the velvet box to reveal a square-cut diamond ring. "I want to be the husband you deserve and a father to our baby. I want every piece of you, every moment and year. Marry me, Katie, and make me the happiest man in Crimson?"

"Yes," she breathed, and he slid the ring onto her left hand. "I love you, Noah. For exactly the man you are. I want to share my life with you. You're my best friend."

He leaned forward and kissed her. "Let's go home," he whispered and they both laughed as Tater barked from the backseat. As they drove through town, Noah felt a sense of peace he hadn't known since he was a boy. His life made sense with Katie by his side, and he was going to savor every second of it. Forever.

* * * * *

Brian Fortune doesn't think he will ever find the woman he kissed at his brother's New Year's wedding. So when the search for the provenance of a mysterious gift leads him into a local antique store a few days later, he's stunned to find Emmaline Lewis, proprietor—and mystery kisser! Brian has never been the type to commit—but suddenly he knows he'll do anything to stay at Emmaline's side—for good…

*Read on for a sneak peek at
the first book in
The Fortunes of Texas: The Wedding Gift continuity,
Their New Year's Beginning,
by USA TODAY bestselling author Michelle Major!*

"I'd like to take you out on a proper date then."

"Okay." Color bloomed in her cheeks. "That would be nice." He leaned in, but she held up a finger. "You should know that since Kirby and the gang outed my pregnancy at the coffee shop, I'm not going to hide it anymore." She pressed a hand to her belly. "I'm wearing a baggy shirt tonight because it seemed easier than fielding questions from the boys, but if we go out, there will be questions. And comments."

"I don't care about what anyone else thinks," he assured her and then kissed her gently. "This is about you and me."

Those must have been the right words, because Emmaline wound her arms around his neck and drew closer. "I'm glad," she said, but before he could kiss her again, she yawned once more.

"I'll walk you to your car."

She mock pouted but didn't argue. "I'm definitely not as fun as I used to be," she told him as he picked up the bags with the leftover supplies to carry for her. "Actually I'm not sure I was ever that fun."

"As far as I'm concerned, you're the best."

After another lingering kiss, Emmaline climbed into her car and drove away. Brian watched her taillights until they disappeared around a bend. The night sky overhead was once again filled with stars, and he breathed in the fresh Texas air. He needed to stay in the moment and remember his reason for being in town and how long he planned to stay. He knew better than to examine the feeling of contentment coursing through him.

One thing he knew for certain was that it couldn't last.

Don't miss
Their New Year's Beginning
by Michelle Major,
available January 2022 wherever
Harlequin Special Edition books and ebooks are sold.

Harlequin.com

Love Harlequin romance?

DISCOVER.

Be the first to find out about promotions, news and exclusive content!

f Facebook.com/HarlequinBooks

🐦 Twitter.com/HarlequinBooks

📷 Instagram.com/HarlequinBooks

📌 Pinterest.com/HarlequinBooks

▶ YouTube.com/HarlequinBooks

ReaderService.com

EXPLORE.

Sign up for the Harlequin e-newsletter and download a free book from any series at **TryHarlequin.com**

CONNECT.

Join our Harlequin community to share your thoughts and connect with other romance readers!
Facebook.com/groups/HarlequinConnection

HARLEQUIN

Heartfelt or thrilling, passionate or uplifting—Harlequin is more than just happily-ever-after.

With twelve different series to choose from and new books available every month, you are sure to find stories that will move you, uplift you, inspire and delight you.

HNEWS2021MAX

Get 4 FREE REWARDS!

We'll send you 2 FREE Books plus 2 FREE Mystery Gifts.

FREE Value Over **$20**

Both the **Romance** and **Suspense** collections feature compelling novels written by many of today's bestselling authors.